PRAISE FOR JA

A master of the cliffhanger, creating scene after scene of mounting suspense and revelation . . . Heart-whamming.

— **PUBLISHERS WEEKLY**

A master of suspense.

— **LIBRARY JOURNAL**

One of the best writers out there, bar none.

— **IN THE LIBRARY REVIEW**

One of the top authors in the crowded suspense genre.

— **SHELDON SIEGEL**, NYT BESTSELLING AUTHOR

FORCE OF HABIT

The Complete Series

JAMES SCOTT BELL

Compendium Press

CONTENTS

THE MAKING OF A VIGILANTE NUN

Some years ago my son laughingly offered me an idea. He loves to make up titles and concepts, just for fun. "Hey Pop," he said, "how about a thriller about a nun who is secretly a vigilante? She knows martial arts, and can kick butt when necessary?"

I looked at him quizzically, and then he gave me the (you'll pardon the expression) kicker: "You can call it FORCE OF HABIT."

I cracked up. So did he. But he stopped when I said, "I think I'll do it."

"I was only kidding," he said.

"It's a great concept," I said. "Original, great title, and I think I can do something with it."

What I did was start to write it. On the side, as I had traditional publishing contracts to fulfill. But as I played with this story, I got pulled more and more into it.

My nun I named Sister Justicia Marie (or Sister J, as she's known by those close to her). I thought up her backstory. She is a former child star who grew up into a drug-using actress who then hit bottom. That's when she turned her life over to God and entered into the sacred life.

But during her time before the cameras, she studied martial

arts (particularly for a Steven Seagal film she was in) and those skills have not left her.

And as I like to dig into themes in my books, I thought this raised a most intriguing question: could a devout nun actually justify violence if it was in the course of doing good, like stopping a robbery or murder?

When a cop asks her the same question, I heard her say this about the criminal element: "They are the knuckles. I am the ruler."

I started adding a cast of characters. And then I thought of plot lines, and the idea of a series started to unfold. These would be in novelette form, around 15k words each.

For the first one, I wrote this pitch:

> *When a nun is viciously attacked, Sister Justicia Marie takes it upon herself to find out what happened. The cops don't like that. Neither does her Mother Superior at St. Cecelia's school. But when a couple of hoods try to stick up a liquor store and Sister J brings them down, something is unleashed inside her, something that will either confirm her calling ... or destroy it.*

I'll let Sister J take over from here.

FORCE OF HABIT

Sister Justicia Marie thought it was going to be a beautiful day in LA, full of mercy and grace, until she had to break a man's finger at lunch.

The downward spiral started at Rolling Rock Sanitarium in the northwest quadrant of the City of the Angels. Sister Justicia was doing her rounds, bearing fresh bread from the monastery and offering a little spiritual counsel to the Catholic patients.

One of whom was a three-hundred-pound former truck driver named Elisio Minx.

"I don't think eating nothing but sugar is a good idea," she said in response to his declaration of a new diet.

"But that way I can write poems that are sweet," Elisio said.

They were in the front lounge of Rolling Rock, which had been built in 1964 as temporary living quarters for the influx of workers in the booming aerospace industry. It was abandoned in 1987 when the water table upon which it sat was determined to be a virtual river of fuel runoff from the Rocketdyne facility in the Santa Susanna mountains. It was bought by a private firm in 1999 and the city decided the revenue from the proposed use as a mental hospital was of greater value than the odds of one of the patients developing a green glow.

And so here they sat, counselor and patient, in two frayed wingback chairs. A cracked vase of flowers sat on a round table between them, with several fallen petals scattered around on the surface like discarded potato chips.

Elisio almost hid his chair. His white robe was the size of a pest company's house tent and his feet strained the standard issue slippers like bulldogs in sweatbands.

"You need to stay healthy," Sister Justicia said.

"But my poems are Dr. Seuss zombie poems," he said. "I don't like them."

"Then don't write them."

"That's just it! They pour out of me!" Elisio's voice was higher pitched than one would expect from a man of his size. He sounded a little like that sweating guy, Richard Simmons, whom Sister Justicia had met once in what she called her "former life." Simmons had annoyed her and she slapped him, and he cried. She'd been drunk at the time.

Elisio recited: "Sit at the window, sit there and stew, looking for someone's forearm to chew."

"I see what you mean," Sister J said.

"I will not eat green eggs and ham, but I will munch on Sam I am. I will eat his little brain. I will eat it in the rain—"

"Okay—"

"Do not eat my foot or nose. Do not masticate my toes."

"Elisio, maybe an all Twinkie diet wouldn't be a bad idea after all."

"Is what I'm saying."

"But let's try praying about this first."

"Why are you a nun, Sister J?"

The question came at her like a foul ball, one that conked her on the head. It shook her like a California aftershock. She'd been a nun for eight years, since she was twenty-two. That was her purpose. To serve God. *That* was why she was a nun.

Wasn't it?

Or was she fooling herself? Was she still looking for something to fill the crack in her heart?

That thought had crept up to her of late and she kept trying to fight it back. God was her all in all. So why was she always making trouble at the school, even though she tried not to?

"I am a nun because I was called to be," Sister J said.

"I wish I got called," Elisio said.

"Everyone is precious in God's sight. Our job is to find out where he wants us."

"Does he want me here?" Elisio said.

"Maybe for now," she said. "But he also wants you well. Will you believe that, Elisio?"

"I like you, Sister J."

"Thank—"

"I will not eat your brain or thighs, I will not call you Super Size."

"—you, Elisio."

Sister J's cell phone played *Ave Maria*. A message from the school.

"Excuse me, Elisio, I have to take this."

"Nuns have cell phones?"

It was Sister Amy in reception at St. Cecilia's. "I'm sorry, Sister Justicia," she said. "But something's happened."

"What is it?"

"Sister Grace. She's been . . . oh, it's terrible!"

Northridge Hospital was on Roscoe just east of Reseda Boulevard. It took Sister Justicia twenty minutes to get there from Rolling Rock. She was sure God would forgive a little exceeding of the speed limit, especially in a ten-year-old Saturn. Getting to Sister Grace quickly was the more important matter.

At the hospital she was issued a visitor pass and went up to the fifth floor, found the room, and encountered Sister Sarah, her superior at St. Cecilia's, just outside.

"It was an attack," Sister Sarah said. She was sixty years old and did not wear the habit. She had short, graying hair, a V-shaped face and a disposition out of Dante.

"But by whom?" Sister Justicia tried to catch a look at Sister Grace, but a nurse and another nun blocked the view.

Sister Sarah guided Sister Justicia a few steps away.

"We don't know at this point," Sister Sarah said. "Sister Grace has not been able to speak."

"Where did it happen?" Sister Justicia asked.

"At Boyd-Cross."

Boyd-Cross was a notorious section of the San Fernando Valley. Gangland.

"What are the police doing about it?" Sister J asked.

"They're on this. I'm working with them."

"Working how?"

"Shaping the meta-narrative."

Sister Justicia held back a wince. Sister Sarah, a graduate of the Yale Divinity School, liked to talk in postmodern academic jargon. To Sister J her words always sounded like an oral dissertation by the Mad Hatter.

"But I mean, about finding the one who did it," Sister J said.

"It's more than that, much more. We need this case."

"Need it?"

"Publicity, Sister. Surely you understand the directive."

"Yes, I read it." The directive was from on high, the archdiocese, about the public relations of the Catholic church in general, and the local diocese in particular. "So you're saying Sister Grace is going to be fodder for a sympathy grab?"

"Your paradigm is objectionable," said Sister Sarah. "Virtually post-semantic."

Sister J rubbed the bridge of her nose.

"Sister, I know you are very close to Sister Grace—"

"Closer than my own heart," Sister J said.

"—and in view of that I am willing to overlook what seems to be another in a line of recent. . . deconstructive antipathies. But I am going to have to ask you to leave now and get back to the—"

"But I want to see her."

"That would not be advisable, in my opinion. You're agitated."

"Oh, good call!" Sister J immediately regretted the words. She'd had quite a mouth when she was younger and a complete pagan. Sharp tongues are not easily gotten over, and words you regret can spring out every now and again, like hungry pumas.

But why was it always around Sister Sarah? Sister J knew it was because they had issues that went much deeper than a few sarcastic phrases issuing from her redeemed throat.

"I'm sorry," Sister J said. "That slipped out."

"That will be quite enough," Sister Sarah said. "I would like you to leave now."

"She'll want to see me."

"*Now.*"

Sister J didn't move.

"You are on a short leash," Sister Sarah said.

"With all respect, Sister, I don't think God wants us on a leash at all."

"You defy authority."

"I only seek to do the work of God."

"You have a very unorthodox way of getting there. And do not think that this will not be memorialized."

"I beg your pardon?"

Sister Sarah sighed, lowered her voice. "If you do not, shall we say, shape up, your continuing position as a nun at St. Cecilia's will be over."

Over?

Sister J elevatored to the hospital cafeteria and got some Fritos from a vending machine. Then a Coke. She sat at a table near the wall. So far, she was the only one in the place. Good. She needed time to reflect.

Yes, it could be all over, she well knew. You could get a black mark as a nun, like some insubordinate grunt at Marine boot camp, and your vocation could be snuffed out in an instant.

Much like a movie career could be killed by scandal, something she knew all too much about.

She munched and prayed for Sister Grace. And for her attitude toward Sister Sarah. Then for herself. She so wanted to serve God forever.

Had it been a false vision that had told her to seek vows? Was it all just a fantasy based on a bad experience with the last in a long line of men?

Sister J ate more Fritos. For her, Fritos were a balm, a comfort. There were vows of silence, and vows of chastity and poverty. But there were no vows she knew of to abstain from corn chips.

At least she didn't know of one, and she was going to gorge even though she felt guilty about it.

A man with thinning gray hair, unkempt—wearing jeans, sandals and a Hawaiian shirt that had been washed too many times—passed by her table, taking his time. He was looking at her intently.

She gave him the standard nun smile—the one that said *You are a fellow human being made in God's image and I give you this friendly greeting in the hopes that a little of the light of His love may shine into you, and we now return you to your regularly scheduled life*—and went back to her Fritos.

The gray-haired guy stopped and continued to stare.

Sister Justicia put her hand over her mouth, trying to obscure her face, but it was too late.

"Excuse me," the man said.

Sister J wanted to wave him off, but that would have been rude. So she gave him a curt nun nod, the one that said *I heard you and acknowledge that you have something to say to me and will listen to it because I have taken a vow to be loving to all people, even when I'm eating.*

"You're not . . ." he said.

Sister J waited. Maybe he'd forget the whole thing.

"Yeah, I think you are," he said. "You're Brooke Bailey."

"It's been a long time since I've been called that," she said.

"Yeah! God, I used to have the hots for you!"

Wonderful.

"I'm sorry," he added quickly. "I shouldn't ought to say that to a nun."

"I've heard worse."

He slid into the bench opposite her. "I remember when you did this, went nun. I mean, it was all over the news."

"Pretty old news," Sister Justicia said.

"How come you did it?"

"They covered that, too."

"I know, they said it was drugs or something. Was that it?"

"Excuse me, I—"

"Drugs and sex, right?"

"Please, Mr. . . . ."

"Rudy Bing, glad to know you." He stuck out his hand. Sister J shook it reluctantly.

"Mr. Bing, I put that part of my life behind me. I buried it. It's not something I'm proud of."

"You should be! The *Go-To Girls?* That was a great flick! And that other one you did, with Lindsay Lohan. What was that called?"

"I've tried very hard to forget it, Mr. Bing."

"But that's what I'm saying, there's nothing wrong with entertainment."

"I would not want to repeat those roles."

"How come? Just because you ended up in bed with Matthew McConaughey?"

Sister Justicia felt her cheeks heating up.

"But my favorite of all time has gotta be *The Karate Babe.* Man, you really kicked—"

"Mr. Bing?"

"I heard you trained for real for that."

"That was a long time—"

"Can you still kick butt?"

She could all right, and she felt like kicking something right now. His shin, if not the wall. *Think of St. Francis,* she told herself. *Think of birds and flowers . . .*

Bing laughed then. "A nun who knows martial arts! Now what does the Pope think about that?"

Sister Justicia sent a smile that said: *I know you're trying to be cute and make charming small talk and I will acknowledge the effort but I hope you will move on now, please. Nothing to see here.*

A firmness came to Bing's mouth. "You know, I'm not Catholic."

"That's quite all right," Sister J said.

"But what's with that whole no sex rule, anyway?"

Dryness crept into Sister J's throat. "Mr. Bing, I don't really feel comfortable with that question."

"I mean, especially after the life you led, you know, according to the tabloids and all."

Sister J said, "I have a dear sister upstairs that I must go see."

"I think that's a good thing. See, you're not some pure little virgin off the farm now, are you?"

"That will be all, Mr. Bing."

Sister J started to get up. Bing grabbed her wrist. "Don't go yet."

"Please let go."

"Just talk to me. Like I'm a sinner."

"You *are* a sinner, Mr. Bing. Like all of us. Please—"

He squeezed harder. Shards of pain lanced her wrist. Along with it came the fire of anger that continued to be such a burden to her. Instinctively she made two simultaneous moves. She freed herself by pulling up against his thumb. Then grabbed his index finger and bent it backward.

Bing screamed.

He screamed both the name of God and Jesus Christ in ways they were never intended to be used around children or nuns.

He jumped to his feet. "You're crazy!"

"I'm so sorry," Sister J said. "Please—"

"Shut up!" Bing was holding his finger like a dead goldfish. "I think you broke it!"

"Mr. Bing, I—"

"You're going to pay for this! They're gonna hear about it!"

And with that, Mr. Rudy Bing vacated the eating area.

Two minutes later, so did Sister Justicia. She was shaking, and not just at the adrenaline bathing her nerves.

No, it was something else. She knew it was something she would have to confess, and soon.

She was glad she had broken Mr. Rudy Bing's finger.

And that horrified her.

Sister Justicia walked the halls of the hospital, calming herself. Praying. Asking God for a sign that she was still supposed to be a nun.

She remembered the first sign, the one that came to her as clearly as the sun reflecting off a mirror. It was back when her acting career was tanking, when it seemed like *National Enquirer* was her official publicist. The exact moment was, in fact, the morning she woke up next to a man she didn't recognize.

He turned out to be a wannabe director, and she'd met him— so he told her—at a Malibu party.

But she'd been so out of it she didn't even remember the party.

It was two weeks after her second DUI, and two months after she'd been fired from the new Spielberg film. It was the role that could have taken her from being a "troubled ex-child star" to "serious, Oscar-worthy actress."

A real comeback story, just the kind Hollywood loves. She was riding a PR bullet train, right up to the day she showed up on set hammered to the gills and threw an Evian in Spielberg's face.

She had a vague memory of thinking his direction was favoring another actor in a scene. But she knew that was just an excuse.

In truth she was dead scared, right past spitless into chronic dry mouth. Fearful about being able to perform up to the hype. Terrified she'd be laughed at in her attempt at legitimacy, that she'd continue as the butt of jokes from the likes of Letterman and Conan.

And that's exactly what she was then, waking up next to this guy who couldn't stop talking about "the great Tarantino" and "*mise-en-scéne.*"

Harlan Savage, that was his name. He was in love with his name.

But it was what he said as he was leaving his apartment, she still in bed with a splitting headache. He'd said, "Um, Ms. Bailey, I would love it if you'd be in my film. It's urban fantasy, and it has a female zombie, a former beauty queen. It's not a big role, but people will talk about it. They'd come just to check you out."

Check you out! That's what she had become, an item to be viewed like a freak in an old-time sideshow out of Dirt, Arkansas.

When she had managed to get dressed and look mildly presentable, she walked out to the streets of Santa Monica. It was a day heavy with clouds. She walked toward the ocean, filling her lungs with salt air, her temples feeling like Thor's practice pads.

She got to the railing that looked down a hundred feet to Pacific Coast Highway. She wondered what it would be like to jump. To feel raw sky for a brief instant and then be at rest. Would she feel pain at the point of impact? Or would it happen wonderfully fast, no feeling of anything but the elimination of all fear and anxiety and depression forever and ever?

And as she looked down, the clouds tore open and one of those shafts of sunlight you see in religious paintings came shooting out of the sky and hit the water.

It seemed then that the light bounced off the ocean and beamed directly into her soul. She felt alive with electricity, but not the Taser kind. It was more like connection to something so vast and powerful she thought if she touched the earth with her hand it would spin faster on its axis.

She lost breath.

Then burst into tears.

And cried for about two minutes straight, until she heard a grunt on her left.

It was a homeless man and his stuffed shopping cart, with old clothes and plastic bags and bottles and cans. He was dirty and old and smelled like plumber's handkerchief.

Just a hundred-and-twenty seconds before this, Brooke Bailey would have recoiled in horror at the sight of him. She would have turned her back and walked swiftly away, cursing the man to the lower depths.

But now she looked at this guy with a feeling flowing out of her, something like compassion. Unfamiliar territory.

Brooke Bailey gave him a twenty dollar bill and said, "God bless you."

And as she walked away she knew she was not the same, would never be the same again.

She wandered around Santa Monica. She had no idea how long she did. But when she came to a small church she went inside. It was dimly lit, with candles burning in an alcove and stained-glass windows.

She sat in a pew and looked at the altar and heard herself say, "I'm home."

Now she was in a hospital, skulking around to make sure all visitors had cleared out of Sister Grace's room. Because her calling was in question, her vocation up in the air.

Like she had some self-destructive gene still active inside her.

"I'm here," Sister Justicia whispered, soft enough so Sister Grace wouldn't wake up. And then she said a prayer.

"Sister?"

Sister J jolted at the sound of a man's voice.

"Didn't mean to startle you," the man said. He was dressed in a blue coat and tie, with tan slacks. He was about forty, with deep set eyes that carried a serious and professional expression. His hair was sandy blond, cut short. "I'm Detective Rick Stark, LAPD."

"I am Sister Justicia."

"How's she doing?"

"Sleeping. Thankfully."

"I was hoping to talk to her."

"Can you tell me what happened?"

"We only know where she was found, and in what condition. A boy found her."

"A boy?"

"Ten-year-old. You mind waking her?" Stark moved closer to the bed.

"Can't this wait?"

"I'm working a case, Sister. It has its own schedule."

"Might I talk to you about it first?"

"Why?"

"Detective, this is the second nun who has been hurt in the last two months." In April, a nun named Sister Carmela was walking in Sunland, had been dragged into a car, beaten, and left on the sidewalk. It made national news. "Don't you think we're dealing with a serial—"

"What? Nun abuser?"

"Well?"

"Nah. These are random attacks."

"How do you know?"

"Different parts of the city, for one thing."

"That doesn't seem conclusive."

"You doing my job for me?"

"I'm just thinking out loud. What's to stop someone from targeting nuns in different areas of the city?"

"You're connecting dots that aren't even dots yet."

"It's what I do," Sister J said. "It's all that theological training."

"I don't go in for that."

"Theology?"

"I just do my job."

"Doing your job without knowing the spiritual side of man is like trying to play tennis on one leg."

Stark blinked a couple of times then took a step toward the bed. "Allow me?"

"When she wakes up, Detective. Not before."

Detective Rick Stark shook his head. "Next time I come here, I hope you're not around. All due respect."

And with that he left the room.

Sister J stayed by Sister Grace's side, praying, for another hour.

She still had not awakened when Sister J herself decided to leave.

And as she did, she kept thinking about the broken finger of Mr. Rudy Bing. It floated in her mind like a nightmare digit, accusing her.

Monday.

First day of the new school session at St. Cecelia's. The all girl school in the north end of the Valley had been an educational mainstay in Los Angeles since 1953. The girls wore uniforms, Sister Justicia wore the habit, and minds were prepped for the world that awaited them.

She had fourth grade again.

She loved that age. They were still, for the most part, untainted by the cynicism of the culture. Especially if they had been at St. Cecelia's their entire educational lives.

Sister J thought of the fourth graders as a last chance stop, the place where she could do the most good. If she could keep just one of the girls from following her own destructive path, her entire teaching career would be worth it.

One of the girls this morning was new. Her name was Melissa and she looked as nervous as a ballerina on a shuffleboard court. Her pretty face was marred by an intractable frown.

At precisely nine o'clock Sister J called the class to order.

"Good morning, everyone," she said.

"Good morning, Sister," the class responded in unison.

Sister J selected Katisha Johnson to lead the invocation and then the class was ready to go.

Except for the new girl. She did not open her book when prompted. She did not write a note.

When the first break came Sister J asked Melissa to stay behind. The girl looked as if she were in trouble and kept rubbing her hands together.

"It's all right," Sister J said. "I just want you to know everything is going to be okay while you're here."

The girl said nothing.

"And if you have any questions or concerns, you come tell them to me, all right?"

Melissa looked at her shoes.

"Do you have any questions for me now?"

Melissa shook her head.

"All right, you can go—"

"I don't like it here," Melissa said.

"But you've only just started."

"I want to be with my friends."

"Did your friends go to another school?"

Melissa nodded.

"You know you'll make new friends here, very good friends."

"No I won't."

"If you'll only give it a chance."

The girl shook her head, violently. Out of character for the context of the conversation. There was something deeper in there, but not something that could be reached in a five minute exchange.

Sister J smiled and said, "You can go now."

The girl hesitated.

"Yes?" said Sister J.

"Can I stay with you?"

"You mean you don't want to go outside and play?"

Melissa shook her head. Hard.

"Well, only for today then. But you'll have to do something."

The girl waited.

"Do you like to read?" Sister J said.

The girl shook her head.

"Really? Because you know reading is how—"

"Are you Brooke Bailey?" The girl's face was now alive with interest.

"I used to be," Sister J said.

"I've seen *Go-To Girls* ten times!"

Oh, how can I undo that damage?

"I'm not Brooke Bailey anymore."

"How can you not be?"

"We can choose who we want to be, you know."

Melissa frowned.

"And if you want to have the best life," Sister J said, "you should choose to be a reader. You can start right now with a really good story. Have you ever heard of Anne of Green Gables?"

Melissa shook her head.

"Well let's remedy that right now." Sister J went to the book-shelf and took down a well thumbed volume of the Lucy Laud Montgomery novel.

"How about I read the first chapter to you," Sister J said. "And if you like it, you can take it home?"

For the first time the girl smiled.

The Asian gentleman behind the counter of the liquor store looked as shocked as Charlie Sheen's PR manager. Sister J knew nuns were not among his frequent customers. But surely he'd seen stranger patronage.

Well, maybe not. It was late in the afternoon and school was out and this was a task she wanted to get to before preparing the next day's lesson plans.

"Excuse me," Sister J said, "I don't want to bother you during your working hours, but I am seeking some information."

"Eh?" The man was in his fifties, with black rimmed glasses and teeth the color of wet sand.

"There was an attack on a nun just outside these walls. You no doubt heard about it."

"What you want?"

"I'd like to know if you can help me find out who did it."

"Police. Police on this."

"Have they questioned you?" Sister J asked.

"Nothing to say. You leave now."

"I'm not trying to cause trouble, sir, I just—"

"You go now."

"Please—"

"You go!"

Sister Justicia saw a look of fear on his face just then, and thought she knew now what it was about. He was a potential

witness against someone in the neighborhood. That could actually amount to a death sentence. She knew this because she'd
once been in an episode of *Law & Order*. It was one where that
was the premise—a gang hit and intimidation of witnesses. She'd
played the chief witness and there was talk of her getting an
Emmy nomination.

She didn't get it but that was probably just as well. She was
drunk out of her mind every Emmy, Oscar and Golden Globe
night. And most other nights, too.

"I understand, sir," Sister J said. "I just want you to know, if
you need any counsel, you can come to St. Cecilia's and talk to
me. I—"

The door burst open and two men in ski masks charged in.
With handguns.

One of the men stayed at the door. The other rushed the
counter, pointing the gun in the counterman's face.

"No shoot!" the man said, raising his hands.

The gunman turned his head toward Sister J.

And cursed.

"Hey," he called to his cohort, "it's a f...freak...it's a nun!"

The one at the door shouted, "I can see that!"

"What do I do?"

"Get the money!"

Time slowed for Sister Justicia. She'd once been in a movie
with Drew Barrymore, about boyfriends—what movie with
Drew Barrymore *wasn't* about boyfriends?—and there had been
a moment like this. Two thugs were involved, and a chase, and
then a confrontation at a restaurant. In the film, Brooke Bailey
and Drew Barrymore finished them off with liquor bottles to
their heads. All in glorious slow motion.

Like now. Only this was real. Yet, observing herself, Sister J
felt a strange and wonderful warmth inside. A feeling of
perfect peace in the midst of the most tense moment of her
life.

Not that she was complacent or unaware of the danger. No,

it was more like a sense of hyper awareness, pushing right past the menace into a zone of control.

Sister J took a step toward the gunman. "Put the gun down."

The masked gunman's expression was hidden, but his eyes looked wide and confused. He still had the gun on the counterman, but his gaze was stuck on Sister J.

"What do I do?" he called out.

"She won't do nothing. Get the money!"

"It's sin to murder," Sister J said. "Do you want to end up in hell?"

"Damn! What do I do? I don't want to end up in no hell, Reggie!"

"Shut up, man!" Reggie screamed from the door. "Get it!"

"I can't!"

Reggie cursed and ran to his partner's side. He pointed his gun at Sister J.

"You get on the floor now," Reggie said.

"Both of you need to stop this," Sister J. said.

"That's it," Reggie said. He took two steps and put the gun in Sister J's stomach. "Now I got your attention? You think I care about smokin' a nun? I don't!"

"You should care, Reggie," Sister J said.

"She knows your name!" the other gunman said.

"I know that, loudmouth!" Reggie said.

"God knows your name," Sister J said.

"Shut up about that!" Reggie said.

"It doesn't have to be this way."

"What do I do, Reggie?"

"Just do it!" Reggie screamed, and that's when Sister J knew he was going to shoot the counterman. And she would be next.

Two souls about to commit mortal sins and be damned forever. An innocent man behind a liquor store counter, another death.

Her Krav Maga training came rushing back to her limbs. She'd been in her mid-teens when she started training in martial arts, for a role in a Steven Seagal film. Even though she got dumped for showing up drunk one too many times, she'd kept her training up all the way until her commitment to the church.

Even then, she exercised at night, in her room, going through the moves. Just to keep in shape. She hadn't thought she'd need those skills in life.

How wrong she was.

She brought her left hand up fast, like Muhammad Ali in his prime, grabbed the gun barrel and moved the line of fire. At the same time she rotated her wrist downward and straightened her elbow.

The maneuver turned her body slightly and she went with the movement, taking one step forward and thrusting her fist into Reggie's throat.

The whole thing took less than a second.

In the next second she grabbed the hammer area of the gun with her right hand and twisted the weapon out of Reggie's hand.

She knew she had perhaps one second more to stop the other gunman from shooting.

She would later reflect that what happened next was done without reflection or contemplation or concern. It was as if she was imbued with a power from on high.

She kneed Reggie in the groin and pointed the gun at the other's leg.

And fired.

The sound was louder than she'd remembered on the firing range at the LAPD Academy in Exposition Park. She'd trained there for a Denzel Washington movie that never got made.

As the gunman screeched in pain, Sister J lunged forward and with a kick from her nun-shoed leg she knocked the gun from his hand.

He didn't seem to care as he crumbled to the ground, grabbing his exploded knee. Blood poured onto the floor. Reggie squirmed and moaned behind her.

"I'm sorry," she said to the man with only one knee. "Please forgive me."

She gathered the other gun from the floor and had one second of self-reflection. She was a nun holding two nines in her hands, both ready to fire.

That was weird.

It was also LA, and she knew anything was possible.

That's when she heard the cocking.

She turned and saw the counterman holding a shotgun pointing at Reggie's head.

"What's to be done about Sister Justicia?" Sister Sarah was seated behind the desk in her office, the office of the school administrator. Across from her sat Father Dominic, who was the school's spiritual advisor. At sixty, he had the white hair and training to handle the "problem" that was Sister Justicia.

At least Sister Sarah hoped so. She would need backup if she ever were to take action against the troubling nun.

"I don't know that anything needs to be done, so to speak," Father Dom said. "Has something further arisen?"

"It was her attitude at the hospital the other day. So directly defiant."

"She's a spirited one, for sure. But we can use a little of that around here."

"Are you taking her side?"

"I'm trying to be objective, Sister."

"Well, the time for objectivity is gone. It is my duty to run this school and eliminate the weak links."

"Are you saying that Sister Justicia is a weak link?"

"Yes," Sister Sarah said.

* * *

"I blow his head off!" the liquor store man said.

"You do that and it's murder," Sister J said.

"No, they rob with guns!"

"Put the gun away, sir. Now."

"I kill."

"I will rat you out." Did she really say *rat you out*? It felt strangely good.

The man looked at her, confusion slapped on his face like a beer label.

"Put the gun away now and call the police and order an ambulance."

"No—"

"Now!"

Half an hour later, the scene was under control by LAPD and fire department paramedics. Reggie was in cuffs in the back of a black and white. One Knee was on his way to county hospital.

And Sister J was talking to a senior patrol officer who seemed both surprised and amused.

"This is gonna be great in court," he said after taking her statement.

Yes, now she was a witness. And therefore in the same boat as the liquor store man, who had also given a statement. His name was Kim.

When the patrolman had wrapped up his inquiries, Mr. Kim took Sister J aside. "I am sorry, Sister. You save me from them, and from myself."

"You did the right thing, Mr. Kim," Sister J said. "Now I would like you to do one more thing right and tell me about what you've heard about the attack on the nun."

Kim stiffened like a shot of bourbon. "No! You ask too much!"

"God is asking you, sir. God believes in justice and truth."

He shook his head. "When God come to store, I tell him!"

"Bless me, Father, for I have sinned," Sister Justicia said. Night had fallen over the city like a Jesuit's cassock. Father Dom had graciously consented to hear her confession now. It couldn't wait. "It has been two days since my last confession."

"What sins have you committed, Sister?"

"I have desired to overindulge with certain foods."

"Such as?"

"Fritos."

"Those aren't necessarily bad for you, except in excess. Have you eaten them in excess?"

"No, but I want to. Sometimes I dream of being in bed with ten bags of Fritos and a bottle of tequila."

"Now that is a troubling dream."

"I cannot seem to purge it from my head."

"It takes time to cleanse a past life, my child. More time in prayer would help."

"I do pray. I try to practice the presence of God, like Brother Lawrence." How that ancient monk had managed to find the presence of God in the mundane was beyond her. Cooking, cleaning and laundry did nothing to inspire prayer in her.

"Do not try to be a saint just yet," Father Dom said. "Settle for being a very good nun."

"Yes, Father."

"Any other sins?"

Sister J hesitated. She felt her pulse quicken like a nervous bird in a two-dollar cage. It seemed the walls of the confessional felt suddenly smaller, like a mahogany vice.

"Sister?"

She cleared her throat. "Would breaking a man's finger be considered a sin?"

Hesitation on the other side of the screen. Then Father Dom said, "Would you repeat that please? It sounded as if you said something about breaking a man's finger."

"I did."

With an audible exhale, Father Dom said, "As in, breaking the bone?"

"I mean, under the right circumstances."

"I think you will need to explain this."

Sister J tried to swallow. Her throat was as dry as a three-hour homily. She felt now that this was a turning point, perhaps for her entire life, at least that part of her life she would have called her dedication.

"I'm not sure it is a sin," Sister J said.

"Come again?"

"I've been thinking about it, Father."

"Did you indeed break a man's finger?"

"Yes. At the hospital the other day."

"Was it an accident?"

"No."

"You mean—"

"I *wanted* to break his finger."

"Sister Justicia!"

The rebuking tone sat there between them, hovering, a palpable resonance of reproach.

Now was the time to make the case. She'd been forming the thoughts. It was time to sink or swim.

"I don't think it was a sin," she said.

"How," Father Dom said, "could the purposeful infliction of pain be anything but sinful?"

Sister J, kneeling, leaned toward the screen. "The church has always had a well defined teaching on self-defense."

"Are you saying that is what happened?"

"In a way, yes. I used force to prevent harm. Not only to myself, but to the man."

"I don't follow."

"He grabbed my arm and wouldn't let go." Sister J noticed she was gesturing with her hands, as if she were suddenly an Italian street merchant making a sale. "If I have dissuaded him from trying that again to another woman, have I not prevented the man from sinning himself?"

"You have apparently given this much thought."

"I am thinking out loud with you, Father."

"Let me get back to you on this one."

Did that mean he actually would consider her position?

"Any other sins?" Father Dom asked.

Uh-oh. "Well . . ."

"Go on."

"I sort of did it again this afternoon."

"Did what?"

"Inflicted pain."

"Oh boy—"

"But for a good cause! You see, two men came in to hold up the liquor store—"

"You were in a liquor store?"

"Well, yes."

"Oh boy—"

"To ask a question! About the attack on Sister Grace. Well, you see, two men came in with guns and I had to take the guns away and shoot one of them."

"Dear Lord."

"But in a good way."

"I shudder to ask."

"What if I were able to stop greater harms from being done to innocent people by a little preventive pain? What is discipline, after all? Is it not painful in some way? Either psychologically or physically?"

"I hope you're not going where I think you're going."

"Father, do you remember Dietrich Bonheoffer?"

"You're going to bring the Lutherans into this?"

"He participated in a conspiracy to kill Hitler. He reasoned that this was necessary for the prevention of evil."

"And he was hanged for it."

"By the Nazis."

"Your point?"

"The point is, if I were able to prevent these men from robbing another store, or worse, from shooting someone, would that not be good both for the potential victim and the potential criminal?"

"Go back to the word *prevent*. What exactly do you mean?"

"Just that."

"Using what means?"

"Whatever it takes, I suppose."

After a pause that seemed as long as a biblical epic, Father Dom said, "Sister Justicia, what you are talking about here is being a vigilante."

Sister J took in the word, spun it around in her mind, then came out with: "What is wrong with that, in theory?"

"It's taking the law into your own hands!"

Silence now, and contrition? No, she found that she could not back down. "My hands are only an extension of the hands of God. Does not God care about protecting the innocent and reclaiming the guilty? Is not he the higher law?"

"Dear Lord."

"What is it, Father?"

There was another audible sigh from the other chamber of the confessional. "I think," Father Dom said, "you might be mad."

School, the next day.

It seemed a repeat of the day previous. Melissa had the same look on her face and, when break time came, asked to sit in the classroom again.

Sister J took the girl to the window and sat her in a chair so she could see outside, and took the chair opposite her.

"Suppose you tell me what's bothering you," Sister J said. "I will never tell anybody anything you say to me. It will be just between us."

For a long moment the girl looked as if she might speak, but her expression fell and she looked at her hands. They were entwining again, nervously, like kelp in a strong current.

"Melissa, do you know what it means to be brave?"

She nodded, but tentatively.

"I had to be very brave once, when I didn't want to talk. I had a problem that I wasn't facing up to, and nice people, people who loved me, kept wanting me to talk to them about it, but I wouldn't. And the problem only got worse."

Melissa raised her head, listening.

"One day the problem got so bad I thought I might die. So I went to my friend, who was my manager, and said I needed help. And that's when I finally went to a place that could help me with my problem. That's all it took. Me talking about it. Now, do you feel like you'd like to tell me something?"

The girl opened her mouth, paused, closed it. Then said, "I'm afraid."

Sister J took the girl's hand. "What of?"

Melissa started to say something when the classroom door swung open.

It was Sister Wanda, she of the pickled expression and vacuum where a sense of humor ought to be.

"Sister Justicia," the nun said, "You are to report to the Superior's office at once."

"I'm in the middle of something," Sister J said.

"At *once*."

"Give me five minutes."

"My instructions are to take the class for the rest of the day."

"Take the class?" Sister J stood. "Why is this being done?"

"I suggest you talk to Sister Sarah."

Sister J looked back at Melissa. "We'll continue this another time."

"Don't go," Melissa said.

"You be brave like I said, okay?"

The girl nodded and Sister J thought that at least a partial victory.

One step at a time.

"What's the idea?" Sister J said the moment she walked into the Superior's office. The spare, square space had a desk, two chairs, plants and a framed portrait of the Pope—the *real* Pope—though it was well known that Sister Sarah was not a big fan of the Vatican. She preferred the American strain of Catholicism that bucked the magisterium when it conflicted with their view of social justice.

Which is why this power play by Sister Sarah bugged Sister J so much. It was more than a bit hypocritical, wasn't it, to pull rank when you yourself were selective in your obedience?

"Please do not use that tone with me," Sister Sarah said. "Take a seat."

"I don't want to sit down. I want to go back to my class."

"I'm afraid that's not going to be possible for the near term."

"What does *that* mean?"

"I told you to dial it down a little, Sister Justicia."

"We just started. The class is bonding to me. There's one new student I'm just establishing trust with."

"I'm sorry, but all that will have to wait."

"Why? What have I done?"

"For one thing, you broke a man's finger."

"It was an accident. Almost."

"And now there is this unbearable violence in a liquor store!"

"How did you get this information? Did Father Dom tell you? Because that would be breaking—"

"I got a call from a man named Bing, and then right after that the police! Sister Justicia, yours is conduct unbecoming a nun."

"But—"

"A liquor store?"

"I was not there to buy Jim Beam, Sister. I was there to ask the man some questions about Sister Grace."

"Why is that your business? That's for the police."

"The police are overworked, and may not see the full picture."

"And you can?"

"Maybe."

"I find that incredible hubris. And then what you did to those two men in the store."

"What I did? What about them? They had guns."

"Is that an excuse to use violence?"

"What was I supposed to do?"

"Let them take the money and leave. That way no one gets killed."

"That's not God's way."

"You presume to speak for God?"

"Is not all of our duty toward our fellow man contained in the Lord's admonition, Thou shalt love thy neighbor as thyself?"

"Yes, of course, but—"

"And God wills the welfare of all men?"

"That is quite evident—"

"To stop someone from committing a crime, and to induce them not to do it again, is for their welfare, is it not?"

"What are you driving at?"

Sister J was excited now, speaking rapidly. "As a church, we accept that self-defense is the right of anyone about to suffer harm. But we always think it is purely for the safety of the one attacked. We don't think that it is equally for the benefit of the attacker. You see?"

"No," Sister Sarah said.

"It is God's will, I believe, to stop someone from inflicting harm, and pain may be used to accomplish this. Pain is good. Did not God inflict pain on the nation of Israel for its ultimate good? Does not the Holy Scripture tell us that discipline from God is always good?"

"Again, you are presuming to know the mind of God!"

"It's right there in the Book! Read the Book, Sister Sarah!"

Sister Sarah's cheeks turned cotton candy color. "You are placed on leave, pending a full review of your situation."

Sister J's heart did a flying kick into her throat. "No," she said. "I will not accept that."

"You have no choice."

"I still don't accept that. Why do you have such enmity for me?"

"Because I know your kind. You look down on your elders. You think you are the ones who know what nunning is all about. You dress in the habit and think we are less than devoted because we don't. You have a chip on your shoulder because you came to the church as a celebrity."

"That's not true!"

"It remains that you are placed on leave and will not return to the classroom until I determine that you may. Please use this time for prayer and meditation."

Sister J stopped herself from saying what had popped into her mind—definitely not Vatican II material—and simply turned and left the office.

Outside she found it hard to catch her breath.

She did catch a wire trash can, however. Without a thought she gave it a flying kick and put a dent the size of a toaster in it.

The trash can flew down the stairs of the admin building, scattering its contents of extra auction flyers and crumpled hall passes. The can *ka-thump ka-thumped* twenty yards, coming to a hapless stop.

At the feet of the aghast Father Dom.

The old priest cleared his throat. "Sister Justicia, have you ever considered that your, um, calling might have been, how to say this...a wrong number?"

The thought of that sent her stomach turning like pork on a spit. If she ever thought that she'd be ruined, as a person and not just as a nun. If this had all been a cruel hoax played by her own mind. Dear God, how could you let that be?

"Don't say that, Father Dom. Please."

"I must say what is in the best interest of the church. Certainly if a course correction is needed, God will make that clear."

"I thought he was clear already."

"Many a misguided soul has thought the same thing."

"Misguided!"

"Now, you're not going to kick me, are you?"

Sister J laughed. Father Dom always had a way of making a dark situation light, and many times with a smile.

"You just keep thinking about things," Father Dom said.

"And we'll talk again. Meanwhile, with this time off from class-room duties, you can pray and help in the kitchen."

That's not all I'll be doing, Sister J thought.

The next day, after a session of kitchen duty, Sister Justicia took the bus downtown to Bauchet Street, and checked into the county jail as a visitor. For one Reginald Michael Jones. The desk deputy looked slightly surprised. "We don't get that many nuns down here," he said.

"Perhaps you need more," Sister J said. "I understand you have an overcrowding problem."

"You really think you can solve that? Here?"

"What better place to try?"

The deputy shrugged, then brought her through the security entrance and walked her to the visitor's room. She sat on a stool in front of a Plexiglas window and waited.

A few minutes later Reggie Jones was shown in and sat down on the other side of the window. His expression was pained. He picked up the handset and said, "Man, don't you come here no more."

Sister J said, "You may call me Sister J if you like, but not *man*, is that clear?"

"I don't got to listen to this."

"You certainly don't, but you'd better."

Reggie Jones was momentarily speechless. Then: "Look, it gets out a nun took my piece and laid me out, I'm done! You gotta promise me you won't say nothin'."

"I will have to appear in court as a witness."

"No, no—"

"Unless, of course, you change your plea to guilty and take your consequences."

"Ain't no way."

"Reggie, may I tell you why I came to see you?"

"A nun! Where'd you learn moves like that?"

"I came to help you."

"You some kind of damn Bruce Lee in a nun suit?"

"This is about so much more than your street cred."

"Where'd you learn to talk like that? Who the hell are—"

Sister J put up her hand. "Please do not use any more profanity, all right?"

"Damn!"

"Reggie . . ."

"Okay! I feel like I'm in school."

"You are, Reggie. Life is a school. I want you to promise me that you will do your time and, when you get out, you'll get a job and go straight. Will you promise me that?"

"What are you *smokin'?*"

Sister J leaned closer to the glass. "You don't want to find out," she said.

"You crazy," he said. "You are one crazy nun."

"That's funny."

"What's funny?"

"A priest told me pretty much the same thing."

Reggie said nothing.

Sister J said, "But I mean what I just said, Reggie. You best listen."

He looked at the ceiling as if for celestial help.

"One more thing, Reggie."

"Aw no."

"The nun who was beat up down there. You hear about that?"

"I got nothin' to do with that."

"Not what I asked. I asked if you know anything about it."

He shrugged.

"Reggie?"

"I don't know about that, okay?"

"You hear anything?"

He shook his head.

"You know anybody I could ask? Who would know?"

Reggie said, "You don't want to be askin' this guy."

"Who?"

"Don't matter if you're a nun. He don't care."

"Who, Reggie?"

"Don't you say where you got this."

"I know how to keep confidences."

"He hangs at the India Club. Where he does his business. But you don't want to go there."

"A name?"

"You're gonna laugh."

"Why?"

"The Pope. He calls himself the Pope of Los Angeles."

"I have been told you were at the county jail," Sister Sarah said.

Sister Justicia had been summoned to the office the moment she stepped back onto the grounds of St. Cecilia's.

"I was visiting someone," Sister J said. "As Jesus counseled."

"Excuse me?"

"To visit those in prison."

"Of course, of course. But without my knowledge or consent?"

"I was unaware that following Jesus required consent from another."

"Do *not* speak to me that way, Sister Justicia. You are on thin ice as it is."

Sister J said nothing.

"What was the purpose of your visit?" Sister Sarah asked.

"I saw one of the men from the liquor store. I wanted to encourage him to rethink his life."

"I will give you this warning, out of grace. Your time as a sister here is very nearly over."

"Meaning what?"

"Meaning that if I place a mark on your record, you will not—"

"I'll never pray in this town again?"

Sister Sarah looked like she'd caught a parakeet in her throat. She cleared it and said, "Please leave now, Sister Justicia. I am getting a headache."

It does seem to be what I am good at, Sister J thought. Giving pain. Why God, oh why did you burden me with this ability?

Still smarting from the Sister Sarah smackdown, Sister J pulled in front of the India Club. It was on Cahuenga just off Hollywood Boulevard. Over the door was a street-style rendering of a peacock with the graffiti-esque letters *IC* under it. Coming in from the sunlight Sister J's eyes did not adjust immediately to the darkness inside. She heard voices and the forms of four men gradually took shape. They were featureless at first. But as she walked closer their faces came into focus.

A young woman in a tight black dress that accentuated a surgeon's work said, "May I help you?"

"I would like to speak to the one who calls himself a Holy Name," Sister J said.

"You mean the Pope?" the woman said.

"Why he chooses to call himself that, I don't know," Sister J said. "But yes."

"What is this about?"

"Just announce me, please. My name is Sister Justicia."

The woman raised her eyebrows and gave Sister J a look that was anything but reverent. Then left.

Sister J took a look at the menu.

Good heavens. Eighteen dollars for a hamburger.

Without Fritos.

"Go ahead," the woman said on her return.

The four men at the bar were sharply dressed, down to their gleaming shoes. A power look. She knew it from her Hollywood days. These men fancied themselves players.

The one in the middle was short, blond, and ripped. He wore a black knit shirt over black slacks and an outlandish pair of lavender shoes. He was either the most stylish one in the room, or the kookiest.

They were all leaning on the polished wood bar, regarding Sister J as a curio.

"Well now," the blond one said. "We don't get many nuns in here, except around Halloween."

A couple of the players snickered.

"I assure you this is no costume," she said. "What about you?"

Blondie's smile froze. "Excuse me?"

"I've never seen shoes like that," she said.

"Oh these old things? Berluti Rapiécés Reprisés. Eighteen-hundred a pair."

"Your shoes could feed a family of four for several months."

He shrugged. "How about yours?"

"My what?"

"Shoes."

"Oh these old things? Salvation Army Store, two bucks."

"Your shoes couldn't feed my dog." More laughter. "Meaning no disrespect, Sister. I'm a good Catholic myself."

"Is that why you call yourself the Pope?"

"Only the Pope of LA. I'm not overly ambitious. Now what can I do for you?"

"You can tell me what you know about the attacks on two nuns in recent months."

"Nuns? Attacked?"

"Viciously."

"That's terrible. What's the world coming to?"

"No good end, I can tell you that," Sister J said.

Blondie shook his head. "You are so right. And we both are here to make it a better place while we can, am I right?"

"Is that what you do here?"

"Sure! People come here to have a good time, forget their troubles. That's what I am, a provider of pleasure in this dark world."

"A dark world where you know things. Or can find things out."

"I'm just a businessman." He paused. "You look sort of familiar to me. You always been a nun?"

One of Blondie's minions whispered something in his ear. Blondie nodded. "Oh yeah! Brooke Bailey. You went from rehab to a nunnery. I remember that. You look good."

"Thank you, Mr...."

"You know what to call me," he said.

"I reserve that name for the Holy Father," Sister J said.

"Now I'm curious. Somebody tips you off with my name and says I might know something about nun attacks. I sure would like to know who that person is, who is dropping my name around."

"It seems to me you have a name that gets dropped frequently," Sister J said.

"Sister, with all respect—"

"When someone begins a sentence *With all respect* I have found that it is followed by a sentence that has no resemblance whatsoever to respect."

Blondie looked at one of his men. "I like her. You see that? Why don't you guys speak your mind like that?"

Shuffling of feet at the bar. Blondie turned back to Sister J. "All right, I did hear about the nun attacks. I know a lot about what goes on in town, but that's something I know nothing about. If I did, I would tell you, because I don't go in for nuns getting beat up. If I ever find out who did it, I'd take care of business myself."

Sister J was quite sure he meant it.

"But my business is running a business," he said. "So let me give you some advice. Do more praying and less investigating. It might be healthier all around."

"I will take that under advisement."

"And completely ignore it?"

"Probably."

"I like you, Sister. You remind me of me when I was younger, except I'm not a chick and I'm not a nun, and I've got a lot more money."

"Other than that, a resemblance," Sister J said.

"Right. Now here is what I would do, if I was a chick and a nun with attitude, like you. I'd put myself out there as bait. I'd figure out how to do it, and then I'd go right out there and keep a loaded gun under my habit."

"That'd be a bad habit, boss," one of the thugs said.

"Shut it," Blondie said.

"Thanks for your time," Sister J said.

"Hey, you're welcome here anytime, Sister. Drinks are on the house."

Although she was not supposed to be on the school portion of the grounds, Sister Justicia waited until the children had been dismissed for the day. That was really the spirit of the sanction, after all. Not to be on school grounds when it was *in session*.

After school was over, it was ambiguous whether the restriction was truly in effect.

This, Sister J thought, was how lawyers made their livings.

She went to her classroom—rather, what *had been* her classroom—and found Sister Wanda scribbling something at her desk. The nun looked shocked at Sister J's presence.

"Hello, Sister Wanda."

"What are you doing here?"

"I would like to know how the girl, Melissa Henderson, is doing."

"Melissa? Oh, well, trouble."

"What do you mean?"

"I mean she was trouble."

"Was?"

"Didn't listen. Didn't do the work. Hit other children."

Sister J wanted to shake Sister Wanda out of her complacent tone. But that would not have been justified. *Keep calm.* "Where is she?"

"I haven't the faintest idea."

"Are you saying she's out of school?"

"It's for the best."

"Oh is it? Did you make any attempt to figure out what was going on in her life?"

"Sister, how many years have you been teaching?"

"Why is that relevant?"

"It is highly relevant," Sister Wanda said. "How much experience do you really have with children? And yet you think in a class of thirty you can get through to one troubled child? She should never have been admitted here."

"This is nonsense!"

"You are not wise enough to adjudge nonsense, Sister Justicia."

"Maybe I was born with an instant bull...a nonsense detector."

"I'm not entirely certain what you are trying to say to me."

"I am doing my best *not* to say something."

"Sister!"

Sister J saw no use in continuing the conversation. Instead she went to the school office and asked Heather, the office admin, for the file on Melissa Henderson.

"Um, I believe she was let go," Heather said.

"Fine. I'd like to contact the family."

"Oh, that is just not allowable."

"To show concern for a child?"

"To go outside of normal administrative channels."

"That sounds like alphabet soup. I'm talking about a real kid here."

"We could get in some trouble if we released that information to a teacher."

Sister J, her face becoming like a hot stove, walked slowly to the master file cabinets and pulled out the drawer marked H-P.

"So you are saying that if you were to open this drawer, and hand over to me the file on Melissa Henderson, you would be in violation of rules or laws?"

Heather, mouth agape, nodded. "Please close that," she said.

Sister J rifled through the folders. Found *Henderson, Melissa*, and took it out.

"But if I were to lift it out myself, you would not have handed it over to me, now would you?"

"Sister Justicia!"

"And if I were to copy the information on it myself, that would be no fault of yours." Sister J took a piece of scratch paper from the counter and wrote down Melissa Henderson's address.

"I am going to report this!" Heather said.

"Get in line," Sister J said. She replaced the file and walked out.

Sister J drove out to Griffith Park and hiked to a favorite spot of tranquility, where she often came to pray. It had a view of the East side of Los Angeles, past the train tracks and the concrete wash that had been the free-flowing Los Angeles river once upon a time. Now it was a graffitied pipeline for rain runoff. Every year during the rainy season someone managed to drown or get washed out to the ocean.

Today, however, her prayer spot was for thinking out the connection between Sister Grace's beating and the one that happened to Sister Carmela, the nun from Sunland.

Sister J took out her iPad. A minute of Googling revealed a connection between Sister Carmela and a popular nun's blog called *Nuns Running Off At The Mouth.* Sister J recalled visiting the site once about a year ago. Now she searched the site for Sister Carmela's name and found the most recent entry:

April 21

A young woman was brought into our battered woman's center the other night. In many ways, hers is a cautionary tale about our culture of celebrity and the abuses that routinely occur there.

I am talking candidly about sexual abuse of beautiful young women who have stars in their eyes about the movie and TV business, and are all too easily given to what my grandmother would have called "the casting couch."

Male nature has not changed since Adam. It is predatory. When it comes to sex, there is no subduing that nature. Marriage, backed by the force of the church, used to be the restraining agent in society.

No longer. As marriage has been demoted to a mere ceremony in many quarters, and an excuse for a party, we see a rise in men doing what their nature compels them to do.

Older, successful men cast off wives of longstanding and partake of the victuals set before them. With no consequences.

And nowhere is the food more attractive than in the movie business.

It was one week later, Sister J noted, that Sister Carmela was assaulted.

She jotted April 28 on her notepad and continued searching the blog, and came across an entry for August 14. Her breath left her.

It was by Sister Grace.

One cannot turn on the television or look at billboards without seeing fast food everywhere. And then look at our children. See how heavy they've become. Look at parents, taking them out for Happy Meals and supersizing everything.

It breaks my heart what we're doing to ourselves in the name of food and drink.

Sister J looked at her notes. Sister Grace had been attacked on August 21.

One week after the entry.

Wind swept across Griffith Park, like the whisper of an angel. Sister J's mind clicked and cranked.

Nun's Running Off At The Mouth was run by a Sister Jean at The Goodheart school in Granada Hills. Sister J looked up the number and called. The receptionist put her through.

'This is Sister Jean. How may I help you?"

"I like your blog," Sister J said. "I'm a colleague of Sister Grace at St. Cecelia's."

"Oh yes! Terrible what happened. How is she?"

"Recovering. I'm working on the matter."

"Matter?"

"The case. I think there may be a connection between your blog and the attacks on Sister Carmela and Sister Grace."

"Oh my."

"I would like to ask you a great favor."

"Anything."

"I would like to guest blog. When might I have a shot?"

Two hours later, Sister J was knocking on an apartment door in Reseda.

A man of thirty or thirty-five, swarthy, a face like a belt

sander, answered. It was about three in the afternoon. Sister J heard a TV inside selling Sham Wow.

"I'm Sister Justicia, from St. Cecelia's," she said.

"Oh yeah. Heard about you."

"I wanted to know how Melissa was."

"Now you care?"

"Are you her father?"

"Uncle."

"Yes, I care. I had nothing to do with her leaving school."

"I don't know what you're running up there."

"Is she all right?"

"I don't think that's your business now, is it?"

"May I see her?"

"You may not." He set his jaw like a fist ready to jab.

"Is she enrolled somewhere else?"

"I think we're done here."

He started to close the door. Sister J put her hand out and stopped it. The man looked like he'd just been slapped.

"I'm only trying to help," Sister J said.

"Take your hand away."

She left it there. "Please."

"What the hell kind of nun are you?"

"I get that question a lot."

He studied her face. "Have I ever seen you before?"

"I certainly hope not. May I see her, please? It would mean a great deal to me."

"She's not here."

"Oh. May I ask where?"

The man looked on the verge of shutting the door again. Then his face softened. "You're that nun who used to be in the movies."

Why this, why now?

"Yes," she said.

"I only saw one. I thought it sucked."

"You're probably right. Melissa—"

"Okay. She's with her no-good mother, you want to know the truth."

"I do want to know the truth."

"I take care of Melissa because Rita can't. But she takes Melissa every now and then."

"Melissa should be in school."

"I'm working on it."

"May I help?"

"I don't know," he said.

"If you can't trust a nun, who can you trust?"

"Yeah, but you were on drugs."

"Not anymore."

"I guess everybody gets one second chance. You can come in and wait if you want. They should be back in an hour."

It was actually an hour and a half. Sister J listened to the man, whose name was Ernie Lutz, tell about his sister's fall from normalcy. It sounded very close to Sister J's own story, only instead of being a child star, Rita Lutz was a musical prodigy. Piano. Gave that up for guitar and punk. Had Melissa with the bass player Robbie Henderson, who she married. Then divorced.

Sister J's own parents had divorced when she was nine.

A little after four-thirty mother and daughter entered the apartment.

Melissa ran to Sister Justicia and threw her arms around the nun's waist.

"Who's this?" Rita said.

"Nun from the school," Ernie Lutz said.

Rita gave Sister J a long, hard look. Rita had pink hair, a nose ring and arms too skinny for her body. "So?"

"So I came by to see how Melissa was doing," Sister J said.

"I suppose you're gonna say she's better off living here."

"I wasn't going to say that at all."

"She ain't in school."

"I know that. That's why I came."

"What're you gonna do about it?" Rita said.

"Help you figure something out," Sister J said.

"I don't like that school," Melissa said.

"You see that?" Rita said.

"Shut up," Ernie said.

"You shut up!" Rita said.

"Why don't we all shut up for a while," Sister J said, "and maybe listen to reason."

"Excuse me," Rita said. "Did you just tell me to shut up in my own house?"

"*My* house," Ernie said.

"I mean no disrespect," Sister J said, "but we'll get a lot further along if we quietly assess the situation."

"You sound like a damn fed," Rita said.

"Would you mind not using that language in front of Melissa?" Sister J said.

"What the—"

"Tut! Don't make me stop you," Sister J said.

Rita looked at Ernie with disbelief. Ernie shrugged. He seemed to enjoy this.

"Let me have a word with you alone," Sister J said. "Melissa, you stay with your Uncle Ernie, okay?"

"Okay," the girl said.

"Where can we talk?" Sister J said.

"Out on the balcony," Ernie said, and took Melissa by the hand into a bedroom.

Outside, Sister J said, "Look, I can tell times have been hard.

But you have a little girl you're responsible for and she needs an education and she needs a mother."

Rita ran a wrist under her nose. The ring clipped to a nostril waggled. "You have no right to tell me how to raise my kid."

"Yeah, I do. You are subject to the natural law, and I am a representative of that law. You don't want to mess with me."

"I can call the police and get you thrown out of here."

"Do you want to go to the mat with me?"

"You're just a nun. I don't believe in God. So I say you got no rights here."

Sister J put her face about an inch away from the nose ring. "Listen, girlfriend, I don't care if you believe in God or not. God believes in you and let me tell you, nothing you do escapes his notice, and when there is an innocent child at stake he takes very special care about that. And let me tell you something else. I am not impressed with your punk-ass-rebel angrier-than-thou anti-authoritarian crap show. You need help. If you won't admit it that's on you, but you're headed nowhere and so is your little girl if you keep this act up. And it is an act. We both know that, but your girl deserves more than your self-centered creep show, and it doesn't matter how much you bake or snort or shoot, little girl, you can't get out of yourself without help."

Rita trembled with what looked like Vesuvian anger.

"So I am offering to help you and your girl get back to normal, see? I've been where you are, get it?"

For a long moment Rita said nothing. Then she proceeded to go ape bait. Her screams filled the air like an insane siren. She shot out about seven curse words in three seconds. Her face got pink, then red, and her body stiff.

So Sister Justicia of the St. Cecelia's school for girls slapped Rita Henderson across the face.

After an initial look of shock, but at least a quiet one, Rita came at Sister J with her nails bared.

At the same time Ernie came bursting outside, Sister J

grabbed Rita by the right arm and twisted it out and up, forcing the punk mother to her knees.

"What goes on!" Ernie shouted.

"She needs help," Sister J said, holding the woman down. She saw Melissa inside, crying. "I'm going to take Melissa."

"No!" Rita screamed.

Sister J pulled the arm tighter and Rita stopped screaming.

"No," Ernie said. "I'll make sure Melissa's okay. This is a family thing."

"You get Rita to rehab," Sister J said.

Ernie nodded.

"And don't let me find out you didn't," Sister J said. "I'm sorry I had to do that, Rita, but it's for your good."

She let the mother go and went inside. She knelt and stroked Melissa's cheek. "You obey your uncle, okay?"

"I don't want you to go," the girl said.

"I promise to come back. You're my friend now."

Two days later:

Nun's Running Off at the Mouth is pleased to have as our guest blogger Sister Justicia Marie of the Sisters of Abundant Mercy. Sister J, as she is affectionately referred to, has opinions, as you will soon see. We welcome her!

In Hollywood it's all about the money.
*   I should know. I lived it.*

Oh sure, there are people who care about art. But they are forced to bow down before the Golden Idol.

And if you make money, it covers a multitude of sins.

Jesus said you cannot serve both God and Mammon.

Mammon is a name, the name of a false god.

The god of Hollywood.

It has ever been so. Except, in the "old days," the days of the moguls and the studio system, they loved good old fashioned storytelling. That's what made for good box office.

Now, it doesn't matter what the story is, or how it might affect an audience.

It's always about the money.

Art? Fine, if it makes money.

If it doesn't, don't give the writer or director another job!

A steaming heap? Yes! If it makes money!

(Another good title for this blog would be Nuns Saying Inappropriate Things, but we'll leave it where it is)

Fight back, people. Demand excellence. Teach your children to honor goodness, truth and beauty in their art.

Don't buy tickets to see junk.

She sat back and considered the prose.
Then prayed that it would do the trick.

"We have reviewed your file," Sister Sarah said.

"Who is *We?*" Sister J asked. They were in the Superior's office on a dull Tuesday morning in Los Angeles. The air felt like a wet wool habit.

"Father Dom and a representative of the archdiocese," Sister Sarah said.

"May I know the name of this representative?"

"Not at this time."

"What is this, a Kangaroo Court?"

"Sister Justicia, your attitude is not helping you."

"Story of my life," Sister J said.

"Be that as it may, your suspension is ongoing."

"That's just fabulous."

"Contrition rather than aggression might be the better course."

"Oh, you have not seen me aggressive," Sister J said. "Not by a long shot."

"I wonder if the discipline of being a nun is something you are cut out for," Sister Sarah said.

Sister J said nothing, for she wondered the same thing.

Four days later Sister J got the invitation, via special courier to St. Cecelia's.

Brooke! (I of course mean no disrespect). There are many of us in the community who would love to see you again. Maybe need to see you again. And I thought, Hey, what better place for you to shine a little light than at one of my famous parties?

I tossed the idea by Jules, my assistant and he thought it would be a buzz kill. I told him he needed to open up a little, talk to people who might have actual lives outside the industry.

And who knows? There may be a biopic idea here, if you're of a mind. You could star as yourself (if the Pope would allow it, of course).

I'm blathering. Bottom line is, come to my party next Friday night. You know the way. It's still the same old place out there on Point Dume. I will protect you if need be.

I would just love to see you again. Please come.

Odo

Odo Pasternak, her former agent.

The valets who had been hired at Odo's did not really know what to do about a nun driving an old Saturn that pinged. There amidst the Beemers and Benzes and Hummers came Sister Justicia, in full habit.

She handed the keys to a valet and said, "Watch the dings."

"You sure you're in the right place?" the big valet said.

"As the great Buckaroo Banzai said, 'Wherever you go, there you are.'"

The valet blinked.

Sister J walked past the koi pond to the front door. A rush of memories flooded her mind, the past intruding upon the present. She had turned her back on fabulous homes and money and parties and the world's definition of excitement. But she had to admit there was still a little Brooke Bailey left in her. She was not a saint. And some of the old desire for the elixir of alcohol awakened and made vibrations in her bones. She was uttering a quick, silent prayer when the door opened.

Odo welcomed her in with arms outstretched. His eager kiss

on the cheek nudged her wimple. But she didn't mind. She'd always loved Odo.

And his home. Oh so familiar. Brazilian walnut floors. Vaulted ceilings with hand hewn beams. Odo walked her into the living room and it was like old home week, if by old home you were talking people who were older versions of themselves now, despite what plastic surgeons could do.

There was the dark, brooding Dionisio Purcell from that Coen brothers movie.

Jason Mailer, the screenwriter.

Max Manes, producer of two of her movies.

Dimitra Sterling, another super agent.

Daisy Fantall-MacDowell, who had always harbored a grudge against her. Daisy had been tagged as a "second rate" Brooke Bailey by a critic once, and had never gotten over it.

Each of them, with the notable exception of Daisy, gave Sister J a hearty welcome, wanting to catch up, hugging.

And she had to admit she liked it. She missed the camaraderie of the set. The good times, the laughter.

But she quickly reminded herself that these same things led to her downfall. It was all still an open wound.

Finally, Odo got her outside, onto the expansive deck with spa, ocean view, cabana and infinity pool with waterfall. There were less familiar faces here, and more looks of curiosity. What was a nun doing at a party?

"You know," Odo said, "I've never stopped getting offers for you to return."

"After all these years?"

"What a story it would make!"

"But I'm a nun."

"That's what would make it so big! You could star as Mother Teresa, or some other saint. There's a lot of those, aren't there?"

"A few," Sister J said.

"Or you could just do some plain old acting. Why not? The Vatican doesn't have rules against nuns acting, do they?"

If she could justify breaking a man's finger, she thought, maybe she could justify this.

No. The old temptations would be too great.

"Thank you, dear Odo," she said. "But I have other duties to perform."

"At least let me get you something to drink. Martini was your poison, right?"

"Not anymore. A Coke would be fine."

"I'll be right back."

And off he went, leaving her alone to listen to the talk from the spa, where two women and a man sat in bubbling water, looking like a beer commercial.

"Brooke," a voice said.

She turned around.

"God, it's good to see you," Harlan Savage said.

He had aged since she'd awakened in bed with him. But the playful blue eyes were the same. A ten-year-old's eyes.

In spite of her efforts, she felt her face flush.

"Hello," she said.

"You look great. I mean, as far as somebody in that get up can."

"It's called a habit."

"I know what it's called. It's kind of an amazing thing. You know, I never made that zombie picture."

Sister J said nothing.

"I can't believe this," Harlan Savage said. "I wish there was someplace we could go and just talk."

"That would be a scandal, wouldn't it?"

He leaned in. "You're dead in this town only if you're ignored."

An hour later they were headed up Pacific Coast Highway in Harlan Savage's convertible BMW. They had figured out a way to avoid the scandal, with Sister J leaving first and parking her car in the far corner of a Safeway lot. Savage picked her up there and off they went.

With the top down, it was a little hard to talk. Savage shouted out his résumé and the details thereof, over the last ten years.

Sister J spoke Hollywood Puffery fluently, and knew it was an undistinguished list of credits. Doing second unit stuff with Vin Diesel was as close as he'd gotten to the dream of directing his own film.

Finally, Harlan Savage pulled off the main road and hit a private track that took them down near the water. Savage killed the engine.

The sound of the waves hitting the beach was one Sister J normally loved. Tonight, though, it sounded like snakes hissing. Savage got out and sat on the hood of his car. The moon was aglow. Sister J heard Harlan Savage sigh.

She got out but did not sit.

"Isn't this nice?" Harlan Savage said.

"Funny, I thought it would be you," Sister J said. "Even before I knew for sure."

Savage paused. "Knew what?"

"That you've been beating up nuns."

Savage said nothing but his silence spoke volumes.

"You were the one who told Odo to invite me to the party, weren't you?"

"That's fantastic," he said. "How did you figure it out?"

"Well, it makes a perverse sort of sense. You were always a movie nerd. And you worked on *Seven*."

"It was my first job in the industry."

"You loved the movie. You couldn't stop talking about it when I knew you. A serial killer who uses the seven deadly sins as an MO."

"I *still* love it."

"So that was the connection. The two nuns you beat up had each posted something on their blog that had to do with sin. The first post was about lust, and the second one was about gluttony. You've been scouring that website looking for sins, just waiting for the right order. So I went on and published one about greed. It drew the perpetrator out. I only guessed that it might be Harlan Savage."

"That's brilliant!" he said. "You are some kind of genius."

"I try."

Harlan Savage said, "You turned me down. You thought you were better than me. You thought you were better than being in my movie. I was going to save your freaking career, your life! And you never returned my phone calls."

With closed eyes, Sister J said, "Harlan, I underwent a change of my very life that next morning. I have not looked back."

"And then you made a big play in the news about going nun."

"I made no such play. I did not seek publicity."

"All high and mighty. I decided you needed a lesson in humility."

"We're nuns, Harlan. What threat is that to you?"

"No threat at all, and that's what makes it feel so good."

"You're sick, Harlan," Sister J said. "You need help."

"No, you need help. You need discipline. And I'm going to give it to you."

"I wouldn't go there, Harlan."

"And stop calling me Harlan! You don't have that privilege anymore."

"Let me help you," Sister J said. "Let me get you to—"

"Shut up!"

Harlan Savage slapped Sister Justicia across the face. The blow was quick, she never would have anticipated it. A shock wave banged through her skull and down her spine.

His hand came back the other way, preparing for a back of the hand blow. Sister J shot her right arm up and blocked it.

Apparently this surprised Harlan Savage. He took a step back and just looked at the nun, up and down.

"What the hell was that?" he said.

"A block," Sister J said. "Please don't hit me again."

Savage snorted. "Or what?"

"I promise you I will come with you to the police, and help you in any way I can."

Now he looked stunned, as if he could not believe anyone was talking this way. Sister J couldn't blame him.

"You expect me to go to the cops?" Harlan Savage said.

"It's the best thing for you."

"I'm going to have to kill you now. I don't want to."

"I'm touched."

"But you'll go to heaven, so what's it to you?"

"I am not finished with my work on earth."

"What work is that, Brooke?"

"Sister Justicia. And it's helping people like you not do bad things."

"How do you expect to do that?"

"Force," she said.

Savage laughed savagely. "I'm a black belt in Tang Soo Do."

"Well," Sister J said, "I'm a black habit in Down You Go." And with that Sister J shot her right leg out and hook kicked the back of Harlan Savage's left leg.

Down he went.

But not for long.

With a Bruce Lee squeal he was up on his feet, raining jabs and punches at Sister Justicia's face. She fended them off by instinct, her hands and arms taking the brunt of punishment. She knew that at this point it was all speed and attempted intimidation, the way Westerners think Eastern martial arts should be practiced.

She would wait for her opening.

But Savage was full of wild-eyed energy and that made him as dangerous as a runaway John Deere in a flower bed.

Wham.

One of his blows smacked Sister J's left cheek. Stars came out behind her eyes and glowed bright, hot little balls of gas in the universe of her brain. Rationality swirled out of control like a nova, and she heard Savage laughing in a distant galaxy.

He would have no trouble finishing her off if she didn't get up and back into it soon, that much she knew. It was a still small voice that seemed to tell her to get up.

Still dazed by the hit she willed her body to roll and her feet to plant and her arms to push.

The left side of her face throbbed like repeating sonic booms. But her eyes were clearing and she could see the figure of Harlan Savage moving in for the kill.

She arm-blocked one blow, and her right foot found purchase in the headquarters of male fertility.

Harlan Savage screamed like a coyote howling at the moon. It was eerie and unsettling, as if he were a shapeshifting monstrosity from a YA novel about high school love among things that want to eat each other.

Sister J said, "I'll take it easy on you if you'll just give yourself up now."

From his doubled over position, he threw out a curse, something that never should be told to a nun and that rhymed with *itch.*

"That will not help you, Harlan," Sister J said.

"Stop calling me Harlan!"

And then he limped around to the back of his car. Sister J heard a pop.

The trunk. He'd popped the trunk and maybe had a weapon there.

Sister J jumped on the back seat and slammed the trunk down. It hit something hard—a cranium. Harlan Savage shrieked and howled and cried and cursed. He stumbled backward from the car like a blind man staggering through a bar.

"I'll kill you!" he shouted, then started running toward the beach.

Sister J gave chase. It was not easy running in pumps and a nun's habit, but it could be done if she held the habit up in the front. She only hoped she could catch him.

The sand beneath her feet was like the shifting ground in her soul. Uncertain, threatening, but the only thing to run on now. Forward motion. Committed.

It occurred to her then that this was a turning point, a Rubicon. If she crossed it, there would be no turning back. In her head she heard the voice of Father Dom, suggesting she might not be in full control of her faculties. And then she thought of St. Joan, and what the priests all said about *her*.

Joan, can you hear me? Can you save me? Can you tell me what to do?

She kept running. The form of Harlan Savage not pulling away, telling her she could catch him if she kept after him. He only had the beach or the ocean to go to. He could run, but he could not hide.

Nor could Sister J. Not from God or Sister Sarah or Father Dom or reality itself. If she turned back now, no harm, no foul. She could go to the police and tell them what she knew.

But with only her word against Savage's, that was unlikely to move the needle.

And Harlan Savage would not have paid for his sins.

What should she do?

She ran on. And that was her answer. Her body had told her,

her heart had told her, her head would follow along. She was here for a purpose, and this was it.

Harlan Savage was a moral monster and he was trying to get away.

She would not let him. She would never let this happen again on her watch, come what may.

Closer now, she heard the water gently slapping the beach.

Harlan Savage looked over his shoulder. "Get away from me!"

"You can't outrun God, and you can't outrun me."

"Stop it!"

Sister J jumped, feet outward, a flying kick. She got his legs and down he went into the brine. Sister J grabbed his right arm, bent it back behind him. Hard. Savage bawled into the suds but was powerless to move.

"I want you to say that you're sorry," Sister J said. "I want you to admit that you have done wrong, and then you are going to turn yourself in to the police."

Harlan Savage told her to do something to herself that a nun could never do.

Sister J broke his arm.

Savage shrieked louder than that seal on YouTube that screams like a man.

"Someday," Sister J said, "you'll thank me for this."

Using his broken arm like a joy stick, she had no trouble guiding Harlan Savage back to his Beemer. He cried and cursed a few times, but at each offending word she gave his arm a little twist, and that stopped the verbal flow.

He fainted. Sister J put him in the trunk.

To the nurse at the emergency room Sister J said, "If he starts using foul language, just sort of accidentally on purpose tweak his arm."

"What kind of a nun are you?" the nurse said.

"That seems to be the question of the month," Sister Justicia said.

Sister J wheeled Sister Grace out to the courtyard of St. Cecilia's. It would be a couple of months of physical therapy before she would be able to walk again.

They sat in the sun looking at the rose garden. Sister J brought one of Sister Grace's favorite books, *Giant* by Edna Ferber. Sister Grace came from Texas, so that explained it. Sister J began to read.

After chapter one, Sister Grace said, "You are so kind and gentle, Sister Justicia."

"Well, I don't know about that."

"You are. Such a gentle spirit. How do you do it?"

"Prayer and Fritos," Sister J said. "They do wonders for the soul."

On Monday Sister J got a call from Ernie Lutz. "I just wanted you to know Rita's in rehab," he said.

"That's a good thing," Sister J said.

"It's because of you," he said. "Though your methods are little odd."

"Whatever works, I always say. How's Melissa?"

"She doing okay. Got her in the public school here. She really wants to see you."

"Then I'll come by, just after my appointment."

The appointment was with Detective Rick Stark, who had requested she come see him.

Detective Stark said, "The word from the hospital is that a nun who did not leave her name was behind the breaking of a man's arm."

"Really?"

"Was it you?"

"I cannot tell a lie," Sister J said.

"So, was it?"

"I also cannot be compelled to answer questions. That's in the Constitution, you know."

"You're refusing to talk to me?"

"We can talk about the Dodgers if you like."

"Don't mess with me, Sister. Don't you do it. You're just asking for trouble."

"What if I'm preventing it? What if I'm making the streets safer? Isn't that the work of God?"

"It's the work of the police, Sister."

"Last time I checked God held a higher office than the Chief of Police, and even the City Council, though some of them forget it."

"I don't want to see you end up dead, is what I'm saying."

"Everyone owes God a death," Sister J said. "He who pays early doesn't have to pay later."

"Sister, there are some very, very bad people out there on the streets, don't you realize that?"

"Of course I do."

"So?"

"They are the knuckles. I am the ruler."

Detective Stark said nothing more.

For a long time after Sister Justicia Marie left, Detective Rick Stark sat in his chair, staring. Until Sergeant Singleman came in.

"You okay?" Singleman said.

Though he was not Catholic, Detective Rick Stark felt a need to cross himself. And then he said, "Heaven help us."

FORCE OF HABIT 2: AND THEN THERE WERE NUNS

One generally steps into a chapel to pray, not to kick someone's butt.

But if two thugs are stealing Jesus, all bets are off.

Those thoughts bumped together in the mind of Sister Justicia Marie the moment she saw the men sneaking out with the large, silver crucifix. She knew the thoughts were not reverent. Talk of *butts* and *bets* were from her old world. When she was the child star and later drug-addled actress Brooke Bailey, that kind of language was mild compared to what usually came out of her mouth.

But even now, at thirty, and a Benedictine nun at that, the old thoughts sometimes came calling. At those times Sister J wondered if she'd ever fully heal.

She'd come to the chapel near midnight. This was at a Franciscan retreat center nestled in the mountains of Malibu, California. She was here with other faculty and staff of St. Cecelia's school. A silent retreat it was supposed to be, but whenever Sister J was around her superior, Sister Sarah, words pounded against Sister J's teeth, trying to get out. Sister Sarah seemed to have it out for Sister Justicia, and had ever since Sister J had come to St. Cecelia's two years ago.

It was worse now that Sister J had started using martial arts to stop bad people from doing bad things. As Brooke Bailey, she'd taken Krav Maga and street fighting in preparation for a Steven Seagal movie she got fired from due to her drinking.

But she kept on with the training for several years and was considered a star student of Sensei Bobo Portugal.

And then, after taking out two gunmen at a liquor store, Sister J felt she was being called by God to stop violent people, using violence itself if necessary. She thought she could justify that theologically, but old Father Dom, her confessor, was not so down with the idea.

In fact, he thought she might be going nuts.

Maybe he was right. Which was why she came late to the dark, empty chapel to pray. She was in the back when she saw the shadows moving up front, slipping out the side door with the silver crucifix.

She ran to the door, and outside, and heard the start of an engine. She grabbed a large stone from the rock garden and heaved it at the windshield of what turned out to be an SUV.

The windshield cracked.

And brought two young men out of the vehicle, cursing.

One of the words issuing forth was the B word.

Sister J felt her right hand rise up and slap the one who said it. He was a skinhead, about eighteen or nineteen. The faint glow of a wall sconce bathed him in amber.

"Don't ever use that word about a nun again," she said. "Or anyone else, for that matter."

The other gangsta wannabe said they could call her whatever they effing wanted to call her, only he did not use the word *effing*.

Sister J slapped him, too.

"Don't you do no more slapping!" Gangsta Number One cried.

Sister J said, "Now you two look like a couple of boys who could do some good in life. But not if you go around ripping off churches. Do you really think God doesn't see what you're doing?"

"Don't believe in no God," Gangsta Number Two said. He was the slighter built of the two, but they looked like they'd been dressed by the same Gangsta designer—hard casual.

"You broke my window!" Number One said.

"Better than your soul going to hell," Sister J said. "Now give me back the crucifix and we'll drop the whole theft thing."

"I ain't giving you back nothin'," One said. He held the icon behind his back.

"That's not the answer I'm looking for," Sister J said.

"Only answer you gonna to get. You can't do nothin' to us."

"You don't want to test that theory," Sister J said.

The two would-be outlaws looked at each other like Bing Crosby and Bob Hope, wondering what was next on the road to ruin.

Sister J said, "Honestly, I think you boys have a lot of potential."

"I don't want to listen to no nun!" One said. Sister J was starting to think of them in Seussical terms, Gangsta Two and Gangsta One, standing before her with nowhere to run. Which one should she slap? Which one should she spank? Which leg to disable? Which collar to yank?

Sister J said, "You don't have to pretend you're from the street. Why do you want to come up here and commit felonies? You think ending up in jail is going to do you any good? Think you're going to get tough in there? Get cred? It's a fool's game.

And you two should not be playing it. You have to think about your futures."

"I don't like this," One said. "I don't like listening to this at all. Come on."

"Now, wait a minute, Chris," Number Two said.

"Shut up!" Chris said.

Sister J pounced on the name. "Chris, you need to hear this. This could be the defining moment of your life."

"How come your voice sounds like I heard it before?" Chris said.

"That's just an illusion," Sister J said.

"No, no. It's like I know you."

"I don't think so."

He frowned at her a moment, then said, "Who's gonna pay for my window?"

"I think you two should pay for it yourselves," Sister J said. "You can make some good money mowing lawns in the neighborhood, or running errands for some of the old folks on your street. Now give me back the crucifix and we'll call it even. But you have to promise me that you will concentrate in school and stay off drugs."

"Who says I'm into drugs?" Chris said.

"Please," Sister J said.

"You are freakin' me out."

"The crucifix?" Sister J said.

"No way," Chris said.

"Give it to her," Two said.

"Shut up!"

"Now, boys, think about this. I am letting you go. But you have to give me back what does not belong to you. That's what law is about."

From somewhere up in the canyon, party laughter echoed through the night. A lot of Hollywood wealth lived up here. And Sister J knew all about that scene. It had once been her world, and then her downfall.

"What's it going to be?" Sister J said. "Do you give it to me quietly, or do I have to muss you up?"

The two boys, who might have been Eagle Scouts in another life, looked at each other again. "What kind of nun are you?" Chris said.

Then she saw his eyes widen. He was looking over her shoulder. His mouth dropped open and Sister J prepared to turn.

She didn't make it.

Something whacked her on the back of the head. She thought, *I'm falling,* as the night grew darker and the stars disappeared, and as she floated into blackness where all thought ceased.

Sister Xuan was kneeling in prayer when the voice came to her.

You are being called. Attend.

She began to weep.

At twenty-three, Sister Xuan was the youngest of the novitiates at St. Cecilia's. Raised a Catholic, she had always wanted to give herself to her beloved Savior and serve him all of her life. She had never felt comfortable in the world.

In part that was because, when she was growing up, there weren't many Vietnamese-American Catholics around her neighborhood in Ontario, California. But even more than that, she'd always had a feeling that she was, well, incomplete. That she'd been born with some sort of lack, a hole in her soul, and she was desperate to fill it.

She thought becoming a nun would do just that. She thought she would finally connect.

But lately her prayers had seemed like so many empty words cast heavenward to a God who no longer listened.

And now this, a voice at last. She was here with the other nuns of St. Cecelia's, in what was supposed to be a silent retreat. She wondered if the sound of her crying displeased God.

"What is it I should attend to?"

No answer.

"Please, tell me what it is I am to do?"

Silence.

"Please!"

Sister J woke up with a headache like the rock fissures of Fredericksburg. Also the remnants of a shattering nightmare. A giant malevolent face was staring at her, about to consume her for breakfast.

Then she realized it was the face of the Superior, Sister Sarah, in the room with her. Sister Sarah had short brown hair and wore a simple blue button-up blouse and a cross necklace. A normal post-60s, Vatican II nun's look, except when one is waking from a bad dream.

"Where am I?" Sister J said.

"Don't you remember?" said Sister Sarah.

"I'm not sure."

"At the Junipero Center," Sister Sarah said.

Oh yes. Malibu. Overlooking the ocean. Parties in the canyon . . . Two boys . . .

"We came up for a retreat, do you recall that?" Sister Sarah said.

"Yes," Sister J said. Her head felt like a dried grape on the sole of a fat man's shoe. "Who hit me?"

"Hit you?"

"Yes. From behind."

"You fell down, in the rock garden."

"No!" The outburst clanged her head. "I need a couple of aspirin."

"We are arranging for that.," Sister Sarah said. "In fact, we are arranging for you to be taken back to St. Cecelia's."

"I don't need to. I can complete the retreat."

"That is a matter of opinion," Sister Sarah said.

Sister J closed her eyes and tried to will the pain away. It wasn't just the pain in her head, but also of being constantly thumbed down by a superior who did not approve of her.

"I will inform you when the paramedics have arrived," Sister Sarah said.

"Paramedics!" The last time Sister J had been with paramedics she had OD'd on Ecstasy.

"We will talk of this later," Sister Sarah said.

"The crucifix."

"I beg your pardon?"

"The two boys."

"Two boys?"

"They were stealing the silver crucifix from the chapel. I tried to stop them. Then somebody hit me."

Sister Sarah shook her head slowly. "I don't know what you mean."

"In the chapel?"

"Yes, I know the crucifix, the one that's been there since 1953."

"Yes, it's gone. Stolen."

"But Sister Justicia, I just came from there, a few minutes ago. The crucifix is not missing. It's right where it always was."

That little news item made Sister J's head pound even more. "But..."

"You need some rest."

"No—"

"Back at St. Cecelia's."

Sister J tried to sit up on the bed, couldn't. "There was an attempted theft, and I was attacked."

"Sister Justicia, you were found on the ground, and there was some blood on a rock near your head. You must have tripped."

"No!" But had she tripped? Was she tripping now? Had she had some drug flashback owing to her wicked past? Dreamed this whole thing?

Ten minutes later two nice paramedics arrived at Sister J's room. Sister Sarah was behind them, giving orders as if she were a director and they were actors working for scale.

Sister J was sitting on the side of the bed now. "Thank you for coming, gentlemen," she said. "But reports of my demise have been greatly exaggerated."

"Huh?" one of the paramedics said. He was young, perhaps twenty, with a football player's build.

"No trouble today, please," Sister Sarah said.

"No, no trouble at all," said Sister Justicia, even though she knew that's exactly what she had been over the course of the last few weeks. About a month earlier she had broken a man's finger in a hospital, then beat up two liquor store robbers. Her Segal-inspired martial arts training had just bubbled up to the surface, manifesting itself in defense not so much of herself, but of the liquor store man who might have been shot.

The training also came in rather handy when a former lover and mediocre film director, Harlan Savage, tried to beat her up a scant two weeks ago.

Now this business with the two crucifix thieves. But then, why wasn't the crucifix gone? *And who had knocked her out?* She did not fall!

She was going to stay and find out.

"I do not wish to be removed from the premises," Sister J said.

"It is for your own good," said Sister Sarah.

"I beg to differ. Being here to finish the retreat is for my good,"

The second paramedic, older and more portly, said to the Superior, "We can't take her if she doesn't want to go."

Sister J said, "Thank you for coming. I wish we had some lovely parting gifts for you."

"This will force the issue," Sister Sarah said. "When we return, I will have no choice but to begin proceedings."

Before Sister J could say another word, her head entered a vice and the vice clamped shut.

Night came again, blacker than the last.

This time Sister J woke up in a hospital bed. A severe concussion, she was told. They wanted her to stay for observation. She checked herself out at two.

She caught the cross-valley Metro bus at two-fifteen. At

three she was back on the grounds of St. Cecelia's school for girls, in the nuns' quarters. She had managed to avoid the administration buildings altogether, and at five she was in the confessional with Father Dom.

"Bless me, Father, for I have sinned. It's been five days since my last confession."

"What sins have you committed, my child?" Father Dom's voice sounded tired. Sister J wondered if he was tired in general, or of her in particular. She loved Father Dom and wished she could please him.

"I'm not sure," Sister J said.

"Not sure?"

"I slapped a couple of boys who cursed at me."

"Slapped!"

"In a nun-with-a-ruler sort of way."

"Sister—"

"The world continues to get worse and I feel called to do something about it."

"How do you feel you have been called?"

"By the voice of God. Like Joan of Arc."

"May I remind you that Joan was burned at the stake?"

"And am I ever glad we don't do that anymore."

"But there are things that will burn the soul just as much. Like getting kicked out of St. Cecelia's."

"I love it here. But what am I to do when I believe God has this work for me?"

"What is the work exactly?"

"To stop people from inflicting pain upon the innocent."

Father Dom said, "Did I not tell you before that your idea is nothing more than vigilantism?"

"But how can that be?" Sister J said. "Why is it not the very same thing God does when he disciplines us? It may turn a soul to heaven, and it keeps that soul from hurting other people."

"Sister Justicia, this is not a healthy thing for you. May I suggest that you undertake a period of penance and cleansing, forget all about this cockamamie theology you're cooking up?"

"Cockamamie? What if it is exactly what God would have me do?"

"Sister Justicia, you have recently suffered a head injury that may interfere with your thinking."

"But—"

"And you have a history of drug use."

"Now that is unfair, Father. I have long since given up drugs and have been cleansed body and soul."

"There are consequences to sin that long linger."

"And there are sinners of consequence who linger too long. Father, I am going to find out who hit me and I am going to compel that person to confess."

"Hit you?"

"On the back of my head."

"They say you fell."

"*They* weren't there. I got hit. And I'm going to seek justice."

"Vengeance is mine, saith the Lord."

"Then the Lord and I are on the same page."

"I think you'd better read that page again," Father Dom said.

An ax blade of fire cut into her head then, and Sister Justicia found she couldn't form a coherent thought.

"Sister?"

She could not talk as she put her hands on her skull to try to ease the pain. When the pain stayed, she left the confessional without another word.

Four days later, she finally felt she could run.

In her sweats and with her hair free in the wind, Sister J should have felt truly alive, not lost. Running was supposed to make you feel unencumbered, in motion, heading toward something good. Better health, for one, which is why she did it—to keep her body strong and her mind off thoughts she struggled with.

Running sometimes made her feel connected to God. But today there was nothing, just the occasional barking dog or car driving by along this hillside street in Studio City.

She ran around a corner and was immediately side-by-side with a man who had come from the opposite side. He was in color-matching shorts and athletic shirt, and in great shape. In fact, he could have been on the cover of GQ. Sister J made him out to be an actor or game show host.

She gave him a curt nod and slowed her pace to let him pass.

He slowed his pace, too. "My, isn't this a coincidence?" he said.

"Not really," Sister J said. She said it in a friendly manner, but wanting to make clear this was a nothing-to-see-here-move-along moment.

He didn't move along. "You run here often?"

"I'm sorry, I'm on my own right now."

"I would love to do something about that."

"Would it help if I told you I wasn't interested?"

He stayed close. "Now, how can you know something like that without getting to know me?"

Sister J stopped, put hands on hips. "Please move on."

He mirrored her position. "You seeing someone?"

"I'm a nun."

The man laughed. He had perfect white teeth. So white they reflected the sun. His black hair was thick and roguish. "If you mean you're not into men, I can change all that."

"That will be quite enough," she said.

"Come on, can't you take a joke? You were joking *me*."

"It's not a joke. I am really and truly a nun. I'm just not wearing my habit."

The bright smile faded and he looked her up and down like a hungry man at a donut display.

"A real pity," he said. "I mean, look at me. You can have all this if you just say the word."

"The word that I'm thinking of is not one a nun should say. Please leave me alone now."

She started to run back the way she came. But in two seconds the man was running alongside her again.

"I was just having a little fun," the would-be pickup artist said. "I didn't really mean anything by it. I just wanted to meet a beautiful woman. Does the fact that you're a nun have to interfere with that?"

"The fact that I am a nun interferes with everything. You seem like a nice guy, but I am not for you."

She kept running, down a tree-lined street with Spanish and Tudor style homes. It was quiet in the late afternoon, and from the hills and she could smell sage. Normally she loved that smell. But not—

She heard the squeal of tires and instinctively jumped onto the sidewalk. The moment she did the pickup artist was right there beside her. A black Mercedes screeched to the curb five feet away from them.

A man in sunglasses and a black suit emerged from the car. She thought for a moment he was stopping to help her. She was about to say she didn't need it.

Then Pickup Artist said, "Get in the car."

The man in the sunglasses stood behind the Mercedes, arms folded. He was Latino and watched impassively.

"What is this?" she said.

"Someone wants to talk to you," Pickup Artist said.

"I'm not going anywhere with you."

"I think you are," Pickup Artist said. He grabbed her left arm and squeezed. She tried to jerk out of his grip but it was an iron trap.

Which meant she had to hurt him.

She hated to do it.

Part of her, anyway.

An increasingly small part, she realized, in the millisecond it took her to dispatch Pickup Artist. He was gripping her arm with his left hand across his body, rendering him without defense to the left side of his face.

Sister J cupped her right hand and banged it against his ear.

The man let go his grip, grabbed his head and stumbled around, cursing. The ear pop had worked exactly as designed, messing up the inner ear and causing momentary pain and confusion.

Then she saw the guy in the shades pointing a handgun at her.

"Don't try to run," Shades said.

"A gun? Really?"

He took a step forward, gun at the ready. "In the car."

Her next several moves were swift and simultaneous. She brought her right hand down and grabbed his wrist, at the same time turning her body out of the line of fire. With her left hand she grabbed the barrel of the gun.

Which went off.

She twisted the gun against his thumb and disarmed him, then dropped the hot weapon to the ground as she thrust her heel into Shades's knee. He went down with an *Aieee!*

Sister J picked up the weapon by the butt and stepped back.

Pickup Artist was on his back. A sickening splotch of red besmirched his shirt, his hands over the wound as he wailed.

A woman screamed from the front door of an adjacent house. She was an older woman in a plain, yellow housedress.

"Call the police!" Sister J shouted.

The woman put her hand to her mouth.

"Now!"

Sister J heard a grunt, turned, and saw Shades coming at her with a knife.

"I am concerned," Sister Sarah said to Sister Xuan.

"Yes, Sister?" The young nun fiddled nervously with her beads. That was not something that was supposed to be done, but she could not help it. If she didn't have a tactile outlet she thought she might go mad.

"Your performance in the classroom," Sister Sarah said, "has recently dropped off, not to put too fine a point on it."

"Dropped off?"

"And it's showing in the test scores. Are you aware of this?"

"I—"

"And that the reputation of St. Cecelia's is at stake?"

"—will try—"

"And that two parents have called me just within the last week to express their concerns?"

Sister Xuan said nothing. In spite of the beads, hot tears came to her eyes. She blinked hard to keep them at bay.

"Now, there's no need for that," Sister Sarah said. She pushed a box of Kleenex across her desk to the distraught nun. "If we didn't know the problem, then perhaps a tear or two would be understandable. But since we do, we also know the solution."

"I'm sorry," Sister Xuan said. "I do not understand.'

"It's fairly simple," the Superior said, leaning back in her chair. "It's your association with a certain influence that is hurting you."

"It is?"

"Bad company corrupts good morals."

"Company?"

"Come now," Sister Sarah said. "I'm talking about Sister Justicia Marie. You know very well she is on thin ice around here, and it's not doing you any good to be associating with her. She has influence on some of the younger sisters, and it's got to stop."

Sister Xuan felt a crevice opening up inside her. Surely the Superior could not be suggesting she stop talking to Sister Justicia altogether?

"I am suggesting that you stop talking to Sister Justicia altogether," the Superior said.

"But she's my friend."

"Sometimes friendship must be sacrificed to do the will of God."

"I..."

"Now, let's not speak of it again. Let's just accept that you will no longer associate with Sister Justicia."

"But—"

"She is not for you."

"But Sister," the young nun said. "I don't think Sister Justicia is as you say."

"You don't think that her violent tendencies are a danger to a life of consecration?"

"No," Sister Xuan said quickly. She felt the need to rise to the defense of her friend. "I do not think Sister Justicia is violent at all!"

Sister Justicia kicked Shades in the face.

His head snapped back.

She followed with a kick to the command center of male fecundity.

He doubled over like a Victorian butler meeting the Queen. He hovered for a moment then fell over on his side.

And dropped the knife.

The woman on the porch screamed again.

"Will you please stop that and call the police!" Sister J winced at her harsh words. But she needed to prod the woman into action.

She picked up the knife, then attended to Pickup Artist, who was bleeding and coughing. His eyelids fluttered like a neon sign on the fritz. His shirt was soaked with sweat and blood, the spot partially obscuring the shirt logo, a rendering of a peacock.

"Easy now, don't try to move," she said. "Help is coming."

He shook his head.

"Who sent you?" said Sister J.

Under his breath, but with crystal clarity, Pickup Artist uttered the F bomb.

"Sir," said Sister J, "you have been shot. The police are going to want to know all about this when they get here." She looked up and saw the old woman looking out of her curtained window. *If* they get here.

"Don't move," she told Pickup. "You're seriously hurt."

Sister J left him and ran to the front door of the house, which was partially open. She didn't bother knocking. When she stepped in the woman screamed again. But then Sister J realized she was holding the knife in one hand and the gun in the other.

"Did you call?" she said.

The old woman opened her mouth, said nothing, and fainted.

Sister J found a phone in the kitchen and called 911. She gave as much information as she could, hung up, went back outside.

The Mercedes was gone.

And so were the two men.

The patrol officers were not pleased.

One of them was a ruddy faced youngster who looked like he'd stepped off a hay bale in Kansas. When did cops start looking too young to vote? The other was the seasoned one, a woman of about forty. Her nameplate said *Mansfield.* While Ruddy was inside attending to the old woman, Mansfield questioned Sister J.

"And you say they just got up and left?"

"That's right. Just disappeared in a black Mercedes."

"Did you get the license plate?"

"I was a little preoccupied."

"You say one of them had the gun and then the knife?"

"That's what I said."

"Uh-huh." Mansfield scribbled something on her report form, which rested on top of a clipboard.

"Officer," Sister J said, "you don't seem to believe me."

"I'm just trying to piece it together in my mind. I mean, you said you were a nun, right?"

"Yes."

"And you were out running?"

"Yes."

"And you disarmed two men, one of whom was shot?"

"You can see the blood on the sidewalk."

"I'm just trying to figure out how a nun can do that."

"Is it really necessary to explain?"

Mansfield leaned close and whispered, "Personally, I love it. I just have to convince my captain, you know?"

Sister J whispered back, "I'll do what I can."

The questioning took another twenty minutes. Sister J jogged back to her car, an old Saturn she called *Ping*, and thought about the peacock logo on Pickup Artist's shirt. She knew that logo. And she was going to follow it.

After showering and getting back in the habit, Sister J drove over to Cahuenga Boulevard in Hollywood. There was a club there, the India, which used that peacock logo. And inside was a man who liked to call himself the Pope of Los Angeles.

Which was a fancy name for a thug who knew people.

Sister J had come to him once before, when searching for a serial nun abuser. He had given her a tip about how to catch the guy, offering herself as bait, and it had worked.

Now there was a connection of a different sort.

Since the last time she'd been here Sister J had learned that the "Pope" was really named Troy Dickinson, and had come from Chicago. His grandfather had been a bootlegger with Capone. Nice family thug-genes.

The India Club ran a fancy lunch hour for the business interests in Hollywood. Sister J entered and was greeted by a hostess in a dress so tight it could have cut off circulation in a flamingo's leg. The hostess recognized her from last time, told her to please wait.

She returned a few minutes later and showed Sister J to the back and through a door marked PRIVATE.

Dickinson sat at an ornate desk in what could have been the office of an old-time movie mogul. Framed eight-by-tens of stars and politicians hung on the walls. He had a cigar crammed in the corner of his mouth and was talking on the phone. He waved Sister J into a chair and continued talking.

"You tell him if he doesn't come through on this we're done, you got that? This is business, not Xbox."

He took the cigar out of his mouth and blew a long, languid trail of smoke. Sister J coughed. It reminded her of her father, a cigar smoker and former Green Beret. He was a driven, show business dad who had disappeared from her life when she became a nun.

Now the smell of Dickinson's cigar brought back how much she missed her father before the whole TV and movie thing had ruined their lives. Mom had died when she was thirteen, which is when she started drinking heavily. Still, Sister J had long since forgiven her father and wanted desperately to see him again. But he had not left a forwarding address.

Dickinson put down his phone and said, "You messed up a couple of my boys."

"They asked for it," Sister J said.

"Not the way they tell it."

"Are you going to take their word over the word of a nun?"

"Everybody lies."

"I don't."

"Then tell me what you think of me," Troy Dickinson said.

"I would rather—"

"And don't lie."

"All right. I see a man who loves power more than people, and who is a lonely man because of it."

His expression switched from open and friendly to closed and cold. "I got lots of friends."

"That's not what I mean," Sister J said. "It is possible to be surrounded and still be the loneliest man in the room."

"We were talking about you messing up two of my boys."

"Sir, if you do not want your boys to be, as you say, messed up, then you should not dispatch them to perform assaults."

"Now I caught you. You *are* lying. They didn't get any assignment to do any assaulting."

"Then what was all that rough stuff, with the gun brandishing and the knife?"

"Gun? They don't carry."

"I took the gun from him. The Hispanic gentleman."

Dickinson stuck the cigar back in his mouth and rubbed his head. "Sister, I don't know what you're talking about."

"I'm talking about the two men, the one with the smile like he was going to sell me a car, the other, a guy in a Mercedes."

"I'm talking about a couple of kids who are only eighteen."

Sister J shook her head once, as if to clear it. "The boys who were stealing the crucifix?"

"What crucifix?"

"Didn't they tell you about that?"

"They only told me about *you*."

"Wait, wait. Are you saying you did not send those guys on the street out in Studio City?"

"No idea who you're talking about."

Sister J rubbed her temples. "Well then who—"

"Sister, I can't be responsible for all the toughs in LA now, can I?"

"Maybe you should take that on. It would do as penance."

Dickinson removed his cigar. Then he smiled like he'd just won on *Wheel of Fortune*. "Maybe you're right, Sister. Maybe you're right. But . . ."

"Yes?"

"I don't want our interests to conflict, if you know what I mean."

Sister J stood. "Then tell me what you're doing with those boys, why are they hanging around you?"

"Now Sister—"

"I'll make a deal with you."

"Deal?"

"Right here, right now."

"What have you possibly got to offer me?"

"Not making your life a living hell." She smiled. "Cops, newspaper, internet, television."

Dickinson put his cigar in the large glass ash tray. He placed the palms of his hands on his eyes and made small circles with them.

"Just one address," Sister J said. "And I'll relent."

"That's good," the Pope of Los Angeles said.

"For the time being."

"Meaning?"

"Meaning," Sister J said, "I may ask you for a service someday."

"You sound like Vito Corleone," Dickinson said.

"In that case," Sister J said, "Consider this an offer you can't refuse."

Outside the sky was overcast. The sign on the old Pantages theater was lit up. The faded glamour of Hollywood making a last neon stand at the wrong end of the Hollywood strip. All the action was moved to the touristy glitz around the Dolby Theatre. Sister J remembered the last time she walked a red carpet there, back when it was called the Kodak. She was blitzed and hanging onto either George Clooney or John Goodman, she couldn't recall who.

Now the old feelings came flooding back, and she was sure the Pope of Los Angeles and his power had something to do with it. He was like a mythic guardian of a dark cave, and in the cave were the forbidden things that Brooke Bailey had once indulged.

God, deliver me. If this is going to be my calling, do not let me fall into the hands of temptation.

"Yes?"

"You are Chris's mother?"

"Yes, but...I'm sorry, who are you?"

"I am Sister Justicia."

"And you know my son how?"

"May I come in?"

The woman hesitated, then opened the door. Inside it was mid-century modern. Vaulted, open-beamed ceiling, large picture windows and old paint. There was no rhyme or reason to the interior design. It was an eclectic collection of poorly framed posters (AC/DC and Aerosmith) and a color scheme that could have been matched by Stevie Wonder. Sister J believed that someone's home reflects their inner life. If so, this woman was dazed, confused, and probably hurting.

Then Sister J noticed the prominent crucifix over the fireplace.

A quick perusal of the rest of the items in the room gave the impression that a man did not live here, but an adolescent did. A skateboard leaned against the French doors, with a football close by.

"Now," the woman said, "please tell me what this is about."

"May I sit down?"

"I guess."

In the muted daylight Sister J could see prominent crows' feet around the woman's eyes. The feet of those particular crows were larger than the woman's age might have called for. She was dishwater blonde and her face evidenced a run of hard years.

She sat opposite Sister J on a pitiful recliner, without reclining. "Now, is this about Chris?"

"It is. I wonder if—"

"What is she doing here?" It was Chris, hustling into the room. He was in a T-shirt and baggy shorts.

"Chris," his mother said, "do you want to tell me what's going on?"

"Yes Chris," Sister J said. "Why don't you?"

His face was flushed and eyes red-rimmed. He might have been crying but more likely he was baked. Sister J could smell the slightest whiff of marijuana wafting in from his direction. He also an ugly black bruise under his left eye.

"How'd you get this address?"

"An associate of yours," Sister J said.

"Who is she talking about," the mother said.

"You just get out," Chris said.

"Chris, I would like to know—"

"Shut up, Mom! Don't say anything!"

"Hey," Sister J said, "Honor your father and mother. It's a commandment."

"Get out!"

"Chris!" the mother said.

"Ma'am," said Sister J. "I wonder if you might let me talk to your son for about five minutes, alone."

"No," Chris said.

"Good idea," the mother said. She was swift getting to her car keys and shutting the door behind her.

When they were alone in the living room, Sister J said, "What is it with the attitude? The look? You come off like a bad imitation of The Rock."

Chris blinked a couple of times. "You know about The

Rock?"

"Why wouldn't I know about The Rock? I don't live under one. I have an idea about popular culture."

"You just don't think a nun will know about The Rock."

"He a hero of yours?"

"I dig his movies. Like *The Rundown.*"

"That had its moments. Christopher Walken is always worth watching."

"You know about Christopher Walken?"

"I was in a movie with him once. Nice guy."

Chris shook his head. "You?"

"I used to be in the business," Sister J said. "But it didn't do me any good. And crime isn't going to do *you* any good, either. Or drugs. I just don't want you to end up like The Rock in *Faster.*"

"You saw *Faster?*"

"Nuns have to relax."

"But it was rated R!"

"Nuns can take it."

Quietly, Chris said, "Awesome movie."

"It might have been. But they messed up the ending. And that's going to mess up your life."

"What do you mean they messed up the ending?"

"The Rock is close to redemption. He's in that revival tent. He's been growing in compassion. Then he executes Billy Bob Thornton."

"Which Billy Bob Thornton deserved."

"But that's just it, you see? What he should have done was wound him and wait for his cop partner to arrive. Leave Thornton to the justice system. As is, The Rock just becomes another nihilistic assassin no one could care less about. Instead, it might have been a little action classic. The Rock should have waited for the cop partner, she comes at him with a gun. He takes the gun from her and says, 'Don't follow me.' She says, 'I have to.' And then he says, 'I know,' and *then* he drives off. That's would have been the right ending."

"I can't believe I'm talking to a nun about the meaning of a Rock movie!"

"It's your lucky day. Because the lesson is this. Don't try to be like some movie or game. Life isn't like that. Go back to the basics. Learn to live with real courage, which doesn't come from brandishing a gun or pretending morality doesn't apply to you because you're a lone wolf. I don't want to see you end up dead."

"You got to live your own life."

"Of course, but you're not going to find your life where you think you are. You're going to end up miserable and then dead."

"Why do you even care about me?"

"It's my job to care. And I like my job."

For a long moment Chris sat there, and it looked for one second as if tears might form in his eyes. He seemed about eight years old then, and Sister J wanted to engulf him in a hug and tell him he could make it, he could—because he was what she was ten years before. Angry, lost, confused, arrogant. She wanted to squeeze all that out of him and pour in the light.

"You need to tell me something, Chris. You need to."

"What?"

"How'd you get that black eye?"

Chris said nothing.

"I have a feeling the night you came up to steal that crucifix, and my being attacked on the street, are related. You want to talk to me about it?"

"I can't. I mean . . ."

"You can. There's an old saying, maybe you've heard it. Confession is good for the soul. Don't hold in the bad things."

"Don't be so nice to me, will you? Why don't you just leave me alone?"

He got up and started for the door.

"Chris . . ."

He didn't turn back.

Sister J offered up a prayer for Chris and his mother as she drove to a seedy section of North Hollywood, where rents were cheap. She'd had her eye on a storefront that was for lease. It occupied a corner and had been unused for years. This was not what the real estate agents would call a good *location, location, location.*

There was trash all over the cracked parking lot and the residue of homeless encampments on either side of the building.

Which made it perfect for Sister Justicia.

The owner of the building, a pot-bellied smoker named Ron Daley, met Sister J at the locked front door. He took a drag on his cig then crushed it under his shoe. "You sure about this, Sister?" He was balding, about forty, and wore a knit shirt tucked into his slacks. The latter decision accentuated his rotundity to an almost uncivil degree.

"I'm exploring options," she said.

"Gotta tell you, I don't think your do-gooding is gonna do any good for this crowd."

"Maybe you'd rather see a strip club here?"

He shrugged. "Tried. City said no. Frankly, I don't know if they'll go for the Catholic church setting up shop."

"It's not the church. It's just one vision to help the poor."

"It's your nickel. You do realize it's going to cost more than a nickel, don't you?"

"We can talk money later."

Ron Daley took another smoke from his shirt pocket, lit up. "I like to talk money up front."

"Show me the inside," she said.

And he did. The place smelled like 1972.

After the tour, and a little haggling, Sister J told Daley she'd get back to him. He said he wasn't going to hold the property for her. She didn't tell him she wasn't afraid of that.

He drove his Lexus away, trailing smoke out his window.

Sister J was about to get in Ping, her Saturn, when she happened to look up.

Her breath jumped out of her like a skydiver from a plane. Across the street was the Latino guy from the Mercedes, the one who had pulled both gun and knife on her.

He ducked into an apartment complex.

Sister J wasn't sure if he'd spotted her. She ran across the street and into the courtyard. It was filled with cracked cement walkways, some children's toys, and patchy grasses poking defiantly through the cracks.

She heard the sound of booming salsa from someplace on the second level, but no sign of the man she was trailing.

For a moment she could have been on a desert island that piped in hot Latin music through the trees.

Then a door to her left opened. A shirtless man who was a walking advertisement for prison tats stepped outside, almost kicking a toy fire truck that was sitting there waiting for a kid.

"You lost, Sister?" he said.

"Actually, I'm looking for someone."

"Nobody here."

"You are," she said.

The man was about six feet tall, Hispanic, well muscled. On

his chest was emblazoned *CABALLOS* in gang script, and under that a depiction of two wild horses snorting at each other. Above the name, various gang symbols stretched up to his neck and spread out like spider legs.

"I believe someone just went into your apartment," she said. "I want to talk to him."

"Mistake to be here, Sister."

"I think not."

He said nothing but looked like words were struggling in his throat. Sister J walked toward the open door. The man gripped her arm.

"You want to lose that hand?" she said.

El Caballo laughed.

With a quick snap of her hand, and an upward pull of her arm, Sister J loosed herself and got hold of Mr. Caballo's index finger. She bent it back and sent him to his knees.

"Deliver my message, please," she said.

She let him go. Caballo cursed and scrambled inside the apartment, slamming the door behind him.

She heard several voices inside, yammering.

The door opened and a guy who practically filled the whole thing appeared. He was white and skinheaded, at least six foot seven, and maybe five feet across the chest. He had crags and crevices of muscle and skin. He was an iceberg in jeans. He wore a black T-shirt with a skull on the front.

"A nun?" He smiled. He had a gold tooth in front. "Really?"

"Really," Sister J said.

"I don't believe in God," he said.

"He believes in you," said Sister J.

"I'm telling you, I don't think you're anything special. You're a chick in a penguin suit, that's all."

"That's pretty cheeky for a half-naked guy to say."

"I beat up my women," he said. "I'll do the same to you if you don't get out of here."

"There's somebody I want to talk to in there."

"Not gonna happen."

The first guy, the one with the prison tats, said, "Elmo, she's a nun, man."

"So?" Elmo's look was fire, and he was no saint.

"You don't mess with a nun."

"Go inside."

The Hispanic man shrugged and disappeared into the darkness.

Sister J said, "The English underestimated St. Joan. Don't make the same mistake."

"You're kinda cute, you know that?"

"And don't try street charm, either. You're like a blacksmith trying to cut a diamond."

He frowned. Then reached behind his back and came out with a big knife. He started cleaning his fingernails with it.

"Am I supposed to be impressed?" Sister J said.

"You have ten seconds," Elmo said.

"Are you going to kill me?"

"Haven't made up my mind yet."

Sister J sighed, then slowly removed her wimple and hood. She placed the wimple on the ground and wrapped the hood around her left hand. "Protection," she said. "In a knife fight, you have to be ready."

"You kidding me?"

With her right she picked up the toy fire truck. It was about eight inches long, but with a pointy ladder sticking off the back-side. "Don't make me use this," she said.

Elmo laughed.

"I don't want to hurt you," Sister J said. "It would pain me greatly to do it. It would mean I would have to finish the job until you are of a mind to repent. It would be much better if you did so now, voluntarily. Put the knife away and let me talk to the guy inside. You can tell him I'm not—"

From inside a voice said, "She's not kiddin', man! She can take you down!"

The guy from the Mercedes came out, pushing past Elmo.

"Okay, what is it you want?" he said. "Put away the blade, Elmo."

The giant looked confused. But he put the knife away in the back of his pants.

"So what're you following me for?" Mercedes Guy said.

She placed the fire engine gently on the ground. "I want to know who sent you to pick me up."

"You don't want to know."

"I do."

He shook his head. "No, Sister. You got to believe me. You don't. I know all about you. The way you got lucky a couple of times, with me and some other guys in a liquor store. But the word is out on you. You're not gonna surprise anybody again. Why don't you go set up shop in another city, huh?"

Elmo said, "No way she could take me."

"I don't want to beat it out of you," Sister J said, feeling the surge of adrenaline that always accompanied her threats of violence. "Although, it would be for your ultimate good."

"I can't take this no more!" Elmo said and, with a giant step and grab, took Sister J's arm and twisted it behind her back.

Without hesitation she stomped her heel on his foot. This caused a slight lessening of pressure. She gave him an elbow to the gut. He *oomphed* and Sister J yanked free, spun one-eighty, and gave Elmo a Moe Howard double finger poke to the eyes. She lunged forward for a Gracie-style Brazilian Jiujitsu *Baiana*. Bending at the waist, she jammed her shoulder into Elmo's stomach. At the same time she reached around and grabbed both of his legs at the knees. She pushed with her own legs and got Elmo off the ground a few inches, pulling his knees at the same time. They both went down, Elmo hard on his back and Sister J on top where she put him in an old fashioned, LAPD chokehold.

Elmo's eyes bugged as his face turned crimson.

Sister J paused a moment like that, then stood back up.

Elmo stayed on the ground, wheezing.

"You really are crazy, just like they say," Mercedes Guy said.

She heard Elmo struggling for breath as he got up. He pointed at Mercedes Guy. "Don't you say nothin' to nobody about this."

And then through the gate came two uniformed police officers. Two men, one white, one black.

"What's going on?" the white one said.

Mercedes Guy said, "There she is."

"This one?" the cop said.

"You called the police on me?" Sister J said.

The cop looked at Elmo, then at Sister J, then at Mercedes. "You're kidding, right?"

"No, officers, she is disturbing my peace. She's trespassing and making threats."

"A nun?"

"A crazy nun! Get her out of here."

The black cop tried to suppress a smile.

The white cop said, "I guess I have to ask if you have an invitation from any of the tenants to be here."

Sister J said, "Just making my rounds."

"Like a snake she's making her rounds," Mercedes said.

"What's she done that's so bad?" the white cop said.

Maybe this whole thing was bad, she thought. Her emotions and thoughts and hormones were blasting all through her now, exhilarating and frightening at the same time. She *enjoyed* taking the man down. Too much she enjoyed it! She sensed herself becoming a wholly other thing that was as yet undefined, but which drew her as if she were a nail caught in a magnetic field.

When the cops finally broke it all up and said she could go, she almost said out loud, *Go where?*

It was well past dark when Sister J got back to St. Ceclia's. She had to run. She had to sweat. She had to keep ahead of the waves of doubt. She was just getting into her sweats when she heard a gentle knocking on her door.

Sister Xuan meekly asked if she could talk. The young novitiate seemed nervous, as if she'd spilled ketchup on her wimple and didn't know what to do about it. She sat on the edge of Sister J's bed.

"I have heard something about you," Sister Xuan said.

Sister J said, "Why am I not surprised?"

"May I say?"

"By all means."

"That there is something violent in you."

Sister J looked at the nervous nun with tenderness. "Would you care to explain further?"

"I am sorry if I have offended you!"

"No, no, it's all right. I just would like to know the substance of what you've been told."

"I *have* offended you!"

"It takes a lot to offend me these days. You're not getting anywhere near the line. In fact, you're in Philadelphia compared to the line. So don't worry about that anymore, okay?"

A little bit of a smile came to Sister Xuan's face. Then quickly faded. "The Superior has advised me not to associate with you."

As much as she did not want it to, that report hurt Sister J deeply. She sat on her bed and said, "I'm afraid I'm doomed here. It's probably best to avoid me."

"But I don't want that!"

"Thank you for that. But you are a wonderful teacher. I've seen you with the children. They respond to you. That is much more important than what we are talking about. We are only two people, two nuns who want to serve the Lord. But our service has to be where we are called, and I am not called here. You are."

"But what if that isn't true? What if the Lord is calling me to something completely different?"

"We must continue to pray," Sister J said. "But decide nothing now."

"Is any of it true?"

"Is any of what true?"

"That you are somewhat violent?"

Sister J sighed, and allowed herself a rueful smile. "I have the ability to kick people's butts, yes. I'm trying to find a proper theological way to say that. Father Dom thinks I'm crazy, and he may be right, and that is why you should be careful about talking to me or being around me. I may be unbalanced."

Sister Xuan breathed in deeply, let it out slowly. "I do not think that you are."

"I hope and pray you are right," Sister J said.

On Thursday Sister J drove her Saturn up to the Junipero Retreat Center. It was overcast by the ocean, wet and thick air pushing back against her windshield.

She drove up the winding driveway and parked near the rock garden at the exact spot where the Escalade had been that night.

An examination of the garden revealed a fresh spot where a

rock had been removed, leaving its dirt imprint behind. As there were no other rocks with blood stains, it was clear why this one was missing.

Sister Justicia took the walking path to the back entry way, went in, and turned right into the chapel. There was no one inside, but sure enough the crucifix was.

"May I help you, Sister?"

It was Father Bartolome Berryman, who ran the center. He was what medieval monks would have called *stout of build and ponderous of bearing.* He wore the Franciscan robe, a dark brown cassock with hood, and a rope belt. He was perhaps fifty-years-old.

"Father, what do you know about the night the crucifix was almost stolen?"

"Stolen? Our silver crucifix?"

"That one, over there. Two boys tried to steal it, and I was confronting them when I got hit on the head."

"Why, I thought you fell. That's what I was told."

"You were told wrong."

The priest cleared his throat. With his hood on he looked like a boxer entering the ring. "But there was no theft."

Sister J felt another headache coming on. She pressed her palm against her forehead. "Father, it seems to me there were some other people here at the same time we were."

"Yes, a small group of Presbyterians."

"Do you happen to know how many?"

"Oh, however many were chosen." He chuckled. "A little Presbyterian humor."

Sister J tried to force a smile, but her mouth fought back. "Would the office happen to have a list of names?"

Father Berryman wrinkled his formidable forehead. "You are not suggesting—"

"I'm asking."

"It would be a violation of my office to give you that information."

"Of course," Sister J said. "And I would not want you to do anything that would cause your conscience concern. I will not bother you with this further."

But that did not mean she could not bother someone else.

Sister J made her exit by way of the front office. A young woman named Anna was behind the desk. Sister J had spoken with her before, at the last retreat. She was a helpful sort, anxious to please. Like if you had a headache . . .

"Are you all right?" Anna asked.

"Just a headache," Sister J said. "Would you happen to have any, oh, Tylenol?"

"I can go see in the back," Anna said.

"That would be nice," Sister J said. "Thank you."

And as soon as Anna was out the back door, Sister J went to her chair.

She figured she had about a minute.

She opened Excel on the computer. Checked under *Open Recent* and found a file named PRESBY13. She opened it, saw a roster of names and addresses.

Fourteen records.

She clicked the printer icon.

The printer on the credenza started to hum.

It was not one of the fastest printers on the planet.

Sister J quit Excel.

Thirty seconds gone.

The print icon on the dock started bouncing up and down.

What?

Sister J grabbed the mouse and clicked on it. A window came up and reported OUT OF PAPER.

Paper! Where did they keep the paper?

Forty-five seconds gone.

Please let them be out of Tylenol.

Am I really praying that?

Opening the credenza doors, Sister J saw no reams of paper, no paper at all except some brochures and one standard size sheet of printed text and a title: THE STORY OF FATHER JUNIPERO SERRA.

Almost a minute!

Sister J grabbed the paper and looked on the back. Blank!

She pulled out the paper tray. Wait. Which way to place it so it would print on the blank side?

Which way, which way?

In the hallway a door closed.

Sister J put the paper in, print side down.

The printer hacked and wheezed.

Come on!

Just as the door opened, the paper spat out. Sister J grabbed it, looked, saw that the names had been printed over the text, transliterating into a rural form of Mandarin Chinese.

"Oh, I see that you are looking at my humble contribution," Anna said.

"Excuse me?"

"I'm the one who wrote that biography of Father Serra. I hope I did all right."

Sister J gave the page a quick glance and smiled. "Highly original," she said.

Anna smiled. "Really? You really think so?"

"It's unlike anything I've ever seen on Father Serra before." She quickly folded the page and slipped it into the pocket of her habit.

The only legible name was the first one. Ralph Cleat. Sister J knew it. Cleat was a top criminal defense attorney in Los Angeles. When she was Brooke Bailey, one of her best friends was another child actress who fell into drugs, Sophia Demure. She killed her boyfriend, an actor named Roman Andreesen. Apparently Roman was roamin' a little too often. Sophia did not like that and, while in a drug induced haze, confronted him with a ball peen hammer. What happened after that was a matter of who you believed—Sophia, the prosecutors, the police, or Ralph Cleat, who wove a tapestry of reasonable doubt so beautiful in its complexity that the jury wept after issuing Sophia a full acquittal.

Now, a criminal defense lawyer of Ralph Cleat's magnitude would probably be an asset in Sister J's investigation. He could have seen things. Or at least noticed them.

In her Saturn, Sister J pulled out her iPad and did some Googling.

Ralph Cleat had a Wikipedia page of some length, with two standout entries. One on the Sophie Demure case, the other on the William "Skeets" Quigley case, Cleat's first big victory. Quigley had been a hitman for the O'Fallon crime family out of Boston. He was convicted of three counts of murder and sentenced to life without the possibility of parole. But Ralph Cleat, then a young associate in a prominent firm, got a reversal. While out on bail, Skeets Quigley disappeared and was never apprehended. That was fifteen years ago.

Shortly after that, Ralph Cleat came to Los Angeles to open

up his own firm. Some said Cleat was funded by money from the crime family Quigley had once murdered for.

Sister J looked up Cleat's office number and placed the call.

A woman with a voice like Lauren Bacall answered. "Mr. Cleat's office."

"My name is Sister Justicia Marie, of St. Cecelia's school. I would like to see Mr. Cleat on a matter of some importance."

"Did you say *Sister?*"

"I am a nun."

"What would this be regarding?"

"I am not at liberty to say over the phone. It may involve information that Mr. Cleat would rather keep on the down low, as they say."

Pause.

"Naturally, Mr. Cleat is extremely busy. He will be coming back from lunch and has to go right into a deposition. Perhaps if I took your number he can contact you."

"I am afraid this can't wait."

"I'm sorry, but—"

"I can be there in half an hour."

Downtown Los Angeles hosts many high-rise buildings. Ralph Cleat had his office on the fortieth floor of Two California Plaza on Grand. Sister Justicia parked in the lot near Pershing Square and walked over. It was nearing the end of lunch hour, and there were not a lot of nuns strolling around. Mostly young professionals in pursuit of high rise dreams, too preoccupied on their phones to notice much of anything around them, let alone a nun.

Sister J walked into the reception area, which smelled of fine leather and fresh carpet. The waiting room had an antique feel to it, and the impression of classic elegance mixed with shark.

A receptionist, looking like a model out of the Sports Illustrated swimsuit issue and dressed in a style that was at once professional and provocative, looked up in surprise. She forced a smile and said, "May I help you?"

"I am here to see Mr. Cleat," Sister J said.

"I thought I made it plain over the phone—"

"I believe in miracles," Sister J said.

At which point a well-dressed man with a full head of silver hair and an attitude of total control came through the door.

"Mr. Cleat?" Sister J said.

"Well, this is a surprise. I didn't expect—"

"Can we talk?"

"Would you like some coffee?"

"No thank you."

"I think I would. Lacey, would you mind?"

The receptionist nodded and got up. Cleat showed Sister J to his corner office which had a breathtaking view of the city and, on this clear day, the ocean.

Sister J sat in a fine leather chair across from Cleat's desk, an impressive work fashioned from the cut of some majestic tree. The rings of the tree were clearly seen under the glass, like ripples in marble.

"My father made this desk," Cleat said. "He was a carpenter. Like Jesus."

"Ah," Sister J said.

"Have you ever wondered if Jesus was always perfect as a carpenter?"

"I've never thought about it," Sister J said. "He came as a babe and must've had to learn things."

Cleat nodded. "And now, what must I learn from you?"

"You were recently enjoying a retreat at the Junipero Center."

"Yes, I was with a group of men from my church. May I ask how you know about that?"

"I was there at the same time. The teachers from my school were up there for the same purpose. While I was there a couple of young men attempted to steal a silver crucifix from the chapel. I happened to catch them and was speaking to them when I got hit on the back of the head."

"That's terrible! Do you want me to sue somebody?" He rubbed his hands together. "The Catholic church is loaded."

"Please, I would only like to find out who may have done it."

"I'd think you would be," Cleat said. "But how do you think I can help you?"

"Your powers of observation are well known. Plus, you're a criminal defense lawyer. You've represented some of the most notorious criminals in Los Angeles. That gives you a certain connection with the criminal element."

"I don't follow."

"I am just asking the question. You are the only lead I have."

"I'm sorry to disappoint you."

"Then maybe you can give me a little advice. I intend to follow this matter up. The person who hit me is a sinner. As are we all. And this is a sinner much in need of correction, and it is my duty to find and help administer a lesson."

Cleat smiled. "That almost sounds like a threat."

"I have a certain way of doing things."

"Then that makes us kindred spirits," Cleat said.

"I've never been kindred spirits with a lawyer before," Sister J said.

"Nor I with a nun. Only in LA, right?"

There was a knock on the door. Lacey the receptionist babe entered with a cup of steaming coffee, placed it on Cleat's desk, and left.

"Drink a lot of coffee, do you?" Sister J said.

"Gotta keep sharp," he said.

And as he lifted the mug to his lips, Sister J noted the peacock on the side.

"Would you mind if I asked you some pointed questions?" Sister J said.

"Pointed?"

"Cross-examination."

"You want to cross-examine *me?*"

"Nervous?"

"Why should I be?" Cleat said. "The only people who should be nervous on cross-examination are those who lie."

"Then we are agreed," Sister J said. "When did Troy Dickinson become your client?"

Cleat paused, a flinch skittering across his face. "That's a question that assumes an answer," he said. "Like, *When did you stop beating your wife?*"

"And I assume that is the only reason you're drinking from an India Club mug. It was a gift from Dickinson. It does not fit the décor of your office. You probably would not keep it around, except that Dickinson might at some point be in your office and you would not wish to insult him. And the only reason he would be in your office is that he is your client. So, when was it?"

"All right," Cleat said, squaring himself up in his chair as if to get ready for a fight. "So he's my client. I have lots of clients, and very prominent ones, too. You ought to know that."

"But now I see a connection," Sister J said. "Triangularity. If you can get three points to connect you probably can see what's in the middle. There is Dickinson, who employs young men to do his dirty work. There is you, Dickinson's lawyer. And there is the Junipero Center, where you recently were with a group from your church. In the middle of the triangle is me, with a knot on my head. And I want to know why."

Cleat said nothing, but his cheeks did a shimmy.

"I find your unwillingness to be helpful a bit puzzling," Sister J said.

"You shouldn't. I am a lawyer. I don't just hand out information."

"You take money for it?"

He smiled. "Sometimes. But only ethically, you see."

"Would that include having a partial interest in the India Club, undisclosed of course."

A chill veil dropped over his face. "That is an outrageous thing to say."

"It may be," Sister J said. "But the main question is, is it true? Because that would give you an interest in what goes on there. And what goes on there is not always, to use your word, ethical."

For a moment he did not move, did not allow any indication of his inner life to be let through his cool gray eyes. And then he put on the sort of warmth the used car salesman adopts when he reminds you his real title is *Pre-owned automobile associate.*

"I am due in court," Cleat said. "Good day."

Sister J stood. "Mr. Cleat, what shall it profit a man if he should gain the whole world, yet lose his own soul?"

"How much interest can you collect on a soul?"

"Oh, you get your preferred interest rate. God prefers that you be interested in eternal life."

"Right now," Cleat said, "I'm only interested in you leaving."

She left.

Well, you can't win them all, Sister J thought as she walked up Grand to Temple Street. She was going to attend afternoon mass at Our Lady, the cathedral that opened in 2002 to serve the Archdiocese of Los Angeles.

She paused at the corner to look at it. The exterior was a plain, sandy-brown, and always reminded Sister J of plywood. Yet that was what the church in the world was supposed to be—unadorned and practical. Inside, reflect the glory of God. Outside, help the weak, the hungry, the naked, the widows, the orphans.

And right across the street from the cathedral was the courthouse, which operated on a whole different set of rules. Talk about the sacred and the profane! Sister J always expected a small storm to break out on Temple Street as clouds from the two buildings met in the middle.

Next to the courthouse was the Los Angeles Hall of Records. And there. . .

Hall of Records. . .

Triangularity.

And a hundred watts went off in Sister J's head.

She forgot all about mass.

"Sister, how nice to see you again," Father Berryman said.

She was standing on the bluff at the Junipero Center, looking toward the ocean. She'd been waiting for the Franciscan friar. He had his hood on, looking medieval as usual.

Facing him, she said, "Father, has it ever occurred to you what a fine piece of property this is? That whoever owns it could get a lot of money for it."

"We are blessed indeed," he said.

"Even though ownership resides in a private holding company."

Berryman blinked a couple of times.

"That means," Sister J said, "this land could be sold out from under us at any time."

"Ah," he said, "but it is God's will that we are here."

"God's? Or the O'Fallon crime syndicate?"

Pause. "I am sure I don't know what you mean."

"I'm sure you do, Father Berryman. Or should I say Skeets Quigley?"

The ocean waves crashed on a Malibu beach. It was getting to be a cool afternoon, clouds rolling in.

And the face of the ersatz priest seemed to be fighting with itself. Still playing ignorant?

"Let's see," Sister J said. "These grounds were bought almost fifteen years ago. According to the Hall of Records, the transaction was through a development company out of Boston. That's where the O'Fallons are based, though their interests are nationwide. I was curious about the law firm that handled this. Did you know those records were sealed? Except for one document that apparently passed notice. It was a document that gave power of attorney to a local lawyer. By the name of Ralph Cleat."

The man's face began to flush.

"And it was fifteen years ago that Skeets Quigley disappeared. After this same Ralph Cleat won an improbable appeal. I'm sure the O'Fallon family, owners, had no trouble putting in a fake priest here. What a perfect life for a hitman on the run. Not a place the Feds would look. Three squares a day, ocean view, and a little crime on the side. Tell me, did the two young men you hired come here on their own? Or did you ask them to?"

"Sister . . ."

"Stop with the *Sister.* I suspect they were here to steal the crucifix. You had conveniently left the chapel doors unlocked. And when I interrupted the proceedings, you came up behind me and clobbered me. How am I doing so far?"

It was then that the faux Father slowly pulled off his hood.

He had dancing Irish eyes that crinkled as he smiled. "How'd you figure it out, a little girl like you?"

"Oh, we girls have come a long way. We think and everything."

"Damn," he said.

"That word applies to you," Sister J said. "You have posed as a priest, and that is bad news in the eyes of God. I can arrange for you to confess and receive absolution before you go back to jail."

He snorted a laugh. "Are you for real? Do you realize you're talking to Skeets Quigley?"

"For a while now," she said.

"You're a nun, right? I can say something to you and you'll keep it confidential?"

"Anything you say to me will be just between us."

"Good. I've killed twelve people in my life, two of 'em chicks who were going to rat me out. I don't believe in God, so there's nothing to stop me from offing you now, is there?"

A chill wind whipped up from the ocean, carrying with it the smell of salt and seaweed. Sister J took in a deep whiff. It smelled like violence.

"You have a moral conscience," she said. "You've turned it off, but it's there. You know there is good and evil, but you chose the path of evil, and the good you kicked to the curb. You have this one chance to get it back, to save your soul. It's not too late. God keeps the door open, but you have to walk through."

"You see those rocks down there?" Skeets Quigley said, pointing down just over the bluff. "That's where they're going to find you. You slipped. You came out here and down you fell. Tragic."

"You have one chance, Skeets. Kneel down and ask for forgiveness."

That is exactly what he began to do. Slowly. Dropping. Bowing his head.

Then shooting out with his fist.

Sister J wasn't surprised, turned her head. The blow glanced off her cheek.

She gave Skeets Quigley a right fist to the gut. What did surprise her was the hardness of it.

And his reaction, swift. Wrapping his arm around her neck he started pulling her toward the edge.

Up above the bluff, in his infinity pool, director Steven Spielberg glanced down at the Junipero property. He called to his wife. "Honey, come tell me if I'm seeing this right."

"See what?" came the voice from inside.

"I think there's a nun and a priest down there, and I think they're fighting."

Sister J dug her heels into the sod but found no purchase there. Her right foot took out a chunk of earth and the foot itself hovered over the cliff.

When in danger of being overpowered, resist not.

She dropped to her knees and pulled on Quigley's cassock. Even as she did she was angry at the way he was profaning the garb that had been passed down from St. Francis himself. This was no friend of the birds and the trees. This was no mouth that would ever utter, "Lord, make me an instrument of thy peace."

But she did not want him to die with his sins on his soul.

She just wanted him to feel great pain and fear.

But he was on top of her now. Slobber from his mouth dripped onto her chin. He bared his teeth.

Sister J reached for his white, fuzzy hair, grabbed a handful and pulled his head down.

And bit his ear.

Hard.

Tasted blood. And flesh.

"Hurry!" Steven Spielberg screamed. "A camera!"

"Which one?" Kate shouted back.

The coppery taste of her opponent's blood sent sparks through Sister J's own.

This was not what she wanted when she took vows. But this is what was God's will.

She hoped, as she spit out the torn remnant of lobe.

Skeets Quigley wailed and wrapped his hands around her neck.

Sister Justicia Marie planted both feet on the ground and pulled her knees up.

If I should die . . . my soul to take . . .

She pushed up. Hard.

Skeets Quigley somersaulted over her head.

And as he screamed his last, Sister J felt herself sliding, sliding, to follow him.

"I can't find it," Kate said.

Steven Spielberg said, "You can't find a camera in Steven Spielberg's own house?"

Folded over the precipice, Sister J grabbed at the grass.

Her face was planted in the dirt.

And she was falling.

If this be thy will, I shall take it.

The grass she held came out of the earth.

Her regret was for the children, the ones she would never get to teach.

And then a burning on her wrist.

No, a grip.

She stopped falling.

And was, amazingly, actually being pulled up.

"I'm sorry," Kate said. "What about your phone?"

"Just write this down," Steven Spielberg said. "A nun fights a priest to the death, and wins."

"Are you sure?"

"Yes!"

"No one is going to believe that."

It was Chris.

"What?" Sister J said, fighting for breath.

"I saw what happened," he said.

"What are you doing here?"

"I came to see him. Mr. Quigley. I was going to kill him."

She looked into the youth's eyes and saw they were wet.

"But why, Chris?"

"He thought he was so tough. Thought he could punch me out just cause I did what he would've done if he'd been me."

"Like what?"

"Like stealing that cross. So what? He didn't own me! He said he'd kill me if I ever talked, so I was gonna kill him first."

"That's not the way," she said.

"But he's dead!"

"At my hands, not yours."

And then she embraced him. "Your hands are clean," she said. "We're going to keep them that way from now on."

She felt him shake his head.

"I'll show you how," she said.

"Bless me, Father, for I have sinned."

The words sounded wooden to her as Sister J spoke them to Father Dom. His voice sounded sad as he asked for her sins.

"I have to leave St. Cecelia's," Sister J said.

"I know," the priest said.

"I don't want to leave with sins on my soul."

"What sins, my child?"

"I killed a man."

Pause.

"Father?"

"Give me a second."

The sound of a deep, labored breath.

"Now," Father Dom said, "you want to run that by me again?"

She told him the story.

Father Dom waited a long time before answering. "How does that make you feel?"

"Like cr . . .terrible. And yet . . ."

"There's a *yet?*"

"The death of a criminal may have led to the salvation of a young man's soul."

She told him then about Chris.

Pause.

"I don't know how to counsel you anymore, Sister."

"I'm sad about that."

"I am, too. Just . . ."

"Yes, Father?"

"If you do continue along this path . . ."

"Yes?"

"Try not to kill anyone else."

"I will miss you, Father."

"You always know where to find me, my child. God be with you."

Three months later...

Sister Justicia Marie put the final touch of paint on the outside of the newly renovated building at a prime corner of North Hollywood real estate.

That is, if prime included apartment houses with drug dealers in them.

All in good time, she thought. All in good time.

The sun was going down over L.A. and soon it would be time for prayers in her new quarters in the back of the building. She would say a prayer of thanks. And ask for validation of her calling.

She would feed the hungry and clothe the naked here.

And, on occasion, save someone from a life of sin by breaking some of their bones.

Or by giving them something productive to do.

Like Chris. The young man had volunteered to work on weekends, no questions asked. If only she would teach him how to defend himself.

Which gave her another idea altogether—teaching the children in the neighborhood the same thing. So they could stand up to bullies. And respect themselves.

A knock on the door took her out of her reverie.

It was one of the last people she expected to see.

"Sister Xuan! What are you doing out here?"

"I came to join you," the little nun said.

"Join? But what about St. Cecelia's?"

She shook her head. "I had a vision. I was punching a very bad man in the face. And you were showing me how."

Sister Justicia pulled Sister Xuan into the building and closed the door. "Do you realize what you are saying?"

Sister Xuan nodded. "I have waited all my life for a calling like this. I want to be with you. I want to help you. I want to start an order with you."

"Just the two of us?"

"There will be more," Sister Xuan said. "And I have even thought of a name. With your permission?"

"Do tell."

"The Sisters of Perpetual Justice."

Sister J smiled. "Done."

"And will you teach me?" Sister Xuan said. "Will you teach me to fight?"

"Oh yes," Sister J said, looking across the street at the apartment buildings. "Oh very much, yes."

FORCE OF HABIT 3: NUN THE WISER

"Bless me, Father, I may have sinned."

"Hoo boy."

"Excuse me?" Sister Justicia said inside the confessional.

"I'm recovering," Father Dom said from the other side. "Just a moment. All right, now, let's begin again. It sounded to me as if you said you *may* have sinned."

"That's what I did say."

"You really said it?"

"Yes, Father."

"Hoo boy."

"You see, Father, I am not convinced that I have sinned in thinking something. I have had a thought, and then a feeling, and I don't know if it is sin."

"I think you had better tell me about it."

"As you know, I have employed certain means to stop certain individuals from engaging in certain acts."

"You mean you beat people up, don't you?"

"Well, yes. Broken a bone or two, sure. And you know what I think about that. I believe that violence employed to stop evil is actually a good. If there is no other option, of course! It prevents the evil and saves two victims!"

"Two?"

"The potential victim of the evil, and the perpetrator. If he is prevented from committing a murder, that is a good thing, is it not?"

"But your methods!"

"They are consistent with Catholic teaching father. The Just War principle on an individual scale."

"This is a matter for a higher authority," Father Dom said. "Since you will not listen to me."

"But I am listening, openly, but I think it should be a two-way street."

"This is a confessional! It's one way!"

"May I speak freely, Father?"

"What have you been doing?"

"I think the idea of constant confession may not be God's will after all."

"Hoo boy."

"But I have come to you to ask something about this feeling I have."

"Perhaps we can postpone this."

"Postpone?"

"I need to go outside and have a smoke."

"Please, this one question. It is beginning to bother me."

"Good! You need a little bothering! No, check that. A *lot* of bothering!"

"Please, Father."

"All right. It's against my better judgment, but go ahead."

"Here's the thing, Father. The other night I went looking for trouble."

"Stop. I need to go outside and—"

"In order to stop the trouble. In the neighborhood around the shelter, there is much trouble, and can I turn a blind eye to it? Would that honor God?"

"You are called to a life of prayer and service, not looking for people to harm."

"But it is *not* harm to prevent them from evil. So I walked around a corner and saw a man and a teenager. The man was holding the teenager by the shirt and shaking him. He was demanding money. He was using the most foul language. And the teenager's face was full of fear. I came up to the two of them and asked what was going on. The man looked at me like I was from another planet."

"I withhold judgment. Continue."

"The teenager said, 'He sold me bad drugs!' The man then slapped the boy and was about to do it again, so I grabbed his arm and bent it backward. That's all. Just to stop him. Well, he did not like that."

"What a shock."

"And he took a swing at me. I ducked the punch, grabbed his other arm, and bent it even further than I had the first. There was a little cracking sound—"

"Hoo boy."

"And he pulled out a knife. So I gave him a straight-fingered jab to the throat and he went down. He didn't move for quite awhile. In the meantime, the teenager was saying, 'That was so cool! Can I stick him?' But I told him that was not an option, and I told him to give me the drugs. He turned to run so I tripped him. I sat on his back and searched his pockets until I found the baggie. It was bad. It was ice."

"Ice?"

"Crystal meth."

"Crystal meth?"

"Crank."

"Crank?"

"Very, very bad stuff, Father."

Father Dom cleared his throat.

"By this time, the drug dealer was on his feet. I went over to him and said, 'Do not let me catch you in this neighborhood again. And if I ever see you selling drugs anywhere, I will bring down on you the wrath of God.'"

"Now hold it right there, Sister Justicia Marie! Do you dare to speak for God?"

"Only his wrath, Father."

"I really need to go outside—"

"Here is what I need to talk about, Father—"

"You mean this isn't it? Hoo boy!"

"Father, I enjoyed it. I enjoyed what I did."

Silence.

"Father?"

Sister J looked through the mesh. The confessional was empty.

She found Father Dom outside the doors of the chapel at St. Marie's, filling his pipe.

"I just need a minute," he said.

"Father, I do not mean to cause you distress."

"I thought that's what you enjoy doing!"

"Do I need help?"

"An exorcist, maybe."

Sister J very nearly burst into tears.

"I am sorry," Father Dom said. "I did not mean that."

"I have to go now."

"To prayer, I hope."

"Something like that," Sister J said.

Sister Justicia kicked the dummy between its artificial legs.

"Your job," she said to Sister Xuan, "is to incapacitate the act of evil,"

"And how do we know when such an act might occur?" Sister Xuan said, wincing. In her sweats, out of her habit, she looked like an extra in a movie about humble villagers about to take up arms against a band of outlaws.

Sister J, in her own sweats, standing in the middle of the workout room at the back of the Sisters of Perpetual Justice Homeless Shelter, said, "It's like what a Supreme Court judge said about obscenity: I know it when I see it."

Sister X giggled.

"Go ahead and stop him," Sister J said.

"The dummy?"

"I don't see anyone else here. Make him feel it."

"I...don't....know...."

"He's about to shoot a store owner! Kick him!"

Sister X's eyes opened wide, then the little nun led out with her foot and tapped the side of the dummy.

"Harder!"

Another try, barely more than the force of a fly swatter.

"We have work to do," Sister J said.

"It is so different than prayer!"

"That's why we're here, two of us, alone! Do you believe in what we're doing?"

The young nun nodded, but not with great force.

"If I see evil, and have the chance to stop it, and I do not stop it, is that just or good?"

Sister X pondered.

"You must be fully convinced of this," Sister J said, "or you won't be able to do it when the time comes."

"Do what?"

"Whatever it takes," Sister J said. She put a gentle hand on Sister X's shoulder. "We will be opposed. There will be those within the Church who do not understand us. Can you live with that?"

"What does Father Dom say?"

"Father Dom mostly says, 'Hoo boy.'"

Sister X took in a deep breath. "I am ready. I feel that God has called me to work with you."

"You trust me then?"

"I do."

"Good," Sister J said. "Then kick this dummy in the *huevos rancheros*."

Sister X giggled.

"Now!"

The young nun obeyed, kicked the dummy with all her might.

"Nice," Sister J said. "That's a breakfast he won't soon forget."

"Good evening, and welcome to Community Chat. My name is Thad Hamper, and each week here on PBS we bring you a guest from Los Angeles who is making a difference in their neighborhood, and talk with them about it. Tonight, my guest is Sister Justicia Marie, a local nun who has undertaken a most unusual project. Welcome to Community Chat, Sister."

"Nice to be here, Thad," Sister J said. She was no stranger to the camera, of course. As Brooke Bailey, child actress, she'd practically grown up in front of one. The camera raised her, you could say, in lieu of the father who saw her as a commodity and then tried to abscond with her money. You could also say the camera captured her crack-up, too, for all the world to see.

So it wasn't the electronic eye that caused Sister Justicia Marie a slight set of nerves—it was Thad Hamper himself. She'd consented to be on the show to gain some much-needed public support for the homeless shelter she'd opened with Sister Xuan. The local pols were making noises about denying her a permanent zoning permit. They could use some backup from the community to push it through.

Thad Hamper had seemed all peaches and cream on the phone. But there was something in his voice now, a kind of snark, like a coiled snake on a hot rock.

He said, "I understand that you have done something that is very unorthodox for a Catholic nun, in that you have started a new, I don't know what you call it, order?"

"To begin a religious order requires a certain process, Thad, and must be ultimately sanctioned by the Vatican. I am modestly beginning at the community level, trying to help the homeless, and in some way let the neighborhood reclaim its own streets."

"Isn't that something for social agencies?"

"Government hasn't exactly solved the problem, Thad. People can do much more on their own than they can waiting for the inefficiencies of politicians."

"How many nuns in this new order?"

"Just two of us."

"Two! How do you expect to get anywhere with two?"

"There is an old saying: *God and one is a majority.* So think how much better it is to have God and two."

Thad Hamper frowned. He had once been a weatherman in

Los Angeles, but was canned when he got drunk one night and claimed global warming should be blamed on Dick Cheney. PBS offered him a talk show a few months later. "Can we talk about your movie career?"

"I'd rather not. That part of my life is behind me."

"When you were Brooke Bailey you were raking in the money, your father was your manager. What happened?"

"I said I would rather not talk about it, Thad, if you don't mind."

"I think our viewers would love to know. When someone of your background comes into a neighborhood to take up residence, people would like to know what kind of person they can expect."

"What I'd like to talk about is how people should treat each other in a more humane fashion, how we can return to civility, how we might live together and form a decent society."

"Pardon me, Sister, but that sounds like pie-in-the-sky."

Sister J thought, *Oh no, there it is again. That feeling that I really like to hit annoying people.* She would have to confess to Father Dom soon.

"I understand you have a major donor by the name of Joseph Fount McTeague," Thad Hamper said.

"We do not discuss those who donate to our work."

"Are you denying that Joseph Fount McTeague, one of the richest men in Los Angeles, is one of your supporters?"

"As I said—"

"Come now, Sister Justicia, it's a simple question."

"With you, Thad, there appears to be no such thing as a simple question."

"The Catholic church takes in enough money, doesn't it? What is it that Joseph Fount McTeague is getting from you in return?"

"Nothing—"

"He is a major developer in this city. Does he have designs on your property? Are you secretly in league with McTeague?"

The smile again. The same thought coursing through Sister J, wanting to set him straight with a rap not to the knuckles, but to his teeth. The thought scared her.

"There is nothing to hide, Thad. Now can we talk about what we do to help put people back on their feet?"

"I understand," Thad Hamper said, "that you sometimes take people *off* their feet. Isn't that right?"

"I don't—"

"Isn't it true that you have actually resorted to violence to hurt people?"

"Is this a community show," Sister J said, "or an inquisition?'

"Inquisition! Now there's an odd word coming from a Catholic nun!"

Sister J put her head in her hands.

"Praying?" Thad Hamper said.

Driving back from the studio in Ping, her ancient-yet-determined Saturn, Sister J took in the "Universal Canyon," which is what she called the stretch of freeway running past Universal Studios. Now a glitzy tourist trap, the old movie studio location had been turned into a collection of overpriced shops, restaurants, movie theaters and parking structures known as City Walk.

Just like Hollywood, she thought, to create a fake city over a fake city. It reminded her of something some old comedian said once: If you look under the tinsel of Hollywood you find the real tinsel underneath.

She marveled at how her reaction was always the same, a

small jolt of longing mixed in with a heavy dose of regret and relief. As a child star, she loved what she did for a living—acting, pure acting, creating a role (partly to hide from a hideous and exploitative home life). There was some talk of her winning an Oscar one day, but that was before she became a cliché and industry joke—the party girl, the drunk, the druggie, the rehab queen. All that she left behind for good by going into the sacred life.

With some skills intact, like the years of martial arts training under teacher Bobo Portugal.

She got off the freeway at Vineland and headed north toward the shelter. When she was a block away she felt a sense of dread. Sister X called that a sixth sense that God had given Sister Justicia. Whatever its source, it usually proved accurate.

And when she turned the corner, she knew it had proved right again. There were three police cars, lights flashing, in front of the Sisters of Perpetual Justice Homeless Shelter.

Sister X met her at the curb. Sister J saw there was also a news van pulling up, from Channel 7.

"What on earth?" Sister J said.

"A dead man," Sister X said.

"One of ours?"

"We do not know. His body was found in the dumpster."

"Have you been questioned by the police?"

"Not yet. The man in charge is over there."

Sister J looked and recognized Detective Rick Stark. He was talking to a uniformed officer. He turned his head and made eye contact with Sister J. With a half smile he excused himself from the uniform and approached.

"Detective," she said with a polite nod.

"Sister, nice to see you again." Stark was in his forties, good shape, with brown hair and eyes the color of Los Angeles at night. He was clean shaven but swarthy, giving the impression of a freshly scrubbed pirate.

"What happened here?" Sister J said.

"Dead man in your dumpster," he said.

"That much I know. Who is it?"

"Don't know yet. Officer who answered the call said he had no ID on him, but there was something a little odd."

"Yes?"

"He doesn't look like your average homeless guy."

"How does the average homeless guy look?"

"Let's just say, not like this guy. He has a nice haircut."

"Which average homeless guys never have?"

"Now, Sister, don't start with me."

"Just saying."

"Okay—"

A woman in a burgundy suit came up, holding a Channel 7 microphone, followed by a camera guy. "Christine Wong, Channel 7 News. What've we got?"

"Nothing yet," Detective Stark said.

"A body in a dumpster?"

"That's all we know."

Christine Wong stuck the mike in Sister J's face. "Sister Justicia, you're the head of this shelter, is that right?"

"I don't know any more than the police at this point."

"Is this the first time someone has died on the premises?"

"We don't know that the death happened on the premises."

Stark shot her a look.

Sister J took Detective Stark by the arm and led him away from the reporter. "May I look at the body?"

"Didn't you see my don't-play-detective look?"

"This is our property, Detective. I know the layout. Perhaps I could offer a word or two of help?"

"I've seen your help before," Detective Stark said. "Somebody usually ends up in the hospital."

"That is not my intent."

"It's the outcome that worries me."

"The body?"

He sighed. "Come on."

He led her to the sky-blue dumpster on the west side of the facility. There was yellow police tape across the gap between the homeless shelter and the Laundromat wall on the other side of the alleyway. They ducked under the tape. The black, heavy-plastic double-lids were in the up position. A mechanic's light had been attached to the side of the dumpster, illuminating the receptacle.

Sister J looked inside. She took a breath and stepped away.

"You okay?" Stark asked.

"I know him."

"He one of yours?"

"In a manner of speaking," Sister J said. "It's Joseph Fount McTeague."

"Do you have any idea why one of your biggest supporters would be found dead inside your dumpster?" Detective Stark asked.

"None."

"Was McTeague due to pay you a visit?"

"He would drop by from time to time, but nothing was scheduled." She looked back at the body. "No ID, you say?"

"Nothing," Stark said. "Meaning robbery."

"I don't think so."

Stark gave her a rebuking look, but waited for her to explain.

"If you rob someone," Sister J said, "you take the money and run, right? You don't hang around and go to all the trouble of putting the body in a dumpster."

"I'll grant you that."

"And furthermore, it was probably two people."

"Two?"

"You know how hard it is for one person to lift a body?"

"Of course I do," Stark said. "But we're still gathering witness statements. Let's not jump to conclusions."

"The cause of death is yet to be determined?"

"Medical team is on the way."

"Good, let's see what else—"

"Now hold on, Sister. You realize your facility is now a crime scene."

"And so?"

"We have to clear it out and search it."

"That's going to be a problem," Sister J said.

"We will accompany you as you get the people out."

"This is home to some people."

"Be that as it may—"

"You can try to get a search warrant," Sister J said. "But you will have to show probable cause for every room."

"Hey—"

"The body of Mr. McTeague was found outside. You are free to search the outside. But if you want to come in, you will have to get a judge to tell you that you can."

"Look—"

"But I will cooperate with you, and accompany you when you question possible witnesses."

"What? No—"

"We have a joint interest in this matter, Detective. I can help you."

"It seems to me we've had this conversation before."

Indeed they had. Sister J once had to break the arm of a movie director named Harlan Savage, and put him in the trunk of his own car. Detective Stark did not think such methods were appropriate for nuns.

Inside, Sister J and Sister X got the residents, currently fifteen, and those who had just come in the night before, to the dining hall. It was an amalgamation of sights, sounds and smells that is only possible in urban relief centers.

"Quiet!" Elisio Minx shouted. Elisio was a large man who had come out of a sanitarium Sister J visited on occasion. He needed a job and he was the perfect overseer of the facility. He had the respect of the guests and he could enforce the rules if need be.

"I need to make an announcement," Sister J said when everyone quieted down.

"No!" Someone screamed. It was Theda Metcalf, an ex-mental patient. She was middle-aged and built like a mailbox. She had a mass of tangled black hair in which she sometimes found living things. She had come to the shelter asking Sister J if she could get a screenplay to somebody. And that's when Sister J knew the cliché was actually true: Every living person in L.A. was working on a screenplay.

"Just one announcement, Theda," said Sister J.

"Announcements are of the devil!"

"A friend of this facility named Joseph Fount McTeague was found dead outside."

Murmurs.

Theda Metcalf shouted, "Death is of the devil!"

"And I am going to have each one of you talk to a police detective and his partner."

"The police are of the devil!"

Otto Ledbetter, an 85-year-old former Shakespearean actor, shook his head and said, "What fools these mortals be!"

"Please be cooperative with Detective Stark," Sister J said. "He's here to help."

Theda Metcalf said, "The man with no eyes did it!"

Sister J walked over to Theda. "What's that mean?"

"I saw a man with no eyes here today!"

"No eyes?"

"*Cool Hand Luke!*" Theda said.

Detective Stark said, "What's it mean, man with no eyes?"

"Sunglasses," Sister J said. "Isn't that right, Theda?"

Theda nodded. "Sunglasses, and a hoodie."

Sister X came to Sister J and Detective Stark. "I talked to that man!"

"When?" said Stark.

"Earlier today. He was in here, and he made threats."

"Against McTeague?"

"No, Sister Justicia."

"What kind of threats?"

"He said there would be hell to pay, and hell always collects."

"Any idea what that means?" Stark said to Sister J.

"Yes."

"Well, what?"

"It means somebody needs to rewrite his dialogue."

Stark frowned. "I think you better take this seriously. You have a way of attracting trouble."

"You say the nicest things, Detective."

"Part of my job."

"It's also your job to inform Mr. McTeague's widow of her husband's death. I suggest you go now."

The next afternoon, Sister Justicia herself went to see Evelyn McTeague. She had called Sister J late, after Detective Stark left her house, which was located in a posh section of Brentwood.

Evelyn answered the door. "Sister Justicia, thank you for coming, I..." Tears pooled in Evelyn McTeague's eyes. She turned her face away. Evelyn McTeague was raven-haired, olive-skinned and in her middle thirties. Twenty years younger than her husband. It had been, Sister J knew, the second marriage for both.

"I'm so sorry," Sister J said. "I'll do anything I can to help."

"Please come in," Evelyn McTeague said, brushing her black blouse with her hands as if to give them something to do.

The home was large, moneyed, and like Cary Grant's hair— nothing out of place. Even Evelyn McTeague, in her despair, was done up to the proverbial nines.

"May I offer you a drink?" she said in the living room, then quickly added, "I'm sorry. Just force of habit, I guess."

Force of habit, Sister J thought. *I like that.*

"Thank you," Sister J said. "Nothing for me."

"Do you mind if I?"

"Of course not."

Mrs. McTeague went to a fully stocked bar and selected a bottle of Stolichnaya. Sister J knew that label well. It was her go-to booze when she was in the grip of drinking and drugs. Evelyn poured a generous vodka into a glass, opened a small refrigerator and took out a plastic container of orange juice. She added the juice to the vodka, then some ice, and returned to Sister J. They sat in the two chairs in front of the fireplace.

"Joe was very fond of you," Evelyn McTeague said.

"And I of him."

"He believed in your work."

"Mrs. McTeague—"

"Call me Evelyn, please. The reason I asked you here is that I think you may understand things the police do not."

"In what way?"

"The religious way."

"Certainly."

"I think whoever did this to Joe, did it because he hated the good Joe was doing. Hated it, like the devil hates God."

"It's rare, I think, for that to be a motive for murder, Evelyn."

"I can't think of any other reason. Joe didn't have any

enemies. He was kind and big hearted. Our religion is very important to us."

"He was a man of substantial wealth and influence," Sister J said. "Such men inevitably make enemies, even if it is through no fault of their own."

Evelyn McTeague was quiet then, drifting for a moment into her own thoughts. Sister Justicia scanned the living room and its decor—fine vases, a mantel with framed photos of the happy couple, a painting of a woman on a horse at sunset, furniture of the best quality and design. Someone with a well-trained eye had laid all this out.

"May I ask," Sister J said, "how your husband came into his money?"

"Not at all," Evelyn McTeague said. "He was proud of his accomplishments, where he came from. He was born in The Bronx. Did you know that The Bronx is the only city in America with a *The* in front of its name?"

"Now that you mention it."

"That's because it was originally the land owned by a settler named Jonas Bronck. When the family later began to sell it off, it was said that people bought a piece of the Broncks' land. Joe was fond of that story, because he wanted to own land himself. And he does. Or...did." She paused and reached for a wad of Kleenex in her pocket.

"Anyway, he dropped out of high school and worked his way across the country, ending up in Los Angeles. As you know, he was a good-looking man. In his twenties, he was drop dead gorgeous. You should see pictures of him back then. He put George Clooney to shame."

Sister J remembered the time George Clooney put the moves on her at a party, when she was Brooke Bailey. He could have used a little shame back then.

"So," Evelyn McTeague continued, "he was natural prey for the rich ladies in town. One of them was a powerful agent, and got him into modeling and acting."

"Mr. McTeague was an actor?"

Evelyn smiled, "Under another name, Chase Bryan. But Joe very quickly got tired of all the Hollywood. . ."

"I know exactly what you mean," Sister J said.

"He taught himself the real estate business and started flipping high end homes. Eventually he developed sites on his own. And that's how he made his fortune. Not that he didn't sometimes think what might have been had he become a big star."

"I'm rather glad he didn't," Sister J said. "I think your husband did so much more good the other way. Was he always religious?"

"No, that happened after his divorce. It hit him hard, and led to a lot of soul searching. He had been raised a Catholic, and returned to the church. I met him shortly after that."

"And you have been married how long?"

"Twelve years it would have been, this August. . ."

"I'm sorry. Perhaps I've overstayed my welcome."

"No, please. It was I who asked you here. I think the police just don't understand spiritual matters. I have sensed these things in my soul. A spiritual darkness, if you will."

"Is there anyone you can think of," Sister J said, "anyone at all who might have had some interaction with your husband, of a spiritual nature?"

Evelyn McTeague thought about it for a long moment. "One incident, it happened a couple of years ago. We were coming back from a boat trip we took to Cabo, on our yacht, *The Wings of Desire*. We were coming up the dock when a man who seemed to be waiting for us approached. Joe stepped in front of me. The man looked like he meant business. Joe wasn't afraid of anyone. But I was."

"Can you describe this man?"

"I can do more than that. I can give you his name. An alert dock worker saw our confrontation from afar and knew the car the man had driven up in. A red corvette. He got the license plate and from that Joe found out his name. Dan Malvolio. And where he lived. He never did anything about it, never reported it to the police. I urged him to, but he said it was just hot air. I don't think it was."

"What makes you say so?"

"Because of something this Malvolio said to my husband."

"What did he say?"

"He looked in Joe's eyes and said, 'There is going to be hell to pay.'"

Sister J said, "You say you have the address of this man?"

"Yes, written down."

"Can you get it for me?"

She nodded, went out of the room for a moment. Sister J noticed what appeared to be tickets, large and colorful, sitting on a glass table. She took the opportunity to see what they were for—*The Magic Castle,* a private club in Hollywood.

Evelyn returned to the room and handed Sister J the address. She looked down at the glass table. "Oh no," Evelyn McTeague said, her face flushing. "I couldn't."

"What is it?" Sister J said.

"The Magic Castle. Joe and I were going to go tonight."

"I'm so sorry."

"I can't possibly."

"Of course not."

"Would you take them?"

"Me?"

"Have you ever been?"

She had. Back in the Brooke Bailey days, she'd gone to the Magic Castle a couple of times, but got too drunk to remember anything that happened there.

"Then please, take them as my gift."

"But—"

"I insist." Evelyn gathered up the tickets and handed them to Sister J. "You need to get a little relaxation from time to time, yes?"

She thought then that Sister Xuan might need a diversion,

after all that had happened. She could leave the shelter in the able hands of Elisio Minx and get away for an evening's diversion.

And maybe that would be just the thing after the next call she was going to make.

The East side of Los Angeles, just down the hill from Boyle Heights, is a collection of brick and concrete buildings once used for industrial and commercial, but now coming back as lofts for the urban dwellers. Neighborhoods once lost to the darkness of grime and crime were showing new life, in a demonstration of resilience peculiar to city renewal.

That's where Sister Justicia headed after finishing her conversation with Evelyn McTeague. She was still processing the information Evelyn gave. Could this Dan Malvolio be the same man who had been in to threaten Sister X the day before?

The address was a three-story red brick building on Santa Fe Avenue just off of Seventh Street. Sister J parked Ping in a two-hour zone and approached the iron fence that guarded the parking area and access to the building.

There was a call box for buzzing in and a directory. Twelve names on the directory, but only one with initials: DM. That was listed as 3-B.

Just then the gate hummed and rolled open. A woman in a Jeep pulled out to Santa Fe, giving Sister J a quick and surprised glance. A nun in a habit standing outside a security gate is not your everyday Los Angeles tableau.

Nor is it the most threatening image. The Jeep made a left toward Seventh, and Sister J strolled into the parking lot.

There was an outdoor stairwell, the kind all industrial buildings had back in the day. She took the stairs to the third floor and entered. The corridor gave her two turns before she came to 3-B.

She heard a baby crying on the other side of the door. She knocked.

The baby kept crying. A man's voice yelled something and a woman's voice yelled something back. Then a third woman's voice yelled something and the man yelled another thing, laced with words no baby should have to hear.

She knocked again, louder.

The door whipped open. A man thirty or so, heavily muscled, wearing a black tank top, glared at her through brown eyes of fury.

'What is this?" he said.

"Are you Mr. Dan Malvolio?" Sister J said.

He looked back into his apartment, like he didn't want something inside to be seen.

"What do you want?"

"A reclamation."

A dumb haze dropped over the man's eyes. "A what?"

"The police will want to talk to you, I believe."

"What about?"

"You were seen threatening a man who is now dead."

"You shouldn't go around saying stuff like that, sis."

Another man appeared at the door. He was so big he looked like he'd have trouble getting *through* the door. He was a skinhead and wore a Lakers jersey, one that could have once belonged to Shaquille O'Neal.

"What's goin' on?" the big guy said. His voice was higher than his massive bulk would have suggested.

"Nun," the other man said. "Wants Dan."

"Neither one of you is Dan Malvolio?"

"What's it to you?" the big man said.

"She wants to save your soul," the other guy said.

The baby was still crying.

"May I speak to him, please?" Sister J said.

It turned out the big man could fit through the door after all, because he came out to where Sister J was and looked down at her.

"You got a message, maybe I can deliver it," he said.

"It's personal," Sister J said.

"He doesn't know any nuns."

"Everybody should know a least one nun."

"Are you really a nun?"

"Don't I look like one?"

"You could be faking."

"Why would I fake being a nun?"

He shrugged his massive shoulders. "It's L.A."

"Good point."

A slamming noise spilled through the corridor. It sounded like someone was coming in through the same outer entrance and using a little too much force.

Then the sound of running footfalls.

The big man's eyes widened. Moving like frightened elephant he backed into the apartment and shut the door.

One second later two men with nylon masks over their heads, and guns in their hands, charged the apartment.

Then stopped. The mashed-in faces behind the nylons registered astonishment.

Sister J assessed the situation in an instant. The weapons were submachine guns. The guys in the masks were here to clean out the apartment, baby and all.

She had one second to use the surprise factor.

Her mind envisioned the entire thing before it happened. She had two men to disarm and would have to use the domino effect—use one man to knock down the other.

With one, continuous action she stepped in front of the first man so he was the sandwich meat between her and the other guy. With her left hand she knocked his right arm—the one holding the weapon—out to the side. Using her right hand like a spear, she shot her fingers into his throat. The resulting shock and loss of breathing capacity would blank his mind.

She withdrew her right and opened her hand so she could grip his entire face like a volleyball. She pushed the volleyball into the face of the man behind, landing a perfect strike.

The front man collapsed.

The back man showed a bright red splotch under the nylon, where his mashed nose was.

But his right hand was bringing the gun up and around to killing position.

Instinct and the teaching of Bobo Portugal told her that in close contact with an armed opponent, don't move back or to the side—move in.

Sister J put her chest into the chest of the assailant, wrapped her right arm around his back and locked her left arm down on his right, effectively keeping the barrel facing past her.

The gun went off, spraying bullets around the corridor.

The shooter tried to extricate himself. Sister J hung on and they spun around like crazy dancers on Ecstasy. He was big and Sister J had no leverage. Her feet were off the ground.

She managed to glimpse the guy who'd gone down. He was trying to get to his feet. Which would mean another gun loose on the premises.

She had only seconds to disarm both of them.

"Where is Sister Justicia?" Detective Stark asked.

"I'm not sure," Sister X said. There were in the front hallway of the homeless shelter.

"I'm not asking for sure. What's your best guess?"

Sister X looked at the floor of the shelter.

"What aren't you telling me, Sister?"

With a heavy sigh, Sister X said, "I believe she went looking for the man with no eyes."

Detective Stark slapped his sides and looked at the ceiling. "She's going to cause trouble!"

"No," Sister X said. "She is not. Sister Justicia Marie is no trouble at all!"

Sister J broke the man's arm at the elbow, doing a reverse nutcracker move that snapped the joint like a chicken wing.

He would not be doing any shooting with that arm for some time to come.

Sister J let go and kicked the other man in the face as he was coming into shooting position. She grabbed the barrel of his weapon and pulled up against his thumb, removing it as she would a toy truck from a three-year-old's fist.

The apartment door swung open and the big guy in the Lakers jersey and the other guy jumped out into the hall with their own weapons drawn.

They stopped short when they saw the two splayed bodies with the nun standing over them.

Sister J collected the two weapons of the nylon-masked men.

"Call the police," she said.

"Forget that," the smaller guy said, and pointed his handgun at the head of one of the masked men. Sister J executed an old fashioned karate chop on the guy's arm. He dropped the gun with a wail.

"There will be no killing!" she said.

"They came to kill *us*," the big guy said.

"The threat is over. And I will not have it!"

The big guy blinked.

"Now go back inside and call the police."

"Uh..."

"You don't want the police because you possess illegal weapons and God knows whatever else, right?"

"Well, maybe."

"Give me your gun."

"What?"

"Do you want me to take it from you?"

"You can't," he said.

Sister J took it from him.

"Hey!"

Now she had all four weapons—two Uzi-types and two handguns. She held one of the handguns in shooting position, pointing at the ground. "You tell Dan Malvolio I want to talk to him. Tell him I'll be down on the street."

"What about those two?" the big guy said.

"They're coming with me."

The nylon-masked men groggily got to their feet. "You try to run away," Sister J said, "and I will shoot you in a very painful place. Do you understand?"

The masks looked at each other. Then one of them made a break for it.

Sister J fired the handgun, aiming for his legs.

He went down with a scream.

Sister J looked at the other masked man. "Any questions?"

The masked man shook his head.

"Then help your friend here make it downstairs, and try not to get blood all over everything."

The little guy said, "What kind of nun are you?"

Sister J ejected the magazines from the two handguns and tossed them on the ground. To the two apartment dwellers she said, "Don't even think of following me."

Sister J held the two thugs at gunpoint outside the gate, and called the police. One thug was on the ground, bleeding from his hamstring, groaning. The other stood by cursing at her with every word he'd ever learned with a hard K sound. Absurdly, they both still wore their nylon masks.

After the cursing guy ran out of words, Sister J said, "Have you ever considered going into some more productive line of work?"

"What do you know about it? Why don't you shove your—"

"Quiet now."

"If you didn't have that gun I'd kick your—"

"What part of *quiet* don't you understand?"

He answered with more hard Ks.

"If you don't stop that, I'm going to have to hurt you."

"What have you *been* doing?" he said. And then he called her a name that only a drunken Teamster in a waterfront bar should ever utter.

Sister J stomped the heel of her shoe on top of the soft Nikes of the foul-mouthed criminal. He screamed like a little girl. When he started cursing his pain she heeled his other foot.

He fell to the ground and rolled around.

Oh God, don't let me like this, she thought. She pointed one of the submachine guns at her grounded prey and waited. Ten minutes later a black and white pulled up.

Two uniformed officers got out of the cop car, guns drawn. The lead was a tall African American. "Put down your weapon, ma'am . . .uh, Sister . . .just put down your weapon!"

She did. The other cop, a white male of younger vintage, went over and gathered up the two submachine guns at Sister J's feet.

The lead looked at the men on the ground, then back at Sister J. "Just what goes on here?"

"She shot me!" the bleeding thug shouted. "Violated my civil rights!"

"You shot him?" the cop said.

"Well, yes," Sister J said.

"Why?"

"He was trying to get away. I told him to stop. He didn't stop."

"She shot me in cold blood, man!"

"Then what are you doing in those nylons?" the cop asked.

Like synchronized swimmers, the two criminals froze for a moment then, at exactly the same time, whipped off their masks.

The cop started laughing. His partner tried to hide a smile.

"What's so funny?" the wounded thug said. "Arrest her, man!"

The thug's companion said, "I saw the whole thing!"

"Let's go sort this all out," the cop said.

At the station, Sister J called Sister X and told her she was being detained. Then she prayed in an interview room until a detective came in with a notebook and a confused expression. He was mid-fifties. He sat in the only other chair in the room.

"Yadda yadda," Sister J said, "I don't need an attorney, and I waive my rights and I'll answer any questions you have."

"Then let me see if I've got this straight," the detective said, brow furrowed. "You shot a known gangbanger in the back of the leg?"

"I don't know about him being known for anything," Sister J said. "But yes, I did shoot him."

"I've seen your name around. You were on TV, right? You're that kick-butt nun?"

"The Vatican has not recognized that designation, but yes."

"And you're a real nun?"

"Hail Mary."

The detective started laughing. "When this gets out, it's not going to do that guy's street cred any good."

"Am I going to be charged?"

He sighed. "That's the problem, right? You shot somebody. A scumbag, yes, but the law doesn't allow you to do that."

"I'm entitled to make a citizen's arrest if a felony has been committed, correct?"

"Well, yeah."

"And I am entitled to use reasonable force if such force is necessary to arrest or keep the arrestee from fleeing. Now, since the young man was fleeing and I had taken away weapons, and there were two of them, I could not afford to leave one and chase the other, because he might grab the weapons back. So I fired."

"Boy, this is going to be a tough one. I have a feeling there are going to be lawsuits. These bangers have mothers and sometimes fathers, and they sue the police all the time, and the city can't afford it."

"Am I under arrest?"

"No, Sister—"

"Then I'd like to leave. I have a date tonight."

The detective raised his considerable eyebrows.

"With another nun," Sister J said, getting to her feet and leaving the law behind her.

He stepped onto the stage with a sweep of his left arm. On his wrist was a bracelet with glistening diamonds—or else the best fake diamonds money could by.

Sister Xuan giggled excitedly at the grand entrance. She had never been to a magic show of any kind, and now here she was at the most famous venue of prestidigitation and legerdemain in the land, the Magic Castle of Hollywood.

He was billed as X-Acto the Magnificent, and was the picture-perfect magician in his tuxedo and plastered black hair. His eyes were wide with the wonder to come. "Good evening, ladies and gentlemen. What are you going to believe? Me, or your own eyes?" He picked up a large red cape that was lying on the stage. He threw it up in the air and it floated down, fully open. He caught it and showed both sides. Then he held it for a moment at his side, smiled, and yanked it away.

And there stood a gorgeous woman in a tight blue bathing suit with rhinestones all over it. She wore high heels and a neon smile.

X-Acto bowed to her. She kissed her fingers and placed the fingers on his forehead.

"Maybe after tonight's performance, I'll get lucky," X-Acto said. The audience laughed.

Sister J cleared her throat.

"But not as lucky as the lovely Merilee, who will now transform before your very eyes."

Music began to play and X-Acto went into his choreographed routine. Two male assistants who looked like they came off the covers of romance novels, walked out, shirtless, holding a large trunk between them. They placed the trunk in the center of the stage and opened it.

X-Acto took Merilee's hand and helped her step into the trunk. She sat down, smiling at the audience, and with a final wave squeezed entirely into the trunk. The beefy assistants closed the top and latched it with two large metal locks. Then they lifted the trunk once more. X-Acto pounded twice on the side. From inside the trunk two pounds were heard in return.

With a wave of his hand X-Acto motioned for the assistants to complete a full revolution with the trunk. They walked in a circle showing the audience the front and back and the front again of the enclosure.

With a snap of his fingers, X-Acto ordered the assistants to lower the trunk. He then tossed something in the air. Whatever it was caught fire and burned brightly, but only for a second. Then the magician caught the thing on its return. He held it up to the audience.

It was a key. He handed it to one of the assistants. The beefcake unlocked the two heavy locks, took them off and threw the lid open. With the help of the other assistant they tipped the trunk forward so the audience could glimpse the inside. And as they did, a large white puma jumped out onto the stage. It had a blue outfit with rhinestones around it.

The audience screamed.

The puma gave a little hiss, then walked over to X-Acto, who patted its head.

X-Acto said, "Teeka! Ah ha!" He snapped his fingers. The puma obediently jumped into the trunk. The assistants closed the lid but this time did not latch it. They waited until X-Acto clapped twice. When he did something thumped twice within the trunk. The assistants opened the trunk and up jumped Merilee, arms outstretched.

The audience burst into applause. X-Acto helped her out with his right hand and said to the audience, "I like 'em wild."

Sister Xuan clapped with glee. "How did he do it?" she said to Sister Justicia.

"Very well," Sister J said.

Then the room went dark, replaced a second later by the flickering lights of a spinning disco ball on the ceiling. A musical theme piped in, heavy on the drums. On the stage, two flashing blades appeared—swords in the hands of Merilee. X-Acto had disappeared.

Merilee danced, whirling around the stage, waving the implements of death, every now and again hitting them together so they made a metallic noise.

Then the two shirtless aides pushed out a large cage, inside of which X-Acto stood, blindfolded.

Merilee began to dance around the cage.

The assistants turned the cage around, one full revolution, then took a step away.

With a theatrical flourish, Merilee placed the tip of a sword at the upper corner of the cage. When she pulled it away, a black curtain fell.

The bulky subordinates turned the cage once again, showing that all four sides had curtains.

When they were done with this, they left the stage.

Merilee was alone with the swords.

Smiling—wickedly, it seemed to Sister J—she drove one of the swords through the curtain, from the side. The curtain withdrew somewhat from the pressure. But when Merilee let go, the sword stayed, as if stuck in something.

Then she repeated the move from the front, the second sword also remaining in place.

The two muscled sidekicks came back on and mimed their shock at what Merilee had done.

She waved her hands at them, menacingly, and they stepped back as if afraid.

And Sister J couldn't help thinking, *Don't give sharp things to women in rhinestones.*

But then Merilee pulled out one sword, followed by the other.

In the flickering light there was actually something like blood on the blades. The effect was so stunning the entire audience exhaled a collective gasp.

Including Sisters J and X.

The twin acolytes pulled the curtains down.

Nothing was in the cage.

At the same time, from the back of the theater, X-Acto came running down the aisle. He jumped onto the stage.

He approached Merilee and stuck out his hand.

Sheepishly, she handed him a sword.

He looked at the bloody blade, then turned to the audience. "I'm only down a quart!" he said, then wiped the blade with his handkerchief.

"But this can never happen again!" he shouted. "Guards!"

The two beefcakes rushed out and took Merilee by the arms, holding her as she pretended to struggle.

A stagehand, this time another provocatively dressed woman, pushed something out onto the stage—a guillotine.

Then the woman reached into the basket where, presumably, a head might drop and pulled out a watermelon. She placed it into the headstock, stepped back and tripped the lever. The heavy blade fell and sliced the watermelon in half.

As the audience *oohed*.

The woman pulled on a rope and returned the blade to the top of the guillotine.

The men strapped Merilee to the guillotine now, and placed her head in the stock. They turned the guillotine one full revolution. When they finished, Merilee's profile was toward the audience, her head on one side of the stock, her body on the other.

X-Acto stepped to the front of the stage, and said, "She always said she wanted to lose ten pounds!" Then with a theatrical twirl, he turned to the guillotine and said, "Any last words, my dear?"

Merilee shouted, "Just wait till I get you home!"

The audience laughed.

X-Acto the Magnificent turned to the wing of the stage and someone tossed him a basket. He placed the basket under Merilee's head.

"Comfortable, my dear?" he said.

More laughter.

"You always wanted to be the head of the family!"

Even more laughter.

"Now it's going to be true!" And with that, X-Acto reached up and tripped the lever.

The blade fell with a deadly scraping sound, and thudded to a stop—cleanly slicing off the head of Merilee, which fell into a basket.

This time the screams of the audience were loud, frightful, panicked, horrified.

Sister Xuan grasped Sister J's arm.

The men gave the guillotine half a turn, so Merilee's feet were toward the audience.

Sister J heard several women crying.

X-Acto waved his hand, and the other woman pulled up the blade. The two men undid the restraints and lifted off the stock.

At which point Merilee, intact, stood and raised her arms.

Cheers from the audience!

The woman brought the basket around to X-Acto, who reached in and pulled out...a watermelon.

The curtain fell.

Most of the audience jumped up for a standing O.

Sister J noticed an older woman passed out in her seat.

After the show, Sister J and her able-bodied but somewhat shaky aide lingered in the Magic Castle, looking at framed photos and getting looks from the club crowd.

They paused to listen to Irma, the "ghost" that played the piano. Someone would call out a song and the keys of the piano would start to play it.

Then it was getting late—nun late, that is, around ten o'clock. One of the hosts, a nice looking man in a tuxedo and red tie, asked if the sisters were enjoying the evening.

"Very much, thank you," Sister J said.

"Mr. X-Acto was quite exciting," said Sister X.

"One of our favorite stars here at the Castle," the host said. "That's why he's on our wall of honor." He turned then and showed a row of framed photos. In the middle was an 8 x 10 of X-Acto and Merilee, with some other people around them. Everyone looked happy.

Sister J leaned in closer. She rubbed her eyes and leaned closer still.

"Anything wrong?" the host asked.

"No, nothing," Sister J said, even though something surely

was. For one of the happy people in the background was Joseph Fount McTeague.

Ten minutes later, in the car heading home, Sister J discussed the matter with Sister X. Was this just a wild coincidence? Mr. McTeague knew a lot of people in Los Angeles. Or was the photograph sending a message? Ghosts and magic castles? Clues from beyond the grave?

The sisters laughed it off, but warily Sister J noted.

It was going on midnight when Sisters J and X got back to the shelter. But the front lights were on and Elisio Minx was waiting for them.

"They've arrested Mr. Ledbetter!" he said.

"Whatever for?" said Sister J.

"Murder! Of Mr. McTeague!"

The next morning at nine sharp, Sister J entered the LAPD station and asked to see Detective Stark. He was there, but kept her waiting for more than an hour. When he was finally ready to talk he seemed in a most sour mood. Perhaps that was because his office was a mere cubicle, and her presence in it filled the space.

He offered her a chair, then said, "You're here because one of your guys is—"

"Otto Ledbetter! Just because he expressed his outrage at Mr. McTeague you arrest him?"

"You know me better than that, Sister. Or at least you should."

"I presume then you have evidence?"

"I do."

"What is it?"

"That's cop business."

"You know I'll find out eventually."

"I can wait."

"Would you like me to get a court order?"

"On what grounds?"

"Guardianship! As long as anyone is in our care, I am official guardian."

"That's only for juveniles!"

"Under the California Code, it applies also to those who have mental disorders, which Mr. Ledbetter has."

"Let him get a lawyer."

"See you in court." She got up to leave.

"Okay, okay. Just to save myself the time and paperwork. You want to know the evidence?"

She sat once again.

"Your Mr. Ledbetter is some kind of Shakespeare fanatic."

"The term you're looking for is former Shakespearean actor. He was quite good in his day."

"That day is long past. Do you know about his Shakespeare underwear?"

Sister J shook her head.

"Boxer shorts with Shakespeare's face all over them," Stark said.

"You can't be serious."

"We found that underwear rolled up in the corner of the dumpster."

"So?"

"They belong to Otto Ledbetter."

"And you know this how?"

"Because on the inside waistband, in ink, it says, Property of Otto Ledbetter, Actor."

"That *is* a community dumpster, you know."

"Except that with this underwear McTeague was strangled."

The picture of it did not make sense. Otto Ledbetter using his Shakespeare underwear to strangle Joseph Fount McTeague? In a dumpster?

Sister J said, "What would be his motive?"

"I suggest you ask the NoHo Shakespeare Theater."

"What's that mean?"

"Ask them about Ledbetter's behavior toward McTeague."

"You're being very stingy with your facts."

"Do I have to do all the heavy lifting?" He paused. "All right. I'll give you the last bit of evidence, the best, in fact."

She saw his cat-with-canary expression, and waited.

"Otto Ledbetter confessed to the whole thing," Stark said.

It took a moment for Sister J to get her thoughts in order, and even when she did they did not add up. "Where is he now?"

"In the lockup. He'll be transferred downtown tomorrow."

"I want to see him."

"Guardian?"

"You better believe it."

"With you I've learned to believe it. I'll give you ten minutes."

"Otto, what on earth are you doing here?" Sister J spoke to him through the bars. Otto Ledbetter, wearing an old-fashioned nightshirt and slippers, looked a skinny as the bars themselves. She hoped he wouldn't try to escape.

Otto Ledbetter said, "An old man, broken with the storms of state, is come to lay his weary bones among ye."

"Otto, this is not a play."

"Farewell! A long farewell to all my greatness! This is the state of man."

"You're not well, Otto. I'm told you have confessed to a crime."

"Confess yourself to heaven. Repent what's past, avoid what is to come!"

"Curtain! Intermission!"

Otto Ledbetter's face changed into a state of awareness. "How was I?"

"The audience is weeping."

Otto Ledbetter nodded. "How's my makeup?"

"Perfect. Now, Otto, did you kill a man with your underwear?"

The old thespian folded his arms. "That's my business."

"And how did you put him in a dumpster?"

"The time and my intents are savage-wild, more fierce and more inexorable far than empty tigers or the roaring sea."

"The curtain is not yet up, Otto."

"Ah. May I smoke?"

"No."

"Fie upon't. Ah fie!"

"Otto, you need a lawyer and you need medical attention. But I cannot believe that you killed Mr. McTeague."

"A pox upon thee, woman! I did, and I would do so again! He was a scoundrel and a cad! And my brain is as healthy as a young whelp's!"

This was getting her nowhere, except perhaps to the unthinkable—that maybe Otto Ledbetter, in a fit of theatrical rage, actually *was* able to kill Joseph Fount McTeague. In an alley. In a dumpster? With his underwear?

"Otto, do not say anything more to anyone until you are represented by a lawyer. Is that clear?"

"I would not put a thief in my mouth to steal my brains."

"Perfect."

Back in Stark's cubicle, Sister J said, "He's obviously mentally incompetent."

"That's not for me to decide."

"Someone else did this."

"I don't think so."

"And I'm going to find out who."

Sister J went to see Troy Dickinson. His office was in the back of a club he owned, The India, just off Hollywood Boulevard. The place wouldn't be open until that night, but Sister J knew Dickinson was there. He was always there.

After a few words with the security guard, and a wait while he checked, Sister J was escorted through the cool, dark interior to an office behind the bar.

"Sister Justicia!" Troy Dickinson was sitting behind his desk. He had blond hair and a boxer's body. He wore a magenta knit shirt, the better to show off his arms. He was a Chicago import, with family roots that went back to Capone. He fancied himself one of the key players in the seamy underbelly of Los Angeles crime, and loved his self-designated moniker: The Pope of Los Angeles.

Sister J never found that amusing.

"How are you, Troy?"

"Amazed."

"At?"

"You. I mean, I was impressed before, but you have outdone yourself."

"How do you mean?"

"I mean the two guys you took down at the loft."

She paused, studying his face. As usual, he had a passive-aggressive smirk. "Yours?" she said.

Dickinson laughed and opened a wooden humidor on his desk. He withdrew a cigar and then a gold cutter. He snipped off the end. "Oh, sorry." He picked up the box and offered a cigar to Sister J.

She rolled her eyes.

"Just trying to be polite," said Dickinson. "You know me."

"I'm afraid I do," Sister J said. "So it was the guys in the apartment who were yours."

Troy Dickinson lit his cigar and blew out a plume of smoke.

"You're breaking a city ordinance," Sister J said.

"So sue me," Dickinson said.

"What is it your boys are into?"

"That's my business."

"Do you realize there was a *baby* in that apartment?"

"Sure. I'm her godfather," the Pope of Los Angeles said.

"Godfather! Do you even know what that means?"

He shrugged. "I get the respect of the family. And they take my advice."

Sister J put her head in her hand. "No, it means that if anything happens to the child's parents, you are obligated to raise that child in the church and teach her the ways of God."

Dickinson leaned back and thoughtfully drew on his stogie. "Why don't people tell me these things?"

"And what if she was shot? What good would you be?"

Dickinson said, "Don't start with me, Sis. I don't like it when you do that."

"Who is Dan Malvolio?"

"Dan who?"

"Malvolio."

"Sounds like a butter substitute."

"Does he like to threaten nuns?"

"What's that mean?"

"What does he look like?"

"Who?"

"Malvolio."

"Who?"

"Are you denying you know him?"

"I neither affirm nor deny *anything*. I'm not on trial. You have come into my place of business and started throwing your weight around. I know you can fight. *If* you get the drop on somebody. But that's not always gonna happen, so I gotta tell you, I think you should get out of the fighting business and just go back to being a nun."

"Not going to happen."

"I was afraid you were going to say that."

"What do you know about the death of Joseph Fount McTeague?"

Dickinson just stared.

"What is the connection with Dan Malvolio?" Sister J asked.

Dickinson said nothing.

"Why do I constantly find myself in your office?"

The Pope of Los Angeles said, "Mutually assured destruction."

Now it was Sister J who was speechless.

"Like when the Commies and the U.S. pointed nukes at each other. That's what kept them safe. They knew if one of 'em went for it, the other side could wipe them out, too. I think we're heading in that direction, Sister Justicia Marie."

Mutually assured destruction. As Sister J drove from the Pope's club, she kept turning the phrase over and over in her mind. Was that the case with evil in this world? For every good deed there was a bad? And it would all end in the world's demise until God called a halt to the entire program?

Then what good was fighting? Ultimately, it was yin and yang.

Then she heard herself say, "No." She was not going to give up the fight just yet. There was too much work left undone.

The NoHo Shakespeare Theater was located on Lankershim. Sister J knew it to be a special project of Joseph Fount McTeague's. He was a lover of the bard and a major patron of the theater. Sister J parked a meter in front of the theatre, which was currently running *A Midsummer Night's Dream.*

There was no one in the box office window. She gave a rap to the locked front doors. Presently, a young man in blue tights and a skin-hugging, flesh-colored shirt opened the door a crack.

"Yeah?"

"Hi, my name is Sister Justicia, I'm a neighbor."

"Cool."

"Is the theatre manager here?"

"Well yeah, he's in the theater, we're about to run lines."

"May I see him for just a moment?"

"I don't know . . ."

"Let me guess. You're Puck?"

He smiled. "Yeah, that's right."

"That merry wanderer of the night."

"Hey, nice! All right, come on in." He opened the door to the cool lobby. "How come a nun knows Shakespeare?"

"We have books and everything!"

"Got it. Come on."

He led her into the theater, down the aisle. The stage was lit and a forest scene was alive with actors checking their phones. Puck tapped a man in the front row. He was a frizzy-headed forty or so, in a Lakers jacket. He turned and Puck told him a nun was there to see him.

This brought a wide-eyed but curious glare. The man stood. He was at least six-feet nine. Lanky.

"Welcome to the Shakespeare," he said. He had a reedy voice, perfect for a sprite if sprites came in basketball-player sizes.

"My name is Sister Justicia, but most people call me Sister J."

He shook her hand and her hand disappeared for a moment. But his grip was gentle. "My name's Jackson," he said.

"How do you do, Mr. Jackson."

"Not *mister*. Just Jackson. First and last name. I run the place and direct most of the shows."

"Good. I've come to gather some information for a friend of mine, a Mr. Otto Ledbetter."

Jackson's face went from a midsummer night's dream to a tempest. "Then you can just leave now, sister."

"What is it?"

"I know he's been nailed for killing Mr. McTeague."

"Accused, yes."

"Oh, he did it."

"How do you know this?"

An actress said, "Hey Jackson, can we get going? I got a thing."

"In a minute!" Jackson said. Then to Sister J: "He came in here and threatened Mr. McTeague, right in front of his wife and all these donors and everything. Because I wouldn't cast him as Polonius. He thought he was still this big-time actor instead of a nutcase."

"He's seen some hard times."

"Yeah, well he gave us some hard times. We were having a reception in the lobby and he wouldn't leave, and then he stripped down naked and ran into the theater and up onto the stage, and started doing King Lear, and let me tell you something, sister, that's a picture I will never get out of my mind. He kept yelling that McTeague had ruined his career."

"Do you know what that was all about?"

Jackson shrugged. "All I know is he's held some kind of grudge for twenty years. Going back to when Mr. McTeague was an actor named Chase Bryan. I think he got this Ledbetter fired from a soap or something."

"And you think Mr. Ledbetter has held this grudge all these years, and would kill for it?"

"It's acting, sister. People do a lot of weird things to make it in this game."

Boy, did she know all about that.

"What happened after that?" Sister J asked. "I mean, was he arrested?"

"The cops came, yeah."

"Do you happen to recall if they took his clothes?"

Jackson put arms out. "Why would I even want to think about that?"

"Because I'm asking you to."

"Then the answer is I don't know."

"Is there anyone who would?"

"Jackson! Come on!"

The skyscraping director said, "I'm sorry, sister, that's all I got. Talk to the cops. I don't ever want to hear that guy's name again."

As she was exiting the theater, a shadowy figure in the back row whispered, "Sister?"

"Yes?"

"May I talk to you?"

"Of course." Sister J sat in the seat next to the man.

"My name's Al Spooner," he said quietly. "I'm the custodian."

Sister J nodded. In the darkness Sister J thought Al Spooner looked to be in his sixties.

"I heard you talking about the night that man went crazy."

"Yes?" Sister J said.

"I was here. I saw it. I have to tell you, it was scary."

I was afraid of that, Sister J thought.

"Freaked us all out. And right in front of Mrs. McTeague and all. She's a trouper."

"Evelyn McTeague?"

"Uh-huh. She helped clean up the mess he made of things, but then she said something to me I think you need to know about."

"I'm listening."

"She said it wasn't the first time that man made a threat on Mr. McTeague. It was the fourth."

Four threats? If that was true, and could be corroborated, it would reshape the entire matter for Sister J. Maybe not enough to convince her Otto Ledbetter was guilty. But it would certainly make the prosecution case stronger.

Back at the shelter, Sister Xuan was waiting for her comrade. "He came back," she said.

"Who?" said Sister J.

"The man who said *Hell to pay*. He came in the front door and shouted it. He scared everybody. And then he went away."

Dan Malvolio again? Or could it be someone completely random? The neighborhood was crawling with people off their meds. Such people could be deadly. One such specimen had knifed several bystanders at a bus stop on Ventura a few weeks earlier. Evil was certainly on the prowl in Los Angeles.

But now there was food to prepare and needs to be seen to. Sister Justicia and Sister Xuan began the duties they had signed themselves up for. It became a day of work and prayer and ministering to *the least of these, my brethren*.

After the evening meal was served, Sister Justicia did some background checking on X-Acto but was unable to find any connection to Joseph Fount McTeague. She did, however, find a connection to her neighborhood. Mr. X-Acto had offices and a warehouse right there in NoHo. She could actually walk there.

The offices were in a commercial building, and were naturally locked up. It was a little after nine and the night a dark one in the city. The name "X-Acto" was not to be found, but there was an office with a sign that read *Abracadabra Enterprises, Inc.*

Sister J examined a few other offices, then went around toward the rear. Light hit her. Headlights, distant. She put her back to the wall like a character in a prison escape movie. As the lights got closer she surmised they were on a golf cart. That would be a security guard making his rounds. She was glad that her old school habit was black.

So she waited like Steve McQueen until the cart made a turn and continued down the small lane. She came to a row of squat buildings, obviously storage and warehouses. She looked around for the golf cart and saw no lights nor heard its chugging. Using the flashlight app on her cell phone, Sister J took a quick look at the doors of two of the facilities. The second one had, in small script, *Abracadabra Enterprises, Inc.*

And it was slightly open.

Sister J pushed her way in. An acrid smell hit her, like something old and rotten. The place was completely dark. She listened, heard nothing.

Someone had to be here. Why else would the door have been

left unlocked? Maybe someone had burgled the place. But surely that would have tripped some alarm.

What if X-Acto had come in for just a moment? But then, why were the lights out?

"Anyone here?"

No response.

Using her flashlight app again, Sister J was able to get a view of a thirty-foot perimeter. The first thing she saw was the trunk illusion she'd seen X-Acto and Marilee use at the Magic Castle. It sat there like a trap, as if someone walking by too closely would get snapped up into it.

But what was causing the smell?

Then she saw it.

It was an arm.

On the wrist of the arm was a bracelet. With diamonds.

It lay in a pool of blood. A couple of feet away was a leg. And then, further still, a head.

It was X-Acto all right, and if he wasn't performing the greatest cut-and-restore trick of all time, he was most certainly as dead as it was possible to be.

His eyes were open. His mouth was agape. He looked like he was about to say, "Ladies and gentlemen, you will not believe the things you are about to see."

A sound did escape. Only it wasn't from his mouth. It was the sound of a trunk opening.

Sister J whirled around, holding out her phone flashlight just in time to see two gleaming swords in the hands of Merilee, the weapons swishing in the air as they made their way toward her like giant blender blades.

Sister J jumped to the side as a sword hacked off part of her sleeve. She had the presence of mind to stick her phone in her pocket so Merilee could not trace her by the light.

"You are not going anywhere," the deadly assistant said. "We are going to perform the cutting a nun in half trick. Let's practice!"

Practice. She tried to remember what her teacher, Bobo Portugal, taught her about defending against long weapons, like sticks and swords. The most important principle was you had to get away from the long end of the weapon. The closer you got to the assailant, the better. But how was she going to do that in the dark?

If she could get underneath Merilee's arms ahead of a slice, she would be able to get her on the ground and have a chance.

Then the lights came on. Only they were not steady, but were coming from a revolving disco ball on the ceiling. Part of the X-Acto act. And now she could see Merilee advancing. She looked like a slow-motion movie. Slow and deadly motion.

Sister J had to find something to defend herself with. Until she could get to Marilee's body, she had to keep those slicing blades from hitting their mark.

There was a small table with what looked like a cake pan on it. Sister J grabbed the lid and lifted it. When she did a small white dove shot out of the pan.

And that's what saved her life. The bird flew right into Merilee's face. The murderous helpmate yelped and flailed at the bird with the swords. The feathered flapper dodged and took off toward the ceiling.

Now Sister J held a small shield. Too small for long term effectiveness, but would have to do in a pinch. And that pinch was now.

Merilee struck with the sword. Sister J fended it off with the lid, but the impact almost thrust her to the ground. If only she had another weapon, a stick or a . . . she saw just that on the table. A black cane. She picked it up and held it like a sword. She now presented herself as a gladiator, only the shield was barely the size of a plate and the sword was only a cane.

Merilee laughed. "With that you're going to fight me?"

The best thing to do with a stick in this situation was to thrust, try to get the pointed end into a soft spot of the opponent. In the face would be best, but that target was small. Something in the middle was the better choice.

And the more Merilee talked, the better sister Jay's chance to find an opening would be.

"Why, Merilee, why did you kill him?"

"Because all men deserve to die!" She held the twin swords high.

"We cannot make that judgment," Sister J said.

"He was cheating on me, and lying about it. All men cheat and lie."

"Merilee, do you believe in God?"

The question seemed to stun her. She looked at Sister J, the light flickering on her face, looked as if that was the strangest thing anyone had ever asked her.

"God will forgive you if you ask him to," Sister J said.

"I don't need forgiveness. I need to kill you."

"I'll help you, Merilee. I'll stand by you."

"You won't be able to stand at all by the time I'm finished with you!"

Sister J's move would have to be now. She issued a Rebel yell to freeze Merilee for a split second, then thrust at her with the cane.

The moment the tip touched Merilee's chest the cane disappeared and Sister J found herself holding a bouquet of flowers.

Merilee squealed with mocking delight. "What will your next trick be?"

Good question.

Sister J grabbed for anything on the table. Something metallic. And came up holding a ring. No, a chain of rings. Three of them. The old linking rings trick!

A blade flashed in the flickering lights.

Sister J jumped back as it embedded in the table.

Seizing the moment, Sister J made Merilee's head a carnival game, because the rings were the approximate size of a human cranium. At once the picture formed in Sister J's mind, even as she moved forward with Merilee's right arm temporarily stuck on the sword in the table. As a girl, Brook Bailey—as Sister Justicia was known then—could never win that ring toss game. It always seemed fixed to her.

Now she had no choice. She would have to win or die.

The light once again gave off the strange feeling of slow motion, and this is what Sister J saw—Merilee's face, turning toward her, teeth bared like an animal, eyes burning like twigs on fire.

Sister J's hands, as if acting on their own, held the top ring and thrust it forward, then up, then down.

It was a winner!

The ring dropped over Merilee's head with just enough snugness that she would need both her hands to get it off.

Sister J pulled on the third ring in the chain, jerking Merilee's head. Merilee let go of the sword in the table and swung wildly with the sword in her left hand.

Sister J was behind, holding Merilee like a dog on a leash, pulling so as not to give Merilee a chance to get her balance.

But she was strong and wiry and wild with screaming and slashing motions.

At that moment Sister J remembered fishing with her father, back when he was a good man and not the louse he later turned out to be. They were in a boat near Paradise Cove when her father hooked a small shark. As he pulled it above the water it thrashed and thrashed with the survival instinct God had placed in it.

As did Merilee now.

Only this shark had a long, razor sharp fin. Which Merilee now snapped back over her head, in hopes of catching some part of her captor.

The blade clanged off the rings, barely missing Sister J's fingers.

As soon as the sword retracted, and before Merilee could deliver another strike, Sister J dropped the rings, moved to

Merilee's back, and got her in a Portugal Death Hold. Bobo Portugal had taught her this hold as the ultimate stabilizer, if you could get behind your opponent.

It was her left arm around the throat, her right arm thrust up and under the right of the opponent, where it joined the other wrist. This close, the sword was not an issue. But Merilee still was.

"Drop the sword," Sister J said. "And I'll let you breathe."

Merilee did not drop the sward. She thrashed some more, shark-like, but a shark that knew its days were numbered.

"I don't want to kill you, Merilee." And that was the truth. Taking her life, that would be a bridge too far. She could not imagine what Father Dom would say, what the cops would say, what God would say.

No time for theological speculation now.

Merilee trembled. Sister J was sure she would pass out. Maybe that was best. Just pass out and get the police.

But then the sword dropped.

Sister J let go a little of the pressure. "Are you ready to stop fighting?"

Merilee coughed, nodded.

"I'm not going to let you go yet. We're going to go to the door and we're going outside and I'm going to call the police."

"No..."

"It has to be that way, Merilee. I'll see to it that you get a good lawyer and the help that you need."

"He deserved..."

"We'll sort it out together. Now, toward the door."

In the surreal luminescence of the spinning disco ball, Merilee started slowly toward the other side of the room. Somewhere on the floor were the mortal remains of X-Acto, one of the Magic Castle's most popular acts. As Sister J held on, they moved together like clumsy salsa dancers.

"They'll put me in prison," Merilee said, her voice scratchy.

"I'll visit you in prison."

"Why? Why would you do that?"

"It's part of my job."

"I don't understand you."

"You are not the first, Merilee."

They were almost to the other side, where Sister J could see the outline of the door.

Which Merilee was veering away from.

And made Sister J tighten the hold on her neck.

Which did not do anything to Merilee's legs. Sister J felt, rather than saw, Merilee reach out with her leg and stamp down.

Followed by the sound of something opening.

And a feline screech.

Merilee shouted, "Teeka! Kill!"

Sister J saw nothing...until a flying thing came at her from the side and the bared teeth of the puma made for her neck.

Sister Xuan scanned the main floor, looking for any last trash to clean up before securing the facility for the night.

And then she saw him. The man in the hoodie and shades. At the front doors, staring in.

He was not there for food. He stood still, holding his gaze in her direction, his body language stating he was looking for trouble.

And then, as if to answer Sister Xuan's unspoken question, he reached under his sweatshirt and pulled out a knife.

Sister J turned forty-five degrees and leaned back. The animal whizzed by her, growling. She could smell its fur and fury.

With her left hand reaching up almost of its own accord, Sister J grabbed at the passing puss, and closed around something rope-like and fuzzy. The momentum of the furious feline was cut short, and Sister J found she literally had a tiger—or, rather, a cougar—by the tail.

Going with the flow, Sister J swung the predator around and around like an Olympic hammer thrower, then let fly at the stationary Merilee.

The puma hit Merilee full on.

Merilee screamed and stumbled backward, falling against something, her body prone now, like she was falling out of a window backwards.

Only it wasn't a window.

It was the guillotine from the show.

The violent way Merilee hit the terrible instrumentality of death triggered the blade.

Down it came.

And Merilee performed the woman-cut-in-half trick for the last time.

Sister J ran for the door. Heard the puma hiss behind her.

She jumped out and pushed the door closed.

And heard a *thump*.

Just as lights hit her.

"Hey, what goes on?"

Sister J turned toward the golf cart. "Call the police," she said.

"You shouldn't be here."

"Please."

"This is Mr. X-Acto's private warehouse!"

"Show's over," Sister J said.

Detective Rick Stark arrived half an hour later.

"Why am I not surprised?" he said.

"I'm here to serve," said Sister J.

"There's blood on your habit."

"And body parts inside that warehouse."

"What!"

"Mrs. X-Acto did not like the fact that Mr. X-Acto was fooling around. Mrs. X-Acto cut him up with a sword and then tried to do the same to me."

"And what did you do to her?"

"I'm afraid—"

"Oh no."

"I'm very sorry. May she rest in pieces—*peace!* May she rest in peace."

Detective Stark closed his eyes.

"Oh yes, and an angry cat inside."

"Cat?"

"Puma."

"Puma?"

"Puma."

"What exactly *is* a puma?"

"A cat, a very large..." And that's when she knew.

The next morning, Sister Justicia Marie accompanied Detective Rick Stark to the home of Evelyn McTeague. They assembled in the living room.

"Thank you for seeing us, Mrs. McTeague," said Stark.

"Can we get this over with?" Evelyn McTeague said. "I have a tennis lesson." She wore tennis whites and had a sweater around her shoulders, the arms tied loosely around her neck.

"Certainly." Detective Stark took out the booking photo of Oscar Ledbetter. "Do you recognize this man?"

"Yes," she said. "Unfortunately."

"And how do you know him?"

"He threatened my husband at a fund raiser. He made a spectacle of himself."

"In what way?"

"He just...he began yelling and screaming. He said he was some Shakespearean actor and that my husband owed him a part."

Detective Stark nodded. "Anything else?"

"What else would there be?" Evelyn McTeague said.

Sister J said, "The fact that Otto Ledbetter took off all his clothes, for one."

"Oh," Evelyn said, "yes."

"And that you helped by cleaning up those clothes."

"Excuse me?"

"You were observed picking up the clothes and taking them out to the back of the theater."

"Yes," Evelyn said. "I am not above doing some dirty work."

"But the Shakespeare underwear somehow did not make it to the trash."

"Shakespeare what?"

"You retained them in your coat pocket. You brought them back with you to use as a murder weapon, implicating Otto Ledbetter."

Evelyn McTeague just stared.

"I spoke to Mr. Al Spooner this morning," Sister J said. "He's the custodian at the NoHo Shakespeare Theatre."

"I know who he is."

"He told me about the Shakespeare underwear. He noticed it the night Otto Ledbetter shed his clothes."

"So what?"

"I checked with the manufacturer this morning," Sister J said. "Shakespeare underwear has not been made by them since 1983. So they had to travel from the theater to your husband's neck by some means."

The room became very still.

"You and X-Acto—what *is* his real name?—used a magician's best friend, misdirection. The body in the dumpster. The false lead about Dan Malvolio. And one more thing. When I visited you the day after your husband's murder, you were wiping something off your blouse. Would you consent to having a search of your clothes for cat hair?"

"Cat hair? We don't own a cat."

"Big cat hair. Puma perhaps? A friendly cat because she knew you?"

Evelyn McTeague stood up straight and tall. "You may not have permission, and I assure you my lawyers will sue someone before the month is out!"

"Then I must secure the house," Detective Stark said, "while I wait for a search warrant. You may now go to your tennis lesson if you like."

Evelyn McTeague glared at Sister J. "You call yourself a nun! You're a snake!"

"I remain your humble serpent," Sister J said. "Servant!"

Sister J felt like a Baptist preaching outside a punk rock concert. Spent and somewhat depressed.

She had killed someone now. Or at least participated in a death. And not a pretty one.

Yes, it was classic self-defense. Yes, it was a murderess who had been coming after her, with an animal no less.

But it was still a human life. And Merilee had not had time to make her peace with God.

A cloud of unknowing covered Sister J, just as it had the old mystic who wrote that famous contemplation.

When she got back to the shelter it seemed like the entire facility was feeling the same way. There was a heaviness about the place, a shroud of unknowing about the future.

And once more Sister Justicia Marie wondered if she was slightly crazy, or maybe mostly mad, and not leading the life God had called her to.

She wouldn't think about it. Not tonight. Her mind was too tired to put together rational thought. Her spirit too fragile to take in any revelation.

What was the prayer you were supposed to utter after you killed someone with a guillotine?

Wearily, she pushed through the front doors and saw in the middle of the main room a knot of homeless looking toward the rear.

Theda Metcalf was the first to see Sister J.

"The devil is inside!" she shouted.

"What is it?" Sister J said. "What's going on?"

"Hostage!"

"Hostage?"

"Sister Xuan! She is behind that door! The devil is holding a knife to her throat."

"Did you call the police?"

"He said no police! Or he'd kill her. And take her to hell. He said there would be hell to pay!"

"Stay here," Sister J said. She went to the kitchen door and knocked.

"Who is it?" The voice was low, almost a whisper, but one that held menace poised behind it.

"I'm Sister Justicia Marie. May I come in?"

"Don't try anything, or this one dies."

"I assure you I won't."

"Come in slow."

She pushed through to the kitchen.

He had a hoodie and sunglasses. He also had a blade of six inches held to the neck of Sister Xuan.

"What is it you want?" Sister J said. She tried to comfort Sister X with her eyes.

In that same, low, threatening voice, like you'd hear over the phone, he said, "What's coming to me."

"And what is that?"

"Money."

"How much do you want?"

"How much do you have?"

"Not much at all. We are a poor order."

"Don't give me that."

"First, let Sister Xuan go. I will stay here and talk to you."

He shook his head. "I know all about you."

"You'll have to speak louder."

"You'll have to listen harder."

"I give you my word I won't try to hurt you."

"The word of the Catholic church? What's that worth on the open market?"

"You don't want to do this," Sister J said. "If it's money you want, I'll see what I can do. But first you must let her go."

"Not gonna happen."

Sister Justicia Marie assessed the situation in a moment, in a flash, and once again saw it all unfolding before it happened. Was this a vision from God or from her own fevered brain? She had to make a decision, and decided that faith in the former was better than apprehension about the latter.

Sister J said, *"Huevos rancheros."*

The man with the knife said, "What?"

"I think what you need is *huevos rancheros!"*

Sister X took in a breath and seemed to gather strength with it. And with that she flexed her right leg, snapping her heel into the middle of the knife wielder's legs.

At the moment of contact Sister J leapt like...a puma! She had only a split second to get Sister X out of harm's way.

When confronting an attacker with a knife, the first order of business is knocking the blade hand away from its slash zone and taking that opportunity to deliver an offensive blow.

She came down with a chop on the man's right wrist. He dropped the knife. Sister J cupped her hands and clapped them over his ears. The popping inside his eardrums sent him reeling backward, disoriented.

In one second Sister J had him face down on the floor.

In the next second she called to Sister X to get the twine.

In less than sixty seconds she had the man's hands tied up behind his back.

"Now," she said, standing, "we call the police."

The man started laughing.

"I'm sorry we had to hurt you," Sister J said.

"Yes," said Sister X. "I am very sorry about the *huevos rancheros."*

The man laughed even harder. Then he took a breath and said, "You hypocrite!"

"Call the police," Sister J said.

"Yes," the man said. "Tell them to come down and arrest your own father!"

The police arrived fifteen minutes later. Two blue-suited patrol officers, a man and a woman, came into the kitchen where Sister J had her father tied to a chair. He had refused to say a word until the cops arrived. And in that odd twilight zone of waiting, Sister J looked and looked upon the man she now recognized, the man who had done so much to hurt her. Her mind told her she had to forgive him, but her heart was leather and she knew that was wrong.

When her father saw the cops he yelled, "I want my fair share!"

"Fair share of what?" the male officer asked.

"The money she's got stashed away."

The cop looked at Sister J. "What's this about, Sister?"

"He's my father," she said. "And we have no money here."

"She's lying!" her father said.

Sister J looked at him, anger coursing through her. "Hello! Nun! Vow of poverty!"

"Don't give me that," he said. "You owe me!"

"For what, exactly? Huh? What!" She almost jumped at him then, but Sister Xuan's worried look stopped her.

"I made you!" said Dalton Bailey, for that was his real name.

"Is someone going to make a complaint here?" the cop said.

"I am!" Dalton said.

"Besides you," said the cop.

"Look at me, Dad!" Sister J said. "I'm not what I was. I don't make money anymore, you took whatever I had, and now I'm poor. That's it! Poor and happy!" But she didn't feel happy.

"Lies! You . . ." Dalton Bailey put his head in his hands. "I got nothing."

She looked at him long and hard and her first instinct was to tell the cops to take him in. He had been the one who started her drinking. He told her it would ease the work. He was the one who got her into drugs. A little Mary Jane never hurt anybody, he'd said. At one point in her past life she had wanted to kill him. She remembered that vividly.

But she had never in her life seen him weep. As he did now.

The police officers looked at her as if her next move would be the crucial one.

Sister J took a deep breath. Her pitiful father...they'd gone fishing once...

"How are you fixed?" she said.

"What?" her father said.

"You have a place to stay?"

"No."

"You want to stay here?"

"Here?"

"We have a bed for you, if you want it."

"You'd do that?"

"Christ commands it," Sister J said.

"No complaint?" the cop said.

"I suppose not," Sister J said.

"What if he tries something?"

"We can handle it ourselves." She looked at her father. "Can't we, Dad?"

Her father winced. Sister Xuan looked sheepishly, but not unhappily, at the floor.

When the police were gone Sister Justicia Marie looked at her father and said, "If you stay here, there will be conditions."

He said nothing.

"No drinking."

"But—"

"No drugs."

"I—"

"And no trouble. You've made enough for one lifetime." She saw in his face some hurt then, and her heart softened a little.

"Is it a deal?" she said.

Dalton Bailey paused, nodded.

"Okay then," she said. "For the time being, you can call this place home."

"Thank you," he said. "You know..."

"Yes?"

"I've been working on a screenplay. Can you get my screenplay to somebody?"

Sister J closed her eyes.

Just then Theda Metcalf stuck her head through the kitchen door. "We've got to go get Otto from the jail!"

"That's right!" Sister J said.

"He called. He said somebody needs to bring him some underwear!"

FORCE OF HABIT 4: THE NUN ALSO RISES

"I let you go this time," the big gangbanger said. "But no come back no more."

"This is my neighborhood, too," said Sister Justicia Marie of the Sisters of Perpetual Justice. "We're going to have to get along."

It was night, around eight, and Sister J had been on her way to check in on an old man named Arturo. He was one of the homeless they'd taken in at the shelter, now back with his sister in an apartment building a few blocks away in North Hollywood. She wanted to follow up, make sure he was doing all right.

She expected it to be a short visit.

What she didn't expect was a drug buy in front of the building.

This section of North Hollywood—or NoHo as most Angelenos called it—was in a sort of no man's land. It was two blocks away from the start of the theatre district strip along Lankershim, a place of roaming hipsters and old movie-money retirees. This block was also out of the notorious "box" of concentrated gangland between Tujunga and Fair. Here you found single-family homes with iron fences, and small four- or five-unit low-rent apartment buildings.

And on the corners at night, like right now, you could find young men on the road to county jail or Quentin.

Which Sister J always seemed to find, the way those metal detectors picked up loose change on the beaches of Southern California.

But, but! Perhaps this was God's will. She could stop a sale of drugs, but more importantly serve notice: she was going to clean up this corner of the Valley. If the overworked police couldn't do it, she'd have to. For the children and the old folks and the good people who just wanted to live quiet lives.

And she would also do it for the dealers. By stopping them from perpetuating their sins, she would move—or kick—them closer to redemption.

Or so she hoped and prayed.

After a pause of ten uncertain seconds, the big banger who wore a red bandana and had a face like clumsily chiseled rock slipped a knife out of his waistband. He held it up, smiled, twirled the blade a couple of times.

"Please don't do that," Sister J said.

There were four other bangers around, and one buyer. The buyer was not dressed in gang colors. He was dressed like a high schooler who thought he could score dope and not get caught. Now his eyes said he wanted out of there, but one of the bangers held him by the arm.

The smallest of the assembled gang, a miniature version of the leader, frowned and said, "Maybe we go, huh?"

"Shut up," the big one said. "She goes."

Sister J touched the cross she wore around her neck. "I have a much better idea. Why don't you boys go to mass this Sunday? I'm sure you have mothers or grandmothers who would love to see that."

"Mass!" the banger said, and laughed

"And after mass, you'll all come over to the shelter for coffee or hot chocolate," said Sister J. "You can help us clean up around the place. It'll be good, honest work."

"Enough," the banger said.

The small one said, "I don't like this."

The leader jabbed the knife at his face and the small one shut up.

Sister J said, "Why don't you put that away, huh?"

He smiled. "I like this knife. Killed a guy with it."

"Then you need to get to confession. Put it away."

The banger said, "Why don't you take it?"

"It would be better if you put it away," Sister J said.

His answer was to wave the knife around some more, his face taunting.

"I don't want to cut you," he said.

"Come on," the small one said.

The big banger slapped him across the face.

"God forgive me," Sister J said. She pushed off her left foot, spun a one-eighty. Her back to his chest, she grabbed his knife arm with both hands and snapped his elbow across her knee.

The knife clattered to the sidewalk.

The banger shrieked. He grabbed his broken wing with his good hand. His screams turned to curses.

Sister J went over and scooped up the knife, turned, pointed it at the stunned assemblage. "No more weed. No more drugs. Not here. Not ever."

No one moved.

Until the wounded banger sprang at Sister J.

She jumped in the air and met his face with the heel of her shoe.

He went down.

The gangsters looked at each other.

The buyer looked scared, confused and sober.

Then, as one, they all turned and ran.

Except the big one on the ground.

Sister J pulled her cell and called 911. She told dispatch where she was, that there was a man with a knife and drugs, but he was down and to send a paramedic and police.

The big gangster stirred and groaned on the sidewalk. He struggled to get up.

Sister J pushed his head down with her foot, and held it there.

"Please hurry," she said to the dispatcher.

"Are you all right, ma'am?"

"At the moment, fine."

"Are you sure?"

"No problem," said Sister Justicia.

"We have got to do something about the Sister Justicia problem," Monsignor Stubbs said.

"I quite agree," said Cardinal Fennelly. "I am beginning to think we have a mental issue here, and if she continues to gain popularity, well ..."

The two clerics were sitting in the Cardinal's office at the Archdiocese headquarters on Wilshire. It was after hours and the two had returned from a fine dinner at the home of Preston Makepeace, one of L.A.'s wealthiest Catholics.

Cardinal Clark Fennelly was forty-seven and had been archbishop for two years. He was a round man with much to be round about.

Monsignor Franklin Stubbs was his chief of staff. At fifty, he was still the lean priest that had come out of St. John's *Summa Cum Laude* before donning the collar. His job was overseeing all matters relating to the public relations of the archdiocese.

Which, in Los Angeles, involved a whole lot of overseeing.

"Some are saying she is God's chosen instrument for such a time as this," said Monsignor Stubbs.

"Poppycock," said Cardinal Fennelly.

"Of course, but we have to be aware of public perception."

"Which is, I believe, your job."

"I need direction," the monsignor said.

"We can close them down. What do they call themselves?"

"The Sisters of Perpetual Justice."

"Pretentious name for an order of nuns!" Cardinal Fennelly got to his feet, hitting his knee on his desk. The pain reminded him of his humanity which was always a major pain indeed.

"There are only two of them," said Monsignor Stubbs.

Cardinal Fennelly moved to the window overlooking the lights of Wilshire Boulevard. From here he could see the façade of the old Oasis Theatre, a once opulent movie palace that now housed a congregation of Protestants.

He sighed.

"My fear is there could be more," the cardinal said. "Young girls, unschooled in the faith, taking matters into their own hands." He turned back to his assistant. "Unless we nip this in the bud."

"It would best be handled on the QT," said the monsignor. "I can be pretty convincing when I'm of a mind."

"And what would you suggest?"

"That she start with an extended stay at St. Martha's. At least a year of quiet reflection in the desert."

Cardinal Fennelly nodded. "Good."

"And then an assignment in Chile or Brazil."

"I like it."

The monsignor smiled.

"But," said the cardinal, "what if she refuses?"

"Then we haul her habit up here and give it to her straight."

"You mean?"

"Yes," said Monsignor Stubbs. "Either follow the dictate or be cast from the church."

"Is what I'm doing the sign of a diseased mind?" Sister J asked.

Sister Xuan said, "Oh no!"

The only members of the order of the Sisters of Perpetual Justice were seated in the kitchenette at the shelter, having just served breakfast to the homeless community. Sister Justicia was still thinking of her run-in with the gang the night before.

"I mean it," Sister J said.

"Why do you speak so?" Sister Xuan was Vietnamese-American, young and anxious. Sister J had been training her in martial arts. The training was not without spiritual conflict for Sister J. Was the training a good thing in the eyes of God? Or was she merely dragging down a good soul?

But because Sister Xuan seemed to be coming out of her shell, at least for the moment Sister J had decided to keep it all going. If God was going to stop her—if he wanted her stopped—then let there be a sign.

"I had to break a young man's arm last night," said Sister J.

"But why?"

"He had a knife."

"A knife! So you had to."

"Did I? Did I have to inflict such an extreme injury? And yet I did, and Sister Xuan, God forgive me, I liked it."

Sister X's eyes widened.

"I don't mean like a sadist," said Sister J. "At least I don't think so. I mean I felt joy that I could stop him. But I feel so guilty about the joy!"

Sister J picked up a butter knife and tapped it on the table.

"If only we could settle all matters with the rules of the joust," she said.

"Joust?" said Sister X.

"Like in the days of the knights. You could get two people to fight it out, not whole groups. Then whoever lost would tell his people to surrender or go away. I defeated one gang member last night, but the gang still exists. Are we doing any good at all?"

With a deeply furrowed brow, Sister Xuan said, "I believe you are good."

Sister J took Sister X's hand. "Thank you for that. But I do think we need a time of deep prayer and reflection. We need to seek God's direction."

"Should we not take this to Father Dominic?"

"I fear I have taken years off of Father Dom's life. Perhaps we should do this alone."

"Quietly?"

"Very quietly. We've had enough publicity. I just want to take care of our people for awhile, including my father. And perhaps for a time no more inflicting pain. Let's see if we can find another way.

"But ..."

"Go ahead."

Sister Xuan looked sheepishly at the floor. "We can go on with our training, yes?"

A warm and welcome laugh bubbled up from Sister Justicia. "Of course we can. The dummy knows no pain, does it?"

Sister X smiled and shook her head. "Not even for the *huevos rancheros*." Then she put her hand over her mouth, as if she'd just uttered a minor blasphemy.

"No, not even that," said Sister J. *Huevos rancheros* was their code for a kick to a man's classified ads. Sister Xuan had once utilized it to save Sister J from a knife-wielding man. They did not know at the time the man was Sister J's own father.

"Now we will add to your repertoire," said Sister J. "Up to the rooftop we go."

From the roof of the shelter the sisters could see a broad panorama of the San Fernando Valley. There to the east was the black tower that dominated Universal City during the daytime. To the north, the San Gabriel mountain range which, if the weather was cold enough and the rains came, would be dusted with snow. But in the summer they were a tinderbox for the firebugs.

The western view was of Valley sprawl, every square inch of it seemingly developed or covered with some form of concrete or asphalt. And then to the south, the hills where old Valley money lived with the occasional displaced coyote.

For better or worse, for richer or poorer—check that, just *poorer,* as required by her vow of poverty—this was her city. It had been put in her lap when she was the child star Brooke Bailey. The booze and the drugs pushed it off her lap and into a nightmare of near self-destruction and tortuous rehabilitation.

But when she entered the sacred life the city took on a new look, absent the false glitz. She'd heard a comedian say once that if you looked under the phony tinsel of Hollywood you could find the real tinsel underneath. What Sister J found were souls starved for meaning, with poor starved for food and clothing, and then, quite by accident, criminals who needed a wake-up call —not with reason, but with body blows. Stopping a criminal was an act of mercy, for both the potential victim and the potential felon.

Sister J opened the small plastic shed and removed Harold.

Harold was the faceless punching and kicking dummy that had been donated to the shelter by her former MMA guru, Bobo

Portugal. Made of black synthetic leather, Harold existed to receive punishment without complaint. His featureless face never complained.

Sister J began the lesson with the side kick.

"Turn your body slightly to the left," she told Sister X.

The young nun complied.

"Now you're going to step out at a forty-five degree angle with your left leg. That's going to become your support leg, okay?"

"Yes," said Sister X.

"On that support leg, you rotate your hips and bring your right leg up, waist level, and kick the sucker ... I'm so sorry, I mean the perpetrator, with your shin bone. You want to get him ... or her ... about four inches above the knee, in the soft blobby part of the thigh."

"Blobby."

"And don't kick with a straight leg, keep it bent at the knee a bit."

Sister X nodded. And then with an enthusiasm little known to nuns who did not kick, Sister X let Harold have it in the leg.

The thud was deep and resonant.

"Terrific!" Sister J said.

"Oh my," said Sister X.

"What is it?"

"I ..."

"Yes?"

Sister X looked down. "I so enjoyed that. Is that a sin?"

Sister J gave her an immediate hug. "If it is, we will find out, and do our penance together. But if it's not ..."

Sister X waited.

"We'll enjoy the heck out of it," Sister J said.

And then she heard some cheering.

There was a small knot surrounding the monitor of the community computer. As one they went, "Oooh!" and "Ohhh!"

Sister J touched a couple of shoulders.

Theda Metcalf said, "You're a star, Sister!" Theda was stout and had wild black hair. She'd done time in a mental institution, but had since channeled her marbles toward more productive ends, like telling everyone else in the shelter what to do.

"What is this?" Sister J said.

"Watch!" Theda said. "Start it again."

Elisio Minx, large and in charge, one of the first residents of the shelter, sat at the keyboard. He refreshed the screen. It was YouTube.

And then it was Sister J facing a gang.

On the screen Sister J said, "God forgive me."

And then it all happened again.

"Oooh!" said everyone as the gangster's arm was broken.

Sister J winced.

"Owww!" cried the crowd when Sister J's foot met his face.

Sister Justicia Marie felt whatever blood was left in her cheeks drain down capillary tunnels toward her feet.

"Your best work in years," her father said. He was standing behind her. Dalton Bailey was in his fifties now. He did not have the svelte look of his youth, but the fatness of one who no longer cared what he looked like, in girth or clothing. He'd once been a Green Beret. Now he was a discarded hat. Sometime between those two extremes Sister J's mother had died, and her father had dropped out of sight. Until one day when he'd shown up at the shelter, wielding a knife.

She had felt compelled to try to help her own father. But she'd had plenty of doubts since.

"That's not my work!" Sister J said.

"It used to be," Dalton Bailey said. "And it can be again!"

"No, Dad. That part of my life is over."

"Not anymore!" Theda Metcalf said. "You can get a book deal out of this."

"Book deals are dead!" shouted a bearded man named Gwin Griffith. He was new to the shelter but from the initial interview Sister J had gleaned that he was once a *New York Times* bestselling author who wrote a novel that was made into a Goldie Hawn movie. His follow-up novel had failed to sell and then he couldn't get another contract.

"You hear that?" her father said. "Your public awaits."

"Come here," she said, and walked to the far end of the lobby. Her father followed.

She heard Theda say, "Let's watch it again!"

"Look, Dad, you are here as a guest of the Sisters of Perpetual Justice. While you are here, you will obey our rules. And you will understand that I am now a follower of Jesus, and not an actress."

"Do you know how big your comeback would be?" Dalton Bailey said.

"And I suppose you would manage me."

"Who else but the one who brought you fame and fortune?"

"You mean, who took my money and got me into drugs."

"Aw, honey. don't you know the commandments of God?" he said.

"Excuse me?"

"Honor thy father," he said. "Or it will go down very bad for you, sweetheart. Very, very bad."

Sister J's heart became a mad hummingbird, fluttering around flowers trying to find nectar, and failing. What if he was right? What if she was a lousy daughter and a lousy nun? What if she could never point someone, especially her father, to God?

"Dad," she said, her voice shaky, "won't you at least attend mass and pray to God for your own soul?"

"Don't talk to me about God!" he said.

"I'm a nun! What do you expect me to talk to you about?"

"Money! Your church is rolling in it!"

"Please stop," she said. "Or I'll do something I don't want to do."

"What's that?"

"Ask you to leave."

"You mean you want me to stay?"

"If you behave!"

He smiled. He was missing a front tooth. "We'll just see about that," he said.

Sister Justicia Marie said, "Bless me Father, for I have sinned. It has been too long since my last confession."

Father Dom's voice was low in the confessional. "What sins have you committed, my child?"

"I was afraid you were going to ask me that."

"Hello! This is called *confession*. I shudder to ask, but what on earth is going on with you?"

"I'm confused about what sin is anymore," she said, her voice catching in her throat. Each time she came to Father Dom it seemed that catch got a little tighter. "I don't know how much sinfulness is in my thoughts. I don't know how much sinfulness is in my actions. If God is telling me to do something and I do it, and I find some sort of satisfaction in that, can that be sin?"

"Sister, is this going to be another of your theological

ramblings, which I have warned you about? Or is this going to be a confession?"

"I am afraid I don't know the difference. I don't know how to confess if I don't know what sin is!" Now her throat started to close completely. It always seemed to happen when she knelt inside the confessional. No peace. No absolution!

"How about if I help you out?" Father Dom said. "When you strike someone in anger, *it is a sin.*"

"Never in anger, Father. Oh no. Always with the intent to stop something worse."

"But you have told me in the past that you felt a sort of thrill or excitement about it, haven't you?"

"Aren't we supposed to be thrilled when doing God's will? Aren't we supposed to find joy in that? Joy in our work, our calling?"

"Hoo boy," Father Dom said.

"Did not our Lord feel a sense of exhilaration when he made a whip of cords and drove the moneychangers from the temple? Does the Bible not say that zeal for his father's house consumed him?"

"My head is beginning to hurt, Sister."

"For that I am truly sorry."

"Have you considered," Father Dom said, "that it is a sin to take years off a priest's life?"

"Oh, Father, I don't want to do that."

"Then let me tell you what to do. Go the rest of this day without doing anything to anyone. No kicking, hitting, or grabbing."

"But what if—"

"Tut! Nothing that may be construed as violence. Is that clear?"

"Yes, Father. I was actually saying the same thing to Sister Xuan."

"What, exactly?"

"That perhaps we should put our physical corrections on hold."

"That's a great idea!"

"For a time, at least."

"Hoo-boy."

"I will listen to you, Father." Sister J felt a tear leak out of her eye.

"Very good, my child." He cleared his throat. "Now get ready for some big-time Hail Marys."

And then she found herself driving her ancient Saturn, Ping, back toward the shelter. Her loyal car was going to break down anytime now and refuse to run again. It seemed a perfect metaphor for her sacred life. How much longer could she keep going? When would she break down? When would God send a repairman to her soul?

As she turned up Cahuenga Boulevard, she was almost side-swiped by a FIAT trying to pass on her left. The suddenness of it startled her. Even more disturbing was the blaring horn and the man driving the FIAT, gesturing madly at her in a most unfriendly way.

Had she, in her reverie, made some traffic mistake that kindled the other driver's anger? That would be all she needed—road rage instigated by her unfocused driving.

The FIAT drifted to the right side of her car and slowed so they were side by side. Sister J looked at the driver. His face was contorted, like a demon in tight shoes. He was around fifty with a mustache and wild brown hair. He was mouthing words at her that she knew were heavy on the K sound, and with his left hand he gave her the one-finger salute.

Surely she had done something to him. She mouthed *I'm sorry* and touched her heart just above the crucifix she wore around her neck.

It only seemed to inflame the driver. His gesturing became absurdly manic. Sister J was mesmerized by his eyes. They seemed almost glowing red, and then she turned to look ahead. Just in time! She jammed her brakes and skidded, almost hitting the woman and child in the crosswalk.

Her tormentor did not stop at all, whizzing by. As he did, she caught sight of a bumper sticker with a Christian cross inside the international NO symbol—a red circle with a slash. Sister J pulled to the curb and jumped out, almost getting clipped by a BMW racing past. The Beemer honked. She was a honk magnet today.

She ran to the mother and child. "Are you all right?"

"What's the matter with you?" the woman said. She gripped her little boy's hand with motherly protection.

"I am so sorry," Sister J said.

"And you a nun!"

Not for long, she thought. "Is there anything I can do?"

The little boy was looking at her as if she were an alien being. Perhaps he had never seen a nun in a black habit before. That wouldn't be a surprise. Full-habit nuns were almost a relic now, replaced by off-the-rack Wal-Mart clad sisters.

She smiled at the boy.

The boy turned his head and grabbed his mother's leg.

Shaking at the near miss and the woman's scolding, Sister J got back in Ping and wondered if she should just keep driving north to Canada. Why stop there? Alaska. No, Russia. Yes, find a Russian convent and live off sturgeon eggs and kasha.

Then she berated herself. Sister Xuan needed her. So did the people at the shelter. Somehow, she'd get back her equilibrium. God, in his mercy would—

The screech of angry tires.

It was him again, the madman, in the opposite lane, burning to a stop so he could ... no ... yes, turn and follow her!

No, more than that.

Bam.

He bumped Ping's rear.

Sister J's head snapped back.

In the mirror she saw his twisted face. Hate shot out of his eyes. His mouth moved in the manner of foul utterances.

Why?

The madman bumped Ping again.

A hot rage filled her, a harbinger of her past. When she was boozing it up as Brooke Bailey, she'd been infamous for her onset outbursts. It felt that way inside her now.

She sped up. But speed was only a relative thing for Ping, which had 153,328 miles on her and needed a new trannie.

The demon car kept on her, separated by only a couple of yards. The grill of the FIAT seemed almost alive as well, mocking her.

Where was a police car when you needed one?

The speed-away plan wasn't going to work. Not just because her ancient wheels were more horse-drawn carriage than race car, but because of the red light she had stop for.

Giving the devil mobile behind her another chance to bump. And honk. And push Ping toward the intersection and the cross-traffic speeding by.

The emergency brake. She hadn't used it in ... ever.

Would it even work?

She had to try. With a mighty yank she pulled up the unfamiliar lever as the car behind her pushed, pushed.

Ping held her ground.

But what would the crazy man do next?

She had to stop him, had to—

Father Dom's voice echoed in her head. *Go the rest of this day without doing anything to anyone.*

But lives, lives!

She opened the door and jumped out. She was aware now of people on the sidewalk, looking. At least one had a phone out ...

No, please, no video!

The demon edged forward.

That was it. The man needed a knuckle burrito or people might die.

Then honking cars blared behind the devil FIAT. The light had changed. Ping was now holding up the cars behind.

She locked eyes on the driver, who was smiling now.

Kick in his window! Knock him cold before he hurts someone else!

... *without doing anything to anyone.*

Her tormentor laughed.

Then turned the car right and squealed around Ping, across the intersection, and sped away.

The other cars behind her did the same. The first was a woman in an SUV, honking at her. The next was an old man in an old car that could have been Ping's half-sister. He stopped and rolled down his window.

"Can I help you, Sister?" he said.

His voice of concern almost made her cry.

"No one can help me," she said.

She got in her car. It screamed in protest as she tried to move.

An acrid smell of automotive distress hit her nostrils.

The emergency brake.

Sister J released it.

And that was when Ping, her loyal and longsuffering Ping, died.

A Good Samaritan—a Cal State Northridge student, male—helped Sister J push Ping to the curb. He asked if she needed a ride somewhere and she almost said, "Philadelphia." But she told him no thanks and proceeded to call Triple A. They said a tow would come in half an hour.

Across the street was the famous L.A. jazz club called *The Baked Potato.* Sister J, standing on the sidewalk, shuddered at the sight. Back in her acting days she'd gone on a date here with Johnny Depp. She barely remembered the details, only the first drink she was served. A Manhattan. The next thing she knew she was at the microphone trying to sing "How Do You Solve A Problem Like Maria," and Johnny was trying to drag her away.

He never called her after that.

Sister J shook her head and crossed herself, just to make sure she'd never go back to drinking again. But what if it happened? What if she were excommunicated? Sister Justicia Marie as plain old Brooke Bailey again. What would that be like?

At just that moment, as if it were some sort of sign, a black stretch limo on Cahuenga zoomed past her, made a tire-squealing stop, then a U-turn. It came back and stopped directly in front of Sister J.

The driver got out. He was as large as the door he had opened and was dressed in a dark suit with a white shirt and black tie.

He walked around to the passenger side and opened the rear door.

"He'd like to see you, Sister," the driver said.

And that's when she knew who it was.

Troy Dickinson, the local crime boss, who liked to call himself The Pope of Los Angeles. His family tree had roots in Capone's Chicago.

Sister J stuck her head in.

"Hiya, Sister," Dickinson said. He was in his mid to late forties, in shape, blondish hair. He was wearing a sport coat and slacks with a black shirt unbuttoned at the top. He held an unlit cigar in the hand he used to motion Sister J in.

"You going to take me for a ride?" she said.

"Imagine how happy I was driving by and seeing you standing there," Dickinson said. "I been wanting to talk to you."

"What could you possibly want to talk to me about?"

"Right. You usually come to me, don't you?"

"Only when I must," Sister J said.

"I think you'll like what I have to say," he said. "I think a little magic might be about to happen."

Well, she'd have to wait for the tow truck anyway. She got in the limo and sat opposite Troy Dickinson.

He offered her a brandy.

She said no.

He offered her a Coke.

She said yes.

He opened up the bar at his left and got a stippled glass, put some ice in it with silver tongs, twisted off the top of a plastic Coke bottle, and poured. He handed her the drink.

Then said, "Sister, what do you think of me?"

Sister J took a sip of the bubbly—CocaCola was her favorite drink now, since she'd been off vodka for twelve years.

She said, "How can my opinion be of value to you?"

"I'm asking," he said. "I really want to know."

"Would it shock you if I told you I don't think about you at all?"

Dickinson smiled. "Not many people talk to me that way, I'll have you know."

"I know you have been involved in criminal activities."

"Hey, nothing has ever stuck to me. I have not served one day in prison."

Sister J she felt her eyebrows rise almost of their own accord. It was the universal expression of incredulity.

The Pope of Los Angeles said, "All right, you have a right to be skeptical. But what if I told you I was going completely straight? And that Hollywood is the land of second, third, and fourth chances?"

Well, that much was true. She had received a second chance when she turned to God and cleaned up her life. Now she couldn't help thinking she would have to turn a new page soon But that page was blank.

"I'm going into the entertainment business," he said. "I'm going to start a reality show. I've already got the star in mind."

"Who?" she said.

"You," he said.

"Oh no no no!" Sister J saw a horror story unfolding before her eyes, her face in millions of homes every week, with endorsements—for sensible shoes and the latest fashions in black.

"You are the biggest thing since the Kardashians," Dickinson said. "Or you will be once I get finished with you. And think of it. Think of all of the good you can do with this publicity. Think of the money that will flow in so you can help the poor and all that nun-type stuff you do."

"Has my father been talking to you?"

"Your father? Do I know him?"

"Nevermind."

Dickinson shrugged. "One thing I do know is how to make money. And you are money on stilts. Are you against success for some reason?"

"I am a nun, Mr. Dickinson. I have taken a vow of poverty."

"Old school! Why would anybody do that when you can be sitting on silk?"

"Sitting on silk is not going to get me into heaven. Or you."

"I'm not banking on a membership in heaven right now. I'm in two country clubs. So tell me why you don't want publicity."

"Someone just tried to kill me," she said.

Troy Dickinson put the unlit cigar in his mouth and folded his arms, looked at her for a long moment. He took the cigar out with two fingers of his right hand and said, "Come again?"

"Someone with a No Christianity bumper sticker tried to run me into cross traffic."

"What is this city coming to?"

"I don't need anymore of that."

"You won't have any more of that," he said. "Consider yourself an asset."

"A what?"

An asset of the Troy Dickinson production company. I offer you my protection. Do you know what that means? To have protection from the Pope of Los Angeles?"

"I'm afraid the Pope in Rome is not going to find this arrangement beneficial to the church."

"You let me take care of that," Troy said. "I'll schedule a trip over to Italy and have a little talk with him. I can be very persuasive."

"Can you save her?" Sister J asked Paulie of Paulie's Auto Repair & Body Center on Burbank, after a tow from Triple A.

Paulie wore a grease-stained blue jumper with his name in red stitching across the left breast. He looked to be 350 pounds, which would have been fine if he were 6'10". But Paulie was Sister J's height, 5'8". The jumper had to be specially made, no doubt, for you don't find that size garment off any rack known to man.

His orbicular face was kindly, though. "If she can be saved," he said, "I'm the man who can do it. But I'll give it to you straight. Parts'll be hard to get. They stopped making this model in 1998. Ever considered just getting a new one?"

"We've been through so much together," she said.

"You're young, Sister. You've got your whole life ahead of you. Your car's had a good run."

"You're trying to tell me it's over, aren't you?"

"I didn't say that. Only trying to be real. One thing Paulie is, is real. Wait a minute. You're that kick-butt nun, aren't you?"

She closed her eyes.

"We love you here at Paulie's! Talk about you all the time. You're the greatest!"

"Not everyone thinks so."

"Well, everyone can eat my socket set. We need more of your kind around this city."

She wondered what a city like that would actually look like.

And what it would look like to the Vatican!

"Whyn't you grab a coffee or something," Paulie said. "Let me have a look at her. I'll give you the straight dope."

Sister J did not like the sound of that.

There was a Coffee Bean around the corner and down half a block. Sister J got the usual nun looks going in. This wasn't Boston in 1885, after all.

She decided to treat herself to a cappuccino and took it to a corner table in the back where she could be relatively alone, and watch people being normal. What that must be like!

The baristas all looked happy. Maybe that was her true calling. Serving people, serving them coffee products, instead of her fists or her advice. And thus staying as far out of trouble as possible.

A couple of cops came in. They were dressed in blue patrol uniforms. The one in front, the taller of the two, glanced at her and did a double take.

He said something to his partner, who stayed in line, and came over to her table. "Hello, Sister," he said. He was about forty-five, with brown hair just starting to gray at the temples.

Sister J smiled and nodded.

"You're the kick-butt nun, aren't you?"

Sister J put two fingers on the bridge of her nose.

"I'm sorry," said the cop. "It looks like I disturbed you."

"No, that's alright," she said.

"May I?" He motioned to the empty chair at the table.

"By all means," Sister J said.

He sat. Leaning in a little closer so he could keep his voice down, he said, "I want you to know, you have a lot of friends on the force. We like your vids."

"They're not my vids," she said. "I wish they weren't there."

"I know what you mean." He slumped a little in the chair. "Could I ask you to say a prayer for me? I'm not exactly a Catholic or anything."

"Won't stop my prayers," Sister J said. "What's the request?"

"Well, see, I'm under investigation right now. I'll be coming up in front of a board of review, and I'm thinking they're going to give me the bum's rush."

"Whatever for?"

"A video! Excuse me, I'll try to keep my voice down. My partner and I were on routine patrol when we saw an old woman on the sidewalk waving her hands at us. So I pull over and ask her what's wrong. She can barely talk and points her finger at a car with an open door parked at the curb. I walk over and see a man and a woman going at it, if you know what I mean. Oh, excuse me."

"I know what you mean," Sister J said.

The cop cleared his throat. "Anyway, the woman didn't have a top on so I told them to stop what they were doing and cover up. They started cursing at me. I made another request, and they told me this was a free country and to go shoot some other poor innocent citizen. There was a blanket in the backseat. I grabbed it and threw it around the woman's shoulders and physically removed her from the car and told her to stand off to the side. She swore a blue streak at me. The man was a little more reasonable. He told me he was just doing what a man does. I told him I was not impressed with his definition of a man. I told him to go sit on the sidewalk next to my partner. I went up to the woman and asked her for some ID. She started cursing at me and said she didn't have to give me any ID. I told her she absolutely did. Then she spat in my face. At that point I told her she was under arrest and I was going to put handcuffs on her. She said there was no way I was going to put handcuffs on her. She tried to walk away so I grabbed her arm. When I did the blanket fell off her, exposing her. I put her on the ground, face down, so she wouldn't be exposed, and cuffed her hands behind her back."

He took a breath. It seemed like his first one.

"Well, the last part of that incident was recorded on someone's phone. If that's all you saw you would think I was assaulting a young lady. But you didn't see the spitting or the cursing. My partner told my superiors exactly what happened, but the news didn't report it. They only showed the bad part. Because the young woman was black, another element was added. They sent protesters down to police headquarters, calling for my racist head. I'm going to lose my job over this, because the brass is too afraid to fight back. And they wonder why murder rates are going up in big cities. The cops are not going to put their careers on the lines anymore. They might end up on the national news."

"I know exactly how they feel," Sister J said.

"So if you could send up a prayer for justice," the cop said, "I would be very thankful."

There were tears in his eyes.

Sister J touched his arm. "Of course I will."

"And I'm going to pray for you, Sister. That someday people will all see what you're really about."

She did not have the heart to tell him that was the exact opposite of what she hoped.

Paulie said, "She's in bad shape."

"Can you save her?" Sister J said.

"You might want to pray over her."

"I've been asked to do a lot of that," she said. "Is it a matter of money?"

"Even with the good citizen discount, which I just made up for you, it's gonna be around nine hundred dollars."

"Oh my!"

"Make it eight hundred."

"Eight?"

"Okay, five."

"Five hundred dollars?"

"No, five dollars even. Consider this my gift to your work."

"I can't let you do that," Sister J said.

"It's done," said Paulie. "Your job is to keep on doing what you do."

"But what if ..."

"Yes?"

"What if I can't?"

With a look that seemed to understand everything, Paulie said, "Sister, in my business we learn never to say *can't*. Same for yours. Now let's get 'er fixed."

Monsignor Stubbs placed the report on Cardinal Fennelly's desk.

"What's this?" the Cardinal asked.

"It concerns the other sister," Stubbs said. "Her name is Sister Xuan."

The Cardinal took up the page and scanned it. "What kind of a name is that?"

"Vietnamese," said Stubbs. "By all accounts she is a gentle and loving servant of our Lord."

"That's more like it," Cardinal Fennelly said. "With all of the violent nun talk that's been going around, it's good to know there are still some serious sisters left. I was beginning to wonder!"

Stubbs issued a supportive chuckle.

"But do you fear," said the Cardinal, "that she might be influenced in a negative fashion by Sister Justicia?"

Stubbs pondered the question. "I truth, I don't think so. I've met Sister Xuan, and it does not seem possible that she could ever strike anyone, not even in holy anger."

"Well," Cardinal Fennelly said, "that is a relief!"

The funeral at the Laffing Bros. Mortuary in Pomona began as a lovely affair. Sister Xuan was there to sit beside and offer solace to Mrs. Viola Marbury, who'd lost her husband Herbert after sixty-one years of marriage. Many years ago Viola had been the favorite babysitter of little Xuan and they'd stayed in touch ever since.

The chapel was half-full with gray-haired friends and neighbors, and a smattering of younger people who knew Herbert, a machinist for forty years in Fontana, as a warm and welcome businessman and father. The three Marbury children—Marvin, Maxwell, and Melinda—sat in the pew next to their mother. Sister X counted seven grandchildren between the adults.

Soft organ music piped in through speakers attached to the front ceiling. An open casket, surrounded by floral arrangements, lay at the front of the chapel.

A smiling chaplain—a ruddy-faced man who looked as if he had been doing this since the day Herbert and Viola got married—entered from a side door and stood next to the coffin.

He gave Herbert's remains a gentle look, and nodded. The music ceased and the chaplain looked at the mourners.

"Beloved," he said, "We are here to pay our last respects to our dear friend and loving husband, Howard Marbury."

Sister X closed her eyes. Several voices muttered around her, and one loud whisper cut through the chatter. *"Herbert!"*

"Yes," said the chaplain without missing a syllable, "Howard was known to all as a gentle and—"

"Herbert! Herbert!"

"—loving man who—"

Before he could fill out his sentence, but with his mouth open and ready to go, a loud voice from the back of the chapel shouted, "It's Herbert, and he was worth nothing! You hear me? Nothing!"

Sister Xuan's heart jumped and a gasp arose from the bereaved. Turning, Sister X saw that the outburst had come from a fat, middle-aged man dressed in a white T-shirt and dirty blue jeans. He was in the last pew, his feet crossed arrogantly in the aisle.

"If you please!" the chaplain said.

"I don't please," the fat man said. His eyes were pellets set in drooping, fleshy lids. "The man was a louse!"

Viola cried out and placed her hand over her mouth.

The chaplain said, "Sir, if you would please step outside."

With a grunt the fat man said, "Why don't you come down here and make me, Padre?"

A small flame ignited behind Sister X's ribs. She sensed a coming moment, a new phase of her faith, and it terrified her.

The fat man stood and lumbered forward. Some of the older men verbalized protests, but the man kept coming, as formidable as a delivery truck.

When he was five feet away, Sister X smelled the liquor on his breath. The flame inside her burst into a wildfire.

She jumped in front of the big man who stopped and stared at her. He was a full half-foot taller and three-times wider than she.

But she entertained only a passing thought on the difference. The voice that came out of her next was barely recognizable to her.

"You will please go outside," she said.

For a moment the fat man's beady eyes narrowed in confusion. Then he found his scowl again and said, "Out of my way, whoever you are."

The heat had overtaken her body now, and Sister X began to feel that holy ecstasy Sister J had once described. So this was what it was like to be a sister of perpetual justice!

"Let us go outside and talk this over," Sister X said. "This is a private family funeral, and they would like to mourn without interruption."

"I don't care what they want," the big man said. "I'm gonna have my say about good old Herbert there, who is right where he belongs."

Viola cried out again. An old man wearing a gray suit and a veteran's pin struggled to his feet and moved into the aisle. Next to the big man he looked like a walking stick.

The old man tapped the fat man on the shoulder and said, "You leave right now, young man."

With a beefy hand the fat man pushed the vet in the chest and sent him sprawling on the floor.

Sister X's vision went to a snow-blown white.

She gave the big man *huevos rancheros*. He doubled over as she sent her right foot into his chin. The kick straightened him up. He tottered there.

She turned her body slightly to the left. She stepped forward at a forty-five degree angle with her left leg, her support leg. She rotated her hips and kicked the man four inches above the knee.

Down he went, to his knees, and as he did Sister X, by instinct more than instruction, reversed the kick she had just performed and did the same with her opposite leg. Only this time the blow to the side of the man's head. He fell flat on his back, thunking his head on the terra-cotta floor.

He did not get up.

Sister X stepped back, more adrenaline than she had ever produced in her life rushing through her like a raging river. She felt faint.

"Oh my," she muttered.

The men in the chapel broke into loud applause.

Viola came to her, hugged her. Just like when she was a little girl.

Looking over Viola's shoulder, Sister X noticed one of the grandchildren, a boy of about fourteen, pointing his cell phone at her.

Two days, two long days later, Sister Justicia Marie found herself seated in front of an ornate, African mahogany desk. Behind the desk sat his robed eminence, Cardinal Clark Fennelly.

The Cardinal reached for a cigar. Sister J wondered what he was going to do with it, as it was illegal to smoke inside buildings in Los Angeles.

"It's electronic," Cardinal Fennelly said. "Vapor. Do you mind?"

"Not at all," Sister J said, hoping it was a soothing vapor, full of mercy.

"I find it steadies the blood and makes thinking clearer, and we certainly need clear heads, don't we?"

"Certainly, Your Eminence."

"Heads that are not filled with foolish visions and delusions of grandeur, eh?"

Sister J waited as Cardinal Fennelly blew a stream of vapor over his desk. It smelled faintly of gardenia.

"It has come to my attention," said the Cardinal, "that you are suddenly a, what's the word, virus?"

A virus! Infecting the entire church!

"I think I've got that right," the Cardinal said. "The kids say you've gone virus."

Some small measure of relief came to her. "I think you mean I've gone viral."

"Is that what I mean?" Cardinal Fennelly said.

"A video of a recent encounter has been put on YouTube," Sister J said.

"Ah, YouTube! They have some funny things. Have you seen those animals that talk?"

"Talk?"

The Cardinal said, "Daytime! Nighttime! Daytime! Nighttime!"

Sister J nodded, wishing it was nighttime now and she was in bed.

The Cardinal cleared his throat and vaped. "In any event, this virus thing and whatever else, show forth a certain record on your part. And that record is oddly, and disturbingly, violent."

"On occasion, and only as a last resort, do I sometimes find it necessary to stop sinful, even lethal, behavior."

"Stop how?"

"A bit of martial arts," she said.

"You mean like Chuck Norris?"

"I should be that good."

"This is not a time for levity," Cardinal Fennelly said.

"I assure you, I'm not joking. If I may?"

"May what?"

"Explain?"

"I don't see how. You are using violence, child."

"Yes, but as I see it, it is only to stop greater violence. If I can stop someone from committing murder, I have saved not only a victim but also prevented someone from committing a mortal sin. Does not God command us to do good? And is that not a good thing?"

The Cardinal squinted through the haze of his own making.

"You confuse me," he said. "You're a nun. You're not supposed to use violence of any kind."

"I am not sure where that is written, Your Eminence."

"Love your neighbor as yourself."

"But I ought to love my neighbor enough to save his life, should I not?"

"Turn the other cheek."

"It's not my cheek I'm protecting. It is my neighbor's."

"Do not return evil for evil, but overcome evil with good!"

"But is it not reasonable that a simple beat down to keep someone from a mortal sin is good?" Her voice was rising and she felt powerless to stop it.

The Cardinal set his porcelain cigar in an glass bowl shaped like a fishing boat.

"My child, violence is never the answer. Never. Under any circumstances."

"But—"

Cardinal Fennelly put up his hand. "We have an image to project to the world. I believe they are calling you the—" he hesitated, cleared his throat—"kick-butt nun?"

"That is not of my choosing," Sister J said.

"*Kick-butt* is not something we want associated with Catholic doctrine. You do understand that?"

Haltingly, she said, "Yes. I do. But—"

"You must also understand that you are on the cusp of something far graver than being denied an imprimatur for your ... order."

That cold and cruel word flashed in her mind—*Excommunication.*

The Cardinal said, "Monsignor Stubbs and I have determined that a year at St. Martha's would be of great value to you."

"St. Martha's?"

"In Tuscaloosa," said the Cardinal.

"But that's where ..."

"Indeed. For the recalcitrants. A year of quiet will do your soul good. And get all this violence out of your system."

"But I can't just leave ..."

"Oh, but you can. The door is right over there. That will be all, Sister."

Down these mean streets...

Sister J remembered a film she did when she was the actress Brooke Bailey. It was from a Raymond Chandler novel, *The Lady in the Lake.* The director was a big Chandler aficionado, and kept quoting one of his famous phrases about the private investigator: *Down these mean streets a man must go who is not himself mean...*

That impressed Brooke, aged fifteen at the time, as being a nice guy to have around.

Now it was she, a nun, walking the mean streets, and she did not consider herself mean. She was on Wilshire Boulevard, walking and thinking, her head roiling with troubling thoughts.

After all she'd been through, was she merely fooling herself? Was she less an instrument of God than an agent of sin and malice?

And yet, lives had been saved.

But what of her work with the homeless in North Hollywood? So many of them had come to depend upon her and Sister Xuan. She could not jeopardize that. If ceasing all violence was the condition for continuing to serve, she would have to stop it.

Unless it was God himself who put that spirit into her. Yes, some of that Old Testament spirit of justice.

Or she was misreading God! Sinning harshly against him!

She stopped next to a vacant building and looked at her reflection in the smoky glass. Her features were dark and immutable, even to her.

She closed her eyes and began to pray. *Show me, O beloved Father, what I should do! Make your sign unto me so clear that I may know and not doubt. If I am to be your servant, be thou my vision. Let me not think any selfish thing. Show me, O Father. Show me ..."*

A scream interrupted her supplications.

Half a block away a shirtless man in jeans and heavy boots was kicking another man lying on the street. The victim was curling up in an attempt to protect himself.

The shirtless man was heavily muscled. A forest of tattoos spread across his chest.

Sister J ran toward them, shouting, "Stop!"

Shirtless did stop, long enough to give Sister J a snarlish grin. One of his front teeth was gold.

The man on the ground groaned.

Shirtless kicked him in the back and screamed something profane and ugly and relating to money the man on the ground owed him.

"No more!" Sister J said.

She stopped five feet from the shirtless man.

Who did not say anything. His look was amused. He was enjoying this!

The poor man on the ground writhed and moaned. Sister J saw the attacker's eyes cast downward. She saw him tense for another kick and knew that within a microsecond the next strike would come ... that it could do lasting damage ... that the victim's spine could be snapped ... or his head traumatized ... and within that microsecond Sister J's mind reeled and raced, her faith wavered and her spirit wrestled like Jacob with the Angel of the Lord. She saw her shelter and the faces within and the visage of the Cardinal, his electronic cigar in his mouth, his disapproving eyes locking on her own.

One microsecond ...

... and she did not act.

And the sound of the shirtless thug's boot striking the man's head sickened her.

As did the thug's laughter.

Her body seemed to be made of marble, unable to move or

even twitch, even if she willed it. But her will was bound in the chains of an ecclesiastical edict. Her thoughts were choked in a Gordian knot of uncertainty.

And then another microsecond ... another kick being readied ... another pitiful cry from the man on the ground ...

And then the dam broke, the dynamite blew, the ball of inert gasses exploded into a nebula of wrath.

Sister Justicia Marie screamed, a cry that came unbidden from the deepest part of her, and she spun around three-sixty, the last ten degrees consisting of her right heel finding purchase on the shirtless man's right cheekbone.

Shirtless slammed into an iron street light and bounced off it like a handball. His momentum carried him into the arms of Sister J. Without a thought, operating on pure instinct and the training of Bobo Portugal, the nun from North Hollywood bent slightly at the knees and placed her left hand on the man's neck and her right hand on what street people would euphemistically call his junk, and with a strength she had heretofore never known felt herself lifting the man into the air, above her head, and with a propulsion born of adrenaline and rage flung the hapless kickster through the air, she knew not where, until she let go and realized to her horror that it was toward the street.

The attacker descended, arms akimbo, legs flailing, and met with perfect timing the windshield of an oncoming car.

The sound was like the cracking of an ice block dropped from a roof onto a hot Indiana sidewalk.

Then the screeching of tires as the body of the shirtless hooligan rolled off the hood of an LAPD cruiser.

"She's just left," His Eminence Cardinal Clark Fennelly said.

"How did it go?" asked Monsignor Stubbs.

"She seemed a little resistant at first, but I believe I got through to her."

"You have that way about you."

The Cardinal vaped. "I have a feeling we won't be having any more trouble with Sister Justicia."

Two cops emerged, guns drawn. But they seemed hopelessly confused about who they were drawing on. Their heads moved from Shirtless, now inert on the asphalt, to the nun on the sidewalk, to the man at her feet.

The first cop made his way to Shirtless but kept craning his neck toward Sister J.

The other cop, holding his gun out and pointed down, moved cautiously to the sidewalk.

"Sister?" the second cop said. He was tall and balding.

"It's under control, Officer," Sister J said.

"What exactly is under control?"

"The man in the street, he was assaulting this man here." She nodded downward. "Call an ambulance, please."

The cop hesitated, looked at his partner, then holstered his gun. He bent down for a look at the groaning victim. Then he went to his cruiser and called for an ambulance.

A small crowd started to gather.

The first van arrived just after the ambulance. ABC Eyewitness News. A young, female reporter hopped out, scanning the scene like a lioness sniffing for jackals. It didn't take long for her to spot the zebra.

"Sister! Kelly Kasey, Eyewitness News. Can I have a word?" Kasey was waving for her cameraman.

"No comment," Sister J said.

The intrepid reporter ignored the request. "You're the kick-butt nun, aren't you?"

Terrific.

"Are you responsible for all this?" said Kasey.

And she knew she was, responsible, for all this and more. For the course of her actions, which were going to be ever more on the public stream.

"No comment," said Sister J, and she began to walk away.

"Hey!" It was the cop's voice.

Sister J did not stop. She felt as if a demon were at her heels, and there was no kicking that specter with mere human shoes.

That night, at the shelter, she tuned to the six-o'clock edition of Eyewitness News. She watched in the office, with Sister Xuan.

Sister Justicia Marie was the lead story.

Kelly Kasey was live at the scene. "Earlier today the kick-butt nun, Sister Justicia Marie, saved a man from a savage beating. And then, like Batman, disappeared."

The video showed her scurrying around a corner.

Sister J groaned.

Cardinal Fennelly groaned.

Monsignor Stubbs groaned.

They sat in the Cardinal's office, watching the local news.

They looked at each other and, together, groaned once more.

"Well," said the Cardinal, "I guess that's it."

"This is it!" Sister J's father said. "You're Batman! You're money in the bank!"

"Please, Dad," Sister J said. She had just turned off the TV in the shelter's dining room. She hadn't wanted to watch the news, but knew she had to. She had to know how bad things were. And they were bad now. The publicity was spinning out of control.

"You have no idea what all this is about," she said. "And I want you to know!"

"I already know!" he said. "I raised you up to be a star, and I made you one. You owe me!"

"No!"

"Owe!"

"For what? For sending mom to her grave with your abuse? For smoking pot with me? For using me as your meal ticket? I was your *daughter,* not your trained monkey!"

"You're still my daughter!"

"In name only!" Sister J said, horrified at her own anger. "Now get out! Get out of here and don't come back!"

"You can't—"

"I will call the police! You're trespassing! You're dirtying up this sacred place!"

She became aware of people shuffling into the room.

Theda Metcalf said, "What's all the noise?"

"Your beloved sister is telling me to leave," Dalton Bailey said. "Listen to how she talks to her own father!"

Sister J was doomed and damned and she knew it. For in her chest was hate, a Godzilla of hate, a raging, screaming monster spewing fire out of its mouth. She was never meant for this life, it had all been a joke, a bad dream, and now it was over.

No one who hated like this could be a nun.

Or even a member of the civilized world.

She wanted to cry then but felt only stone-cold deadness in her soul.

She heard Theda Metcalf say, "If Sister wants you gone, you better get gone. No matter who you are!"

Dalton Bailey said, "What?"

Elisio Minx stepped up to Sister J's father and said, "You heard the lady."

Sister J didn't know if he was referring to herself or Theda, but it didn't matter at this point.

"Out," Elisio said, "before I use your skin for a laundry bag."

"No," said Sister J. "Don't talk that way." But then she thought, Who am I to be giving that advice?

So when Elisio pushed Dalton Bailey toward the door, she said nothing further.

"You'll all be sorry," Dalton Bailey said as Elisio opened the door and, with one mighty, meaty hand, ejected him from the premises. "Especially you, daughter!"

Elisio closed the door.

Sister J went up on the roof. She'd always liked that song "Up on the Roof," the James Taylor version. Many times, drunk or stoned or both, Brooke Bailey sought solace in solitude on a roof somewhere—from Malibu to Hollywood to Huntington Beach to, once, on top of DuPar's restaurant in Pasadena, with no idea how she got there or, after passing out, how she got down.

What was it about roofs? Being above the fray, or being close to the sky? The great "up there." As Brooke Bailey she'd thought it only a soft void, unthreatening, blinking stars at her like friendly ships at sea, but nothing more. Then, when she'd found God, it was the place she was closest to Him.

But tonight, with a slice of moon over Universal City and the artificial glow of City Walk coloring the sky like makeup stains on a black shirt, she felt no closeness at all.

Otto Ledbetter's beach chair was there by the edge. The old Shakesperean actor liked to come up here and sun himself without, er, costume. He once explained to her that King Lear ends up naked, stripped of everything, even his clothing, and that was how she felt now, even in her habit.

All gone.

A crunch of footsteps behind her. Sister J whirled and readied her fists.

It was Sister Xuan.

"Oh my," said Sister J.

"I am sorry to startle you," said Sister X.

"Look at me! I'm ready to pounce."

"You are good at pouncing."

"I suppose I am," Sister J said, "which is not a good thing."

Sister Xuan opened her mouth, then snapped it shut.

"What is it?" Sister J asked.

"I just ..."

Sister J put a hand on the young one's arm. She was clearly distressed. "Please, you can tell me."

"I ... I also pounced."

"You did?"

Sister X nodded.

"Where?" Sister J asked.

"Oh, at a funeral!"

"But how?"

"A man. Making trouble for all."

"What did you do?"

Sister X took in a deep breath, then let it out slowly. "*Huevos rancheros,*" she said.

"Truly?"

"And more. He did not get up."

Sister J pictured it, processed it, then sat on the ledge of the building. Which was not the best move, as her head was starting to spin. And then, out of some deep forgotten well, a gush of laughter came out of her. She could not stop.

"*Huevos rancheros!*" she said between guffaws. "Too perfect."

"You are pleased?" Sister X said.

Sister J's eyes were watering as the laughter continued.

"It's not that," Sister J said, followed by another belly chortle. "It's just ... it's just ..." More cackles, a giggle, then a titter. "I am probably insane! How do you like that?"

Her laughter suddenly stopped as she pondered the enormity of what she'd just said. And what it might mean to a young nun who looked up to her.

A long silence was pierced only by a siren somewhere in the city below.

Softly, Sister X said, "You must not think that."

"And why must I not?" Sister J said.

"Last night I had a dream." Sister X sat on the ledge beside Sister J. "I must tell you."

"Dream?"

"Perhaps it was more like a vision," Sister X said.

"Do tell."

"In this vision I saw a field of flowers. Beautiful, colorful flowers of all types. flourishing. But then weeds began to grow very fast around the flowers, choking them, causing them to droop over and turn brown. And also in this field were some bulls, with horns, and one or two of them ate the flowers, but not one of them ate the weeds.

"Then from the distance came a cow. It was running, and jumping, unlike any cow anyone has ever seen. And it came into the field and began to eat the weeds. And where it ate the weeds the flowers began to show life again. One of the bulls tried to run the cow off the field, but the cow snorted and jumped, and kicked the bull in the face! The bull ran away, whimpering. And then the cow went on eating the weeds and the flowers kept on blooming. And that was my vision."

"That is a strange vision."

"Not so strange," Sister X said. "You are the cow."

"I have been called worse."

"You are the cow and you must continue to eat the weeds."

Sister J threw her arms around the little nun she had come to love so well. A tear coursed down her cheek as she whispered, "I pray you are right. But what if ..."

"Yes?" Sister X said.

"What if I'm the weeds?"

The letter arrived the next morning, by special courier. It came in a manila envelope with the seal of the Archdiocese on it. The letterhead was from the office of Monsignor Franklin Stubbs, SJ:

Kyrie eleison! The Lord have mercy!

In agreement with His Eminence, Cardinal Clark Fennelly, I have arranged for your stay at St. Martha's Monastery in Tuscaloosa, Alabama, for an indefinite term. It is our considered and collective decision that a long period of reflection and service, away from the city of Los Angeles and its many temptations, would be the best for your soul and also the reputation of the Archdiocese.

I have no need to revisit our concerns, as you know them well.

In the matter of Sister Xuan, she will remain and will be undergoing counseling. We believe she can be turned around rather quickly, as the saying goes, but we have also determined it is best that you have no further contact with her.

The facility in North Hollywood must be vacated within a week. Please make arrangements for anyone staying there to leave. A list of suitable shelters in the area is attached to this letter.

It is our sincere hope and prayer that you will take this opportunity to submit to church teaching and authority, and be restored to full service for our Lord. Out of Los Angeles, of course.

In nomine Patris et Filii et Spiritus Sancti. Amen.

And so to her final mass in the city, at the great Cathedral of Our Lady of the Angels.

It was Tuesday, two days before she was to show up at St. Martha's.

And in one final irony, it was Cardinal Clark Fennelly himself who would be conducting the mass.

This had to be God's final message to her. Maybe the church, represented by the Cardinal, was right. Maybe she was just a delusional woman with a crazy theological theory.

Once and for all, Dear Lord, give me a sign of thy will!

But there was only silence, save for the saying of the mass, for the responses of the people.

It was all a valley of dry bones to Sister J.

She placed her head in her hands as the Cardinal continued in Latin.

Until the shattering of the air!

People screamed. A group of black-clad, gun-toting, masked hooligans swarmed inside the cathedral, taking positions in the aisles.

Another volley into the air.

"Nobody move!" said one of masked ones. He held what looked like a small machine gun in his hand. Sister J had seen Gary Busey fire one just like it in a movie where he played a demented terrorist. The thought hit her that she had never seen Gary Busey when he was not either demented, a terrorist, or both.

But these weren't actors.

"You are all captives of the Zarathustra Brigade," the man said. "Anyone using a cell phone will be shot. All hands in the air now!"

The Cardinal, face flushed, said, "This is a house of worship!"

"Quiet! Or one of your people here will die."

On the back of his black shirt Sister J saw the strange symbol that had been on the bumper of the FIAT that day.

She calculated there were eight gunmen, stationed strategically along the aisles and at the exits.

Sister J was just off the center aisle in the middle of the cathedral. She stood.

The leader turned his masked face toward her. "I know who you are."

She waited.

"You're the nun everybody thinks is so hot," he said. "I hate nuns."

"Well, we love everybody, including you."

"Shut up and sit down!"

She knew, at that moment, she could never do what he asked.

To the other gunmen she said, "Are you all crazy?"

"I said sit down!"

"What in the name of God is the Zarathustra Brigade?" Sister J said.

"We have a list of demands," he said.

"You can't possibly hope to get away with this."

"We are going to tape a confession," the leader said. "By the big man there. He is going to confess the sins of the church, and then he is going to renounce God."

"No!" the Cardinal said.

"And if he doesn't, one by one people in here will die."

He meant it. And because he did, Sister J knew he had a cadre of crazies willing to throw away their lives for him. This was some sort of cult, and this guy was the chief nutjob.

Then Sister J heard herself say, "You're not going to kill anyone."

The eyes of the leader squinted through the ski mask. "What did you say?"

She had nothing left to lose. She was a recalcitrant. Her budding order had been ripped away from her. She was damaged goods, but she was not going to stand for this criminal interruption to God's house.

But how could she possibly stop eight armed gunmen by herself? This one, maybe, but the others, what of them?

The answer came instantly.

She said, "How about if I beat you up?"

The gasps of the congregation were muted in comparison to the laughter of head nut.

"For your own good," she quickly added.

The leader swung his weapon toward her chest.

She said, "I challenge you to the rules of the joust."

"The what?"

"In medieval times, it was the joust that determined the will of God."

"There is no God," he said.

"Then you shouldn't be afraid, should you?"

"I'm not afraid of ... wait! I'm the one giving the orders!"

"Chicken," said Sister J. What was she doing? But it felt good! Like Elijah taunting the prophets of Baal on Mt. Carmel.

"You stupid chick ... nun ... whatever. I'm a tenth-degree black belt in Korean Karate!"

"But you don't have the power of God, you uncircumcised philistine!"

He blinked. "You are wack."

"Not so wack. All you have to do is pin me. And then I will make the confession you seek. I will do whatever you ask."

A voice from the back said, "Let's do this!"

Another man in a ski mask was charging down the aisle. He

held his gun in the ready position, almost as if he was aiming at the purported leader.

Something about his movements were familiar to Sister J.

And then she knew.

"Dad?"

He stopped and whipped off his ski mask. "Think about it!"

"What do you mean?" the leader said.

"We can win this thing right here and now," Dalton Bailey said. "All you have to do is put my little girl on the ground, and you will have made your point! She said it was a joust, and God would decide the winner. All you have to do is get her down, and we will show the world we're the ones with the truth!"

The leader appeared to be thinking about it. Or else he was hopelessly confused.

"Dad, whose side are you on?" Sister J said.

"I'm on the side of once-in-a-lifetime entertainment!" he said.

The leader said, "I call the shots around here!"

"Think of the publicity," her father said. "Nothing like this has ever happened before. You've been called out by a nun! She is giving you the best opportunity in the world. Give me a fifty-percent share and I'll turn us into a reality show. We can do this every week. Christianity today, Islam tomorrow. The Jews, of course, and then the Buddhists. We could move on to Democrats next, and–"

"Dad!" Sister J said. "You're insane, you need help."

"What I need are half a dozen phones ready to film this match!"

The leader looked at Sister J. Looked her up and down. Then to Dalton Bailey he said, "You really think so?"

"I'm your head of media, aren't I?" Dalton Bailey said.

"Well, yeah."

"Then I say do it," he said. "But I have to warn you, she's pretty good."

"So am I," the leader said.

"Then it's agreed!" Dalton Bailey said.

Sister J wondered if she was having a drug flashback. It was all so surreal. Men in ski masks with guns? Her own father one of them? But then weird, strange, evil things had been happening in the world. Indeed, it seemed as if Satan was unleashed for his last stand against the church, the earth, the souls of all who breathed. While it seemed absurd that someone could concoct a scheme like this, they were, after all, in L.A. This city had produced the Manson family and O. J. Simpson. An arms-bearing cult fit right in.

"Wait," Sister J said.

She approached the Cardinal. He was standing as if he had never moved a muscle.

Sister J knelt in front of him and took his ringed hand. "Your Eminence, it is entirely up to you. Whatever you tell me to do, I will do. If you want me to stand down, I will."

The Cardinal took a deep breath. He gazed out over the congregation and scanned the aisles.

"Arise, my child," he said.

Sister J stood.

She was trembling.

The Cardinal held her hand firmly, then looked into her eyes.

"Kick his sinful butt," he said.

Sister J and the leader, who kept his mask on, faced off on the floor space before the front pews.

Around them at least two dozen people stood, holding their smart phones in video positions.

"Have your men lay down their arms," she said. "I don't want any cheating."

"I don't need to cheat," he said.

"You will feel the need," she said. "Order it."

He snorted, then told his followers to place their guns at their feet.

Then he said, "I have to warn you, if we start this, I'm going to finish it."

Sister J said, "The fool hath said in his heart, There is no God."

"I'm trying to tell you, you'll get hurt real bad. Give up now."

"You come at me with your little black belt, but I am going to come at you in the power of the living God."

"There is no God!"

"Then bring it!" Sister J said.

Inside the Apostolic Palace in Vatican City, the Pope woke up in a cold sweat.

His breath was short, his head swimming, and now his finger was reaching for a button on the console next to his bed.

Thirty seconds later his valet entered the room, robe wrapped about him.

"Sandro," said the Pope said in their native language. "I must tell something."

"Your Holiness," said the valet, "what is it?"

"A dream. You must help me to know what it means!"

"Yes, yes." The valet sat on the bed as he would have with a sick child.

"I saw flowers," the Pope said. "All kinds flowers. But weeds also. Growing fast. Killing the flowers. And a bull, with horns. Eating the flowers." He paused. "Water, please."

The valet went to the service by the door, poured a glass of water, returned to the bed.

The Pope drank, then put the glass on the bed table.

"But then," said the Pope, "a cow. It was jumping! It was running! And it ate the weeds. Then the bull, it came for the cow, but the cow, oh Sandro, the cow!"

"What of the cow, Holy Father?"

"It was a violent cow! It kicked the bull, and made the bull run away!"

"What do you think it all means?"

"I was hoping that you would tell me!"

Sister J flashed on two things that had been said to her during her own martial arts training. The first was from Bobo Portugal. "Do not think," he would say. "In your mind do not go over moves. Instead, find a color. A vivid color, because that will take your mind off analysis and give you only a feeling. The time to think is when you train. The time to feel is when you fight."

She always used the color orange for this. Hot, blazing orange.

She also remembered something she was told when she worked on a Steven Seagal film. Seagal got somewhat standoffish on the set, but one day when she, Brooke Bailey, was weeping because she thought her career was over, she was surprised that Seagal came over and sat beside her. He said, "This is not a good look for you. I know how you feel. You think the critics are nice to me? Listen, it's all about looking good. If you look good it'll make you feel good. Look at my hair. My hair is perfect. I want everybody to know that my hair is perfect, to look at my pony-tail and know that someone with a perfect ponytail like that has to be tough, or he would not dare to wear it. Looking good is eighty percent of what we do. So look good, sweetheart, and don't ever let them know you're afraid."

And though the film was never completed, she never forgot the sayings of Seagal.

Sister Justicia Marie, now facing the fight of her life, a fight that would influence so many, took a good-looking stance and filled her mind with hot orange.

At that precise moment the leader attacked.

He charged like a bull, trying to intimidate with forward motion and a snort.

Sister J ducked under his sweeping leg kick.

And drove the point of her nun shoe into his kidney.

He grabbed his side with an astonished *oomph*. Through the eye-holes of his ski mask Sister J could see a flicker of doubt in his gaze, and even the slightest tinge of fear. Her own heart beat with an elemental joy. She knew why. The church had given her its imprimatur. Her calling was secure!

And Mr. Ski Mask was picking up the vibe.

He began to circle her.

She responded in kind.

Someone in the crowd shouted, "Take him down!"

Someone else shouted, "Don't let her get to you!"

Her father shouted, "Keep your heads up so the cameras can see you!"

Then Ski Mask came at her again, this time with a combina-tion—feinting with his left fist, coming over the top with a right.

Her left arm came up to block it, but too late.

His fist rang her bell, landing just above her left ear.

But the bell was made of solid steel.

It was startling to the point of astonishment. He had hit her hard with a fist of fury, but her head had taken it easily, as if an invisible but impenetrable combat helmet had been placed on her dome.

Ski Mask backed away, shaking his right hand.

Whirling, Sister J gave him a full foot to the stomach.

He *oomphed* again, bent over slightly, jumped out of the way of her follow-up kick.

"Finish her!" a male voice said.

"Finish *him!*" a woman's voice answered.

Ski Mask was still waving his hand around.

And Sister J said, "We can end this right now. Give up, and repent."

She couldn't see his face but she had the feeling he was baring his teeth at her. With a full-throated scream he came at her with everything he had—flying fists, whirling torso and legs seeking purchase.

Duck, counter, block. Nothing landed on any vulnerable part of the fighting nun—

—who turned sideways and gave the masked man a Krav Maga elbow to the middle of his face.

The crunch of cartilage echoed through the cathedral.

And her opponent fell to his knees.

"Give up now," she said. "I would rather treat you as St. Francis would, not Ronda Rousey."

"Never!" he said, and started to get up with a curse.

Her sweeping right leg made a whooshing sound as it cut through the air. Her right foot landed flush, a perfect soccer kick to a fully inflated ball.

Ski Mask flopped backward, splaying out on the limestone floor.

His mask was damp, obviously with blood.

Sister J bent over and whipped it off.

The FIAT driver stared upward with eyes rolling in his head.

"Even St. Francis had his limits," she said.

"I ... hope ... your ... car ... died," he said.

She shook her head. "No. It was fixed up just fine. Unfortunately, you drive a FIAT."

"Wha ...?"

"That stands for Fix It Again, Tony."

He blinked.

From the back of the cathedral came a booming voice through an electronic bullhorn.

"Nobody move! LAPD!"

What looked like a thousand SWAT officers swarmed in with weapons raised and took over the church.

Two days later, Sister J escaped the hordes of news vehicles, producers, agents, authors, amateur bloggers, nascent filmmakers and assorted others surrounding the Sisters of Perpetual Justice shelter in North Hollywood, by visiting her father in jail.

Dalton Bailey had a crazy look on his face as he spoke to her through the Plexiglas. "We did it! You're a star again!"

"Dad, you need help," she said.

"I need a lawyer."

"You haven't got a lawyer yet?"

"I mean an entertainment lawyer. Can you get me one?"

Sister J looked at her own father, now in a LaLa land of his own making.

And still she loved him.

"I will be back to see you when I can," she said.

"Don't forget!" Dalton Bailey said. "God is not the only God. Cable is also God!"

On the rooftop of the shelter, around noon, Sister J looked at the outline of Universal City. It was the one moment of peace she'd had in a week.

She heard the soft steps of Sister Xuan behind her.

"Are you praying?" Sister X said.

"Thanking the Lord," Sister J said. "For we will stay open, and continue to feed the poor, clothe the homeless, and save criminals from themselves."

"When the need arises."

"And by any means necessary."

"For the glory of God," said Sister Xuan.

"Exactly," said Sister Justicia. "But ..."

"Yes?"

"There are so many," Sister J said. "More homeless than ever. And crime is on the rise in Los Angeles. So, so many ..."

"Perhaps we should pray for help," Sister X said.

"I have been so doing," Sister J said. "Surely the good Lord will provide."

Elisio Minx called to her from the rooftop door. "Sister Justicia, some nuns to see you!"

He opened the door wide and out came four smallish nuns in full habits. Two of them were seasoned, and two were quite young. But they all moved with purpose.

"Welcome, Sisters," Sister J said.

The oldest of the quartet bowed slightly. "Excuse, our English is poor."

"Where are you from?"

"We have traveled far to come here," the old one said. "We

are from a small Greek island. We have come to serve here with you."

Sister Justicia could hardly believe it. God was truly in the prayer-answering business.

"What is your order?" Sister J asked.

The old sister looked at her compatriots, and they all smiled.

"You may call us by our island name," she said. "We are the nuns of Navarone!"

FORCE OF HABIT 5: HOT CROSS NUNS

Sister Justicia Marie of the Sister of Perpetual Justice handed the woman a Styrofoam cup of coffee.

"They stole the cross!" the woman said. She had entered the shelter in North Hollywood looking like she was being pursued by wolves. Sister J knew that look well. Taking care of the homeless, many of them off and on various forms of drugs, had educated her in all manner of horror-stricken visages.

Sister J had brought her quickly into the kitchen, so they could talk in semi-privacy.

"What cross do you speak of?" Sister J said.

"The cross! On the hill! That protects Hollywood!" the woman looked to be in her thirties, wore her auburn hair in pigtail braids secured by bands of Native American design— something a tourist might pick up in Albuquerque. Her eclectic, chromatic clothing could have come out of a local production of *Joseph and the Amazing Technicolor Dreamcoat.*

"You mean the one in the Cahuenga Pass?" Sister J said. "That lights up at night?"

"That's the one! It was snatched!"

"But that cross is so huge. It's got to be bolted to cement or something."

"That's just it! Who else but a team of wicked people in a giant conspiracy could have taken it?"

This had to be a paranoiac vision of some kind. Sister Justicia kept her voice calm. "It's a good question, but what would the motive be?"

"Ah! That I can certainly tell you, for I am a seer."

"May I know your name?"

"I am called Deva Furnois. It means Bearer of Light."

"In what language?" asked Sister J.

"My own. I'm still working on it." She closed her eyes and said, "I see Hollywood in the grip of dark forces."

Sister J resisted the temptation to say, *Tell me something I don't know.* In her former life as the actress Brooke Bailey, she had seen—even more, lived—the darkness, fueled by drugs and alcohol and rampaging pleasures of the flesh. Descending into the abyss—a worse fate even than being cast in an Oliver Stone movie—Brooke was about to take her own life when God reached down with his everlasting light. Abandoning Hollywood for the sacred life, she became Sister Justicia Marie. She'd had no idea her martial arts training would ever be part of her service to the Lord. But apparently the Lord had other plans.

"The cross was the only thing protecting us from total takeover," Deva Furnois said.

"Well, for something as big as that cross, the police will surely handle it."

"Never! No one associated with the government of Los Angeles will do anything."

"Why do you say that?"

"Because they're behind it! They took the cross off the seal of Los Angeles, remember?"

Sister J well remembered. For fifty years the seal of Los Angeles County illustrated the rich cultural background of the City of Angels. It had a fish and a cow for the fishing and dairy industries, two stars for the entertainment biz, a Spanish galleon for the explorers who came to California, and a tiny cross to memorialize the early Spanish missions. Dominating the seal was the figure of Pomona, Roman goddess of plenty. In 2004 the ACLU pitched a fit about the cross, saying nothing about the pagan goddess. The Board of Supervisors caved and removed the cross. They replaced that panel with what was supposedly a mission, but without a cross it looked like a Walmart.

"But why did you come to me?" Sister J said.

"Everybody knows about you," Deva Furnois said. "Who better than a crime-fighting nun to find a hot cross?"

"That makes a certain amount of sense," Sister J said. To keep the woman calm, and also to satisfy her own curiosity, Sister J added, "Let me see what I can do."

And just what would that be? Sister J wondered after Deva Furnois left. Surely this was big national news by now. Sister J never listened to the news anymore. She despised bad fiction.

Wouldn't the proper authorities be all over this?

Walking into the dining area, Sister J saw that Elisio Minx and Otto Ledbetter were at their usual game of chess. They made quite a pair. Elisio, large and pear-shaped, in his late-40s. Otto Ledbetter, a twig of a man in his mid-80s. Otto was a former Shakespearean actor who was constantly sneaking up to the roof for nude sunbaths. Sister J took comfort that Elisio, her subtle enforcer of the rules, had his eye on the erstwhile, nature-loving thespian.

"Take that, thou churl!" Otto Ledbetter said as he slammed one of his knights on a square.

Elisio Minx said, "Wrong square, Mr. Ledbetter."

"Thou mewling knotty-pated pignut!"

Elisio smiled. "You went one square too far, Mr. Ledbetter, so if you just—"

"Thou mammering clapper-clawed scullian!"

Sister J said, "Now, now Otto. We don't allow such language here."

Otto Ledbetter looked up, his gray eyes wide. "This malmsey-nosed pigeon-egg is cheating!"

"Surely you know Elisio better than that," Sister J said. "He is completely trustworthy."

"I shall unsheathe my petard and take a pound of his flesh!"

"That's one sort of diet plan," Elisio Minx said, patting his substantial tummy.

"If you cannot play a civil game," Sister J said, "I shall have to insist we put the pieces away."

Otto Ledbetter stuck out his lower lip and murmured something inaudible. He moved his knight to another square.

Elisio Minx shook his head.

Pointing a bony finger at Minx, Otto Ledbetter said, "Disgorge thy glutton bosom, knave!"

"Let me help," Elisio Minx said. He gently pushed the knight to a proper square. "Okay?"

Sister J said, "Tell him it's okay, Otto."

The man who had once played Mercutio to great acclaim in Des Moines, who had elocuted the Queen Mab speech for fifty-one straight performances without a single gaff, now grunted a mono-syllable.

"Move," he said to Elisio.

As Sister J turned she almost ran into her assistant, Sister Xuan, whose face was etched with concern.

"What is it?" Sister J said.

"Outside," said Sister Xuan. "A boy. Graffiti!"

"Stay here," Sister J whispered. "Otto may need calming. I'll go see what's up."

What was up was a skinny boy, probably sixteen or so, standing proud as peanuts with a couple of aerosol paint cans, spraying the back wall of the shelter. Fair of skin and red of hair, he could have been cast as Tom Sawyer. Only this wasn't a fence he was whitewashing. It was her wall he was defacing.

"Excuse me!" Sister J said.

The boy looked at her. He seemed primed to run. But apparently she did not put enough fright in him to get him to take off.

He shrugged and went back to his "work."

She came to him and looked at the word he had outlined in black.

"Koolyo," she read.

The boy lowered his cans. He wore a black T-shirt and lowrider pants. The waistline of the pants crossed the hemispheres of his backside at the halfway point. Which meant most of his boxer shorts made a fashion statement.

"Yeah," he said.

"You have very good writing," Sister J said.

He just stared at her.

"Unfortunately," she said, "you don't own this building."

At that the boy smiled. "What do you want?"

"I want you to clean this up," she said.

"Ain't gonna happen," the boy said.

"I think it is," Sister J said.

At which point the boy began to run away.

East, toward Vineland Avenue.

Sister J was dressed in her traditional nun's garb, but for reasons explainable only by Divine Providence she was wearing her black Adidas running shoes.

She took off after the tagger.

At the end of the alley the boy stopped and turned around. His hesitation cost him. Sister J was on him like polyester on a Florida retiree. She grabbed the back of his T-shirt in a bunch and knocked the spray cans out of his hands.

"Leggo!" he said. "My boys see me like this I'm toast!"

"If you walk back with me," Sister J said, "I won't make it look like I'm taking you. But if you try to get away I'll catch you and pull your pants down all the way and tie them around your legs. What will your boys say then?"

His eyes widened. "What kind of nun are you?"

"One who respects someone else's property. What kind of thug-in-the-making are you?"

"Come on! Lemme go!"

"Walk or pants?" she said. "Choose now."

A two-word curse issued from the boy's mouth.

Sister J twisted his shirt tighter and bent one of his arms behind his back. "You will not say that again. Now, pants or walk?"

He struggled to free himself. But Sister J had learned the arm lock from her martial arts instructor, Bobo Portugal, when she was an actress. In fact, she had once used it on Steven Seagal when he was being obnoxious on a set, which was, like, always. Seagal never forgave her for that.

"Last chance," she said.

He repeated the curse.

With her free hand, Sister J yanked the boy's pants down to his ankles. For good measure she grabbed his boxers and practically raised him off the ground with an industrial wedgie.

"Stop!" he screamed. "I'll walk!"

His name was Darrin Farrow. He had a North Hollywood High School student ID in his wallet, which Sister J had summarily searched when they got back to her office at the shelter.

"You can't do that!" he said. "I got rights!"

"Darrin, I am not a police officer," Sister J said. "But I am making a citizen's arrest."

"What!"

"You were committing a crime in my presence, young man."

"Tagging ain't no crime!"

"Oh?"

"It's art."

Sister J leaned back in her chair. Darrin Farrow sat defiantly in his. The nun, deep in thought, removed her rosary beads and began twirling them.

"Why are you doing that?" Darrin said, a concerned look on his face.

"The beads? Oh, just practice."

"Practice? For what?"

"You never know," she said.

"Know what?"

"You're just full of questions. Well, I have one for you. Can you paint people?"

The boy smirked. "Anything. I got what it takes."

"Why waste it on graffiti?"

"Not a waste," he said. "Shows everybody I'm here."

"What if you showed everybody what you can do?"

"Huh?"

"They could look at something and say, Wow! Darrin Farrow did that."

He looked like he was trying to understand. For about four seconds. Then he said, "Not interested."

"Cops, then."

"I didn't do nothin'!"

"That determination would be made by a judge or jury," Sister J said. "But it doesn't have to go that far."

"Huh?"

"What if we cut a deal right here?" Sister J said.

Narrowing his eyes, Darrin Farrow said, "What kinda deal?"

"One that will absolve you of the harm you have done to this property, and which will also allow you to put your artistic skills to good use."

"What are you talking about?"

"Darrin, do you think you could do a really big project?"

"Big?"

"That whole back wall for instance."

"You want me to tag the whole thing?"

"Not exactly. I don't want names or signs or words. I'm talking about real art. A mural."

"I never tried that," Darrin said.

"Want to?"

"But what?"

Sister J said, "I was thinking of Jesus in the boat with his disciples, calming the storm."

"Whoa, Jesus?"

"You know about Jesus?"

"My dad says his name all the time."

"Tell you what," Sister J said. "You go home and read the story from the Bible. You do have a Bible, don't you?"

He shook his head.

"Does your dad?"

Again, shook his head.

"I'll let you have one of ours. But you must promise to read the eighth chapter of Matthew. Then bring me a sketch of Jesus calming the storm, as you might paint it on the wall outside."

"Then you don't call the cops on me?"

"That is correct."

"And you let me do the wall?"

"That's what I'm saying."

"But I will need paint and markers, all that stuff."

"You shall have them," Sister J said.

With a big smile, Darrin Farrow said, "You got yourself a deal."

He put out his fist.

Sister J bumped it.

Darrin said, "I need my student ID."

"Ah," said Sister J. "I think I'll just hang onto it until you return."

Anger replaced the smile on Darrin's face. "You can't do that!"

"It's called security," Sister J said. "You keep your end of the bargain, okay?"

Sister J parked her ancient Saturn, Ping, just off Cahuenga Boulevard and made her way up to the John Anson Ford Amphitheater. Back in 1920, this site was purchased by Christine Wetherill Stevenson, the heiress of the Pittsburgh Paint fortune. Stevenson built an outdoor amphitheater for the performing of *The Pilgrimage Play,* which she authored.

Stevenson died in 1922. As a memorial to her and her play, a large wooden cross was erected on the hill above the theater. It was outlined by 1,800 incandescent light bulbs, which were illuminated for evening performances.

In 1965, a brush fire destroyed the wooden cross, but the county responded by putting up a steel-and-Plexiglas replacement.

Then the ACLU stepped in. Arguing its version of separation of church and state, it went to court to get an injunction to prevent county funds from having any connection with the Hollywood Cross.

So the county sold the cross and its plot of land to a preservation group.

The plot, as they say, thickened. Some vandals managed to saw through several of the steel supports, leaving the cross vulnerable to the Santa Ana winds that make an annual appearance in the City of Angels. In 1984, the cross blew down.

But as with Christ himself, the cross was resurrected in the 1990s. A Christian evangelism ministry partnered with the East Hollywood-Los Feliz Kiwanis Club to rebuild the illuminated memorial. Their stated goal was to keep  "spiritual protection" over Hollywood. Now the site was owned by a church in the San Fernando Valley.

And so every night, at the apex of the Cahuenga Pass and overlooking the city sometimes referred to as "Babylon," the cross would light up.

Until it disappeared.

As Sister J started on the path leading up to the cross site, she was surprised by a man in typical security guard garb. White shirt with shoulder mic, black pants, and a fifty-five-year-old face.

"Sorry, Sister, but the path is closed," he said.

"So it's true," she said. "This is a crime scene."

"Yep."

"Have the police been here?" Sister J asked.

"Been and gone."

She looked at the embroidery above his shirt pocket. "Patterson Protection. Private security firm?"

"That's right."

"You don't have authority to take anyone into custody."

"Oh yes I do!"

"Only if someone commits a felony in your presence," Sister J said. "I am going to walk up this path. That is not a felony. Thus, you cannot stop me."

The security guard's face tightened into an angry squint. "You would be making a mistake if you tried to go up there."

"A mistake is not a sin," Sister J said.

The security guard did not follow her.

When she got to the top of the hill, Sister J saw before her a beautiful day in Southern California. A light breeze had cleared the air of pollutants, and a blue sky domed the tableau of Hollywood in the foreground, and downtown Los Angeles beyond that.

A recognizable landmark, the Capitol Records Building, still looked like a stack of vinyl discs, while around it structures both new and old pierced the skyline.

And at her feet was the base of the Hollywood Cross with no cross on it.

Actually, a stub about four feet high was all that was left of the cross, along with the steel struts that secured the monument.

It appeared that the cross had been neatly sliced. The edges of the cut appeared smooth. What could have possibly—

"Hey!"

The voice came from a large man in a gray suit. He looked like a professional wrestler dressed up for a job interview with an accounting firm. There was another man next to him, in a blue suit. They could have been brothers, but the coloring was different. The gray-suited man had curly blond locks. Mr. Blue Suit was a steel-wool buzz cut.

They stood ten feet from Sister Justicia, arms held loosely at their sides, but their ham-sized hands were ready for anything.

Gray Suit said, "You shouldn't be up here."

"It's such a lovely day," Sister J said.

"Don't matter. You need to go."

With a smile made of all sweet accord, Sister J stepped forward with hand outstretched. "I am Sister Justicia Marie of the Sisters of Perpetual Justice."

The suits didn't move.

Sister J lowered her arm. "And whom do I have the pleasure of addressing?"

Gray Suit said, "You need to leave this place. Now."

"May I ask, what gives you authority to make that pronouncement?"

"Pronounce...?"

"Ment. Pronounce*ment*."

Gray Suit said, "Look at us. Look at you. We can tell you to beat it. And that's what we're telling you, nun or no nun."

"A church owns this property," Sister J said. "Are you affiliated with that church?"

"Yeah," Gray Suit said. "We're dickens."

"You mean deacons?"

"Yeah, yeah. Deacons."

Holding back a snort Sister J said, "Well, as good deacons of your church, I am sure you are familiar with your Bible? As deacons you can of course tell me what John 3:16 says."

"John who?" Blue Suit said.

"It's from the Bible, stupid," Gray Suit said. "Tell her."

Blue Suit fumbled with his tie. "Oh yeah. Sure. Um, love your neighbor but not his wife ... I mean, you shall not look at your neighbor's wife or his donkey."

"Thanks for playing," Sister J said. "We have some lovely parting gifts for you."

"We're not the ones gonna be parting," Blue Suit said. "If you don't walk back down the path, we'll have to escort you."

"I don't think you want to do that," Sister J said.

Gray Suit nodded at his companion and they moved forward, one on either side of her.

The element of surprise worked in her favor with Blue Suit, who was on her left. No one ever expects quick movements from a nun. People think nuns move slowly with their hands in prayerful repose, or at somewhat faster—though still modest—speeds when summoned to the Mother Superior's office.

But swift physicality is not associated with those called to the sacred life.

Even less so—in fact, Sister J would say the chances were

exactly zero—do folks connect violent physical engagement with women of the habit.

All of which helped Sister J at this moment.

With a brisk jump to her left, Sister J clamped her hands on the right arm and hand of Blue Suit.

Hooking her fingers across the fleshy part of his palm just below the thumb, Sister J pulled his hand toward her chest while rotating the hand outward, twisting the joint. She brought her other hand up and, pivoting on her right foot, applied the full weight of her body onto the now helpless wrist.

Blue Suit dropped to his knees.

Sister J now twisted his arm at the shoulder and lifted it, forcing Blue Suit's body forward. She placed her left foot squarely in his back and pushed.

Blue Suit face-planted in the dirt.

The entire sequence took three seconds.

Which was the length of time Gray Suit needed to emerge from his dumbstruck torpor to lunge at Sister J.

In her very first lesson with Bobo Portugal, the sensei told her the greatest of all martial arts principles was *Cuanto más grandes son, más duro caen.* The bigger they are, the harder they fall. When a mass of much greater weight comes at you, use the laws of physics and the skills of *jiu jitsu* to bring him down.

Which is exactly what Sister J did to Gray Suit. She half-turned to the left as she grabbed the lapels of his coat and sent him over the back of her right leg. With a whipsaw at the end of the move, Sister J managed to get the hulk to flop on his back with an audible *whump* and a small dirt cloud.

The two men struggled to sitting positions, shaking their heads.

"Shall we depart as friends?" Sister J said.

Gray and Blue flashed angry looks as they got to their feet. They took off their coats and tossed them aside. And began rolling up their sleeves.

"This is unnecessary," Sister J said.

"You were warned," Blue Suit said.

Gray Suit said, "Maybe we should call this in."

Blue said, "No! We gotta take care of this ourselves!" He put his hands up and gestured for Sister J to come to him.

"I cannot be the aggressor," she said. "Kicking your rear ends can be done only in self-defense."

Blue Suit began to move toward her, circling, half crouched.

"I'm telling you to stop," Sister J said, "for your own good." Even as she said it she gathered up her habit like a Roman soldier girding his loins, and tucked the hem in her belt.

With a growl, Blue Suit lunged.

He went low, going for her legs.

Sister J gave a slight jump and landed on Blue's back.

Gray Suit jumped on top of her.

With her fighting instincts on full alert, Sister J executed a scissor move that flipped herself around so she was on top of Blue Suit.

Which, for the moment, made them a triple-decker sandwich, with Gray as the meat.

She grabbed a handful of Gray's hair, yanked his head back, and slammed it into the back of Blue's head.

The archbishop of Los Angeles, Cardinal Clark Fennelly, looked at the white hairs sprouting like heretics on his formerly jet-black hair. Even at forty-seven years of age, Cardinal Fennelly thought the Lord had granted him a special dispensation when it came to the color of his coif.

But no. The white was coming on strong, and it was all because of what a single nun had wrought.

He had been firmly opposed to Sister Justicia Marie's methods. And then one day the Cathedral of Our Lady of the Angels was taken over by a crazy bunch calling themselves the Zarathustra Brigade, and he found himself giving the nun permission to quell the uprising with a fight to the finish.

And it thrilled him!

But then he had heard from the Vatican. The pope had recently replaced the head of the Congregation for the Doctrine of the Faith, the department responsible for defending Catholic teaching. His hand-picked appointment, Cardinal José María Castiglione, apparently watched YouTube and had seen a viral video of Sister Justicia Marie putting the hurt on a knife-wielding gangbanger on the street one fine evening.

Shocked and dismayed, this Cardinal Castiglione fired off an official letter to Cardinal Fennelly demanding a detailed justification for allowing such actions to take place in the archdiocese without severe sanction.

Cardinal Fennelly knew of Sister Justicia Marie's odd theological justification for her occasional bouts of violence. She had done her homework, using everything from just-war theology to the voice of God in her heart á la Joan of Arc.

The latter rationale was enough to bring the white streaming to any archdiocese superior's pate!

But knowing the political winds blowing from Rome, the Castiglione castigation—as he called the official letter—was a clear warning to rein in Sister Justicia Marie and her small order of rogue nuns. Cardinal Fennelly would have to have an uncomfortable conversation with the nun who had saved him that day in the cathedral.

Perhaps, he thought wistfully, God would speak to her about violence no longer being necessary.

Still holding Gray's golden mane, Sister J wrenched his head back and pounded it into Blue's once more.

This time the thugs both went to sleep.

Sister J dusted herself off and made her way down the hill, and was met by the security guard.

"Wait just one moment," he said.

"No thank you," Sister J said.

The guard made a move for something dangling on his belt.

"Don't even think about it!" Sister J said.

Her eyes must have put the fear of God into him, for he froze.

"I'm sorry for speaking so harshly," she said. "But I'm a bit agitated. See to the two men up there. I believe they are concussed."

Back at the shelter, Sister J was met by Sister Xuan and the recently-arrived sisters from a small Greek island who called themselves the nuns of Navarone.

"The police are here!" Sister X said.

"With a man who is most angry," said Sister Agnes, the eighty-year-old superior of the Greek sisters.

"I have them in the kitchen," Sister X said.

"Good thinking," Sister J said. "We can offer them fruitcake."

In the kitchen she found two uniformed LAPD officers, a man and a woman, standing with a man of fair complexion but angry eyes.

"You the nun who runs this place?" the angry man said.

The male officer said, "Let us handle this, Mr. Farrow." Turning to Sister J, he said, "I'm Officer Winter, and this is my partner, Officer Burdon. This man says you have his son's student ID."

Sister J said, "You are Darrin's father?"

"That's right," Farrow said.

"I do have his student ID. It was part of a deal."

"There ain't no deal!" Farrow said.

"There most certainly is," Sister J said. "Your son defaced our wall. He has agreed to do a little cleanup work for us."

"Not the way I see it," Farrow said.

"Please," Officer Winter said, putting his hand in front of the inflamed father. "Now sister, I think you should give him back the ID and we can consider this matter over."

"I'm afraid that would be against the law, officer."

"Huh?"

"How old is Darrin?" Sister J said.

Farrow said, "Sixteen."

"At sixteen, a child is empowered by the State of California to make all adult decisions himself."

"What are you talking about?" said Farrow.

Sister J said, "In California, a sixteen-year-old girl is deemed competent to terminate a pregnancy. It follows that a sixteen-year-old boy can enter into an agreement for services, and all the conditions thereof."

The cop and the father looked at each other.

"I dunno," said the cop. "I never heard of that."

"If you disagree with my interpretation, you can either arrest me or go before a magistrate and attempt to secure a search warrant for the ID. Otherwise, I must ask you to leave the premises."

"She can't do that, can she?" Mr. Farrow said.

The uniforms looked perplexed.

"I can summon the media to help you out," Sister J said.

"Okay, okay," said Officer Winter. "No need to get nasty."

"Heaven forbid," said Sister J.

Mr. Farrow's face turned the color of an overripe tomato. "This ain't over."

"When your son completes his agreement," Sister J said, "it will be."

Entering the community room with Sister X and the nuns of Navarone, Sister J was immediately set upon by Elisio Minx, Theda Metcalf, and Otto Ledbetter.

"We are mounting a production of *A Midsummer Night's Dream*," Otto said. "And we want you to play Hippolyta, queen of the Amazons!"

"My acting days are over, Mr. Ledbetter."

"I'm to play Bottom the weaver," said Elisio Minx.

"I am Puck," said Theda Metcalf. "Aka Robin Goodfellow."

Theda Metcalf was a middle-aged, tangle-haired woman who was as close to Puck as Joe Biden was to a spring chicken.

"It's quite a large cast," Sister J said. "And a lot of lines."

Theda looked at the four nuns of Navarone. "We need fairies. Are you game?"

Sister Agnes said, "What means this, game?"

Otto put his finger in the air. "This is no game! This is Shakespeare!"

"All right, let's settle down," Sister J said. "The sisters and I have some immediate business to attend to."

"You mean the hot cross?" Otto Ledbetter said.

"You know about it?" Sister J asked.

"Just look!" Otto pointed to the wall-mounted television.

It was a news feed. It showed pictures of the cross at night, aerial shots of the site with the cross missing, and some talking heads. At last it came back to the daytime talk show hosted by Carly Caruso, a former actress whom Sister J knew from the old days.

Sister J stepped over to the TV so she could hear what Carly was saying as she looked into the camera from her plush, white chair.

"... and whoever did this, I implore you, bring it back," said Carly Caruso.

Her studio audience applauded. Carly beamed. She was about forty years old, trim and athletic, with short auburn hair.

"If you want to contact me," Carly continued, "let me assure you I will keep it confidential. All we want is the cross returned."

She then reached for a pink can that was sitting on the table next to her. "Now, let me tell you about our new sponsor, Drink-a-Weigh, the incredible weight-loss breakthrough..."

At the Hollywood station of the LAPD, Sister Justicia asked to see Detective Rick Stark.

"I don't usually take walk-ins," Stark said, offering Sister J a chair in his cubicle. "But in your case I'll make an exception."

Stark had been the detective in charge of Sister J's first foray into solving crimes. Ironically, it was another cross theft, but one that was much easier to lift and hide.

"Kind of you," Sister J said.

"Practical," Stark said. "If I don't, I just know something's going to happen out there that will involve you, a criminal, and some broken bones."

"I've been on very good behavior. At least, for the most part."

"It's that most part that concerns me."

"I have some concerns of my own."

Detective Stark closed his eyes and sighed. "Let's have it."

"The Hollywood Cross has been stolen."

"That's not exactly breaking news."

"Who's in charge of the investigation?"

"There is no investigation."

"How can that be?"

"Ask me a question I can answer."

"Why don't you know? This is your jurisdiction."

Stark shrugged.

Sister J said, "It's obviously coming from downtown."

"I can't confirm or deny," Stark said.

"When did you become a politician?" Sister J said.

"Listen, once again you're poking your Catholic nose where it doesn't belong."

"I had this nose before I was a Catholic, thank you. And it tells me something stinks."

"What else is new in L.A.?"

"Thank you for coming in," Cardinal Clark Fennelly said.

"As you wished, Your Eminence," said Sister J. It was Thursday morning, and while Sister J wished to look further into the theft of the Hollywood Cross, she was a nun who answered to authority.

Most of the time.

Cardinal Fennelly indicated that she take a chair. He lowered himself into the massive chair behind his desk and took something out of his ecclesial pocket. They appeared to be two metal balls. Cardinal Fennelly began rolling them around in his hand.

"I believe we must come to some sort of arrangement," he said. "And I am speaking, in a way, for the Pope himself."

Sister J wondered how that could be, but said nothing.

"The Holy Father, or rather his chief theologian, has indicated that the use of physical violence by an individual, especially one called to the holy life, can never be justified. Which puts me in an uncomfortable position, as you well know. I have sanctioned it myself, but now feel I must accede to the request of the Vatican."

"Request?"

"To order you to stop. As you know, we made this request before. Now we must make it again."

"Perhaps I can prevail upon the Vatican with a written justification."

"You mean, a letter?"

"A defense."

"What would you say in such an epistle?"

"Oh, that sometimes a good, swift kick is better than a

prayer. That the law's delay sometimes means a smack in the face is called for. That sort of thing."

"It is highly unlikely that such a defense will have any effect," Cardinal Fennelly said. "I'll tell you a little secret. Things are just as political over there as they are over here."

"We can only try to do our part," Sister J said. "And don't worry. I will put in a good word about you."

"Oh, dear," said Cardinal Fennelly.

"Meanwhile, Your Eminence, you are aware, of course, that the Hollywood Cross has been stolen."

"It has been all over the news."

"I should tell you that the case interests me."

"Oh, dear..."

"I find it highly curious that the police are not active in the investigation."

The Cardinal said, "Shouldn't you rather be curious about feeding the poor?"

"Should not a nun be able to walk and chew gum at the same time?"

"Oh, dear..."

Outside the office building, Sister J was surprised to see Gray Suit waiting there. He had a large Band-Aid on his cheek. The skin around his left eye was black and purple and puffy.

"Don't try anything," Gray said, taking a small step back.

"How nice to see you again," said Sister J.

"I'm warning you. I got a stunner in my pocket. Five million volts."

"In your pocket?"

"That's right."

"Hope it doesn't go off accidentally!"

"I'm not joking here. Mr. Patterson wants to see you."

"Of Patterson Protection?"

Gray nodded. "I got a car waiting."

"I have my own car," Sister J said.

"You're comin' with me." He put his hand in his right coat pocket.

"You don't have to do that," Sister J said. "I'll be happy to drive myself. What's the address?"

Gray Suit frowned. Thoughts seemed to be battling it out inside his head. Finally, he brought out a hand-held device with two electrodes on it, like fangs. "I don't want to have to use this on you."

"Don't be silly," Sister J said. "If you try I'll just take it and use it on you. Now wouldn't that be a shock?"

For a long moment, Gray Suit stood stock still, as if he'd already been shocked into immobility. His face twitched. His good eye squinted. His black eye, almost completely shut, tried to open but didn't.

"But I'll ..." he said.

"You what?" Sister J said.

"I'll get in bad with Mr. Patterson if I don't deliver you myself."

"You're afraid of him?"

Gray Suit nodded. "I gotta make a living, too."

"All right," Sister J said. "We'll take your car. And your boss doesn't have to know about our little chat."

"You'd do that for me?" Gray Suit said.

"Of course," said Sister Justicia Marie. "I'm really a very nice person once you get to know me."

The Patterson Protection office was located on the east side of Los Angeles near Union Station. The building was one of those restored jobs that retained its pre-World War II design on the outside and Art Deco flooring in the lobby.

Sister J allowed Gray Suit to lead her past the security desk and the dour guard who gave Gray a nod. They took the elevator to the tenth floor and into a large office at the end of a corridor.

A receptionist, a svelte woman with dark hair and cat-like eyes said, "Mr. Patterson is expecting you."

Sister J smiled at her and said, "Good morning."

The woman did not smile. She seemed incapable of it. She pressed a button and the door near her desk buzzed and clicked. Gray opened the door for Sister J and led her past some cubicles abuzz with typical office activity. Sister J heard one female voice say, "Patterson Protection, may I help you?"

At the other end of the cubicles was an office whose entry was a dark-wood door. Gray gave a respectful knock and a gruff voice from within said, "All clear!"

Gray opened the door and let Sister J enter, then closed the door behind her. She was alone in a large office with a big desk and a big man behind it. The man stood and moved out to meet her.

He was dressed in business casual—light-blue shirt, khaki trousers. His broad shoulders and rugged face of lines and creases gave the impression of a man in his mid-fifties who would gladly challenge a man in his forties to an arm-wrestling contest.

"So you're the little nun that put the hurt on my men," the man said. "I'm Pete Patterson."

He extended a paw and Sister J shook it.

"Please," Patterson said, indicating a chair.

Sister J sat. Patterson parked himself on the corner of his desk, giving him an elevated position.

"I'll put it to you bluntly," Patterson said. "I'd like you to come work for me."

"I'm a nun," Sister J said. "My devotion is to my God and my church."

"Yeah, yeah, I understand all that. I was a good Catholic myself."

"Was?"

"From about four to fourteen," Patterson said. "Then I had to make my way in the world."

"In this world, faith comes in handy."

"So do two fists," Patterson said. "Now I'm not saying give up your nunship or anything. I just want to hire you from time to time. I need good security in my business, and it's not always the biggest guys who can give it to me, apparently. But you! You got what it takes."

"Mr. Patterson, I don't consider my skills to be anything to be proud of, or exploited. They are used rarely and only if I feel God would approve."

"Did God approve of you beating two of my men senseless?"

"I rather hope that sense was knocked into them," Sister J said.

Patterson grumbled.

"May I ask, sir, what your interest is in the site of the Hollywood Cross?"

"I run a security company," he said. "We get hired."

"By whom were you hired?"

"You know I can't tell you that," he said.

"You can certainly confess it to me," she said.

He cocked his head, the way a dog might at a high-pitched sound. "Confess?"

"Anything you confess to me will be held in strictest confidence, as per the priest-penitent privilege under the law."

"You're not a priest."

"And you're not a penitent. But according to the law, the privilege still applies if what you say to me is something you do not want revealed to anyone else."

"Why should I reveal it to you, Sister?"

"Because I'm asking nicely," she said. "If I don't hear it from you, I will have to dig some more, and when I dig I sometimes kick up dirt."

Patterson shook his head, and the beginnings of a smile crossed his face. "I tell ya, I like you, Sister. You got guts."

"Most of the nuns I've known have guts," she said. "You don't go into the sacred life without them."

"Fair enough," Patterson said. "All I can tell you is, we want to find out what happened as much as you do."

"Where were your men when the cross was taken?"

"Nowhere. My outfit wasn't engaged until after the incident. We're there to keep curiosity seekers away."

"Engaged, no doubt, by the owners of the cross, the church in the Valley."

"I will not confirm or deny."

"So do you have any theory on how the cross could have been stolen?"

Patterson said, "Dead of night, some kind of high-end cutter. Had to be an amazing tool. The cut was smooth. How they got the cross out of there I have no idea."

"Awfully brazen," Sister J said.

"The cops talked to the homeowners on the other side of the hill, on Lorenzo, Cahuenga Terrace, San Marcos. Nobody saw anything. I guess that's life in the big city."

"The Lord gives sight to the blind," Sister J said.

"Maybe he'll give us some answers, too," Patterson said.

As Gray Suit drove Sister J back to the diocese to pick up her car, he said, "Sister, do you believe in hell?"

"My, what a question for a nice drive," she said.

"I'm dead ser...I mean, I want to know." His voice was tremulous, concerned.

"I must," Sister J said, "for our Lord taught more about hell than anyone."

"Is it like they say? Fire and all that, forever?"

"There is perfect justice forever," Sister J said. "God would never do anything that was not perfectly and morally, and in every way, just."

"But all that fire and torture?"

"I don't suppose you've ever read Dante."

"Only if he wrote comic books."

"No, he wrote a poem, part of which is about hell. Punishment is in accord with justice. There are different levels in hell. Jesus told a parable which ended with the lesson that a slave who knew his master's will and did not get ready or act in accord with said will, would receive many lashes, but the one who did not know it, and yet committed deeds worthy of a flogging, will receive a few."

There was a long silence. Then Gray Suit said, "I'm confused about that."

"There is no need to be confused. You can settle your score with God and be ready to meet him when you die."

"I don't wanna die," he said.

"I don't want to get sick. But it happens."

"I can handle gettin' sick."

"We all have sickness of soul. Only the Great Physician can heal us."

"You have a great physician?"

"I certainly do."

"How much does he cost?"

"He doesn't charge a cent."

"He have a clinic or something?"

"Something like that. When was the last time you went to church?"

By the time they got back to the diocese, Sister J had secured Gray's promise to go to church on Sunday. He seemed both shaken and relieved. That was a good combination, Sister J mused. She'd been through that very process herself.

As she opened the car door to get out, Gray said, "Uh, Sister."

She looked at him.

"There's a guy you should see. Name of Fats Dial."

"Yes?"

"He knows things, so they say."

"Where can I find him?"

"Well, it's not the usual place I'd see a nun, but ..."

Two nuns walked into a bar, and the bartender said, "Is this some kind of joke?"

"No joke, I assure you," Sister J said. She and Sister X had entered the dive a little after four in the afternoon. It was located off of Hollywood Boulevard, on one of the those little streets that once bustled with legitimate businesses back in the '40s and '50s, but was now a series of empty spaces interrupted by the occasional tattoo parlor or retro clothing store.

Or drinking establishments where nefarious deals often went down.

The bartender was a beefy man with a beard and years of cynicism in his eyes.

"We don't get many nuns in this place," he said.

"I've heard that before," Sister J said.

"What can I get you?"

"Information," Sister J said.

The barman scowled. "What do I look like, Wikipedia?"

"I'll make it worth your while," Sister J said, laying a ten dollar bill on the bar top.

The bearded bartender looked at it incredulously. "A nun greasing a palm?"

"There's no law against it," Sister J said. "Either man's or God's."

"Well this is a new one on me," he said. He took the bill, folded it once, and put it in the pocket of his apron. "Shoot," he said.

"I'm looking for a man named Fats Dial," Sister J said.

The bartender's eyes widened. He fished out the ten spot and slapped it on the bar top in front of the sisters.

"What is it?" Sister J said.

"Out, the both of you," the bartender said.

"You know him then."

"I'll call the cops."

"To come get rid of a couple of nuns?" Sister J said.

A voice thick with drink said, "She ain't no nun!"

It was an angry-looking dude at a table. He had maybe forty disgusting years hanging on his skin. His head was shaved and he had dark-ink tats on his neck and arms.

"Quiet, you," the bartender said.

Angry Dude spat out a curse word, then said, "They're scam-min' you! They ain't no nuns! You know what they are, don't you? Twenty bucks and you can find out!"

"That's enough," the bartender said, and started to come out from behind the bar.

Sister J put up her hand. "Let me," she said.

"No way," he said with obvious concern. But Sister J was already on her way to the table.

"It will be all right," Sister X said to the barman. "She has a way about her."

When she reached the table Sister J saw the rheumy eyes and despair of life in the drunken accuser.

"Sir, you don't want to do this," she said.

"How much you go for, honey?" He grabbed some of her habit and rubbed it.

Slapping his hand away, Sister J said, "Your mind is in the gutter of hate and alcohol. I understand. I was once there, too."

"Sit down. Lemme buy you a drink."

"I think you've had enough."

"Wha'?"

"It's time for you to go," Sister J said. "I have a recommendation for you. Alcoholics Anonymous."

Angry Dude shot to his feet and wobbled. He put his hand on the table to steady himself. Then he said, "I got a recomm...recomm...I got *somethin'* for you."

His arms went around her like boa constrictors. He squeezed and put his mouth on hers. His whiskers were like iron shavings against her skin.

She shot her arms up and out, breaking his hold, then put the iron clamp of her right hand on his throat. She shoved him hard against the wall, giving his head a firm thrust that made his eyes waggle.

She spun him around and locked his arm behind him. He squealed and tried to fight out of her grip. She bent his arm up higher.

He yelped. "Stop!"

"There's an AA meeting just a few blocks away, at the church on Selma."

"Oww!"

"You can just make it if you leave now."

"I ain't leavin'!"

"Oh no?"

Sister J had him in her complete control, maneuvered him to the door and pushed him out on the street. Before the eyes of a few awed pedestrians she marched Angry Dude half a block to Selma, then let him go with a push in a westerly direction.

"The church is that way," she said. "And tell them Sister Justicia Marie sent you."

Hunched over and unsteady on his feet, Angry Dude wandered down the street, waving his arms around.

Sister J rejoined Sister X and the bartender in the dive. The bartender said, "That was the greatest thing I've ever seen in my life! You can keep your ten spot. I'll tell you where to find Fats."

Darrin Farrow was inside the shelter waiting for Sister J. He was sitting with Otto Ledbetter, who proclaimed, "This kid's got talent!"

On the table in front of them was a large piece of butcher paper. On the paper was a sketch of Jesus in a boat with his disciples on the roiling Sea of Galilee. The Lord was standing, his arm outstretched to the elements.

"It's stunning," Sister J said.

Darrin beamed. "You like it?"

"He's going places!" Otto said.

"I love it," Sister J said. "What materials do you need to bring it to life?"

"Brushes, a Chroma mural paint set, five colors of spray paint, Krink markers, and a ladder."

"Done and done," Sister J said. "I will give you some funds and Mr. Ledbetter will accompany you to the art store."

"I will?" Otto said.

Sister J said, "Begone, thou motley-minded rascal!"

Otto jumped up. "Your servant, M'lady!"

Theda Metcalf burst through the front door. "They're coming for us!"

"Who?" Sister J said.

"The feds! The black helicopters! Run for your lives!"

Theda Metcalf charged toward the stairs.

Through the glass door Sister J saw two vans in the parking lot. One of the vans had a broadcast tower sticking up. News!

Sister J hated publicity almost as much as she hated man buns.

One of the cameramen had a man bun.

She opened the door slightly and said, "Not today, please."

A man with a microphone shouted, "Isn't it true you know who stole the cross?"

"Why, no—"

"What are you trying to hide, Sister?"

"Excuse me?"

"Aren't you a shill for the Catholic church?"

"That is an absolute—"

"Didn't you in fact collude with the Vatican to remove the cross?"

"Sir! How dare you spread such falsehoods."

The man with the microphone turned to the man with the bun and said, "Are you getting this?"

The cameraman gave the reporter a thumbs up.

Sister J took the opportunity to duck back inside and close

the door, and lock it. The reporter grabbed the handle and shook it angrily. "You can't do this to me! I'm from CNN!"

Sister Xuan appeared at her elbow. "All is not well?"

"We'd better get to the bottom of this thing," Sister J said, "before the lies start taking over."

"Would it help to go on television yourself?" Sister X said.

"What do you mean?"

Producing a note, Sister X said, "The show of Carly Caruso called. She would like to have you as a guest."

Sister J shook her head. "Must everybody see everything now?"

"Sadly," said Sister X.

"Call them back, please," said Sister J. "And politely tell them no."

Shayla Ortega was the councilmember (the Los Angeles City Council had long ago purged -*man* and -*woman* from the title) of the 13th District, representing Hollywood, Silver Lake and other adjacent neighborhoods. Her biggest legislative achievement was the "plastic straw on request only" ordinance. She had a picture of a dolphin on her office wall.

"Thank you for seeing me on such short notice," Sister J said.

"Not at all," Councilmember Ortega said. She was a squat woman with curly brown hair and a J.D. from Harvard hanging on her wall. "I've long wanted to meet you."

She gave Sister J a cursory handshake from behind her desk. They sat.

"So you're the kicking nun," Ortega said. "Not exactly the stuff of Bing Crosby movies or Sally Field TV shows."

"I don't put these labels on myself."

"Nevertheless. Do you have plans to stay in Los Angeles?"

"I've had no thoughts about moving."

"Ah."

"Why do you ask?"

With smooth emotionlessness, Ortega said, "I wonder if you and your order might be better off in another state. Like Louisiana."

Sister J said, "Why would you think such a thing?"

"The city is changing," the councilmember said. "One hundred years ago, most people went to church, Catholic or Protestant. That is not so today."

"Something to remedy," Sister J said.

"Is it? Or would that be going backward?"

"You tell me. Do you see the city as safer than it used to be? Are the people here more civil, or less so? Is it *Love thy neighbor as thyself?* Or is it *Love thyself and to heck with thy neighbor?*"

"The answer is further progress, without the prejudices of the old-time religion."

"Is that why you don't want the cross to be found?"

Shayla Ortega stiffened. "What on earth are you talking about?"

"I thought you might know," said Sister J. "Why have the police been called off this case?"

Through a haughty and derisive glare that could have come only from training at an Ivy League school, Ortega said, "I don't like the implication of your question."

"The truth doesn't care if you like it or not."

Ortega stood. "I have nothing more to say to you."

"You are an elected representative," Sister J said. "Answerable to the people. I'm one of the people."

"I don't like people," Ortega said. "Shall I call security?"

Outside Shayla Ortega's office, Sister J looked up at the

Hollywood Hills. On the spot where the Hollywood Cross should have been she saw only empty sky. How ironic, she thought. That spot should be filled with the Cross. It is Shayla Ortega's office that should be empty.

"I'm Fats Dial," the fat man said.

He was sitting in a chair that was crying for mercy. Sister J heard it creak with every movement of the proprietor of Big Man Storage in Newhall. Papers of all kinds—loose, bound, wadded, ripped—made up most of the decor. Somehow there was enough room on the desk for several pink cans of Drink-a-Weigh.

"What can I do for you?" Fats Dial said. He was wearing a Hawaiian shirt that was at least quadruple-X and covered with little surfers riding waves toward palm-treed shores.

"My name is Sister Justicia Marie, and this is my associate, Sister Xuan."

Fats Dial nodded, reached for one of the cans, and popped the top. "Tryin' to drop a few LBs," he said.

"I was told you might be able to help us," Sister J said.

"With what?"

"We're looking for a stolen cross."

As Fats Dial leaned forward, the chair screamed. "What's that got to do with me?"

"You know about the Hollywood Cross?"

"I read about that," Fats Dial said. "You don't think it could be here, do you?"

"Do you?" Sister J said.

Sitting back now, under further protest from the chair, Dial put the diet drink on the table and laced his fingers over his stomach. "We got a little thing in this business called privacy. It's on our contracts. Even if I knew about it, I couldn't tell you, without maybe I get sued."

"Unless you believe there is evidence of a crime," Sister J said.

"Then I'd have to report it to the cops," Fats Dial said.

"Perhaps we should call them now," Sister J said.

"Now look! I don't need trouble, especially from a couple of nuns."

"Is the cross here, Mr. Dial?"

"I got no idea."

"You have video surveillance cameras, correct?"

"Well, yeah."

"And that is not subject to your lease agreements, is it?"

"Well, no."

"You have the right to review the footage at any time, don't you?"

"What are you implicating?"

"Suppose Sister Xuan and I help you review the last two days?"

"Why should I let you do that?"

"Because," Sister J said, "we will pray for you to lose that weight."

Dial said, "I was thinking more along the lines of, you know, money."

"For what shall it profit a man, if he shall gain the whole world, and lose his own soul?"

"Huh?"

"Come, come," Sister J said. "Let us look at the footage and I'll buy you another case of Drink-a-Weigh."

And so they did, covering the last two days, in 2x motion. It was like watching an old silent movie, only with no plot and no main characters. A man with a pickup filled with furniture backed into a space. Another man took a canoe out of a unit and strapped it to the top of his Jeep. A large woman removed a small refrigerator from a medium-sized van. A man and boy and dog on a leash removed three clear-plastic boxes and put them in the back of a Hyundai Sonata.

Then someone in a hoodie, face obscured, parked a small truck in front of a unit, got out, pulled down the ramp, and rolled down something strange.

"Stop here," Sister J said.

Fats Dial paused the playback. The item being un-trucked looked like a robotic arm attached to a movable base, with a thick wire joining the two units.

"What on earth is that?" Sister J said.

"Heck if I know," Fats Dial said.

"Can you zoom in?"

"I think I can," Fats Dial said, and manipulated a trackball. Sure enough, the picture zoomed though the result was fuzzy.

But not so much that Sister J couldn't make out the name on the side of the robot-thing: JAZZEECUT, INC.

"Have you ever heard of this company?" Sister J said.

"Nope," Fats Dial said. "Now if you'll—"

"Wait!" She leaned in. The hooded figure's face could not be seen, but there was something poking out that could. It was ... a braid. With a band around it that had a design.

Sister J said, "Zoom in on the hoodie. I want to—"

The monitor went dark!

"Wait!" Sister J said.

Fats Dial shook his head. "If you're not gonna rent a unit, I must kindly ask you to get out."

As they drove back to the Valley in Ping, Sister Xuan used her phone to search the net. "Jazzeecut, Inc. is a startup. They are making a fiber laser robotic cutting system with articulated kin ... kin...ematics."

Sister J said, "Eureka."

"I do not see that word."

"Oh. It's Greek. It means 'I have found it.' *We* have found it. Because we were meant to find it."

"I am confused."

"It's all been too convenient. Too easy. Someone wanted us to find Fats Dial and see that very video. Someone wanted us to find that robotic arm."

"I do not understand."

Sister J said, "I don't either. Yet."

"Fantastic," Sister J said.

Darrin, a marker in his hand, stepped back and regarded the back wall of the shelter with her. He had primed the wall with white paint and used the marker to sketch out the figures. Now all he needed to add was the color.

"You like it?" Darrin said.

"Love it," Sister J said.

She looked more closely and noticed that one of the disciples had his back to Jesus.

"And why did you do that?" she said, pointing to the faceless follower.

Darrin beamed. "That's Judas," he said. "He is in the boat, but he is against Jesus."

And that's when she knew.

"Brooke!" Carly Caruso said. "I can hardly believe it."

"It's Sister Justicia now."

"Best looking nun in Hollywood," Carly said. "Maybe the world!"

They were in Carly's spacious dressing room on the television studio lot. When Sister J had called that morning, offering to do a TV appearance regarding the stolen cross, Carly's assistant relayed the message. Five minutes later Carly was on the phone saying it would be a ratings bonanza to have the fighting nun on her show.

Carly wore a white blouse and pants, with white sandals and blue toenails. The blue in her eyes matched the polish on her toes. Indeed, everything in the dressing room was some form of white or blue. Spill a little red wine on the carpet, Sister J mused, and it would be downright patriotic in here.

Carly offered Sister J a plush chair and said, "Coffee?"

"Thank you."

Carly thumbed her phone. "Brandi, bring us two cups of rustic shade-grown Tanganyikan roast, if you please. Thank you."

Carly sat in the chair opposite Sister J and said, "I don't think I've seen you since we did that Western with Tom Selleck," Carly said.

"A long time ago, it seems," Sister J said.

"Different paths."

"You've done very well for yourself," Sister J said. "I saw a picture of your home in Hidden Hills."

"Not so hidden, eh?" Carly Caruso said with a chuckle.

"Google Earth," Sister J said.

"You do Google?" Carly said.

"We nuns have come a long way since the Middle Ages."

"I should say! It's amazing what you get away with...I mean..."

"I know what you mean."

"May I ask, then, how you justify it? The violence? If I ask you that question on the air, how would you answer?"

"I usually point people to two examples," Sister J said.

"Do tell!"

"One of them is Joan of Arc."

"Good one. Who is the other?"

"Chuck Norris."

"No one can go wrong pointing to Chuck Norris!"

"I hope the Vatican will agree."

Carly Caruso smiled, but it seemed forced. She drummed her fingers on the soft arms of her chair.

"Is anything wrong?" Sister J asked.

"What? Oh, no. Nothing. About the show, how would you like to be introduced?"

"Before we get to that, perhaps I should give you the information I have. To see if you really want to go through with this."

"Oh, I know...at least, I assume you will have something interesting for the audience. Brooke...I'm sorry, Sister...go ahead. What've you got?"

"The first clue in this matter was the very clean cut that went through the cross, allowing easy removal right off the hill, in the dead of night."

Carly Caruso nodded.

"There was only one way to do that so quickly," Sister J said, "and that was with some advanced kind of industrial laser."

Carly's assistant entered the dressing room with a silver tray holding two fine china cups and saucers. Also, a silver cream and sugar set. She set it down and Carly dismissed her with a wave of the hand.

As she began to pour, Carly said, "Do you take anything?"

"I like it straight," Sister J said. "Like I like answers."

For a moment Carly froze, then continued the pour. She handed a cup to Sister J.

Sitting back in her chair and crossing her legs, Carly said, "Can this laser thing be proved?"

"I did some investigating, and found one in a storage locker in Newhall."

"Oh?"

"Off a surveillance cam. It looks sort of like a robot arm," Sister J said.

"Any markings on it?"

"Only the name of the manufacturer."

"You could see it?"

"I was meant to see it," Sister J said.

"I don't understand."

"And meant to appear on your show to mention the manufacturer's name. That would be massive free publicity. Hype for my appearance came from the reporter who rushed me. Tipped off, I think, by you. The laser company could put out a statement condemning the use of their product for such an outrageous crime, at the same time call attention to it. That could lead to millions of dollars in contracts with industry or the government."

Carly Caruso took a tentative sip of coffee.

"If someone had an interest in this company," Sister J said, "that could mean a lot of money in the old bank account."

"I'm ... it ..."

"It was all a set-up from the start. When I saw the robotic cutter, I also saw the person in a hoodie."

"You saw her ... I mean, him?"

"You were right the first time. Only what I saw was not a face, but peeking out of the hoodie, a braid. With some sort of ornate band securing it. Like the braids worn by Deva Furnois."

"You can't ... I don't know any such person."

"Confession is good for the soul, Carly. I found that out. You can, too"

"There's not...I don't..."

"Who is Deva Furnois? Your sister?"

A man's voice said, "My daughter."

From behind a partition stepped Pete Patterson.

He was holding a gun.

"I'm sorry you got out of your lane," Patterson said.

With a Judas look, Carly rose from her chair and went to Patterson, who kept his gun trained on Sister J.

"How did you figure it, Brooke?" she said.

"It was a hunch," Sister J said. "We were in the same boat. I needed to know if your back was turned."

"Huh?"

"I suspected Mr. Patterson here had something to do with the cross disappearance. That he got me started on the path to find the laser. What I didn't figure, until yesterday, was that you were part of it."

"Enough," Patterson said. "I assume you've got your affairs in order with God, Sister. That should make things easier on both of us."

"Nothing will be easy for you after this," Sister J said.

"The only hard part is disposing of your body," Patterson said. "But that's what I do. Carly, there's some chloroform in my bag. Get it."

She got it.

Sister J said, "I won't let that happen. You'll have to shoot me here."

"Fine by me," Patterson said.

"What about Carly's assistant?" Sister J said. "She'll hear it."

Carly said, "Brandi is twenty-four and wants to make it in this business. She'll do as she's told."

"Now turn around," Patterson said.

Sister Justicia Marie turned her back to the gunman, removing the rosary beads from her belt as she did.

As soon as she felt Carly's arms come around her, she spun and yanked the talk show host's arm behind her, then held her like a human shield in front of Patterson.

With her right hand, Sister J twirled the rosary like a gaucho with his *bola*, and let it fly.

The base of the crucifix hit Patterson in the eye.

Sister J pushed Carly Caruso aside and leapt at Patterson, who was yelping in pain. More pain was added as Sister J's foot slammed the side of his head. As he fell, Sister J kicked the gun out of his hand.

And just as an extra Hail Mary could keep a soul from sin, an extra foot to cranium could keep a criminal from action, which was Sister Justicia Marie's reasoning as she put Patterson to sleep with a final kick to the cranium.

Which was the exact moment Carly Caruso made a dive for the gun.

Sister J made a dive for Carly.

All three—talk show host, nun, and gun—converged in a knot of arms, hands, and steel.

The gun blasted.

And when Sister J flipped Carly over onto her back, and took hold of the weapon, she saw the blood. It was coming from the head of Pete Patterson.

The dressing room was red, white, and blue after all.

Detective Rick Stark had his arms folded. He shook his head. "How do you manage to do it?"

Sister J, sitting across from him in the police interrogation room, said, "God's will."

Stark slammed the table. "A man is dead! And you are accusing one of America's most beloved personalities of fraud, homicide, and ... cross stealing?"

From the pocket of her habit, Sister J removed the digital recording device she'd had on her when confronting Carly Caruso. She placed it on the table and played the entire scene, all the way to the gunshot.

When she clicked it off Detective Rick Stark had a look of stark unbelief on his face.

"I suggest you move fast," Sister J said. "As you know, I am a private citizen, so this recording does not fall under Fourth Amendment scrutiny. You can use it to get a search warrant for her home in Hidden Hills."

"How do we connect the home?" Stark said.

"I will provide you with probable cause to believe that you'll find the stolen cross in her horse stable."

"Just how will you do that?"

"We made a Western with Tom Selleck once. She hated horses. She told me she would never have a horse. But a stable is the perfect size to hide a cross."

"And how would it get there?"

"In one of those long horse trailers, of course."

Stark rubbed his face, and said with a sigh, "But as I told you before, we're off this case."

"Not anymore," Sister J said. "You are going to find it. If you don't, I'm going to blow the lid off this operation, with the LAPD taking orders from Ortega's office. Dancing like puppets on a string. You're going to do your job. Because it's the right thing to do. I don't believe you're one of those who turns a blind eye to duty."

Stark said, "Councilperson Ortega isn't going to like it."

"So much the better, right?"

The detective smiled.

Cardinal Fennelly said, "I cannot believe you used, as a method of criminal prevention, the crucifix! You threw our Lord into someone's face!"

Sister J said, "Surely our Lord, who used a whip of cords to drive away the money changers, would have no qualms about his representation stopping a man from committing murder."

Fennelly palmed his face.

Sister Justicia Marie, along with Sister Xuan and the nuns of Navarone, stood outside with half the shelter residents, admiring the mural on the back wall.

"Beautiful," said Sister J.

"Like a rich jewel in an Ethiope's ear!" said Otto Ledbetter.

Darrin Farrow smiled.

Even his father smiled.

For there was Jesus stilling the waters, with an artistic touch of genius. It would be seen by countless drivers and pedestrians, burrowing into hearts that were hungry for what they knew not. This would help them to know.

Just as the Hollywood Cross would. Recovered from Carly Caruso's stable, it was even now being reattached by the owners back on its rightful spot.

Meanwhile, the evidence against Carly Caruso being overwhelming, she did the currently fashionable thing—proclaimed her innocence and hired an expensive lawyer who threatened to sue the city if charges were ever filed.

After an initial ratings spike, Carly's show tanked and her contract was not renewed. Her lawyer said he was going to sue the network, but before he could file he was indicted by a federal grand jury for tax evasion and mail fraud.

The Sisters of Perpetual Justice production of *A Midsummer Night's Dream* was given a favorable review by the Daily News, with a special mention of Otto Ledbetter's "enthusiastic" performance as Nick Bottom.

FORCE OF HABIT 6: NUN TOO SOON

Los Angeles, Summer, 2020

The blaring voice from the hovering police helicopter cut through the afternoon air.

"Attention! You are in violation of Los Angeles health regulations. You must all put on masks immediately."

Or what? Sister Justicia Marie thought. *You going to open fire?* Then she thought: *Snark is close to sin. They are just trying to do their job. They simply know not what job they do.*

"They can't do that!" Elisio Minx said. "Can they?"

"We'll see," Sister J said. They were on the roof of the shelter of the Sisters of Perpetual Justice in North Hollywood. Eight residents, ranging in age from fifty to ninety, were sitting on beach chairs, nicely spaced apart, as Sister J presided over a twenty-minute sunbath. It was essential in this time of virus panic that the elderly keep up their Vitamin D and not be cooped up inside all day. She wasn't about to let a New York nursing home-type tragedy happen on her watch.

Nor was there a reason for any of them to be wearing masks outside.

But the LAPD was apparently following orders from the clown show in City Hall.

Watch the snark, Sister!

"Repeat!" boomed the copter voice. "Masks on or move inside!"

Sister J held up her arm and pointed to her wrist, indicating they'd go inside after a short time. Short, of course, being a relative term.

"If you refuse, you will be cited!"

Theda Metcalf, the middle-aged former mental patient and current screenwriting wannabe, shook her fist at the helicopter. "Come and get us, coppers!"

"Theda, no," Sister J said.

"I'm not moving," said Otto Ledbetter, the ex-Shakespearean actor. "A pox on all their houses! The tottering motley-minded boar-pigs!"

Otto loved the roof. He often snuck up there alone, *au natural*, declaring that the roof was his "turf."

"Stay as you are," Sister J said. "I'm sure they'll send someone around. I'll explain matters."

"We need a talisman of protection!" Otto said as he removed something from the pants he thankfully wore. He held it up. It was a penny. He placed it at the foot of the roof access door.

"The ill-nurtured malt worms shall not pass!" Otto said. His voice was drowned out by the blaring of a siren. Sister J walked to the ledge and saw a police SUV come roaring up to the front of the shelter.

Sister J took the stairs to the first floor, where Sister Xuan, her assistant, and the four nuns of Navarone stood with wondering expressions.

Two uniformed officers, a man and a woman—dutifully masked—came to the glass front doors. Sister J opened one.

"How may I help you today?" Sister J said.

"Apparently you have several people on the roof not wearing masks," the male officer said.

"That is correct."

"You understand that's a violation of the mayor's order that everyone who goes outside must wear a mask."

"Not so," Sister J said.

The two cops looked at each other.

Sister J said, "The mayor's guidelines state that individuals engaging in outdoor activities must wear a cloth face covering whenever there might be contact with others who are non-household members. And this is their household."

"Isn't this some sort of nursing home?" the male officer asked.

"Not at all," Sister J said. "We are a religious order and provide food and shelter for the hungry and needy."

"Look, Sister," the man said, "give us a break here, huh? We don't like hassling good people like you. If you'll just follow the rules until this all shakes out."

"But we are following the rules," Sister J said. "According to the order, face coverings are not required when exercising outdoors, provided one can maintain a distance of at least six feet from others."

"Aha," said the man. "You are not exercising on the roof, are you?"

"Actually, we are," Sister J said. "We are exercising our First Amendment rights."

Snark...

"But we also do relaxation exercises."

The male officer told Sister J to wait a moment and turned to consult with his partner.

Sister Xuan tapped her on the shoulder. "What do you think they will do?"

"I believe they are as confused as anyone," Sister J said. "One viral video and they could have their lives ruined, even if they are upholding the law. It makes for a very difficult state of affairs for police. We must be kind."

Presently, the male officer came back to the door and said,

"Sister, would you consider coming with us? Someone from the mayor's office would like to meet with you."

"Of course I'll go along," Sister J said. "What you don't need right now is more trouble."

Under their masks, it appeared both cops sighed with relief.

Sister J sat in the back of the police SUV. The male officer's name was Rollins. The female was Hernandez. Rollins drove. To keep them from discomfort, Sister J wore a cloth mask with a rendering of Joan of Arc on it.

"I just want you to know," Sister J said, "that I am behind you. Not just literally, but in every way. I know what a tough job you have."

"Thank you, Sister," Hernandez said.

"My grandfather was a cop," Sister J said. "Right here in L.A."

"Really?" Hernandez said.

"Martin Bailey. Served under William Parker."

Rollins said, "I think my father spoke of Martin Bailey!"

"Your father was a policeman?" Sister J asked.

"He sure was," said Rollins. "He went in because of *Adam-12*."

"The old TV show," Sister J said.

"The one where the police were the good guys," Rollins said ruefully. "Anyway, my dad said Martin Bailey had a granddaughter who went into the movies."

"Her name was Brooke Bailey," Sister J said.

"That's right. She'd be your sister then?"

"She'd be me."

Officer Hernandez said, "No way. You're Brooke Bailey?"

"Not anymore," Sister J said. "I am now Sister Justicia Marie."

"That's crazy," Hernandez said. "When I was a kid I used to watch *Bunny Troop* over and over."

"Oh yes," Sister J said. "I was twelve when I made that."

"It was such fun!"

"In a way," Sister J said, if you include in the word *fun* an older member of the cast getting her drunk for the first time.

"Why'd you give it up?" Hernandez asked.

"The usual crash and burn story," Sister J said.

"Kind of like this city," Rollins said.

Hard to argue with that.

The Los Angeles City Council field office was at the corner of Maywood and Colorado in Burbank. The officers escorted Sister J inside the Spanish-style building. The young receptionist looked at Sister J as if she'd never seen a nun in a habit before. Perhaps she hadn't, considering the dearth of tradition in the Church these days.

"I was summoned to a meeting," Sister J said.

"Um, wait here," the woman said. She got up from her desk and went through a side door.

"We're authorized to wait for you," Hernandez said. "Unless we get a call."

"That's nice," Sister J said.

The woman returned and told Sister J to go right in.

The office was narrow and stuffed with boxes and papers. An equally unkempt desk was under the only window, which had closed slats over it.

Sitting behind the desk was a woman who appeared to be in her late forties. She wore a mask, and had black-and-gray curly hair framing her round head.

"I am Mitzi Van Gogh," the woman said. "Department of Public Safety, Valley Task Force, Virus Division."

Sister J thought a moment. "DPSVTFVD?"

The woman blinked. "Sit down, please."

Sister J sat.

Mitzi Van Gogh folded her hands on the desk. "I note that you choose to wear a mask."

"If I am going to be around non-household people in some public setting, I do wear a mask around others as a matter of Christian charity."

"Christian charity is not an official reason for any action," Mitzi Van Gogh said.

"You'd rather we had no Christian charity?" Sister J said.

Mitzi Van Gogh cleared her throat and said, "What kind of nun are you? I mean, I know your reputation, of course. Your methods are, to put it mildly, unorthodox."

"They said the same thing about Jesus when he healed on the Sabbath," Sister J said.

"Are you comparing yourself to Jesus?"

"Heavens, no! Just pointing out that orthodoxy can sometimes get in the way of being any earthly good."

"Tell me," Mitzi Van Gogh said, "do the authorities in your Church think you are doing earthly good?"

"We are still sort of working that out," Sister J said.

"They excuse your use of violence?"

"Ah, that is the question," Sister J said.

"What is the question?"

"When and where violence may serve a just cause."

"I don't follow."

"Violence used to destroy someone's property or business, that's not good use, wouldn't you agree?"

Mitzi Van Gogh seemed confused and did not say anything.

"But," Sister J said, "if someone is armed and enters your home, violence used to defend yourself is justified. True?"

At the moment, it seemed as if nothing made sense to Mitzi Van Gogh.

Sister J said, "I have on occasion used physical force either to defend myself or another, or to prevent someone from committing a terrible sin, like robbery or murder. That is a positive good, for it stops the sin and protects the innocent."

Mitzi Van Gogh said, "Let's not get too far afield here. Perhaps you and I—by which, of course, I mean the mayor's office—can figure out a way to do each other some good." She picked up a ballpoint pen and clicked it a few times. "It's no secret that you have earned a great deal of respect in this city among a certain constituency. Something you say publicly would carry a lot of weight."

"Something like what?"

"Oh, if you were to come alongside us and help us get the word out on certain issues, we might be able to get more compliance from our citizens."

"I'm not sure my words would be authoritative," said Sister J.

"It would with that constituency," said Mitzi Van Gogh, raising her eyebrows.

"Do you mean Catholics?" Sister J said.

"I mean all religious people. We are having some problems in that area."

"Problems?"

"You know, attitudes."

"You mean," Sister J said, "people wanting to congregate at their place of worship?"

"Exactly."

"You and the governor outlawed meetings for worship inside buildings. But the Supreme Court has ruled against you."

"To a point," Mitzi Van Gogh said. "Protocols must be followed, but we are starting to see more and more violations."

"Which the faithful might describe as obedience to a higher authority."

"There is no higher authority in the city and county of Los Angeles than the mayor."

Sister J tried to let that sink in.

It wouldn't sink.

Sister J said, "I don't wish to be a problem. But I cannot in good conscience make common cause with everything that is going on right now. I assure you, however, that I will not make any public statement regarding your edicts. I simply want to take care of those who have been entrusted to me."

"I'm afraid it's not that simple," said Mitzi Van Gogh.

"Excuse me?"

Mitzi Van Gogh raised her eyebrows.

Sister J said nothing.

Mitzi Van Gogh lowered her eyebrows.

Sister J waited.

Tapping her fingertips together, Mitzi Van Gogh said, "How shall I put this?"

Try English. Snark!

"The city," Mitzi Van Gogh said, "can help you to help those people you say you want to help. On the other hand..."

"Yes?"

Mitzi Van Gogh raised her eyebrows once more.

Sister J raised her eyebrows, too.

The eyebrow standoff lasted ten seconds. Then Mitzi Van Gogh said, "Thank you for coming in, Sister. Here's my card. Give me a call when you're ready to talk sensibly."

The ride back to the shelter was uneventful. Officer Hernandez was genuinely interested in hearing more of Sister J's life story. Sister J complied only because someday either or both of them might know someone who needed a similar deliverance. Or, if they stayed cops in L.A., might need it themselves.

So she told how her father tried to exploit her as a child actress, how she fell into alcoholism and drugs and sexual adventurism, and of the night she determined to take her own life.

How she stood on the bluffs of Santa Monica and was close to hurling herself over to splat on Pacific Coast Highway. And how, at that moment, a shaft of light came from the clouds and filled her soul with ... *Presence.*

"It's really as simple and as powerful as that," Sister J said. "My life was one way, and then in an instant it was another. And it still is."

Silence in the vehicle for a moment, then Officer Hernandez said, "Look at that!"

They had just arrived at the shelter, where Sister J saw the following:

Two thick strips of yellow tape criss-crossing the front of the shelter.

Two uniformed men, large in size, wearing sunglasses and masks, were standing with arms folded in front of the glass

doors. Their uniforms were of the security guard variety. Their
expressions seemed imported from the Federal Bureau of Investigation unit that instructs agents on how to look surly.

Two news vans.

Two mask-wearing pedestrians watching with their leashed
dog, a schnauzer. The schnauzer was unmasked.

"What is all this?" Sister J said.

"Looks like they've secured the building," Officer Rollins
said.

"Who has? Who are those guards?"

"They must be private," said Hernandez.

"Then surely you can get them out of here," Sister J said.
"They're trespassing."

"Let's see what's going on," Officer Hernandez said.

They got out of the SUV.

Two mask-wearing reporters with masked cameramen and
masked sound men, rushed toward Sister Justicia. One was a
woman in a KABC blazer. The other was a man holding a microphone with a CNN flag on it. They shouted garbled questions at
her. Sister J ignored them and headed for the guards. She saw
Sister X and Otto Ledbetter inside the glass doors. The doors
had a heavy chain and lock on the handles.

"What is the meaning of this?" Sister J said.

"Quarantine," said the guard whose face resembled a bucket
of knuckles.

"On whose authority?" said Sister J.

"Department of Public Safety," said the other guard, who
looked like the cheekbone champion of the world.

The reporters kept shouting questions.

Sister J turned to the police officers. "Can they do this?"

Looking perplexed, Officer Hernandez said to the guards,
"Do you have an order?"

Knuckle Bucket pulled a folded piece of paper from his back
pocket and handed it to Hernandez. She scanned it, showed it to

Rollins. He scanned it, showed it to Sister J. She scanned it, crumpled it and threw it on the ground.

"You have no authority here," she said. "I declare this a sanctuary!"

The reporters went into bird-cheep overdrive, talking over each other. Sister J turned to them and put her hands up for quiet.

"I would like to make a statement," she said.

The reporters held up their mics.

"What is being done here is illegal under the laws of God and man," Sister J said. "And furthermore..."

Cardinal Clark Fennelly was dreaming that he was on a sunny beach, waves lightly lapping the sand. Bereft of vestments, dressed only in pineapple-themed trunks, happily soaking up some sun. At long last he was in a place of peace, away from all trouble and care. His Piña Colada was cold and refreshing.

Then the ground began to shake.

Coconuts fell from palm trees. A dancing girl in a sarong screamed.

Fennelly watched helplessly as fissures opened up in the sand. They cracked like jagged lightning down to the water, where they ruptured into chasms.

The dancing girl disappeared into the maw of the splitting Earth.

"No!" said the dreaming Cardinal Fennelly. "Not yet!"

And his body shook with the ground.

"Your Eminence?" a coconut said.

"Eh...what?"

"Your Eminence, wake up."

Cardinal Fennelly opened his eyes. A hand gripped his shoulder. The hand was connected to an arm, and the arm was connected to Monsignor Franklin Stubbs, the public relations director for the Los Angeles Archdiocese.

"What is it?" Cardinal Fennelly said.

"Look at this." Stubbs pointed to the flat screen TV on the wall. There was some sort of news report and—

"Oh, no," Fennelly said.

"Oh, yes," said Stubbs, unmuting the sound with the remote.

On the screen Sister Justicia Marie was talking. "And so this is a now a sanctuary. The people inside are under the protection of the Church, which I represent."

"Can she do that?" Cardinal Fennelly asked.

"She just did," Monsignor Stubbs said.

One of the reporters shouted, "On what authority?"

Sister Justicia said, "Under Constantine's Edict of Toleration, 303 A.D., and the Theodosian Code of 392. And, of course, the Free Exercise Clause of the United States Constitution. And let's throw in all the governors and mayors who have declared whole cities to be sanctuaries. In other words, there's a whole lot of sanctuary going on, and this is one of them. Entry will not be allowed but on my say. I will, of course, be reasonable..."

"Do you think she will be?" Cardinal Fennelly said.

"Fifty-fifty," Monsignor Stubbs said.

"...so if any authority of the city wishes to negotiate with me in good faith," Sister Justicia said, "I will be happy to reciprocate."

"This is going to cost us," Cardinal Fennelly said.

"I'm on it," Monsignor Stubbs said.

"And now," said Sister J, "I kindly request that I be allowed to go inside." Turning to the security guards, she said, "Please unlock the chain."

They didn't move.

To the police officers she said, "These men are refusing to allow me into my residence. Will you instruct them to open up?"

After a moment's hesitation, Officer Hernandez said, "Guys, let her in."

Knuckle Bucket said, "No can do."

Cheekbones said, "We got our orders."

Sister J observed the large keychain on Cheekbones' belt. She huddled with the officers. "Can you force them to open?"

Officer Rollins said, "It could get sticky, especially with news cameras rolling."

"I'm sorry," Officer Hernandez said.

"If I were to use a little force of habit," Sister J said, "might I rely on your indulgence for a moment or two?"

"What are you going to do?" Rollins said.

"Perhaps it's best you don't know." Before another word could be said, Sister J whirled around and snatched the keychain off Cheekbones' belt.

"Hey!" Cheekbones said.

Sister J leapt for the door.

And felt a large hand spin her around.

"Give it back," Cheekbones said.

"Hands off," Sister J said

"Now!" Cheekbones said.

Sister J grabbed the offending hand and wrist, and with a deft turn and twist had Cheekbones on his knees, crying out in pain. Holding him there with her left hand, she looked for a key that had Master© on it. She found it, unlocked the lock and removed the chain.

"You can't let her do that!" Knuckle Bucket said to the cops.

"I'll give her a stern talking to," said Officer Hernandez.

Sister J released Cheekbones, entered the shelter, and used the lock and chain to secure the door from the inside.

"Your Eminence," Monsignor Franklin Stubbs said, waving a hand towel furiously in front of Cardinal Clark Fennelly's face. "Your Eminence?"

"Have a seat, everyone," Sister J said. The front portion of the shelter had tables and benches where meals were served. Now, the residents and the other nuns—Sister Xuan and the nuns of Navarone—sat.

"We are news now," Sister J said. "There's probably going to be activity outside for awhile, at least for one news cycle. I expect some representatives of the city's health department will show up to examine what we're doing. We are going to be nice and cooperative."

"Fie on that!" Otto Ledbetter shouted.

"Including you, Mr. Ledbetter," Sister J said. "We want to clear this up as quickly and painlessly as possible, so we can continue to build up our health."

"Are we going to go to jail?" Elisio Minx asked.

"Not at all," Sister J said.

"I can't go to jail," Elisio said. "I get scared in closed spaces."

"You have nothing to worry about, Elisio. We'll continue on as usual, and trust that this incident will be worked out reasonably and in good order."

That's when something went *BOOM* and rocked the shelter.

Theda Metcalf's scream lasted the longest. She also jumped into Sister Xuan's arms.

The other residents were in various stages of head grabbing and ear covering.

Sister J's own ears rang, but she was encouraged to see the sisters beginning to comfort the afflicted.

One of whom lay bloody on the floor.

Elisio!

Sister J rushed over. Sister Chloe was kneeling at Elisio's side.

"A gash on the head," Sister Chloe said. "Must have hit it on the corner of the table."

"He needs medical attention," Sister J said. "Keep everyone as calm as you can." She took out her phone and punched 911.

Outside the doors people were scattering everywhere. Sister

J couldn't see Officers Hernandez and Rollins. Presumably they had gone to where the explosion—or whatever it was—occurred. Knuckle Bucket and Cheekbones were in the same spot, looking as if they had no idea what to do, in life or anywhere else.

A 911 dispatcher answered. Sister J gave her the information. The dispatcher said they were experiencing an unusually large number of calls and to be patient. Then Sister J remembered that a massive protest had been organized for downtown that day.

"It's on! It's on!" Quincey Robinson, the newest resident of the shelter, was waving his arms. One hand was holding a phone. "Armageddon! The rise of Anti-Christ!"

"Mr. Robinson," Sister J said. "Please keep your voice down."

"The Four Horsemen of the Apocalypse!"

"Not today."

"The wrath of the living God is about to rain down!" He pointed his phone at Sister J. "And this revolution will be televised!"

"If you don't want to incur *my* wrath, Mr. Robinson, sit down and pray quietly, or I'll take your phone away."

The prophet of doom frowned and said no more.

Sister J went back to Elisio. He was still out cold. Sister Persephone came with a damp cloth and gently applied it to Elisio's head.

Sister J went to the front doors, unlocked the chain, went outside. She strode past Knuckle Bucket and Cheekbones without a word. Around the corner she saw the news crews pointing their cameras upward.

A plume of black smoke wafted from the roof.

She found Officer Hernandez. "What was it? A bomb?"

"Somebody said it was a plane," Hernandez said.

"A plane? On our roof?"

"We'll know as soon as the fire trucks get here."

"This is crazy," Sister J said.

"This is crazy!" Cardinal Fennelly said.

"You fainted," Monsignor Stubbs said.

"I know I fainted! Why didn't you?"

"We have to figure out a strategy," Stubbs said. "We've had enough blowback from the mayor already."

"Can we bring Sister Justicia in?" Cardinal Fennelly asked. "Talk to her?"

"Has that ever worked before?"

Fennelly pounded the arm of his chair. What was it with this rogue nun? She had proved herself faithful once by saving the Cathedral from a domestic terror group calling themselves the Zarathustra Brigade. And with his permission, too.

But as the saying went, it's always something with Sister Justicia Marie. And now a claim of sanctuary? This problem was not going to be easily resolved. Not this time.

"Who can we talk to out of the mayor's office?" Cardinal Fennelly said.

"There's a woman named Mitzi Van Gogh who is running interference for him."

"Let's get her on Zoom."

Paramedics arrived and took Elisio Minx to the hospital. Two firetrucks and another LAPD SUV pulled into the lot. So did three more news vans.

An hour later, a fire department spokesman gave the reporters a quick press conference.

"A little after eleven o'clock this morning, a light aircraft, a Beechcraft Bonanza, crashed into the roof of the shelter run by the Sisters of Perpetual Justice. At this time we have no idea how or why it happened. The investigation is ongoing, and we will give you updates as appropriate."

A reporter shouted, "How about the pilot?"

"As I say," the LAFD spokesman said, "we are still in the early stages of the investigation."

"Where is the body?"

"I have no further comment at this time."

While reporters shouted more questions, a fire department investigator motioned for Sister J to follow him. He had serious eyes, which was all she could see due to his mask.

Away from the activity, he said, "We have to treat this as an accident scene, assess damage, all that. When can you have your people out?"

"Excuse me?"

"Evacuated," he said.

"This is their home."

"Yes, but—"

"They have nowhere else to go. They'll be out on the streets."

"I was hoping we could do this with—"

"I didn't see any great damage inside."

"That's not for you to assess," the investigator said.

"We will cooperate," Sister J said. "But we will not evacuate."

He frowned. "Please don't make this a problem."

"I don't intend to, so long as we're clear that my people are going to remain in the only home they know."

"I might not be able to sell that upstairs," the investigator said.

"Then give it away for free," Sister J said. "God will see us through."

"God has nothing to do with this," said Mitzi Van Gogh. "Most of Los Angeles, indeed, most of the country now, does not believe in God."

"We are well aware of that," said Franklin Stubbs. He and Cardinal Fennelly sat at Fennelly's desk, addressing Mitzi Van Gogh via computer monitor and Zoom. "And we have tried to be respectful—"

"It's not a matter of respect," Mitzi Van Gogh said. "It's a matter of who is in charge. And let me tell you, it is no longer the church. And especially not your out-of-control nun, Sister Justifier or whatever she's called. She is a menace and must be cancel—must be stopped."

The gastric juices in Cardinal Fennelly's stomach churned.

"What do you suggest we do?" Franklin Stubbs asked.

"Start by shutting down that shelter," Mitzi Van Gogh said. "Our office can do it, but the way things are, that might tip the public scales too much. Might make us out to be the bad guys, what with her helping homeless people and all."

"But how would *we* look?" Cardinal Fennelly said.

"With all due respect," Mitzi Van Gogh said, with no respect in her voice at all. "Your rep is not all that great at the moment. This might actually be a good thing for you."

Cardinal Fennelly sighed. The words *good thing* had never, in his experience, applied to Sister Justicia Marie and the Sisters of Perpetual Justice.

It was two o'clock when Sister J got the call from Cardinal Fennelly. It was three when she saw the black sedan with the ecclesiastical flag on it pull into the parking lot.

She called for the residents to pay attention. "We are getting a visit from His Eminence the Cardinal. Be on your best behavior."

Otto Ledbetter put his hand underneath an armpit and started to flap farting noises.

"None of that," Sister J said. "I mean it."

"We'll see about that!" Otto Ledbetter said. At least he removed his hand from his pit.

Sister J unlocked the front doors, listened to a few shouted questions from the reporters. When Cardinal Fennelly got out of the sedan, the reporters turned to him. He gave them a papal-style wave and smile, and told them a statement would be coming "forthwith."

Sister J wondered if the young reporters even knew how to spell *forthwith*.

The Cardinal entered the shelter. Sister J locked it up again.

"Quite a scene," Cardinal Fennelly said.

"If you want a scene," Otto Ledbetter said, "I will give you one! How about Pyramus and Thisbe from *A Midsummer's Night Dream?*"

"Perhaps we should talk in my office," Sister J said.

Once ensconced in the small, spare office where Sister J conducted the business of the shelter, the Cardinal said, "Sister, we are not unmindful of the good you have done, and have been doing, and perhaps will do again."

"Perhaps?"

"Let me put it this way. I believe we can find a way to get along, all of us—you, me, the archdiocese, the city—and find common ground."

"That would be fine with me. But common ground does not mean having the ground under us blasted away."

"Precisely my thinking as well. So here is a way to accomplish that. I have it on authority from the city that your shelter can remain up and running, if you would consent to do a series of public service announcements."

"Does the city authority happen to be named Mitzi Van Gogh?"

Cardinal Fennelly cleared his throat. "Someone we all should strive to get along with, eh?"

"It depends on what you mean by get along," Sister J said. "If it means a negotiated settlement, that's certainly a good idea. But if it means acquiescence to everything the city demands, I don't see how the church can do that."

Cardinal Fennelly said nothing.

"Do you?" Sister J said.

"We certainly should get along with the city."

"Would you have said that about Rome in 64 A.D.? Would you have done a PSA for Nero?"

Snark again! What was wrong with her these days? She was developing a tongue of fire. What was it the Bible said in the Epistle of James? *And the tongue is a fire, a world of iniquity. The tongue is so set among our members that it defiles the whole body, and sets on fire the course of nature; and it is set on fire by hell.* Terrific. She was turning into a homily illustration.

"It wouldn't hurt to try to be reasonable, would it?" the Cardinal said.

The whine in his voice was a cry for help. Though he'd been a thorn in her side for months, he was her superior. She owed him at least the effort.

"I will try to be reasonable," she said, and thought, *Like a minnow trying to reason with a shark.* She knew then she had better get to confession, and fast.

The Cardinal stepped outside and gave a statement to the reporters. In the artful way of chief executives, he managed to say very little with an enormous output of words. What Sister J picked up was moderate support for sanctuary, but also support for the city. On that, he said, more was coming.

As his sedan drove away, Sister J went up to the roof to check on the fire investigators. The chief saw her. He had a look of deep concern on his face.

"Did you or any of your people come up here after the crash?" he said.

"No one," Sister J said.

The concern deepened.

"May I ask what the problem is?" Sister J said.

"Keep this in strictest confidence," he said. "But we don't know who was controlling this plane."

"You haven't identified the body?"

"Not exactly."

"Partial ID?"

"No."

"Where are the remains right now?" Sister J asked.

"There are no remains," the man said.

"What?"

"What I mean, Sister, is we didn't find a body in the wreckage."

"But how ...?"

"Exactly," he said. "This plane was being operated like a drone. It has what appears to be a GNS system."

"What's that?"

"Global Navigational Satellite. Very sophisticated."

"Apparently not sophisticated enough," Sister J said. "How soon before you wrap this all up?"

"Hard to say. We'll need a crane to remove it. Maybe tomorrow or the next day."

"We'll be sure your crew has plenty of coffee," Sister J said.

Night crept up on Los Angeles.

At Third and Hope a riot broke out, the mob setting fire to a municipal bus after surrounding it and refusing to move. At least they allowed the people on board to get off, and only beat up the driver.

After a high-speed chase through the Wilshire district and surrounding neighborhoods, a teenager in a stolen Lexus crashed into a palm tree on Windsor Boulevard. He got out screaming at the police that he deserved this car because the owners were "too rich."

And outside the shelter of the Sisters of Perpetual Justice, the news crews were wrapping up their segments. The fire investigation unit was pulling out. And thankfully, the private security guards were gone.

But trouble had set up shop and wasn't moving at all.

Sister Xuan said, "I have tried all the local hospitals. No one has a record of admitting Elisio."

"The way things are now, they could have taken him almost anywhere," Sister J said. "Keep trying."

There came a tapping at the front doors. It was a young man and a young woman, dirty and disheveled. Their eyes were wide and hungry.

Sister J unlocked the doors.

"Thank you, Sister," the woman said. Her coat was once green. It was now a shade of brown. Her hair was black and stringy. "Have you any room for the night?"

In truth she did not, but every such request brought out Sister Justicia's Benedictine inclinations. "Please come in."

"Bless you," the woman said.

"We can pay," the young man said. He had three-day's growth of beard and the weight of the world in his eyes.

"I have no beds," Sister J said. "But you are welcome to sleep on the floor. I can offer you blankets and a pillow."

"That's okay by us!" the woman said.

"Are you two married?" Sister J asked.

"Um, no," said the woman.

"But we're planning on it," said the man.

"Very good," Sister J said. "We will set you up on different sides of our dining hall."

The couple smiled and nodded.

"Are you hungry?" Sister J asked.

"We can pay for some food," the man said.

"That won't be necessary," Sister J said. She turned to Sister Xuan. "What have we on hand?"

"Sandwiches," Sister X said. "And coffee."

"Oh, coffee!" the woman said.

"Come with me," Sister J said. She led them into the kitchen. Sister Xuan went to the refrigerator and pulled out two wrapped sandwiches.

"Egg salad and sliced chicken," Sister X said.

"Thank you," the man said as he took out a pistol and pointed it at Sister J.

"Don't make a sound," the man said. "We can work this out."

Sister J shook her head. This was the price of operating under the Rule of St. Benedict. All guests are to be welcomed as Christ. If they were packing heat, well, do the best you can.

"What is it you want?" Sister J said.

"Money," the man said.

"We have no money. We are simple order of nuns who have taken a vow of poverty."

"I think you do have money," the man said. "And it belongs to me."

"I don't understand," Sister J said.

"I think you do," the man said.

"What you think is of no concern to me," Sister J said. "Now why don't you put that gun away?"

The woman, who had also pulled out a handgun, though she pointed it at the floor, said, "Let's get out of here."

"No," the man said. "Not without our money."

"Why do you think we have anything of yours?" Sister J said.

"Because it was on that plane."

Sister J, the former Brooke Bailey, the one-time child star who'd seen her share of the dark side of life, said, "Drug money."

The man smiled. "So you do have it."

Sister J shook her head. "No one has been near that plane except the fire department investigators."

The man shook his head. "We've been watching them all day. They didn't bring nothin' down with 'em. It was in a duffel bag. So you've got to have it stashed somewhere."

"I have told you—"

"You went up to the roof today. I saw you."

"Briefly," Sister J said. "Just to view the investigators."

The woman said, "I don't think she has it."

"She has it," the man said. "All that money she can use to help the poor."

"I wouldn't touch drug money," Sister J said.

"You don't have to touch it. Just give it to me."

In a tremulous voice, Sister Xuan said, "Coffee anyone?"

"Money," the man said.

"You're not going to shoot us," Sister J said.

"Oh yeah? Why not?"

"It won't do you any good. We're not afraid of death. You have no leverage."

"I don't like this," the woman said.

"In fact," Sister J said, "you will put away your gun and leave us. If you do not, I will have to take it away from you."

He laughed.

And the laugh cost him. For he closed his eyes and rocked back his head. At which point Sister J sprang forward and kicked his gun hand. The gun flew up and hit the ceiling. Giving the man an elbow to the ribs with her right arm, Sister J caught the descending gun in her left. Then stepped back.

With a breathless voice, the man managed to say, "Shoot her!"

"No!" the woman said.

"Sister Xuan," said Sister J, and nodded toward the woman. Sister X went to the woman with an outstretched hand. The woman gave up her gun.

"Now, isn't that better for all of us?" Sister J said.

The man was still catching his breath.

"What I would like to know," said Sister J, "is who sent you."

The man looked up. And shook his head.

Sister J looked at the woman, who said, "I'll tell you—"

"Shut up!" the man said.

"Sister Xuan, please pour a cup of coffee for this young woman and take her to the conference room. I want to have a word in private with the gentleman."

When they were alone, Sister J said, "You don't seem like a hopeless case to me."

He looked crestfallen, like a dog whose bone had been snatched away. "You got my gun. A girl. A nun!"

"You are blessed," Sister J said. "You could have done great damage not only to others, but to yourself."

"You don't know anything."

"I know much more than you think I do. And if you can tell me who is running this drug scheme you're a part of, your soul may find reclamation."

"Recla what?"

"Mation. Salvation."

"I don't believe in that stuff."

"Your lack of belief does not alter the truth. God is your judge. The first step is for you to come clean, tell me who you work for. Otherwise, I will be forced to summon the police."

"Ha ha," he said. "The cops won't do anything. I'll just say I'm a protester and they'll let me go!"

"What are you protesting?"

He frowned. "Crazy nuns."

"You don't want to see my crazy," Sister J said. "And how would it look to your bosses if you did get arrested here? Or were held captive by a group of women who have taken vows of poverty?"

For a long moment, he said nothing. His eyes moved from Sister J to the kitchen door and back to Sister J.

Then he made his move. He leapt toward the door and got his hand on the handle.

Sister J sprang forward and got her hand on his wrist.

A second later he was on his knees, begging to be let go.

"I will have that name now," Sister J said.

Elisio Minx opened his eyes.

It was dark. His head hurt. His head hurt bad.

I need Sister.

"Sister?" His voice was weak. His breath was hot.

Something was over his mouth!

He tried to lift his hands. But they were tied up!

He screamed. Kept screaming. Because he was in a nightmare and if you scream in a nightmare you have to keep screaming because the monster gets closer and closer!

Light. A door opening?

"Quiet!" said a voice.

"I need Sister!" Elisio heard his muffled voice. A mask. That was what was over his mouth.

"You need to calm down." It was a man's voice, a little high and soft.

"Help!"

"Shh. I will help you, but you need to be quiet."

"Where am I?"

"You're among those who can help you."

"I need Sister," Elisio said.

"Of course you do," the man said. "As soon as you are able."

"Why is it dark?"

"Too much light might give you a headache. And we don't want that."

Elisio turned his head slightly, and saw a shadowy form.

"We want you well and happy," the high-voiced form said.

"I can't breathe," Elisio said.

"Of course you can. If you're quiet."

"I can't move."

"For your own good, my friend."

"Who are you?" Elisio asked.

"Friends," the high-voiced man said.

"Please let me go. I don't like small places."

"You would like to get back to your residence?"

"Oh yes."

"And to the one you call Sister?"

"Yes!"

"That would be Sister Justicia Marie, right?"

"Uh-huh."

"Tell us a little about her," the man said.

"About?"

"Yes."

Elisio wondered what to say. It made his head hurt a little more. "She's a nun."

"Go on."

"She takes care of us."

"Does she talk to you?"

"Yes."

"What does she say?"

Elisio thought about it. His temples throbbed. "She tells Otto to be quiet a lot."

"Otto?"

"Mm-hmm."

"Never mind Otto. Does she ever say anything about, oh, let's say, the mayor of Los Angeles?"

"I can't breathe."

"Think real hard, Elisio."

"It hurts my head."

"Well then, we'll just have to let you rest a little bit more."

"I want to go home." A hot tear streaked down Elisio's cheek.

"You rest, and when you think you can tell us some of the things Sister Justicia Marie says about the mayor, or the governor, or anything like that, we'll talk about letting you go."

"But…"

"You rest now. Remember, we're friends."

"Don't go!"

The door closed. Darkness engulfed him. He heard the turning of a heavy lock.

He couldn't breathe.

Troy Dickinson called himself the Pope of Los Angeles, though his connection to the church was on the same level as oil's connection to water. A mover and shaker of the criminal strata, he knew his way around the underbelly of the city, which was becoming increasingly seamy.

Sister J was seated in his office in the back of the India Club, just off Hollywood Boulevard. Once a popular nightspot, it had fallen on hard times—or, rather, had hard times dropped *on it*— like all the bars and restaurants in the city that had been yo-yoed around by the ever-shifting standards of the governor and mayor.

"All these out of town rabble-rousers!" Dickinson said from behind his desk. The veins stuck out on the arms of his well-toned body. "They come here to smash windows and burn police cars! I don't know who's worse, them or the drunk-with-power politicians."

"And none of them being held accountable," said Sister J.

"You got that right! At least I have to keep my nose clean, so to speak."

Sister J cleared her throat.

Dickinson said, "They're making it very hard for businessmen such as myself to conduct our affairs."

"That's a funny way of putting it," Sister J said.

"I'm a funny guy. But you didn't come here for the comedy."

Or to shoot the breeze. Sister J had once needed help finding a stolen cross, and Dickinson had offered her help...in return for her not making trouble for him. She hadn't, except for having to rough up a couple of his henchmen once. But she had stopped them from sinning, which was the point.

"I got a visit from a drug dealer and his girlfriend," Sister J said. "I had to take their guns away."

"I wish I could've seen that. When it's not my guys, I find that amusing."

"Do you know about the plane that crashed into my building?"

"I heard. What's it about?"

"There was no pilot."

"No pilot?"

"It was remotely controlled," Sister J said. "And this young man said there was drug money inside the plane and accused me of taking it."

"Did you?" The Pope of Los Angeles asked.

"Of course not."

"You should have."

"I don't think there was ever any money on that plane," Sister J said.

"Where is this young man now?"

"Probably out of state," she said.

"How's that?"

"I let him go after he gave me the name of the drug lord he

worked for. He told me that his life wouldn't be worth a curly fry if he stayed in California. I told him to try South Dakota."

"Why South Dakota?"

"They're allowed to have normal lives there," Sister J said. "They can breathe. More job opportunities."

Dickinson shook his head. "So what was the name he gave you?"

"Barabbas."

The Pope of Los Angeles sat up straight. "Steer clear."

"You know him?"

"I know all about him. He's from one of the most dangerous cartels in Mexico. This is not a man you want to annoy or steal from."

"Do I strike you as a thief?"

"No, but you do have a tendency to annoy."

"Alas, true," Sister J said. "But suppose I wanted to see this man, face to face. Would he consent?"

"Only if he thought it would protect his money or bring him some more."

"Would you be able to arrange a meeting?"

"Sister, you seem to think I have contacts in some vast underworld."

"Oh my, what would have given me that impression?"

The Pope of Los Angeles smiled. "See, that's why I like you. I'm not your typical thug, and you're not your typical nun. We make a peach of a pair, don't we?"

Sister J shook her head. "If I'm an apple, you're an orange."

"So once again, why should I help you?"

"Maybe a bowl of mixed fruit is what this town needs."

"It sure needs something," Dickinson said. "Or it's gonna die."

Back at the shelter, Sister J found Sister X in the office, shaking her head at the computer screen.

"What is it?" Sister J said.

"I have tried locating every hospital in the city," Sister X said. "I have made call after call. No one has any record of admitting Elisio! Where could he possibly be?"

"He could have been taken in without any ID. You know how he is about such things."

Sister X nodded.

A shout erupted from the main floor.

"Uh-oh," Sister J said. "That sounds like Mr. Robinson." She pushed through the door and saw Quincey Robinson staring out the doors, waving his arms.

"The Beast from the Sea!"

"Mr. Robinson, please." Sister J came over to see what riled him. It was a deputy sheriff holding up a folded paper.

"He speaks blasphemies!" Mr. Robinson gesticulated wildly.

"Please go sit and be quiet," Sister J said.

"If any man have an ear to hear, let him hear!"

"Now Mr. Robinson."

The mad prophet sulked away, looking at his phone.

Sister J unlocked the door.

The deputy handed her the paper. "You have been served," he said.

"Oh joy." It was an order to appear in Superior Court, to show cause why a permanent injunction against the shelter should not issue. The ominous words *shut down* were included.

It was at that moment that Sister Agnes approached. She was

the superior of the four nuns of Navarone. At eighty years old, she was full of wisdom and humility, two things Sister Justicia knew she was deficient in.

"Trouble, my child?" Sister Agnes said.

Sister J showed her the summons. The Greek nun put on a pair of reading glasses and gave the paper a look. "I am sorry, but my English. This is law, yes?"

"Law, yes," Sister J said. She rubbed her eyes. "There is an old saying here in America. You can't fight City Hall. Why must they do this?"

"Your voice is full of sadness."

"Sometimes the fight is too much," Sister J said.

Sister Agnes gripped Sister Justicia by the shoulders. "Never too much for God," she said.

"I know," said Sister J.

"You know up here, I think." Sister Agnes tapped her head. "But not so much here." She touched her heart.

Nodding sadly, Sister Justicia Marie said nothing.

"Ah, but that is when our faith is tested," Sister Agnes said. "And when the test is met, and we do not give up, our faith shall come forth as gold."

"But what can I do?" Sister J asked. "I mean, actually do?"

"God will show you," Sister Agnes said. "God will give you the act, and the words. He will fill your heart with fire, just as he did with our beloved Saint Joan."

"But I am no Joan."

"God decides who is Joan," Sister Agnes said. "And may I tell you another thing?"

"Please."

"You are not, how do you say, chopped liver. Do not give up. Your time will come. And when it does, you will know it."

Holding back tears, Sister Justicia embraced the wise, old nun. An embrace that lasted two seconds, interrupted by Mr. Robinson's explosive voice. "He that leadeth into captivity shall go into captivity!"

Sister J went over to him and said, in her best calming voice, "It's all right, Mr. Robinson. No need to worry."

"I have them!" He held up his phone. "Not one shall escape!"

"You have who with the what now?"

"All of them! From day one!"

"Mr. Robinson, if you'll just—"

"Look!" He turned his phone toward Sister J. It was playing a video of the deputy who had just come to the door.

"And this!" He switched to another video. This one appeared to be of the commotion outside the shelter yesterday, after the plane hit. The news crews, the security guards, the fire trucks, the paramedics—

"Let me see that!" Sister J snatched the phone from him. She watched a moment, then moved the playhead back and watched the same part again.

"Wait here!" she said, and rushed into the office and handed the phone to Sister X. "Upload this video. I want to see it on full screen."

Sister X got a USB cable from the desk and attached it to the phone. Presently, she had the phone open on the computer, found the video file, and played it.

"What are we looking for?" Sister X said.

"Watch," Sister J said. The video played for a little over thirty seconds, then Sister J paused it. "What do you see?"

Sister X leaned closer to the screen. "The trouble. The fire trucks. And...wait! Is that Elisio?"

"It must be."

The picture showed a gurney almost all the way into an ambulance.

"Now look there." Sister J pointed to license plate. "We can make out those numbers."

"Yes!"

"Okay, faithful assistant, see what we can find out!"

Elisio pulled against his restraints. They held fast.

He didn't like the high-voiced man. That man wanted him to say things about Sister. Why doesn't he go ask her himself?

Maybe I'm slow, he thought, but I'm not dumb. He wants me to tattle on Sister!

He tried again to pull his arms free.

Surely he could break out. All his life people told him he didn't know his own strength.

Strength!

He thought of his favorite Bible story. The one about Samson. He liked that story, except for the part where he got a haircut and then had his eyes gouged out by the Philistines. That was terrible! But then he got revenge by pulling down a whole building on top of the Philistines while they were having a party. Ha!

Right before he did that, Samson prayed to God for strength.

"I'll take whatever you can give me, God," Elisio whispered. "I just want to go home."

He took a deep breath, closed his eyes, and pulled.

Snap!

Snap!

He was free!

But those plastic things had cut his wrists. He was bleeding!

The bed he was on had a sheet. With a few rips Elisio had two bandages, and put them around his wounds.

Now to find a way out.

But what if they had guns?

The office landline rang. The number was PRIVATE.

Sister J picked up. "Sisters of Perpetual Justice, Sister Justicia Marie speaking."

A voice, low and slow, said, "You want to meet him, eh?"

"Who is calling, please?" Sister J said.

"This is the way it will be. You will walk to the alley between Vallarta Market and Cleon Avenue. Do you know it?"

"It is a bit of a walk."

"You will park your car on Case Avenue and walk from there. If you bring anyone with you, no deal. If you try to bring cops, we will know and that will be very bad for your people."

"You're threatening me?"

"This will be your only chance to talk to him."

"Just so we're clear, you're speaking of Barabbas?"

"Ten-thirty," the voice said, and cut out.

Sister J put the phone down. "Keep looking," she said.

Sister X said, "You are going somewhere?"

"Yes," she said. "In this city you get to meet some of the most interesting people."

Sister J drove her old Saturn, Ping, to Case Avenue, and

parked. It was an old residential section of North Hollywood, a couple of blocks from the Hispanic market, Vallarta.

She walked there. The market closed at ten, so there was scant activity in the front. Behind the market was an alley that smelled of wet trash wafting from twin dumpsters. *The odor of the new Los Angeles.* How had the city fallen so far? From the land of sunny optimism and family dreams, to this decaying husk filled with mobs, feckless politicians, and people afraid to go outside their homes.

Los Angeles had once been the great land of opportunity. Now it was a landscape of fear and acquiescence. And a growing population of the homeless. Which is why, she reminded herself, she was here. To feed the hungry and clothe the naked is why God planted her in this place, for better or worse.

Headlights blasted across her.

A black SUV with darkly tinted windows pulled to a stop, killed the headlights. Two large men emerged. They were young with dark hair and coats and shirts opened at the collar. As far as Sister J could make out by the light of the moon, one wore a deep-red shirt, the other sky-blue.

But there was no mistaking the bright white teeth of the deep-red fellow as he smiled. Even in the moonlight his pearlies gleamed.

"A real nun," Sky Blue said.

"Shocking, I know," said Sister J.

"Got a mouth on her," Deep Red said.

"Ready to go?" Sister J said.

"What's the hurry?" Deep Red said, giving her a long, lingering look.

"Let's get going," said Sky Blue.

"Hold on," Red said. He took a step closer to Sister J. "I just want a chance to confess my sins."

"I suggest you seek out a priest," Sister J said. "Now take me to your boss."

"See the way she gives out orders?" Red said. "What are you gonna do, take out a ruler and slap my knuckles?"

"You don't want to know," Sister J said.

Red laughed. And then an unmistakable look came into his eyes, a look Brooke Bailey had seen on a studio executive who forced himself upon her years ago.

"Back away," she said.

He did not back away.

"Let's go," Blue said.

They did not go.

"Go wait in the car," Red said.

Blue cursed. "Then just get it over with."

"It's over now," Sister J said. And then she whirled and rammed her elbow into Red's nose, hearing and feeling the crunching of cartilage. She followed with a knee to his masculine identity. This doubled him over, and she was able to see Blue, mouth agape, fumbling under his coat.

She knew what that meant. Just as Blue's hand was emerging with a gun, Sister J was leaping at him. She drove the heel of her shoe into Blue's neck.

He fell back, dropped the gun. He made gurgling sounds as he fought for breath.

Sister J picked up the gun. As she did, she saw Red, wobbly on his feet, drawing his own weapon.

No, no, no! She didn't want to kill him. She didn't want to send a man to hell!

But he had no such qualms about her.

She fired three rounds, aiming for Red's legs. He cried out, fell on his keister. His gun hand flopped outward. Sister J took a step and jammed her foot on Red's wrist. He screamed in anger and agony and grabbed the hem of her habit with his free hand.

No, no, no! She did not want to dent a man's head.

But she did with the gun she held. Red went to sleep.

She took Red's gun and went back to Blue. He was only now beginning to breathe somewhat normally.

"I am so sorry," she said.

He looked at her like she was crazy.

"I don't like to inflict pain," she said.

"Coulda fooled me," Blue said, rubbing his neck.

"Now are you ready to take me to your boss?"

"What about him?"

"Put him in the back. Then you drive. And please, no funny business, or I'll have to inflict more pain, and I just hate doing that."

Blue drove. Sister J held the guns.

They snaked up into the Hollywood Hills, to what seemed like the highest point in the entire city. There they came to a high wall with an iron gate and a call box. Blue took a plastic card from his coat and held it out the window in front of the box.

The gate slowly opened.

A large, circular driveway led to the front of a huge, Tudor-style house. There was a man waiting outside the front door. He had the same look as the other two. Sister J no longer cared what color shirt he was wearing.

She got out, holding the guns butt up. The man on the porch watched her carefully as she approached. She put the guns on the ground near his feet.

"These don't belong to me," she said. "You may take me inside now."

"I have to pat you down," the man said.

"No, you don't," Sister J said.

"I'm gonna."

"Not gonna."

"Turn around."

"You turn around."

"I'm not gonna ask you again."

"Good. Open the door."

The man clamped his hand on her shoulder. Sister J pushed it off.

He made the same move. Sister J leaned left and used his momentum against him. She pulled his arm and then his body across the back of her leg. The package went tumbling down the front steps.

Sister J opened the door and went in.

The interior was all tile floors and beamed ceilings. Sister J followed the odor of cigar smoke to its source in a spacious living room. On a luxurious white sofa sat a rotund man with olive-colored skin. He was in his fifties. He wore a silk shirt from an old Disco movie, open at the neck. Around that neck was a thick, gold chain that nestled into the fibrous shag of his black chest hair. He stared at her with a lit cigar smoldering in his mouth. On his left shoulder sat a small monkey making little squeaking sounds.

"How did you—"

He stopped as the guy from the door lumbered in. "She cold-cocked me!"

"This little nun?" the man on the sofa said.

The door guy said nothing.

"Get out of my sight," said the man.

"But—"

"Get out!"

The monkey shrieked.

The door guy limped out of the room.

"Please sit down," the man said. "You have been granted special dispensation."

Sister J sat in a large chair facing the sofa. "I was unaware that this was an ecclesiastical meeting," she said.

"I don't usually grant audiences. But you intrigue me. You see, I've heard about you."

"And I you, Mr. Barabbas."

"What have you heard?"

"That you are not a man to annoy."

He smiled, nodded.

"Also that you traffic in drugs," Sister J said.

He shook his head. "I am a businessman."

The monkey screeched.

"Quiet, Caesar," Barabbas said.

Sister J said, "I suspect the thing that means most to you in life is money."

"You would be wrong about that. I have a wife and five children in Mexico."

"Do they know what you do?"

"They know that I am in business. They know the world is made up of drug dealers, from pharmaceutical companies to your corner street hustler. I see the world as it truly is, not as an innocent little nun wishes it to be."

"I have no illusions about this world," Sister J said. "I've seen enough of the dark side to last me a lifetime. What I don't want is the dark side trying to snuff out the light."

"Is that what you think I'm doing?"

"Of course it is. And you know it."

He frowned and took a puff on his cigar. "Now, Sister, you are edging toward annoyance."

"I want you to call off your dogs. I don't have your money. I don't believe money was on that plane. I don't know who chartered it or controlled it, but if there had been any drug money on it the police would've found it by now."

The monkey squawked.

Barabbas said, "Caesar wants to know why we should believe you."

"I am answerable to God," Sister J said. "Lying is not one of the things I do."

"Ah, who is answerable to God anymore? Politicians lie with every breath. Even those who call themselves Catholic."

"Fortunately, I am not in politics. My business is taking care of the hungry and homeless, and I would like to go back to my shelter without fear that one of your men will come and try to toss the place."

The monkey squealed.

"Caesar wants to know what is in it for us," Barabbas said.

"In it?"

"Of course. You don't make such a request without offering something in return."

"I do."

"You'll have to do better."

Crossing her arms, Sister J said, "How about I promise not to annoy you?"

The monkey screamed.

"You see?" Barabbas said. "That is not enough."

"It will have to do," said Sister J.

"Do you really know about me?"

"I can only imagine. And what I imagine is not good."

He grinned. "Very good imagination. One less nun in the world wouldn't do it any harm."

Sister J said, "Threats of death mean nothing to me. This life is a trip toward eternity. Making it a little shorter on Earth is actually a blessing."

"That makes it easier on both of us then, doesn't it?"

"Not easier for you," she said.

"Oh?"

"That black soul of yours is pitch for the fires of hell."

When he didn't immediately respond, Sister J knew she'd found the opening she was looking for.

"No doubt you were raised a Catholic in Mexico," she said. "You know about heaven and hell. You know about eternal judgment. But somewhere along the way, perhaps as a youth running errands for a local drug lord, you told yourself to stop believing it. But it's still there inside you, a small voice, one you haven't listened to in a long time. It's there now. You can hear it. You can even smell the fire."

The monkey wailed and started jumping up and down on the sofa. Barabbas gave it the back of his hand. The little primate cried out as it tumbled to the floor.

"No one talks to me like that!" he said.

"You are talking to yourself," Sister J said.

"Antonio!"

The large man from the front door hobbled back into the room.

"Take her back to wherever she came from."

"Do I have to?" Antonio said.

"You have to!" Barabbas stood and pointed at Sister J. "I don't want to see you or hear you ever again."

"I expect the same of you," Sister J said.

Antonio was brooding and silent on the drive back to Sister J's car.

Sister J was not so reticent. "You do not have to stay in this life, Antonio. It will not end well for you. There is a God and he is a God of justice. Vengeance is his, and he will repay. But he is a God of love and mercy, and all you need to do is repent and receive the forgiveness of Christ."

Antonio said nothing.

"You surely must know that you are in constant danger of dying. Being shot by a rival gang, a police officer, or even your own boss."

He flinched.

"Oh yes, your boss is one of those men who will kill on a whim. You know that. Do you want to die with all your sins on your head?"

"Why don't you shut up?" Antonio said.

"Why don't you answer the question? It's the most important question you'll ever ask yourself."

He drove in silence for a time, then said, "You threw me down the steps."

"Please forgive me," Sister J said.

"Huh?"

"Forgive me for doing that to you. I was only trying to prevent you from the crime of battery."

"Yeah? What do you call throwing me down the steps?"

"Mercy."

When they got to Sister J's car, she said, "If you ever need help, I want you to call me."

"Yeah, sure."

"I mean it. Do you want to come in for some coffee?"

"No!"

"Good night, then."

It was quiet back at the shelter. Sister J noticed a glow coming from the office. It was Sister Xuan's laptop.

"Up late?" Sister J said.

"I have sinned," Sister X said.

"Oh?"

"I have hacked into the Department of Motor Vehicles."

"It depends on what you've found."

"How so?"

"If it helps us find Elisio, it's a greater good. If one calls this a sin, it's a bitty one."

"Do you mean venial?"

"Works for me," Sister J said. "You can confess later. What did you find?"

"The vehicle that took Elisio away is registered to the County Health Department."

"That doesn't help us much."

"But there is a listing for an agent for service of process," Sister X said. "Harold Quackenbush."

"What do we know about him?"

"I was only beginning to search."

Sister J pulled up a chair and sat next to her assistant. "Search away."

Sister X typed *Harold Quackenbush* into the search box. The top hit was to the L.A. County Public Health media site. Clicking on the link brought up the site and message from Assistant to the Director Harold Quackenbush.

The Los Angeles County Department of Public Health (Public Health)
works to protect and improve health and well-being in the largest
county in the United States. Los Angeles County is home to over 10
million residents and a travel destination for millions each year.

Sister J said, "I know the answer, but let's make sure who the
actual Director is."

Sister X typed.

Mitzi Van Gogh's page came up.

"Bingo," said Sister J. "Let's see if we can find out where that
vehicle might be. Use your skill to search out county parking
facilities."

Sister Xuan nodded and went into her research. Sister J took
that moment to look out the office door at the shadows of the
shelter. The only light filtering in through the windows was the
dull gray of the streetlight on the sidewalk, and a hint of color
from the 7-Eleven at the corner. It was like the last vestiges of
life were being sucked out of the city. Except in the mansions of
the governing authorities. There they had parties and private
hairdressers, lights galore, and a lot of laughter.

"Here it is," Sister X said. "Likely at the parking garage on
Lankershim."

"Got it," Sister J said.

"Are you going now?"

"We've got to find Eiliso."

Normally, a car could get to the address in seven minutes. It
took ten in Ping. But she got there and drove up to the gate. A

security guard sat in a kiosk, reading his phone and eating a bag of Funyuns. He was thick around the middle, as his diet indicated.

He looked up and quickly put on his mask. He stepped out and said, "No entry."

"I need some information," Sister J said.

The guard's eyes narrowed. "You're that nun."

"One of many," she said.

"Uh-uh. You're causing all that trouble."

"I don't mean to," she said. "But sometimes it's necessary. I would like it not to be necessary now."

"Eh?"

"I need you to give me the record of the last twenty-four hours for this vehicle." She handed him a note with the license plate number on it.

He took it, looked at it. "I can't give out that information," he said.

"Of course you can."

"I just told you I can't."

"What section of the Los Angeles Code are you relying on?"

"Eh?"

"This vehicle picked up an injured man from my shelter, and he cannot be located. You are going to help me locate him."

"I'm trying to tell you—"

"If not, that trouble we were talking about will begin to take shape around you."

Elisio peeked out the door and saw a man, in dim lighting,

sitting in a chair. His head was down. He was snoring. He sounded just like Otto Ledbetter, who had the room next to Elisio at the shelter, and who snored through the walls. It sounded like oil drilling. Sometimes Elisio had trouble sleeping. Sometimes he got mad at Mr. Ledbetter.

But now he thought he would love to hear that sound again, at the shelter. Now he had to get past the sleeping man and get out...where?

His head was pounding and his wrists hurt.

I just have to get out.

It was hard for Elisio to tiptoe. He was never very good at it. Always way too much bulk. But he gathered all his strength and willed it to his feet, and started past the sleeping man. They were in a hallway. It looked like a place with offices. He wondered if bad men were in them. He wondered if—

Squeak!

The floor under his feet made a noise!

The snoring stopped. The man opened his eyes.

"Hey!" the man said. His voice was high-pitched. He burst out of the chair. He was a skinny man whose face was scrunchy.

With the instinct of the cornered tree sloth. Elisio raised his fist and came down on the man's head.

The man crumpled to the floor.

"I'm sorry!" Elisio said. "But you are bad!"

And then he shuffled down the hallway, found a door, and went out into the darkness.

The next morning Sister Justicia Marie, masked up out of

Christian charity, appeared in the courtroom of Judge Willis Hugard of the Superior Court. This in response to a petition for a permanent injunction to shut down the shelter. She noted the prominent bas-relief of Lady Justice on the wall behind the judge's bench.

Sister J went to the barrier between the gallery and the attorney's tables. The bailiff—a deputy sheriff who had eyes like Denzel Washington—was standing. She almost said, "You ought to be in pictures," but then recalled what a hell hole the picture business was.

"May I help you, Sister?" he said in a slightly muted mask-muzzle tone.

"Yes," Sister J said. "I am here representing the Sisters of Perpetual Justice."

"Oh, yes. Your case is up first this morning. Is your lawyer with you?"

"I have no lawyer."

"Excuse me?"

"Just me."

The bailiff pursed his lips. "I've seen a lot of people represent themselves. Never a nun."

"Then I suppose I'm here none too soon."

The bailiff was blank-faced for a moment, then threw back his head and laughed.

"What's so funny?" A tall, thin, slope-shouldered man in a navy-blue suit had approached.

The bailiff said, "City Attorney Frank Faylen, this is ... I'm sorry ..."

"Sister Justicia Marie," said Sister J.

"Is your lawyer here?" Faylen said.

"I'm representing myself," she said.

Faylen looked at the bailiff, who shrugged.

"Well," Faylen said. "Good luck to you."

"I don't believe in luck," said Sister J.

A few minutes later the bailiff said, "All rise!"

Judge Willis Hugard came out and took the bench. He was middle aged with fluffy eyebrows the color of his robe. Most of his head was bald. When he sat, everyone in the courtroom sat. Except the bailiff.

Judge Hugard said, "On the record now in the matter of County of Los Angeles versus the Sisters of Perpetual Justice. Are the parties ready?"

"Frank Faylen on behalf of the County. Ready, Your Honor."

"Sister Justicia Marie for the Sisters, Your Honor."

The judge said, "It is my understanding that you wish to go forward without a lawyer."

"Yes, Your Honor," said Sister J.

"I feel it is my duty to warn you that that is unwise."

"I believe the issues are simple enough even for a nun."

"Very well. Mr. Faylen, you may proceed."

"Thank you, Your Honor. As the sister puts it, the issue is very simple. The County of Los Angeles is empowered in matters of Public Health emergencies to take whatever steps it deems necessary to protect its citizens. In the case of the current pandemic, we have determined, along with all of the scientific experts, that mandatory mask wearing whenever someone is outside will protect the health of not only the wearer, but anyone who might come in contact with them. We also have the power of enforcement. When the Sisters of Perpetual Justice refuse us entry, they have made it impossible for us to determine whether or not they are taking proper precautions. They have made a medieval declaration that their shelter should be considered a sanctuary. Well, we are not in the Middle Ages. We're in the City and County of Los Angeles. And we are in the middle of a global pandemic. The County has issued safety protocols that the respondent has consistently ignored. Therefore, we ask this court to issue an order shutting down this facility and evicting the tenants."

Frank Faylen resumed his seat.

The judge nodded. "The respondent may answer."

Sister J stood. She wondered if she indeed was an example of the old legal saying, that a lawyer who represents himself in court has a fool for a client. She prayed silently for something coherent to say. And then it came to her.

"I believe it was a famous Supreme Court Justice who said, 'Even a dog distinguishes between being stumbled over and being kicked.'"

"That was Oliver Wendall Holmes," the judge said. "Very impressive."

Not so impressive if he knew it was a line from a legal thriller she had been in once, starring Matthew McConaughey.

"Well, Your Honor, we in America are beginning to see we have been kicked by our government. We have witnessed how the onerous restrictions imposed on them by public officials to allegedly fight the virus simply do not apply to certain, favored groups. When many went to the streets to engage in 'political' or 'peaceful' protests—"

"Your Honor," Smith said, standing. "I want the record to reflect that Sister Justific...Justasif..."

"Justicia," Sister J said.

"That she put air quotes around the words *political* and *peaceful*."

"I would like nothing better than that the record reflect this," Sister J said.

"So ordered," the judge said. "Continue."

"These, um, gatherings refused to comply with the pandemic

restrictions, and the County did absolutely nothing. Indeed, public officials encouraged these 'protestors' to—"

"You can dispense with the air quotes," the judge said.

"—encouraged these protestors to, and this is a direct quote, express their rage. And without masks. Yet when a truly peaceful protest by small business owners was held outside City Hall, it was quickly shut down. I will also note that while the city and county have allowed big-box stores and marijuana dispensaries to have people indoors, it has denied this to churches. This offends both the First Amendment of the Constitution but also the guarantee of equal treatment under law. For these reasons, the County is acting capriciously and discriminatorily, as well as irrationally and maliciously."

"That's a whole lot of adverbs," the judge said.

"If the adverb fits, they must wear it," said Sister J. "I rest my case."

"I will take this matter under advisement," Judge Hugard said.

"Your Honor," Faylen said, "in view of the danger posed by the flouting the guidelines, may we ask for an order, pending your decision, that all residents of the Sisters of Perpetual Justice shelter be required, henceforth, to wear masks, both inside and outside the facility?"

"How about when we are all alone, on the roof, or in a car?" Sister J said.

"Of course," Faylen said.

"And when we eat?"

"Mask on between bites, as the governor has ordered."

Judge Hugard said, "I find that a bit extreme, myself."

"Even so," Faylen said, "it's the law."

"It is not the law, Mr. Faylen," the judge said. "It is an order from an executive without legislative direction."

"Your Honor," Faylen said, "we all know the legislature does whatever the governor wants."

"What a fine argument," Sister J said.

Snark!

"I'm getting a headache," Judge Hugard said.

Elisio Minx stumbled through the twilight.

He had been hiding in a Dumpster behind a store. All day he hid, so the bad men wouldn't find him.

Now he needed to get home.

He was sure home was just up ahead. It had to be! That sign, that colorful sign for the 7-Eleven, that was near home, wasn't it?

But how far away was he?

Lights from an oncoming car hit his eyes.

HONK!

Elisio screamed. The lights veered around him. A man yelled a bad word at him.

Why?

Because he was *in* the street.

Stupid!

What is wrong with me?

Help me, God!

Sister J went up on the roof to pray. The plane wreckage had been cleared by a large crane while Sister J was in court.

It was dusk now in Los Angeles. The orange ball of the sun was dipping behind the mountains separating the San Fernando Valley from the west side and the Pacific Ocean. The lights at Universal City were coming on in a sad reminder of what was missing up on that hill—people. The draconian lockdown of the city had dried up most social venues. No wonder there was an uptick in suicides, substance use, and domestic abuse. Yet these dismal realities moved none of the Mad Hatters in City Hall.

Something moved down on the corner. Something big and clumsy. Or confused. A person. A man ... could it be?

Yes. Elisio!

It took Sister J all of thirty seconds to get down the stairs and out the doors. Thankfully the press had gone home for the day, and the private security guards were gone, too.

Sister J got to him as he leaned into a streetlight, grabbing it as if it were a life preserver. She touched his arm. "Elisio?"

He turned to her, and even in the dim of the streetlight she could see his eyes were vague and unfocused.

"Sister?" he said.

"Yes, it's me. Are you hurt?"

"I'm scared."

"Walk with me," Sister J said, and draped his arm around her shoulder and started them toward the shelter.

Inside, all was quiet. There was a small room—a former broom closet—they used as an infirmary. Sister J got Eliso down on the cot.

"Elisio, where have you been?"

"What?"

"Where have you been, Elisio? The hospital?"

"Dark!"

"Did a doctor see you?"

"Doctor?"

"Were you in a hospital?"

"Dark! A man..."

"A doctor? A nurse?"

"He asked me questions. I don't feel good."

"What sort of questions? About how you feel?"

"No..."

"Easy does it. You're okay now. Rest a moment."

Sister J went to the sink and wet a washcloth with cool water. She squeezed it and folded it. She returned to the cot and placed it on Elisio's forehead.

"There," she said. "Now about this man. What did he ask you?"

Elisio closed his eyes. "About you."

"Me?"

"About the things you say. About ... the mayor ... my head hurts."

"Try to think, Elisio."

"What you say about him. Why did he want to know?"

"Elisio, you may have to go to a real hospital."

"No!" He grabbed her wrist. "I want to stay with you."

"Sh, all right." She patted his hand until he loosened his grip. Then she placed his hand on his chest.

Sister J went to a cabinet and got a thermometer. She took Elisio's temperature. Normal. From another cabinet she took out a bottle of aspirin and had Elisio take two with water. She unwrapped his makeshift bandages and looked at his wrists.

"What happened here?" she said.

"They tied me up," Elisio said.

Fighting back rage, Sister J got a fresh washcloth and patted the wounds, then applied antibiotic cream. She wrapped his wrists with gauze.

"Tell me a story," Elisio said.

"A story?"

He nodded. "David and Goliath."

She did. When she got to the part where David is about to cut off Goliath's head, Elisio was asleep.

"Good cliffhanger," she muttered to herself, then went upstairs to the roof to finish her prayers.

All dark and fairly quiet. The only interruption was a chopper overhead. Quite a common occurrence in Los Angeles. A police or traffic helicopter was a ubiquitous reality in the city. There was always crime and there was always traffic. Add those two to death and taxes if you lived here.

But this chopper was exceedingly loud.

Because it was getting lower and lower. Because two rappelling ropes dropped from the chopper. And because two men dressed in black rappelled onto the roof.

The history of rappelling dates back to a French mountain climber named Jean Estéril Charlet. In 1876 he made his descent from a peak in the French Alps by using a rope, his feet, and gravity. This brought him some degree of celebrity. Soon rappelling became a sport, with the inevitable evolution of equipment and techniques.

In 1911, a German climber named Otto Herzog, introduced the carabiner—a metal, spring-gated loop. His wish that this piece of equipment be called "the Otto" or "the Herzog" went unfulfilled.

Eventually, rappelling was adopted by SWAT teams as a possible tactic for dropping into hot spots. In Los Angeles, SWAT rappelling was limited to a few public demonstrations in order to deter potential terrorist events. There had yet to be an actual tactical event involving cops dropping from choppers.

Which raised an immediate question in Sister J's mind. *Why are two men rappelling onto my roof?*

But there they were. Dressed in black and ski masks.

The chopper sped away.

"We've come for the money, Sister."

She recognized the voice. "Antonio!"

"Aw, man!" He whipped off his mask.

Sister J said, "So you've made your choice. You really want to go down this road?"

"Man's gotta eat," Antonio said.

"I can offer you food," Sister J said. "I also have coupons for Arby's, if that's more your line."

Antonio came closer. And he pulled a gun.

"You know what I mean," Antonio said.

"Your boss wanted you to lay off," Sister J said.

"Not working for him no more," Antonio said.

"He won't let you off that easy."

"He won't be letting anybody on or off again."

"Oh, no," Sister J said.

"Oh, yeah," Antonio said.

"Murder."

"I don't call it that," Antonio said. He nodded toward the other man. In his getup Sister J couldn't tell if he was Mr. Red, Mr. Blue, or some new associate.

"Whatever you call it," Sister J said, "it's a mortal sin, and you both are heading straight to Hell."

"Yeah, yeah. Now—"

"Don't *yeah, yeah* me. I'm telling you to repent right now. That will mean turning yourselves in. It will mean some years in prison. But you will gain an eternity in Heaven."

"Let's get on with this," the other man said. Sister J couldn't make out the voice. What she could make out was the long sword in his hand.

"I don't have your money," Sister J said. "So if you kill me, you won't get it anyway."

"Who said anything about killing *you?*" Antonio said. "We'll go through your people, one by one."

Human evil. Its permutations were never ending. Sister J said, "This is your last chance. You and your buddy. I'm telling you this in the name of the Lord."

"Where's the money?" Antonio said.

"All right!" Sister J said. "It's over there."

She started to move. Antonio and his comrade exchanged looks, as if they couldn't believe what was happening.

Which is exactly what Sister J needed to get between the two and the roof access door.

Nor was she lying, for she remembered the penny Otto Leadbetter had placed at the foot of the threshold. She picked it up.

"Here you go," she said, and tossed it lightly to Antonio.

The spilt-second diversion was all she needed to jump-kick Antonio in the face. She knew on contact that it was a solid strike. He went down in a heap.

Now she had to deal with the sword guy.

Thankfully, when she was the actress Brooke Bailey, she'd worked as the kick-butt lead in the straight-to-video *Ninja Hotties.* Her martial arts teacher, Bobo Portugal, had been the technical advisor and showed her exactly what to do when unarmed against a man with a sword.

You have only a split second to make your move, and it all depends on the angle the sword wielder takes. If he comes at you with the sword upraised in preparation for a downward thrust, you have your best chance. For once he is committed, the blade will cut its path all the way to the finish. Your move, then, is to sidestep until the blade passes in front of you, then step in with all your might and hold his arms down with your left hand while giving him a sledgehammer strike under his chin with your right.

If the sword come in from the side, you have to step *into* oncoming slice, reducing its lethality. At the same time you use the opponent's momentum against him by collaring his head with your arm and flipping him over your body.

But what if he comes at you with a stabbing motion? This is the most difficult of all because you're going to have to hit the blade with your arm and there's a good chance blood will flow. In such a case, if at all possible, the best tactic is to run away.

The swordsman chose to stab.

Sister J chose to run.

Though she did not have much real estate to run on.

Which she knew. Because there was one last move forming in her mind.

She looked over her shoulder and saw him closing in. Fast.

Ten feet away.

Then five.

She stopped and ran in place, looked back again, and when the swordsman was but a blade's-length away Sister J dropped onto her back and put her feet up with knees flexed. The attacker's momentum carried him into the soles of the holy footwear. Sister J's heels dug into his groin at the same time she straightened her legs. The effect was to turn Sword Guy into a human catapult. Only there was no moat below the two-story building, only a strip of alley asphalt. Sister J heard an awful scream. Then silence. She rolled over and looked down. Sword Guy was motionless and face down on the pavement, the sword jutting out of his back.

She got up, sick to her stomach, crossed herself and said a prayer for his soul's purgation. Then she turned her attention to the inert Antonio. His gun was lying next to him. Sister J picked it up, ejected the magazine and the round in the chamber. She threw these off to the side and took out her phone and called the police.

In the morning Sister J checked on Elisio. He was feeling better. He wanted to hear about David cutting off Goliath's head. In view of what had happened the night before, Sister J said she would tell him another time.

A bullhorn voice from outside said, "Attention! This building is now under quarantine and subject to inspection! You will unlock your doors immediately!"

Even through the tinny vibrations of the bullhorn, Sister J recognized the voice and cadence of Mitzi Van Gogh.

"What is it, Sister?"

"You stay put, Elisio, okay?"

Out she came, and saw Sister X and the nuns of Navarone standing just inside the glass doors.

Outside were cops, reporters, and news vans. This was obviously an organized assemblage, the handiwork of the head of the Department of Public Safety, Valley Task Force, Virus Division.

Officers Hernandez and Rollins were there. Hernandez sheepishly held up a folded document. It looked official. Sister J indicated that Hernandez should slip it through the mail slot in the door.

She did. Sister J read it. Official sounding gobbledygook. The line that stuck out was *Probable cause to believe an outbreak of COVID-19 may occur.*

"What does it mean?" Sister Xuan asked.

The answer was given by Sister Agnes, who touched Sister J's arm with her seasoned and loving hand. "It means your time has come."

The words filled Sister J's heart with fire.

"Everybody stay here," Sister J said. "And whatever you do, do not unlock the door!"

Up on the roof, Sister J looked down at the crowd and waited for the TV cameras to find her.

She shouted down, "Are we live?"

The Channel 7 reporter gave her a thumbs up. The Channel 2 reporter nodded. The Channel 5 reporter—a young, telegenic man who looked like he was on his first major story—yelled, "You bet!"

"Citizens of Los Angeles," Sister J said in her theatrically-trained voice. "It is time for all of you to take a stand for the freedom that is your right. It is time to stop being sheep! What you are seeing here today is an attempted shearing. We will not let it happen! Inside these walls we are healthy and secure. The attempt to turn one of us into an informer has failed. For you reporters down there, I will be naming names and giving you evidence. This is called news. It would be good of you this time around to actually report it."

Mitzi Van Gogh tapped Officer Hernandez on the shoulder. "Stop her!"

"How's that?" Officer Hernandez said.

"I said stop her!"

"I'm sorry. I can't understand you with that mask on."

Mitzi Van Gogh snapped her mask below her chin and pointed an angry finger at the policewoman. "You go up there and stop her!"

"Please stand six feet away," Officer Hernandez said. "If you're going to continue yelling, make that twelve feet."

"Stop her!"

"What law is she breaking?" Officer Hernandez said.

"*My* law!" said Mitzi Van Gogh.

"I'll have to look that up at the station."

"Why ... you ... how ..."

"Mask on, please."

Sister J continued. "Our Lord said we should render unto Caesar that which is Caesar's, and God that which is God's. Our souls do not belong to any king, emperor, governor, or mayor. Live your lives! Be kind, be loving, but also be smart. Our Lord said be gentle as doves and wise as serpents. Treat people with compassion, but don't allow yourselves to be treated like a doormat or a goldfish. You are a human being, created in the image of God! You have a mind. If you use it, you can determine when you are being lied to. It takes work to think. It takes no work to sit back and just do as you are told."

The rooftop door opened and Sister Xuan ran to Sister J, holding out her phone. "Look!"

Sister J took the phone and read the text of the news item. *Judge Hugard denies County request to shut down the Sisters of Perpetual Justice.*

To the crowd below Sister J said, "Have you all checked out the latest news? The court has denied the County order to shut us down. Look it up for yourselves!"

Reporters whipped out their phones. Thumbs tapped away at the screens. Mitzi Van Gogh looked questioningly at someone who was standing with her. The someone was looking at her phone. A moment later she handed the phone to Mitzi Van Gogh, whose face changed from annoyance to fury. She glared up at Sister Justicia. For a long moment their eyes locked. Then Mitzi Van Gogh lowered her mask and cried out, "This isn't over!"

Sister J noted the irony, but said nothing, recalling the proverb *Answer not a fool according to his folly, lest thou also be like unto him.*

Evening.

Sister Justicia Marie gathered all the residents and nuns in the dining hall.

"We can all rest easy tonight," she said. "For the moment, at least. We are proving how we can remain healthy and sane at the same time. The city, county, and state do not want to hear it. They won't hear it. For them it is not about facts or even science, but power and control. We had a miracle today in the form of a ruling from a single judge. No doubt the county will appeal the decision, so we must all be in prayer."

"Let's get us a good lawyer!" Theda Metcalf said.

"There's no such thing!" Quincey Robinson said.

Otto Ledbetter said, "First thing we do, let's kill all the lawyers! Henry VI, Part 2."

"That's quite enough, Otto," Sister J said.

"Nay, wench! You want a lawyer?"

"I don't know," Sister J said. "He or she would have to agree to represent us *pro bono.*"

"Hold!" Otto said, and scurried out of the hall.

With a shake of the head—a gesture often associated with the goings, comings, sayings and doings of Otto Ledbetter— Sister J said, "We must remember our Lord's admonition to love our neighbor as we love ourselves."

"I love myself!" Quincey Robinson shouted.

"And have compassion on those who persecute us," said Sister J. "For truly they know not what they do."

"I'll tell 'em what they can do!" Quincey said.

"You will not," Sister Justicia said. "As St. Paul tells us, 'Let your speech always be gracious, seasoned with salt, that you may know how to answer any man.' "

"I'll give 'em some salt!" Quincey said.

Sister J rubbed her temples.

"And now!" shouted the returning Otto Ledbetter. He had a satchel of some sort over his shoulder. He plopped it on a table in front of Sister J.

"Let's get ourselves a lawyer," he said.

Sister J paused, then unzipped the satchel. Inside was money. Lots of money.

"Otto! This isn't..."

"It is!" Otto said.

"But ... how?"

"The roof is my turf! By accident most strange, bountiful fortune! I slipped up there the moment after it happened, like a spectral presence, like Hamlet's father! And there it was, out in the open."

"But why did you keep it a secret?" Sister J said.

"Frailty, thy name is woman!"

"Oh, put a cork in thy mouth," said Theda Metcalf.

"But what are we to do with it?" Sister Xuan asked.

"Drug money," Sister J said, as she thought it over. "Blood money. Certainly not to be given to the drug lords. And just as certainly not to the city and county of Los Angeles, which will make it disappear down some dry and worthless hole. Perhaps God has provided us a way to buy more food and supplies for our brothers and sisters suffering in the streets."

"Which means us, too?" said Elisio Minx with a hopeful bob of his eyebrows.

Sister J smiled. "We are a household and it is almost dinner time. What would you say to five extra-large deep-dish pizzas for dinner?"

"I'd say huzzah!" Otto said.

NOTE

Thanks for reading *Force of Habit.* If you enjoyed it, I would be grateful if you could leave a review on Amazon. Here's the link!

Link to Amazon Review Page

ABOUT THE AUTHOR

 James Scott Bell is a winner of the
International Thriller Writers
Award, and the author of many
bestselling novels and books on
the craft of fiction. He lives and
writes in Los Angeles.

FREE BOOK

I'd love to keep you informed of my new releases and special deals. To sign up for my occasional, short and sweet, no-spam emails, and to pick up a free book in return, go to:

www.JamesScottBell.com

Click on the FREE BOOK menu item and enjoy.

Jim

ALSO BY JAMES SCOTT BELL

The Mike Romeo Thriller Series
(in order)

1. Romeo's Rules
2. Romeo's Way
3. Romeo's Hammer
4. Romeo's Fight
5. Romeo's Stand

"Mike Romeo is a terrific hero. He's smart, tough as nails, and fun to hang out with. James Scott Bell is at the top of his game here. There'll be no sleeping till after the story is over." - **John Gilstrap**, New York Times bestselling author of the Jonathan Grave thriller series

The Ty Buchanan Legal Thriller Series

1. Try Dying
2. Try Darkness
3. Try Fear

"Part Michael Connelly and part Raymond Chandler, Bell has an excellent ear for dialogue and makes contemporary L.A. come alive. Deftly plotted, flawlessly executed, and compulsively readable. Bell takes his place among the top authors in the crowded suspense genre." - **Sheldon Siegel**, *New York Times* bestselling author

The Trials of Kit Shannon Historical Legal Thrillers

Book 1 - City of Angels
Book 2 - Angels Flight

"With her shoulders squared and faith set high, Kit Shannon arrives in 1903 Los Angeles feeling a special calling to practice law ... Packed full of genuine, deep and real characters ... The tension and suspense are in overdrive ... A series that is timeless!" — **In the Library Review**

Stand-Alone Thrillers

Your Son Is Alive

Long Lost

Blind Justice

Don't Leave Me

Final Witness

Framed

Last Call

The Sister J Vigilante Nun Series

Force of Habit